PRAISE FOR
THE BURN ZONE

"Fast, unrelenting, and uncompromising, *The Burn Zone* is an adventure you won't want to miss."
—*New York Times* bestselling author Mira Grant

"Between the bone-crack tension, the fertile cascade of ideas, and the neon-bright setting, *The Burn Zone* is a hell of a ride." —National bestselling author Richard Kadrey

"A thought-provoking thrill ride that evokes themes touched upon by the novels of Octavia Butler and films like *District 9* and *Minority Report* and *Dark City*. *The Burn Zone* surprised me with its depth and Decker's ability to tell an intimate story . . . with a more grand backdrop and potential to take a larger series to many different places. An early contender for one of the top SF novels of 2013."
—SFFWorld

"With a tricky plot, a fascinating alien race, and a resourceful heroine whose story deserves many follow-ups, this series debut should please fans of Peter Hamilton, William C. Dietz, and John Scalzi." —*Library Journal*

"[A] fast-paced world . . . grounded and plausible, taking equal parts *District 9* and Arthur C. Clarke's *Childhood's End* . . . and it hits a lot of the right buttons. It's got plenty of action, a cast of smart characters, [and] an intriguing plot." —GeekExchange.com

continued . . .

D1407683

Also Available from James K. Decker

The Burn Zone
Ember (A Penguin Special)

FALLOUT

JAMES K. DECKER

A ROC BOOK

ROC
Published by the Penguin Group
Penguin Group (USA) LLC, 375 Hudson Street,
New York, New York 10014

USA | Canada | UK | Ireland | Australia | New Zealand | India | South Africa | China
penguin.com
A Penguin Random House Company

First published by Roc, an imprint of New American Library,
a division of Penguin Group (USA) LLC

First Printing, February 2014

 REGISTERED TRADEMARK — MARCA REGISTRADA

ISBN 978-0-451-41341-3

Printed in the United States of America
10 9 8 7 6 5 4 3 2 1

For Mom, Dad, and Kim.

Acknowledgments

Big thanks to my editor, Jessica Wade, for all of her efforts on this project and also to Jesse Feldman—both have been a huge help. Thanks also to Brad Brownson, Rosanne Romanello, Jodi Rosoff, and everyone else over at Roc who helped bring this book from my head to you. Thanks to Dave Seeley for another fantastic cover, which captures the mood of the book perfectly. Special thanks to my agent, Ginger Clark, who is not only a great agent but who has always been nothing but helpful and encouraging in a business where those things are huge. From a technical standpoint, thanks to Karin Hsieh for helping me with the Mandarin in spite of the fact that, because it was all out of context, I think she began to suspect I might be insane. Lastly, thanks to my parents for supporting my writing since elementary school, and to my wife, Kim, for being patient and supportive of my long hours scribbling.

Chapter One

Alexei, you ready? I sent over the 3i chat. His little heart icon beat in the tray that floated just in front of my eyes.

Almost. U here?

We're here. Start packing up.

Vamp and I headed down the hallway of the Jianwei apartment high-rise's top floor, and I could feel him watching me from the corner of his eye. When his look lingered, I pulled one strap of my tank top down to flash him a tattooed shoulder and he laughed.

"Sorry."

"It's okay," I said, cocking a bony hip at him. "I guess I am pretty irresistible."

He let it lie at the joke, but I'd stalled his advances for months. I'd have to get serious about it sooner or later, one way or the other.

But not tonight.

Outside the hallway's windows Hangfei sprawled as far as the eye could see, a sea of liquid neon color and blazing white. Streams of aircars flowed past, layers crisscrossing over one another as they zipped between buildings and the congested streets below. I slowed as we passed by, and then stopped for a minute to look. I'd seen the city and the haan ship that had crashed inside it a thousand times before, but these days it all looked different somehow. Through the window I could make out the arc of faint blue from the haan force-field dome, which glowed around their massive ship. Above it, the defense shield they'd constructed for us made a dark pocket of shadow in the sky near where the star of Fangwenzhe, the size of a large coin, shined. The clusters of hexagonal panels hung suspended high in the air, each part of a roughly spherical array. The filaments that connected them looked hair thin from the ground but I knew each panel was the size of a building's footprint and the tethers were as thick around as railcars. Channels on the surface of the shield panels flickered with soft orange light, making it look like an angry, flaming eye that stared out toward the sea as if daring the foreigners' forces to try to approach.

"You okay?" Vamp asked.

I nodded. "It went up so fast."

"They say the haan have made more progress in Hangfei in the last six months than they did in the ten years before that."

Six months. The six months since they attempted to destroy the Pan-Slav Emirates to the north, and failed. Six months since their shell got peeled back almost, but not quite, far enough to let everyone see that they had a lot they weren't telling. They'd used that time to shower us with tech, pull back on their calorie demands, and get very close to the city's new governess. Public opinion had always leaned in their favor, but now more and more of their detractors had begun shifting their positions.

"They think they're running out of time," I said.

"Are they?"

I'd always believed the haan were our friends, that they were gentle, fragile, intelligent, and kind. I learned the hard way that while they were certainly intelligent, and that they could be gentle, they were very powerful and not always kind. They could be brutal, and while their previous female, Sillith, had failed to wipe out the Pan-Slavs and earn much-wanted space for her people, before she died she'd released something into our world that even now festered in the streets below.

"They think they are," I said. "That's all that matters."

Vamp looked down at the streets below, his breath fogging the window.

"You think it could really be true, what the haan told you?" he asked.

"Who knows?" I said, but the truth was that I believed it. Maybe that's why the city looked different to me now. It was different. Everything was.

"Our dimensions overlapped, and then merged, collapsing your universe. . . . After the collapse the field surrounding our world broke down, and in your universe's last moments, your instance was pulled through to replace ours. It began at the opposite side of the planet, and circled the globe in hours. In our last minutes we managed to reestablish a field around the facility, to stop the collapse there, but by then it was too late. All that was left is what you call Shiliuyuán, the facility where the experiment took place. . . . Your universe is gone. It died with my world."

The haan ship hadn't crashed here. It had never moved. The world around it had been overwritten by ours until they stopped it and a quarter million of our people were displaced out of existence by Shiliuyuán, and as crazy as it sounded, I believed it. We now lived in the universe the haan had lived in, though almost no one knew it. The haan, with the help of our government, had managed to keep it a secret in spite of the fact that the harder you looked, the more obvious it became. The generations who might have known certain stars and planets hadn't existed before the haan arrived had begun to die off. All contact with the world outside our borders had been cut off, lies were streamed over the wire, and anyone who tried to tell the truth disappeared.

"How do you think the haan will react when the truth gets out?" Vamp asked, stopping to look out at the ship with me. The black specks of scaleflies swarmed past the light of the dome.

"I don't know," I said. "Knowing them, they probably won't. They'll offer us something even newer and shinier, something to distract us. It's security that will react."

"And how do you think they'll react?"

"Badly."

Alexei's chat popped back up.

Sam?

Yeah, yeah. Hold on.

"Alexei's asking where you are," Vamp said.

I laughed a little, and Vamp joined me as I stepped away from the window to continue on.

"He loves that chat," I said.

"So, how are things going with him?" Vamp asked.

"He's doing better."

"Yeah?"

"You'll see. He's getting there. He's been through a lot, you know?"

It felt like kind of an understatement. His father had been killed near the Pan-Slav border zone, and then Alexei got rounded up in a refugee camp and handed over to the haan. He'd seen his mother die in front of him when she and Dragan, my adoptive father, rescued him but he saw even worse, I think, down in the ruins underneath the haan ship. He'd been eight years old then. After Dragan had saved me from the brink of death at the hands of Hangfei meat farmers, he'd taken me in, just like he'd taken in Alexei. I'd given him years of grief in return, years of lashing out before we became as tight as we were. Alexei had decided to give me a run for my money, spending months almost catatonic before he began to crack at the seams.

"How's Dragan holding up?"

"He's holding up."

"Did he get assigned to secure the protest in Xinzhongzi?"

"No, we shouldn't run into him there."

I felt a tickle through the surrogate mite cluster before I ever even saw the haan. I turned the corner and saw a young woman up ahead, walking in our direction while cradling a squirming bundle against her chest. From the cocoon of blankets, I saw the glasslike, spindly little haan fingers pawing at the air. Then it peeked its head up. It had detected me, too, and its eyes, like orange embers, found me. My stomach growled, then, as the connection formed. The little haan hadn't eaten, and his hunger was contagious.

The stray signal sent an empty pang through my chest, but even so, I found myself savoring it. He saw me see him as we got closer and he reached toward me, groping with his delicate little hands. I disabled the junk filter, and let him in for just a second. Right away, a chat window popped up in the air in front of me.

hi

I gave him a little wave and felt a surge from him. Excitement and a rush of happiness that made my throat burn even as I smiled. I missed it. I really missed it. In spite of what I knew about them, nothing quite compared to that connection and when I quit the program it had left a void behind I hadn't been able to fill.

His surrogate saw me looking and smiled back at me, bouncing him a little in her arms. I put a block on him before he messaged me to death, and we both slowed down as Vamp continued on.

"You're a surrogate," the woman who held the little haan said. She had dark circles under her eyes.

"Was."

She didn't ask what happened. Most people who left the program were booted out because of a failed imprint. She saw the look on my face, though, and nodded toward the kid.

"You want to hold him a minute?"

I nodded. She handed him over and I held him to my chest. He felt cool, and I thought his next feeding must be soon. He put his little arms around my neck, and as his stream of happiness and contentment flowed into my mind, I felt my eyes start to get wet.

"He's cute," I told her.

"Yeah."

I wanted to hold him longer, to feel that connection longer, but I made myself hand him back, giving his bald head a stroke before letting go. The connection dwindled, and then he cut away to reconnect with his real surrogate.

"Looks like he's keeping you pretty busy," I said.

"Sorry?"

"You look tired."

"Oh," she said, looking down at the floor a little embarrassed. "No, I'm just . . . I'm having trouble sleeping."

"I remember."

She looked me in the eye, and her expression changed. She kind of looked back and forth a little and then lowered her head toward me to whisper in a conspiratorial voice.

"Did you hear the message, too?"

The question surprised me so much that I just stared back at her. After a moment, her lips quivered like she might cry. She swallowed and then forced a smile back onto her lips.

"Sorry," she said. "Never mind."

"The foreigner," I said, and it was her turn to stare. She shook her head, backpedaling. Any contact with the foreigners at our borders would land you in prison, but I could see it on her face. She'd heard them trying to reach us through the mite cluster, in our dreams.

"Sam?" Vamp called from down the hall.

"Keep your pants on, would you?" I called back, but when I turned back to the woman, she'd moved on. She hurried around the corner, and before I could even try to go after her, she'd gone.

I hustled to catch up with Vamp as he reached Dao-Ming's apartment and punched him in the arm. When I knocked on the door, Dao-Ming answered. Behind her I saw Jin sitting at the tea table.

"Hello," she said. "Alexei is just getting his bag. Please come in."

The first time I'd ever seen Dao-Ming and Jin had been in the scrapcake plant where the former Hangfei governor, Hwong, had sent us to be turned into black market street meat. After we managed to escape, we'd been on our way out and I handed off some supplies we'd found to Jin, who had taken charge of getting the other prisoners back to Hangfei. Dao-Ming had been with him, standing near him and shaking in spite of the heat. Her long hair had been plastered to her neck and shoulders, and as I approached them she'd stared through the tangles like some kind of wild animal. When she realized I'd freed her, though, she'd crossed her arms over my back and pulled me close, pressing her lips to the side of my neck and trembling. She'd looked so scared, back then, almost like a child, mute, as she chewed on her thumbnail.

Not anymore. Now her hair and clothes were always perfect, and neither her faint wrinkles nor the thin, white scar that ran across her neck did much to detract from her good looks. She always had this glint in her eye like she might lash out and cut you or something, and she made both Jin and Vamp nervous sometimes, but I'd spent time in chains too, waiting to die, and I got Dao-Ming. I liked her, and Alexei loved her.

Jin, next to Dao-Ming's beauty, came off a bit homely with a gaunt face and bushy eyebrows. His thinning hair was a little tousled, as usual, maybe because the only time I'd ever seen him comb it was with his fingers, and his face was shadowed by his perpetual stubble.

Jin told me once that Dao-Ming had never been the same, after her time in the scrapcake plant. Because the people shunted over from Hwong's prisons had them so backed up, Jin and Dao-Ming had both been stuck inside those cages for months. They'd been given the barest minimum to keep them alive before butchering and never let out, not even once. She'd been positioned so that the butchering blocks were in plain view, something I understood all too well. I'd endured weeks, not months, and it still haunted me.

Vamp and I stepped into the apartment, and Jin waved us over to him. He reached into his jacket pocket and removed a flash drive, which he held out to me with two fingers.

"It's all set?" I asked, taking it.

"The completed video is five minutes and thirty-four seconds long," he said. "Once the broadcast begins at the Xinzhongzi protest I don't think even Vamp will be able to keep control of the signal any longer than that, but it should suffice. It doesn't include everything we know, but it covers what is most important. The people will know the truth about the haan."

"And you're sure I can't be recognized?" I asked.

"Your face can't be made out," he said. "And I've altered your voice to the point where no identification can be made. With your hair so short, they may have trouble even determining sex."

I couldn't say that sounded like any kind of compliment, but the last thing I wanted was for anyone to recognize me, since airing an illegal broadcast would pretty much land you in prison and this one would be about as illegal as they came.

Alexei came from around the corner, his thick Pan-Slav hair bushy around a pale face. He'd turned nine a few months ago, but he seemed little even for his age. When he saw me, he waved.

Hi, Sam, he sent over the 3i chat.

"Out loud," I told him.

"Hi, Sam." His Mandarin was getting better, but that accent . . .

"Hi, Alexei."

"Lex, you ready to roll?" Vamp asked.

Alexei nodded, putting his little backpack over one shoulder. I could see the cuff of the gonzo robe peeking out from under the flap as he passed by to go see Vamp, and I gritted my teeth.

"Don't worry," Dao-Ming said.

"I don't like it."

"Nor do I," Dao-Ming said. "Don't worry. One way or the other, this will end."

"I just don't get it. I mean, his mother was killed by a haan. He should hate them, not worship them."

"Maybe it's a way to come to terms with it. It will be better if he disassociates himself with them of his own accord. If he doesn't, Dragan will take care of it."

I hoped that would be true, but I wondered. In reality, Dragan had ended up butting heads with gonzo church members and even their leader, Gohan Sòng, himself over this, with the only result being getting into trouble and pushing Alexei even farther away. His status as a security officer took him only so far. Gohan had connections that went way over his head.

"Dragan doesn't need any more bullshit."

"Then I take it he still doesn't know of our plan, then?" she asked.

"No."

"Are you going to tell him?"

"No. Better he can tell security he didn't know, if he has to."

"Then we meet tomorrow night at the protest site?"

"Tomorrow night."

"Good-bye, Alexei," Jin called. Alexei, still at Vamp's side, waved back.

"Alexei, say thank-you to Dao-Ming and Jin," I told him.

"Thanks Dao-Ming," he said. "Thanks Jin."

"You are very welcome," Dao-Ming told him. She approached him and knelt to tuck the gonzo robe back into his pack. "Remember what we talked about."

He nodded, and then Vamp and I led him out into the hallway, where he ran ahead of us around the corner toward the elevators.

"Should be fun getting him settled in for the night," Vamp said.

"That's Dragan's problem tonight. I've got him tomorrow."

The elevator lobby had been covered in posters I hadn't noticed when I got out of the car on the way in. All of them had faces on them, faces of men, women, girls, and boys. I took a look at the closest one, which had a picture of a young man on it.

MISSING, it said. JUN BAO WEN.

They all had the same theme. People had always gone missing in Hangfei, thanks to the scrapcake trade. Meat farmers turned them into a valuable commodity, but never in numbers like this.

No one said anything as we climbed into the car. Alexei hadn't asked about it, and I didn't want to talk about it in front of him. He knew not to wander around in Hangfei by himself, he knew it wasn't safe. I didn't want to have that talk with him. Dragan could do that.

"Don't miss out on the latest phase six haan technology," the A.I. spouted from the ad box. I took a deep breath and punched the ground floor.

"I won't."

"Which phase six technology would you like to hear about?" it asked. "Graviton suits, or Escher Housing?"

"Neither."

"What would you like to hear about?"

"I want to hear about the missing people," Alexei said, out of the blue.

The A.I. logo bobbed on the screen for a moment.

"Government investigations show there are no mass disappearances," it said.

"Who said anything about mass disappearances?" I asked.

The A.I. clicked a few times.

"Graviton suits, however, are expected to be one of our most popular choices for future fun and travel."

"Uh-huh."

"I could talk to you about hand lotion," it said. I elbowed Vamp.

"I think it's talking to you."

"Ha-ha."

"I am talking to you, Sam Shao," it said. "New advances in RNA retroviral skin cream can literally reverse skin damage. There's no need to endure the embarrassment of scaly, unattractive hands."

I looked at my hand and its chewed nails.

"My hands aren't scaly."

"Perhaps," the A.I. said, uncertainly. "Still, I think even you would have to admit that . . . "

The elevator doors opened and we headed out through the lobby to the city streets.

Hangfei buzzed in the summer's night heat. In the district of Ping Xi every scrap of sidewalk had been claimed by street vendors whose carts had merged into continuous rows, where pedestrians and bicycles flowed past in either direction. People broke from the flow like stray stones tumbling downstream to join the masses huddled under signs of flashing lights and flapping canvas flags. In between it all, four lanes of street traffic inched past, vehicles tricked out in light paint that depicted rows of colorful images and stylized hanzi. Above, through the canopy of street signs, rows of aircars flitted past between the buildings.

Through it all, swarms of scaleflies drifted across the sidewalks and streets. They'd gotten much worse over the past six months, and even though the air still stank faintly of biocide they just kept coming.

I caught Vamp kind of looking my way, and I knew he wanted to hold my hand. It had been months since the incident in Shiliuyuán, which meant months since our little grope session in the bed at Wei's hotel. We'd kind of started to go all the way more than once, but each time I'd panicked and we ended up back where we'd started, with me tied up in knots and him waiting. He'd been playing it cool, waiting for me to give him some kind of signal, but so far all I'd given was the occasional kiss so I wouldn't lose him completely. He'd gotten pretty frustrated. Even I knew it wasn't fair.

I reached over and took his hand, taking a little solace in the way the hard look disappeared from his face and his smile returned.

"You ready for this?" he asked, nodding at the flash stick. I'd been turning it over and over in my free hand.

"I'm ready," I said. "You?"

"A walk in the park."

"Uh-huh."

He tapped at his phone and then angled the screen toward me so I could see.

"I can tap into the Xinzhongzi screens from here," he said. "Give me the flash and I'll upload the video now."

"I want to go over it first, one more time."

"No problem. Just bring it when we head to the protest, I'll upload it there."

"Will do."

"You know, we don't even have to be there."

"I want to be there."

I felt a tickle on the back of my right hand and saw a scalefly had landed there. I went to shoo it away, but instead of flying off it just crawled across my hand, down into my palm.

"Stupid thing . . ."

I clenched my fist, expecting to squish it but I never felt the crunch. I opened my hand, and the fly was gone.

"What the—"

The world tilted under my feet as a strange, but somehow familiar feeling overcame me. I was dizzy, like I'd stood too quickly, and then darkness rushed in and the city around me faded. My foot came down on the pavement in front of me but my whole leg felt numb and crumpled out from under me. I felt myself fall, stumbling sideways into a streetlamp pole. I hooked one arm around it and managed to hold on as I slid down to the ground.

"Sam? What's wrong?" Vamp's voice sounded far away.

I saw a flicker in the darkness, then. It grew brighter and brighter until an image filled the void all at once. In an instant I found myself somewhere else, still in Hangfei, but somewhere else, and the eyes I looked through were not my own. The body I inhabited belonged to someone, or something, else.

It's a haan, I realized. I'd experienced this before. Haan were able to share memories with each other, and those memories were transferred by the scaleflies. Twice before the haan had managed to share their memories with me—Sillith had done it by accident, and Nix had done it on purpose—but they'd used the surrogate mite cluster to do it. I hadn't sensed any signal at all this time. I still didn't, and yet the memory felt very clear. So clear it had shunted out the world, almost shunted out my own sense of self as I moved down the unfamiliar alley somewhere out there in the maze of Hangfei.

The streets and buildings around me were almost unrecognizable. I could see several feet through each building wall, through layers of wiring and pipes into the rooms on the other side. I could sense vibrations in the pipe-work and rapid pulses of electricity coursing through each wire. The street ahead revealed a sewer tunnel below, so that I appeared to float through it all. Around me, the air swirled with particles, hundreds and thousands of them. Pheromones danced there from humans, haan, and scaleflies. All of it flowed into my consciousness, all of it information pouring into the haan's brain even though I could perceive only a little bit of it.

... Eat.

That one drive formed in the core of my thoughts, and I felt the hunger then, a hole that yawned inside me, threatening to pull everything else inside. I needed to eat. I needed to eat soon.

I moved down the street, not able to make sense of the movements my body made as I went. I felt secure that I appeared as a human, but my body image, my human body image, didn't fit with this memory. Arms, legs, feet, and hands were not part of this body. Unfamiliar movements, hundreds of them, all worked in harmony to carry me forward with almost no effort at all.

Eat.

The haan didn't know the name of the area it had wandered to, only that it had arrived in a place where humans didn't matter, not even to other humans. No authority watched here. Reports of crimes went unheeded, and cries for help went unanswered. A human could disappear here, and no one of importance would ever know.

I flowed into an alleyway, and then settled down low to the ground to face a basement window. Through the plywood that had been set there I could see down into the dark room, where the fading heat signatures of human footprints led away.

I felt the rough edges of the plywood on what felt like hundreds of tiny fingertips, and then it came free, moving away to be placed against the brickface. My body changed, oozing through the tiny window. Parts of me felt the rough floor beneath it even as other parts still rested on the damp sidewalk. Then the rest made its way inside, and my body resumed its original shape.

I followed the ghost footprints deeper into the basement, until a wall with a door in the center appeared in front of me. As I moved closer, my gaze moved through it all to see three men on the other side.

They appeared as skeletons, surrounded by soft tissue

and giving off billows of heat and particles. I sensed that none of them was alarmed. None had so much as heard me enter. They lay on bedrolls, their hearts and breathing slowed as they slept.

With the door in front of me, I reached out with an appendage, black and covered in deep pores, and knocked three times on the door.

I sensed the haan's amusement at the concept of knocking, something all humans did. Haan saw, knew, and shared everything, but not humans. They could not know if anyone was inside, and those inside could not know who was out. A knock became a moment of possibility, something that could evoke apprehension, excitement, or even secrecy if the human inside chose to ignore the knock and pretend to be elsewhere. The haan found all of it endearing.

It knew, though, that this knock would evoke fear, and I sensed regret at that fact. All three men jolted awake at the sound of it, and all at once, their cottony hearts began to beat faster as they stirred. One reached to an electronic device in the middle of their arranged bedrolls and switched it on to fill their cubby with light.

I knocked again, and after some hushed discussion, one of the men stepped forward and opened the door a crack to look out.

All he would see would be another, unfamiliar human and I sensed him relax a little as he encountered not a dangerous human, or a security officer, but an unassuming old man.

"Who the hell are you?" he asked, his tongue working inside his skull and pinpricks of electricity zipping through the mass of his brain.

I hesitated, wishing the whole thing weren't necessary. I wanted to apologize, somehow, but knew that prolonging this in any way would only make things worse for these humans who felt fear so keenly in the face of death. I didn't want to be the cause of that fear, but the hole inside of me had grown so big and so empty.

"I asked who the hell are you?"

When I didn't answer he moved to close the door but found he could not. He shoved at it again but couldn't budge it.

I pushed it open fully, forcing him back inside with the others who all stood as, once inside, I closed the door behind me. Their hearts began to beat faster then, brains buzzing with activity, adrenaline entering their bloodstreams.

I grabbed all three at once, feeling the heat in the skin of their necks, feeling the flexing of the cords that worked there, feeling the pulsing of blood within. The patterns of activity inside each brain changed abruptly as the oxygen flow stopped and their bodies went limp. I held them that way, dangling, until the impulses in each brain fluttered away to nothing.

Should I take them to the safe place? I thought. *We should take them to the safe place ... but to move them ... in this case it would mean even more risk, and the hole inside me. The hole ...*

I dragged the closest man closer still and then felt hundreds of tiny fingertips arrange themselves on either side of his skull.

Their kind will not survive on this world, I told myself. *Mine will. This is necessary. This is justified. . . .*

The guilt persisted, though, even as the fingertips poked through the scalp, and then the skull itself to perforate it from the forehead to the back of the neck. Then, like cracking a melon in two, they pulled the man's head apart to expose the brain inside.

I pushed my face into the warm mass and felt the feeding tube slither out. In seconds the calorie-rich brains, blood, and fat were coursing into me, filling the pit inside of me, and the pleasure—the pure, greedy pleasure—of that made everything else fade away. The rib cage sprang apart in front of me, bones popping free to reveal the treasures inside, and I became lost in the gorging—the sheer ecstasy of it—as ...

The images snapped away. I found myself back in Ping Xi, sitting on the sidewalk with one arm looped around a streetlamp. People streamed past me on either side as both Vamp and Alexei stood in front of me, looking worried.

"Sam?" Vamp asked.

"Yeah."

"What the hell just happened? Are you okay?"

I looked around. Everything had returned to normal.

"Yeah," I said. I managed to get back up onto my feet, still a little disoriented. "Yeah, sorry. I'm okay."

"Are you sure?"

That wasn't a dream, I told myself. *That was real. That was a haan memory. It had already happened.*

"Yeah," I said. "Just got light-headed there."

U sure? Alexei sent on the 3i. I tousled his hair and managed a smile. I didn't want to tell them what I'd seen. I didn't want to scare Alexei and Vamp . . . I wasn't sure he'd believe me. I wasn't completely sure what I even believed myself.

Sure, I sent back.

"Come on," Vamp said, handing me back the video flash. "We've got trouble to make."

I took the flash, turning it over in my hand. If everything went according to plan, we'd broadcast the truth about the haan to the whole country. Everything we knew, so far.

But as I remembered the sensation of eating from the haan memory, remembered how even while it turned my stomach I'd liked it, telling the truth no longer seemed like enough.

Chapter Two

I lay facedown on frozen blacktop, shivering in the bitter cold while the wind ruffled my clothes and hair. I didn't know where I'd awoken, but somewhere a long way from Hangfei's steamy summer heat. The city sounds had gone leaving only the whisper of wind, and I smelled wood smoke as flurries of snow drifted down to melt on the back of my neck and shoulders.

"Sam?"

Gray light stabbed into my eyes as I cracked them open and saw a fog of big white flakes drifting down around me. A thin blanket of snow had formed on the pavement of the alley I found myself in, and dusted the edges of a rusted metal trash bin stenciled with Pan-Slav lettering. On the brick wall, a paper notice fluttered in the breeze. It had a picture of a boy on it, framed by words I couldn't understand but felt sure said the boy had gone missing. Farther down the street, more posters had been pasted on a brick wall. Hundreds maybe, overlapping one another all down the length of it. "Sam?"

I recognized the voice, and knew I had to be dreaming. I wasn't in the Pan-Slav border territories. I couldn't be, and Nix couldn't be there with me. Not anymore.

I lifted my head and turned toward the source of the voice. A haan stood there in the alleyway, his wide head turned down toward me while the cold wind ruffled his draping suit jacket. I recognized his face, handsome, and familiar. I knew his figure, too, even at a distance, the lithe but powerful body of a dancer or martial artist. The bond we'd shared since he'd been an infant began to tickle at the edges of my consciousness, making me happy and sad all at once.

When he approached, I could see the honeycomb pattern of his rib cage through his translucent smoke gray skin, and behind that, the shadow of his throbbing heart. His sunset pink eyes glowed softly in the approaching dusk, lighting up the inside of his skull where his two brains floated in their bath of fluid. When he spoke, the soft green light at his voice box flickered.

"Hello, Sam."

"Nix," I said, struggling to speak through my bone-dry throat. "You can't be here."

He approached and knelt down next to me so that his draping suit touched the ground. The mass of his larger brain shifted underneath the dome of his skull, while the smaller one quivered underneath it.

"It is good to see you, Sam."

"You can't be here, Nix," I told him. "You died."

"I don't think I did."

"You died. I saw it," I said.

He seemed to consider that for a moment. Then he turned and looked up at the sky through the falling snow.

"You are troubled," he said. "I can feel it."

"Yeah."

"About what?"

"I think I saw something," I told him. "The other night. I think I saw a haan memory."

"Of?"

"Eating," I said. "Eating people. I think it was one the haanyŏng."

"Haanyŏng?"

"It's what I call them. People are being changed, Nix. Changed into haan."

He didn't respond to that one way or the other.

"I could sense his thoughts," I said. "It felt like they were mine."

"That is expected."

"He said something about taking the bodies to 'the safe place.' . . . Do you know what he meant?"

"I don't. I'm sorry."

"Why am I the only one who can see these memories?"

He held up one hand so that the flakes drifted down between his long, thin fingers. When he spoke again, his tone turned grave.

"I have been looking for you," he said, his voice box flickering softly beneath his upturned chin.

"What?"

He lowered his hand and looked back toward me. His palm felt warm on my cold skin as he gripped my forearm gently.

"I hope that I find you, soon. You have to—"

All at once he stopped. He'd frozen, and the light from his voice box glowed steady, caught in midflicker.

"Nix?"

A whine of static jabbed into my ears, followed by a loud crackle.

"*. . . what you are experiencing is not a dream,*" a voice said. It belonged to a foreign man, American maybe, speaking in Mandarin. "*. . . field prevents traditional communication of any kind. . . .*"

"Nix?"

"*. . . to target the implanted alien receiver, what you term the surrogate mite cluster, in an attempt to reach . . .*"

The voice ended in a pop of static, and Nix began to move again.

"—help me," he finished.

"What?"

"Something terrible is going to happen," he said. "Ava, the haan female who replaced Sillith, is—"

A loud crackle made me reach for my ears, but Nix, frozen in place, still had my arm. The signal cut out again, and he unfroze.

"What?" I asked, confused. "What about Ava?"

"Do not trust her."

"No," I said, and tried to pull away again. "She helped me. She helped all of us."

"She has merged with—"

His voice cut out again, and he stuttered like a corrupt video stream.

"Nix, let go," I told him. He gripped my arm tighter.

"Please," he said. "Soon you will cross the point of no return. You are the only one I can turn to. . . ."

"Nix, I said let go."

His skin grew cold and a shiver ran down my spine as his hand turned from smoke gray to tar black. The fingers stretched like worms, slithering around my forearm as his arm began to change, too.

"Nix, let go."

"A time will come, soon . . ."

His voice slowed down, growing deeper until it became nothing but a low, rumbling hiss. Clicking sounds, like the legs of many insects, began to bubble up from the white noise.

Pockmarks appeared on the tarry surface of his skin, collapsing into deep pores that scaleflies began to scurry out from. I tried to pull away, but his grip felt like iron. As I pushed back with my heels, the cold worms coiled further around me, and Nix's arm began to divide into several others. The new appendages reached for me as well, oozing over my neck and shoulders.

". . . when you must decide what it is you believe."

His eyes, the color of a Hangfei sunset, turned to coal black as his body melted into a shivering mass. The heart inside pulsed faster, and harder, as the mound began to grow.

"Nix, let go! Let g— "

I snorted awake to the sound of a TV feed, the room lit only by the flickering light from a screen. On it, a camera drone swooped between two buildings to focus on the faint blue dome of the haan force field, which glowed in the distance. A cigarillo sat smoldering in a glass ashtray on the sofa arm to my left, a thread of smoke trickling up toward the ceiling. Alexei lay on his side next to me with his head in my lap, where he'd fallen asleep. I felt a tickle and glanced down to see a scalefly sitting on the back of my right hand over a bead of blood where it had bitten me in my sleep. It began cleaning its legs, and I blew on it, causing it to flit away. The fly buzzed my head and I waved it away, causing Alexei to murmur something, still half in sleep.

"Sorry," I said and stroked his hair.

I put one hand on his shoulder, enjoying his closeness. Since I'd quit the surrogate program, he'd become the closest thing I had to that kind of bond, and though I'd never say it out loud, it didn't quite compare. I couldn't feel his emotions through my brain band cluster as I did with the haan. I could only know what he chose to share.

The smoke stinks, he sent over the 3i chat. He'd been picking up the language pretty well, but still had a tendency to lean on the translator.

I know.

You shouldn't smoke.

On the feed screen, the drone did a sharp dive to zoom down, past the blackened ruins surrounding the ship, then on toward the Jinzhou military base where our new governess, Cai LeiFang, stood at some posh ceremony in full military regalia. In the distance I could make out the American naval forces off the southern coast, huge ships clustered like some giant, floating city that bristled with cannons and nukes.

Cameras watched as the new haan female, Ava, approached LeiFang through rows of guards who stood at attention, her cloak flowing behind her as she went. When she reached the governess, she bowed her large head and Lei-Fang bowed in return. In less than a week, Ava would become the first haan to be officially granted dual citizenship, and they had a huge televised ceremony planned. It had some people happy and others furious, but it had me more worried than anything else. Ava had, in her way, helped me fight Sillith and by extension the former governor, Hwong. I hadn't expected her to get so comfy with the Hangfei government and certainly not so soon.

"Do not trust her. . . ."

The dream lingered, feeling too real for comfort. What could Nix have meant by that?

The marquee that crawled below speculated that Ava would make a case for the opening of the controversial Xinzhongzi colony at their meeting after the ceremony. The ticker that crawled past the bottom of the screen below the marquee showed the food index was down again by several points across all six feedlot platforms, which could only work in Ava's favor. Only sixty-seven percent of all processed food now went to the haan. That was down almost sixteen points from less than a year ago.

I remembered the haan memory, or dream, or whatever it had been, and shuddered. The thought that had been stuck in my mind turned over again.

If the haan had begun to spread, then how could the food index be down? Even Hwong believed things would get worse before they got better, and he didn't even know what Sillith had planned.

What are they eating?

I tried to tell myself that things had just improved with Ava in place. Sillith had hated humans. She'd blamed us for destroying her home world, as if we'd caused the disaster and not them. Ava had been born here. She understood, or so I thought. She'd made us a priority. I told myself that, but I couldn't quite believe it.

I checked the time and gave Alexei's shoulder a little shake.

"Up, kiddo. I've got to get ready to go."

He got up long enough for me to slide off the couch, and then he lay back down on the warm spot. I headed to my room, crooking my neck to bring up my 3i implant's holo-display. As I closed the bedroom door behind me, I plucked Vamp's contact icon, a beating candy red heart, from the tray.

Vamp, where are you?

Just took the gate into Tùzi-wō. The sitter show up yet?

Not yet.

I opened my closet door and pushed the hanging clothes to one side. I took the twistkey from its hook and put it in the socket of the small gate that I'd picked up on the underground market. I turned the key, and the wall at the base of the closet shimmered then disappeared. It opened into a dark concrete tunnel. I crawled through, and everything slowed to a near stop for a beat. The sound of the television faded, and the air turned cold.

On the other side, I could hear the faint howl of wind from far above me—the never-ending storm of the Impact rim, the ruins that surrounded the haan ship. I grabbed the flashlight I'd left next to the wall, and switched it on.

Your signal just got worse, Vamp sent.

I'm in the black hole drop, getting the flash.

I cast the beam down the narrow hallway that served as my off-the-grid hiding spot. It ended at a rusted metal door, which I was able to open only a little, enough to see that it opened into a much larger space. Up ahead, sitting on a cardboard box, were stacks of rations, paper money, and a passport, in case I decided I had to get out of Hangfei in a hurry. Among them, I'd stowed the flash drive with Jin's video on it. I picked it up and dropped it into my pocket.

Okay, got it, I sent. *You ready on your end?*

All set. I'll see you soon.

I headed back, through the gate and into the closet. I turned the key, and the tunnel disappeared again.

Back in the living room, Alexei had fallen back asleep on the sofa while the feed had started to cover the Xinzhongzi protest again. The crowd outside the colony had gotten massive, a sea of bodies packed into the square while security cars and news drones circled over them. The jumbo screens on the surrounding buildings showed the same footage, making the crowd seem even larger and louder.

As I watched, an A.I. adbot icon drifted on screen, hitching a ride on the news ticker. I looked away, but not fast enough.

"Sam?" the A.I. asked. It shrank the protest footage and pushed it into a small box in one corner, then brought up a digital catalog containing the upcoming batch of phase six haan goodies. I took a drag off the cigarillo, telling myself the haan could shove their gifts, but as I blew the sweet, spicy smoke from my nose I found myself staring at the thumbnail of the girl in the bikini.

"What do you think?" the A.I. asked. "Not bad, huh?"

"I've got the catalog already."

The thumbnail expanded, and the A.I. used the opportunity to morph the woman's face so that it looked more like mine but prettier. She had a killer body. I couldn't help but want, just a little, to have a body like hers. Maybe more than a little.

She has big boobs, Alexei pointed out. The fascination, it seemed, started early.

"I can see that."

"Phase six is just around the corner," the A.I. said. "You could get on the list now, if you're willing to make a down payment."

"No, thanks."

Hanzi and pinyin scrolled next to the fantasy image, telling all about how easy, painless, cheap, and natural the procedure would be. No barbaric surgery, no scars, nothing at all to suggest the results were anything but natural.

"We all have things about ourselves we'd like to change," the A.I. said. "There's no shame in it. The haan don't want to change who you are, they only want to make you better, and happier. The BeauVisage Corporation has set up an exclusive deal with—"

"Beauty's only skin deep," I told it. "Isn't that what they say?"

"Who says that?" the A.I. asked.

"I don't know. 'They' do."

"Well . . . I doubt 'they' mean it even if they do. Certainly none of the sales representatives at BeauVisage ever says that."

"I'll bet."

"If not for yourself, then maybe for that special someone? Isn't there someone you wouldn't mind giving a thrill?"

I snorted. Vamp would, no doubt, be thrilled if I did it but it took an effort just to keep him in check now. If I showed up at his place looking like the render on the screen he'd probably go berserk and start humping my leg or something.

I flicked my finger again, and swept the catalog off the screen. I used to look forward to the catalogs like everyone else, but nowadays the new offerings worried me a little. They always promised new and better things, irresistible things. There didn't seem to be any end to what the haan could do, or would do, as long as we kept the food, water, and power coming.

Toys, I thought. *That's how they bought us.* Almost no one had any idea what the haan were all about. They didn't care about the haan past the quality of life they let them enjoy, and the toys—shiny, spinning watches that they all stared at, hypnotized—while the truth crept by right under their noses.

A soft knock came at the front door and I jumped, my breath catching in my chest. Alexei stirred on the couch. He sat up, and I made my way to the front door as the soft knock came a third time.

I unlocked the door, turning the two extra bolts I'd installed. When I opened it, I found Yun standing in the hall, tapping away on her phone while glancing off to one side like she also had a chat going on her 3i implant. A braided lanyard dangled from the wet drive plugged in behind her left ear, sticking out from her short, spiky hair. She wore a little fake-leather jacket, and a short, frilly black skirt that fanned out from her narrow hips like a puffball perched on a pair of bean pole legs in striped stockings.

"You're late," I said.

"Streets are all backed up," she said. "Security's got everything snarled. Total gridlock."

"No problem. Come on in."

"Hey, Lex," she called, stepping inside.

"Hi, Yun." Alexei smiled. He liked Yun.

"He can't stay up later than ten o' clock," I told Yun.

"Come on," Alexei whined. I crossed the room, gave him a hug, and kissed him on top of his head.

"You're practically passed out now. Ten."

"Sorry kiddo," Yun said.

"Thanks for watching him," I told her.

"Anytime."

"I'll be late," I told her. She had her phone out again, one thumb tapping away without her even looking, like it had its own tiny brain.

"Cool," she said.

I glanced over at Alexei, who had turned the channel to some cartoon. The protest still raged in the TV's corner inset. Yun gestured at the crowd and made a little snort.

"Look at those idiots. Why bother?"

"Not everyone likes the idea of Xinzhongzi, I guess," I said.

"But who cares if the haan get another colony?" she asked. "No one's going to care if people protest. They're just going to get arrested."

"Probably."

"Xinzhongzi is a pit anyway," she said. "Let them have it. At least the place won't suck as much."

A message from Vamp popped up on the holodisplay between us. *Sam, I'm here. Buzz me in.*

Yun just showed. Hang out—I'm coming down.

"I've got to go," I said. "Thanks again, Yun; Dragan having to drop him off was kind of a last minute thing. Call if you need anything."

"Yeah, yeah." She'd become engrossed in her phone again. "Me and Lex got it under control."

"Okay."

"Stay out of trouble," Yun called as I hustled out the door to meet Vamp.

Chapter Three

The protest had gotten a lot bigger since the start of the week, and people had actually begun to camp out in front of the security wall erected around the colony. Vamp and I navigated through the square, skirting through throngs of security officers and protesters with signs. Makeshift shelters had begun to pop up, clusters of tents and wooden frames covered with sheets of industrial plastic. Groups of scrawny men and women sat in and, among them, people with signs on sticks propped against bony shoulders. They called for the cancellation of the Xinzhongzi project, the ousting of the haan, and the return of the original residents to their homes. At least, the nicer ones did. The meaner ones went after Gohan himself, his church, and even the haan. Some called for their extermination altogether.

Security aircars cruised slowly above the sea of protesters a few stories up, their blue and red lights casting an angry strobe over the square.

Guys, we're here.

I sent the message scattershot to the four of us, and Dao-Ming responded.

Follow my marker, she sent. *We're in the square.*

On our way.

A passing figure made me jump as, from the corner of my eye, I spotted a wet, black, undulating mass. It surged through the crowd around it like a living wave, but when I turned to look, I saw only a little old man on a rickety bicycle.

"Sam?" Vamp asked.

"It's nothing," I said, trying to shake it off. "Come on."

I walked a little faster, forcing Vamp to keep up, slipping through a small group of haan who lingered near the street corner. Their numbers had grown over the years, some said too fast. I could see the glassy domes of their smoke gray heads bobbing among the sea of hair and sweat. The pedestrian traffic weaved around pockets of the frail, fragile creatures as if they were eggshells.

A Reunification Church gonzo caught my eye as I passed his little sidewalk shrine. He knelt before the spinning wax apple that floated above sticks of burning incense, threads of smoke trailing from the bright embers. When I passed, he looked up at me.

"Are you ready for Second Impact?" he asked.

I gave him the finger. "Screw you."

The gonzo gave an indignant start. "Only He can move the stars, bitch."

We made our way through a crowd that grew thicker by the step, until we reached the hub of the squatter population. The shelters had begun to cluster together there into something resembling a small settlement. Huge canvas signs propped up on wooden supports flapped in the wind over our heads, displaying whatever their messages were to the camera crews filming from above. Jin and Dao-Ming stood together near a streetlamp pole, waving for us to cross over to them.

"What's up?" I asked.

"Take a look," Dao-Ming said, pointing up toward the face of one of the buildings that looked down on the square.

I looked up to where she pointed, a spot about thirty stories up the face of the building across from us. A group of men and women could be seen in the windows up there, all dressed in gonzo robes and waving flags with haan symbols on them.

"They're protesting the protest?" I asked. "Can they do that?"

"Showing their support, I guess," Jin said. "They've been up there for the past hour or so. It seems they've barricaded themselves into the adjacent offices."

I squinted up at them, their robes flapping in the wind.

"Yeah, that'll stop security," I said under my breath.

Through the crowd, I spotted rows of security officers with shields. They held the line to keep the protest from spreading too far, but I couldn't help but think that in Hwong's day this would have never happened. If people had expressed this level of dissent, right out in the open like this, he would have sent in as many of his forces as needed to stamp them out. There would have been arrests, and people would have had examples made of them. It stood as a testament to just how different LeiFang's governorship was that these makeshift shelters hadn't been bulldozed.

"They should be arrested," Dao-Ming said, watching the ledge, "and their leader, Gohan, executed."

"They have a right to make themselves heard," Jin said.

"Next to Hwong, Gohan Sòng is the worst thing to happen to Hangfei," she said, her voice airy but insistent. "If he thinks he can just callously scrape off the people of this city so he can give it to the haan he's going to learn the hard way what their limits are. Blood will come next."

A few people looked over at that. Bad-mouthing the government or making threats could get you brought in, and doing both would almost guarantee it. None of the approaching security officers seemed to have heard, but they could have, and, if she kept it up, they would.

"Violence will only create more unrest," Jin said. "It won't sway public opinion, which is what we need to do in order to—"

"Nothing sways public opinion like violence, Jin. You know that as well as I do. That man has sold out his own race to gain favor with the haan, and one of these days, he'll pay for that. He's the head of that organization. You cut off the head, and the rest will die."

"Guys, take it easy," Vamp said, slipping the video flash into the bay on his phone and then triggering something on the screen. "We're on."

Jin opened his mouth to silence her when, as one, each of the six jumbo screens that populated the square switched off. A short murmur swelled in the crowd as everyone looked up to see what had happened.

"In three . . . two . . . one," Vamp said.

The screens all came back on, but the images of the protest, all from different angles, had been replaced with a common image. A woman in silhouette, that woman being me, sat in front of a white backdrop. With my head and shoulders filling the giant screens, I looked huge, and in spite of myself I smiled. The protest itself was news enough to have millions of viewers. That number was about to go up.

The loudspeakers shot up in volume, creating an angry buzz that rose above the crowd, and I watched as, in a voice that had been electronically lowered, I began to address them all.

"Hello," my murky, altered voice boomed. "You don't know me, but I am a citizen of Hangfei, like you. Like many of you, I was born here, after the arrival of the haan."

Everyone had begun to stare. Even the security guys had begun to stare up at the screens, and I couldn't help it—my smile cracked wider.

"I am not here to tell you to hate the haan," my voice continued. "They've helped us in so many ways, and they may even have our best interests in mind, but they have not told us the truth."

A lot of the security troops were still stunned, but they'd begun to recover, no doubt as calls came in from their superiors demanding they shut us down yesterday. Orders were barked, and security officers began to move even with their attention still divided between the mob and the spectacle on the screens above. Even Dao-Ming looked a little awed by it.

"This world no longer exists in the universe we knew," my voice said. "The haan have transported us, and our entire world, into theirs. While this may sound fantastic, there is concrete proof of this in front of us every day."

An image of Fangwenzhe, the biggest star in the sky, appeared in place of my image on the screen.

"The star of Fangwenzhe does not appear in any images, or on any star charts prior to the arrival of the haan," my voice said. "Our government, with the help of the haan, has gone to great lengths to erase this fact by destroying records, cutting off access to the outside world, and imprisoning anyone who tries to reveal the truth."

The image on the screens changed again. Footage recorded by Dao-Ming while caged in the meat farm filled them all. A collective gasp passed through the square, and many looked away as they were confronted with the butcher's block. I'd debated including it, but wanted to be sure I'd have everyone's attention. I had it. I'd decided to let the scene linger, but not for too long, before cutting away. Uniformed men now stepped through the rows, meeting with men in butcher's aprons, shaking their hands on-screen.

At that point, both the crowd and the security troops surged. A shocked vibe passed through the square that turned angry fast.

"Anyone who dissents is made to disappear," my voice said. "The government has sold such dissenters to facilities like these, and worse, the haan have bought them from those same facilities. The haan are not what you believe."

The image changed again, this time showing a still shot Vamp had recovered from my recorded eyebot session six months before. In it, you could clearly see a soldier holding up a discarded human skin. The skin had belonged to a small girl with ringlets of blond hair. The same girl, completely unharmed, still dressed in the same outfit that hung from the soldier's rifle barrel, torn and blood soaked, stood only a few steps away. She watched him with interest.

"They have begun to alter us," my altered voice said. "They have begun taking our places, and have already—"

My voice cut out and echoed down the streets as the screens all went blank.

I turned to Vamp. "What the hell?"

He shook his head while looking at his phone's screen. He tapped away with both thumbs.

"I'm trying," he said. A beat later, the screens all came back on to display the protest again. We'd been cut off.

Security had begun to buzz, additional troops moving through the crowd while the ones with the shields held the perimeter.

"Sorry," Vamp said. "Someone figured out where I came in and—"

"Hey, check it out," someone called.

Jin saw it first. He nudged Dao-Ming, and pointed up to the building face, where the gonzos there had begun to actually climb out of the windows, and stand on the ledge.

"Holy shit, they're coming out," I said.

Even security had begun to stare up at the new spectacle. The gonzos up on the ledge got into position and then unfurled a big banner between them so that it snapped in the wind. There were at least twenty of them altogether, men and women. A security aircar hovered a little ways away from them, shining a floodlight on them and shouting something over a bullhorn.

"What does the banner say?" I asked. Jin squinted up at it.

"I can't tell; it's moving around too much."

Whatever they were playing at, they'd gotten the attention of both security and the news outlets. One of the towering screens across the street stopped showing footage of the square and switched to the people up on the ledge as more camera drones moved in. I expected them to be kids, pulling a stunt like that, but once they came into focus I could see they were all older, around Dragan's age.

They're stealing our spotlight, I thought. *What the hell are they doing?*

"They're out of their minds," Vamp said. "Ten yuan says one of them slips and falls."

As the camera passed over the line of protesters, I could see that each of them held on to the window frame behind them by little more than their fingertips. It made me nervous just to watch them.

"People of Hangfei!" a voice boomed from above. Everyone looked up at the gonzos on the ledge, and I saw that the man positioned more or less in the center of the banner had held up some kind of bullhorn or amplifier out in front of him. I had to admire them. Our fancy attempt to hijack the video screens got shut down, but this guy had every news drone broadcasting him on purpose. His face showed plain as day, and he'd be arrested right after, but for now, he had the audience that had been ours just a moment ago.

He waited for the mob's attention to turn fully to them. One by one, the other LCD screens in the square switched angles, zooming in on him until he had the audience he desired. Once he did, he continued.

"Lies," he sneered, glaring down at the crowd. "What you just saw on those screens were all lies. The haan have pulled us from the brink of disaster, and you repay them with nothing but lies."

He stared down at us from above like a disapproving parent, and then raised his voice to a shout.

"Your gathering here in the new Xinzhongzi colony is unjust," he cried. "The haan have been oppressed too long, and you are all complicit."

Boos rose up from the crowd, and I saw the line of officers near the security wall raise their shields and begin moving in a little to herd the protesters away. They'd had enough. Above, a second aircar had joined the first and now both were barking something, which I couldn't make out, at the people on the ledge.

"You are being lied to," the man continued, "but not by the haan. It is the government who has lied about the haan, and it has lied about the Impact."

The tone of the crowd began to change a little, then. A group of younger men nearby had begun to laugh. I glanced over at Jin and saw he'd turned from the protesters themselves to look at one of the big screens where a camera did a slow pan across the banner the protesters held.

"Jin, what is it?"

"The banner," he said, pointing. I looked. It didn't say anything about Xinzhongzi at all. Instead, elaborate hanzi spelled out the message:

THIS UNIVERSE BELONGS TO THE HAAN—ONLY HE CAN MOVE THE STARS

"The person who made that video told one truth," he said, the angry parent returning. He scanned the crowd below, far too distant for him to make out anyone's face. "I can't see you, but we know who you are. This is not our world. We imprison the haan inside their ship when we aren't fit to even gaze on them!"

Another aircar whipped over our heads, then flitted across one of the LCD screens as it headed up toward the ledge. Two more followed, rippling the big canvas protest signs in their wakes. When they passed the screen, I saw the camera had begun zooming in on the people above, framing them as they struggled to hang on while keeping the banner steady.

One of the two security aircars moved in closer, and the door flew open. An officer leaned out while the driver screamed at the protesters and aimed a rifle in the man's direction.

"Holy shit," I gasped. The whole crowd had begun yelling and pointing.

The officer with the rifle took aim at the man on the

ledge holding the bullhorn. He was going to shoot him—I was sure of it. A third aircar joined the two above as the forces on the ground began marching toward us, moving us out of the way in case they shot the man and he fell.

"The haan will return," the man screamed. "Rapture will see the return of the haan to their rightful place and only the most devout humans will have a place in their world! We don't deserve them! They—"

The officer fired, and the man cringed as the round struck the concrete building face to his right. Instead of backing down, he raised his bullhorn again.

"We know who you are," he rasped, his voice beginning to go. He looked down again, as if trying to find me. "Look at my face. This is the face of belief. Watch, and—"

The officer fired again and I waited for the man to jerk and then fall, but he didn't. The bullhorn sparked and exploded in his hand. His voice squealed into silence as the device began tumbling end over end down toward the street.

Either the bullet or shrapnel from the amplifier had struck the man's head because on the big screen I could see the blood that trickled freely from his hairline. The wind pushed the droplets across his face, streaking it with red lines as the mob in the square screamed.

I couldn't look away from him. The expression on his face changed, and I saw tears form in his eyes as he looked to his left. He seemed to be looking at one of the other gonzos, and he mouthed something I couldn't make out before looking back down over the ledge. He took several deep breaths, drops of blood spitting from his mouth and nose.

He closed his eyes, and at some unseen signal, the people on the ledge dropped the banner. It fell, fluttering into a tangle as the wind carried it toward the streets below. Then they all let go of the window frames, stood up straight on the ledge, and let themselves fall forward.

"Oh my God," Dao-Ming said, putting one hand over her mouth.

The crowd gasped as one by one they fell, white robes rippling around them as they sailed headfirst toward the pavement below. No one needed security to make them move at that point. Those close to ground zero started pushing back against the crowd behind them in an attempt to get out of the way, but were not fast enough. We were close enough for me to hear the crack as the first head hit the sidewalk. I turned away, not wanting to see, but the LCD screen across from us caught the whole thing. People turned, shielding themselves as they were spattered with blood and chunks of gore. The next body struck, then the next.

"Come on!" Vamp shouted. "We're getting out of here!"

Eyebot showed a swarm of orange markers closing in on our position as security struggled to control the impending riot. More bodies rained down from above as the four of us broke, shoving our way through the crowd as best we could.

The square turned into a giant surging mob as people stood clustered on top of vehicles and clung to fire escapes in an attempt to get out of the flow. Security tried to hold the line, but the streets turned to complete chaos. Just ahead, a protester collided with a security officer who grabbed his arm. When the man tried to twist free, the officer hit him with his stunner and the man dropped. While he struggled on his hands and knees, the officer bashed him in the head with his collapsible baton. Someone else tried to push him away and got shoved back onto the pavement as two more officers appeared.

"This way!" Vamp yelled, waving us toward him. The gate hub had started to queue up, and in less than a minute it would be completely swarmed. We shoved our way through the crowd, Vamp taking the lead as he struggled to make a path to the closest one.

I fought to get out of the flow of people, joining Vamp,

Jin, and Dao-Ming underneath a building's awning on our way toward the nearest gate. When I looked down at my hands and my shirt, I saw that I'd been misted with blood from one of the jumpers.

"Move!" Vamp yelled at a clot of bodies blocking our way. "Go, or get out of the way!"

Something boomed near the edge of the crowd, and a beat later a pile of bodies were bowled over in a huge splash of cold water. I turned to see a riot cannon mounted on a security truck, the turret rotating a little to the left before it fired again. A compressed ball of water shot out under enough pressure to lift a man into the air and send him tumbling into the other protesters.

It seemed to be happening in a dream. All I could focus on were those falling bodies—all those bodies—sailing down, silent and almost peaceful, until they struck the ground. What could have been going through their heads as they fell? How could they do it?

"This is the face of belief. . . ."

"Sam!" Vamp called. I didn't realize he'd addressed me directly until he grabbed my arm, and I jumped, turning back toward him. Dao-Ming stood to his left, trying to hold her ground. A single blotch of blood had stained her shirt, spreading out like the petals of a flower.

"Everyone stop what you're doing and get down on the ground!" one of the cops bellowed over an amplifier. Officers with body armor and shields continued to close in, trying to move the mob back away from the security wall. "Get down on the—"

Something struck him in the head, and he dropped the amplifier, which fell to the ground in front of him. The officer stumbled back, as something else—a bottle, I thought—shattered against his helmet.

In response, the officer next to him turned and fired at the man who'd thrown the bottle. The bullet hit him in the forehead, and a gout of blood popped from the back of his skull. As his body slumped, the people around him screamed. One woman stared in shock, her face painted red.

The square, already a pressure cooker, exploded. Two young men, one spattered in his comrade's blood, clawed their way through the crowd and over a parked security car. They jumped the officer who had fired before he saw them coming and one dragged him down to the ground as he fired a single shot into the air. Then both men were on him. The other officers who'd been with the shooter were overwhelmed as the angry mob surged over them. More shots banged through the streets as rocks, bricks and bottles began to strike the wall of shields.

"We have to get out of here!" Jin shouted, his voice hoarse.

Another uniformed officer climbed up on top of a parked aircar and pounded the roof with his palm. The driver fired up the graviton emitters and took them up just out of reach of the crowd; then the man on top aimed a shotgun down at the spot where the protesters had begun beating the fallen cops. He fired, and I saw a woman's shoulder explode as she fell facedown onto the ground. He fired again and again, sending mists of red into the air above them.

"Dao-Ming!" Jin yelled, his voice hoarse. The crowd had begun to push her away from him, and one of the men fell as a bullet caught him behind one ear. "Dao-Ming, look out—"

He started in surprise as a dark spot appeared in the middle of his throat. He looked confused, then moved his hand to his neck where blood had begun to spill out.

Dao-Ming screamed. She fought her way through the mob, eyes wide, as Jin took a step back, then fell onto the pavement.

I stared as Vamp rushed toward him, pushing people away so no one would trample him and so Dao-Ming could get through. She reached Jin, and went down on her knees next to him. She put both hands over the wound, trying to stop the blood but it just gushed through her fingers.

I heard the cannon, but never saw the shot coming. Out of nowhere, the pulse of icy liquid slammed into my chest and pulled my feet up off the ground. My back slammed into the side of a box truck, and I caromed off to pitch face-first onto the ground.

"Sam!" Vamp cried. "Sam!"

I could barely breathe. It felt like I got hit by a car or something, and my legs didn't want to work anymore. I struggled to my feet, stumbling, and turned in time to see an elbow whip through the air as someone struggled with two more officers. It connected with my forehead, and I fell back.

"Sam!"

The sounds grew distant as I fell, fading into silence before I even reached the ground.

Chapter Four

I had no memory of being moved away from the riot. I had vague memories of the transport afterward, the lurch as the aircar lifted off, and men—doctors, I thought—at either side of me. I remembered a prick at the crook of my elbow, then more blackness.

Out of that blackness, I found myself back in Xinzhongzi square. The protesters were gone, leaving it completely empty except for the group of people up on the ledge.

"... if you are receiving this message, we have successfully been able to bypass the alien screen and establish a connection through what you call your surrogate cluster."

A man's voice crackled in the darkness, a Westerner, speaking Mandarin. His voice had become almost familiar, but I found it hard to focus on his words. Up on the building's ledge, the people let themselves fall. They sailed silently, like falling flakes of snow, toward their deaths below.

I caused that, I thought. They did what they did because of the video we showed.

I remembered the man, the way he'd addressed us, addressed me, and I felt sure of it. He sacrificed himself to drown us out, and when the others saw him, they followed.

"... you have to do something ..." the strange voice said.

"I want to," I told it. "I want to do something."

"... have no way to know exactly how this transmission

will be perceived by you," the voice said, *"but if you can hear it, listen carefully to my words."*

"No more words," I said. "No more protests."

Dao-Ming had been right all along. Words and protests, even unprecedented ones, were empty gestures that would in the end do nothing.

". . . and don't seem to see them, even when facing them directly . . ."

Those jumpers believed. They believed in what they said so much that they backed it up with their lives.

". . . if you fall to them they could become unstoppable. The world is in grave danger . . . you have to act, now, before it's too late. . . ."

I turned away from the falling bodies and looked off at the curve of faint blue light, the arc of the haan force field dome with the star of Fangwenzhe shining near its edge. Nix appeared, across the square, and stared back at me with those warm, sunset eyes. It all bled together, blurring through tears of shock and frustration.

"It's not fair," I said. Why did I have to be the one who saw what I saw? Who knew what I knew? What could I do about it?

". . . you have to act. . . ."

"There's nothing I can do," I told the voice. The haan were too powerful. Security was too powerful. The haan had all the power, and we had nothing.

". . . you have to bring down the force field. . . ."

"There's nothing I can do. . . ."

". . . take control. . . ."

"But how can I?" I whispered. "They have all the power. All the power . . ."

My voice drifted off, as I continued to stare at the haan force field. The voice continued to chatter on as I just stared, not listening. Something had almost clicked. Something . . .

Power.

I followed the dome's arc across the sky.

"Wait . . . that's it," I said to myself.

We provided the haan with three things . . . food, water, and power. No one could do anything about the feedlot or water distributions, but if the haan lost their power . . .

"The force field would go down," I whispered. In the distance, Nix began to call out to me, but I couldn't hear what he'd shouted.

Cutting their power would bring down the force field, but that wasn't all. It would bring down the rest of their tech, too, including whatever they used to change our perceptions of them. Just like under Shiliuyuán, when the power got cut for a few seconds. We'd see things as they really are. Everyone would. We could . . .

I snapped awake. I lay in a bed in a darkened room lit only by a small, soft light on a nightstand next to me. I could hear breathing, and someone snored over the occasional beep of a monitor.

"You're awake," a woman's voice whispered. I turned and saw a nurse standing over me at the opposite side of the bed. She wore a bright white uniform whose lapel had been spattered with blood, a squiggle surrounded by five frantic drops. A name tag had been pinned just beneath the stain:

QIAN CHO

She put one hand on mine, and I felt a scalefly crawl across my fingers. We were in a hospital wing where rows of beds had been set up, some surrounded by plastic privacy curtains. Most of the people in the other beds looked asleep.

"What happened?" I asked.

"They turned the riot cannon on you," she said. "You were badly bruised, including three of your ribs. You were also struck in the head and knocked unconscious, but all things considered, you were lucky. You suffered no serious damage."

I tried to sit up, but my body didn't want to cooperate. I had to lie back down.

"Don't try to move," Qian said. "You took quite a beating."

"I got off easy," I said, trying to get my breath back. Qian frowned.

"Many people here now were not so lucky," she said. "What those officers did tonight is unforgivable."

I looked around at the other beds. I caught glimpses of bloodied gauze and, in the dim light, I saw that the man two beds away had one wrist that ended in a bloody stump. He moved out of focus, and the room felt like it began to tilt.

"You're okay," Qian whispered.

"You . . ."

"I gave you a painkiller. You're still woozy." She stroked my hair, careful not to brush my forehead. "Sleep now."

She turned to leave, and I struggled to sit up again.

"Wait," I said. She stopped, and leaned closer to me so she could hear.

"What is it, dear?"

"My friends . . . ?"

"They're here. They're all fine."

"I need Vamp."

"You should get some rest."

"Vamp . . ."

She nodded and stepped out of view behind a curtain for a moment. I heard her heels rap across the floor, then her voice as she spoke softly.

"Mr. Vamp? She's awake. She's asking for you."

I heard her start back, a heavier set of footsteps following. When he stepped out from behind the curtain with Qian I saw his white shirt still had bloodstains on the front and collar. Qian gave a curt head nod, and continued her rounds, giving us some privacy.

"Sam," Vamp said. "You okay?"

"Yeah." I rubbed my eyes, and felt a dull ache even through the pain medicine. "I think so."

"You don't look okay."

"She says I'll be okay." I squinted, focusing as he tried to split in two. "What happened?"

"You took a nasty blow to the head," he said. "I managed to get us through the gate, but you were knocked out cold."

"What about the others?"

Vamp hesitated a little, and all at once it came back to me how Jin had fallen. How Dao-Ming had rushed to him, his blood spilling from between her fingers.

"Jin didn't make it," he said.

I didn't know what to say. I'd known him, and liked him, but I'd never been close to him like . . .

"Dao-Ming?" I asked.

"She's . . . not taking it well," he said. He didn't elaborate, but I could imagine. Dao-Ming lived close to the edge on any given day.

"Does Dragan know about any of this?"

"Dao-Ming wanted to call him but I figured you'd kill me if we told him you got knocked out by security while protesting in Xinzhongzi," he said. "The doctor said you'd be fine. They just wanted to rule out concussion, and they did."

"I have to get back," I said. "Alexei—"

"I called Yun for you. She's going to stay overnight," he said. "You can check out as soon as you feel like you're ready to go, but I'd coast until morning, if I were you. You took a hell of a hit."

"Yeah . . ." Whatever they'd given me, it had really floored me.

"You okay?"

"I dreamed of Nix again," I murmured.

"Yeah?"

I nodded. "I miss him, Vamp."

"I know."

"I feel like I should hate him, for lying, but . . . I miss him."

He pulled up a chair, and leaned close across the bed.

"You always believed in the haan," he said.

"Yeah."

He stroked my hair. "You were the one who convinced me. It seems like you hate them, now."

I started to contradict him, to say I didn't, but the words never came. I struggled with them for a while, not exactly sure how I felt.

"You know, in some ways, I still love them," I said. I smiled, feeling more stupid than happy. "I'll see a surrogate, out on the street, and it still makes me want to cry. I miss them so bad ... but I do hate them a little, too, and ..."

Vamp waited for a bit, and when I didn't continue, he prompted me.

"And?"

"I'm afraid of them, too."

"Even Nix?"

I pressed my lips together.

"They all lied ... even Nix ..."

"Sometimes people are afraid to tell the truth," he said, and even through the fog of painkillers I could see he meant me. "They think people can't handle the truth."

"Vamp ... it's more than that."

"What, then?"

Vamp knew about the burn, and he knew about the haanyŏng, too, but the one thing he didn't know, the one thing I'd kept from him, and everyone, was just how much I'd come to question not just the haan but everything around us. If the haan could control what we saw, what else did they control? Did they control what we felt? What we heard, smelled, and even tasted? How far could they bend our minds?

"I don't know what's real," I said. A tremor had entered my voice, and Vamp took my hand.

"We'll figure it out," he said. "I'll help you."

I struggled for something to say, but he just smiled, and changed the subject.

"That nurse really took care of you," he said.

"Qian?"

"Yeah, I was really worried about you. Some of the people brought in were really bad, but she made sure you didn't get lost in the shuffle. She said you reminded her of her daughter."

"Don't tell me to be quiet!" Dao-Ming's voice carried from the waiting area. Vamp looked back, worry in his eyes. "She's freaking out," he said. "After you got knocked out, the shooting got worse. She's talking about arming ourselves."

"Like . . . guns?"

"More than just guns. She needs to tone it down. She keeps spouting off like that and security will come after her." He looked back at me. "Don't worry about it right now."

"Okay." I leaned back, letting my head sink into the pillow. He leaned closer, looking at my forehead. "Is it really that bad?"

"It's pretty bad." He watched me for a while, and then something he saw on my face made him crinkle his brow. "What is it?"

"I . . . thought of something."

"You thought of something?"

"In my dream."

"You thought of something in a dream?"

I nodded. "I know what we have to do. . . ."

"Huh?"

I concentrated, trying to keep the slur from my voice. "I know what we have to do."

"What's that?"

"We can't wait anymore. We have to do something."

"That didn't go so good tonight."

"The foreigners can see them," I said, keeping my voice low. "They send messages, and I hear them in my dreams, they say—"

"Sam, take it easy. Would you listen to yourself?"

"I'm telling you, it's true. They come in through the mite cluster. You can't hear them, but I can."

"Sam . . ."

"We have to do something. Something real. Come closer."

He leaned in close and held my hand. "What is it?"

"We have to do something real. No more protests, no more talk . . ."

Whatever they had me on had begun to really tug at me, trying to pull me back under. Vamp seemed far away.

"Sam, just rest for now. We'll talk more tomorrow when you're feeling better."

"I'll forget."

"No, you won't forget. Just—"

"I know how to get to the haan . . . I know how we can expose them."

He glanced back over his shoulder. "Sam, take it easy."

"We cut the power," I said.

"What?"

He shot another nervous glance back over his shoulder, and then leaned in close to whisper in my ear.

"Sam, be careful. A lot of people can hear you."

Struggling to focus through the cloud of narcotics, I crooked my neck, wincing at the pain that managed to peak up over the drugs, and brought up the 3i front end to chat with him privately.

We have to cut the power off, I sent. *Cut off their power. Bring down the force field, and whatever tech they use to control what we see.*

His expression changed, at that. He looked concerned.

Is that what you believe? he asked. *You think they control what we see?*

I felt a small panic, and wanted to backpedal but the drugs had me confused, and I felt so tired.

They make us not see.

Not see what?

Them.

His expression of concern grew worse, and the longer he

looked at me like that, the more my throat tightened. I felt tears begin to come.

What does that mean? he asked.

The haanyŏng . . . they weren't made to look like us. They don't look like us. Nothing is what we think.

But what does that mean, Sam? Tell me.

Tears ran down my cheeks, one trickling back into my ear.

Kill the power, and you'll see, I told him. *I swear. Please. I don't know what's real. . . .*

Okay.

Please, Vamp. I know it's a lot but please. . . .

Okay. He squeezed my hand. *Sam, okay.*

"Sam," he said in my ear. "It's okay."

Can you do it? I asked him. *You and your hacker friends? Could you do it?*

He frowned and leaned close.

"I'll look into it," he whispered. "Okay?"

"Promise."

"I promise. Now rest. And don't say anything more about this, to anyone. Do you understand?"

I reached up and patted his cheek, which in my semilucid state came out as more of an awkward slap.

"Vamp?"

"Yeah, what is it?"

"Thanks."

"For what?"

"Being here."

He smoothed my hair back, then leaned forward and kissed me on the lips. I think he intended to just make it a short one, but I kissed him back as best I could and managed to flop one arm up around his neck. He let it linger a little longer, but then broke away and kissed my cheek instead.

"*Now* you get like this?" he asked. I giggled, and he kissed me once more before he began to pull away.

"Wait," I said, and he stopped.

"What?"

"I want to tell you." It had gotten difficult to focus, but I felt like I wanted to tell him everything, just then. To tell him about my years on the street, what I'd done to survive, all of it. I wanted to tell him all of the things I'd been too afraid to tell him over the years. I felt like if I could tell him that, and he still accepted me, I could . . .

"Tomorrow," he said.

I shook my head. Tomorrow I'd be too scared to do it, again.

"Tonight."

"I won't listen," he insisted.

"Why not?"

"You're drugged out of your mind. You'll regret it tomorrow if I let you, so I'm not going to."

"You suck," I breathed.

"Yeah, I know," he said.

"I do. . . ."

"You do what?"

"I want to be . . . with you."

He smiled, but just a little. I couldn't read his look.

"It's been a long time, Sam," he said.

I think I managed some kind of noise that may or may not have been an actual word before whatever drug they gave me pulled me back down. I felt Vamp stroke my hair again, and then he began to fade away, with the light.

Chapter Five

The next time I opened my eyes, morning had come and light streamed in through a row of windows at the room's far end. Some of the beds had been wheeled out during the night, while others were still occupied. A TV mounted in one corner showed news footage of the riot with the sound turned down, and several nurses had gathered around it to watch.

I crooked my head, and winced at the deep throb of pain between my eyes. The 3i front end popped up and I grabbed Alexei's contact icon.

Alexei?

Sam, are you okay?

Yeah, I'm okay.

Yun said you got hurt.

Just a bump. Everything okay over there?

Yeah.

"You're awake."

I turned and saw the nurse from the night before, Qian, as she approached my bed. She smiled as she removed a small penlight from her uniform pocket.

Alexei, I've got to go. I'll be home soon.

Okay.

See you.

"Sit up, please," Qian said.

I did, wincing at the pain in my ribs. Qian shined the light in one of my eyes, then the other before switching it off.

"You'll be in some pain for a few days, but you'll be fine," she said, pocketing the penlight. "You appear to be quite the popular young woman."

"Huh?"

"You have another visitor. Your father is here."

"Oh."

She must have seen my face fall, because her smile dropped a notch and she lowered her voice.

"Would you like me to tell him you're still sleeping?"

"No," I said. "No, it's okay. You can send him in."

She nodded, and left. A moment later, I heard heavy footsteps approach. Dragan stepped through the doorway on the other side of the room, kitted out in full uniform, and scanned the beds. I saw him make note of some of the more badly injured patients, his eyes lingering for a moment on the man whose hand had been blown off.

"Hey, old man," I called.

He turned, and I saw his face fall. He started toward me, picking up his pace as he approached. I braced myself for him to be angry, and to start in scolding me, but he didn't. He stopped at the side of my bed and looked down at me, his hands held out in front of him like he wanted to touch me but wasn't sure if he should.

"What?" I asked.

"Nothing. I . . ."

I found my phone on the bed stand and turned on the camera, pointing it at my face so that the screen framed it. A huge knot had formed in the middle of my forehead, with a purple-green bruise spreading out around it. The bruise grew darker as it went down the sides of my nose, and then turned to two big, black shiners under my eyes.

"Great," I muttered. I switched the camera off and tossed it back on the stand.

"Sam, are you okay?"

"I'm fine," I told him. "It's just a bump on the head."

"You could have been killed, you know," he said.

I couldn't exactly argue about that, sitting in a room full of people with cracked heads and gunshot wounds, so I just nodded.

"Sorry."

"I'm just glad you're okay."

"Who told you?"

"Dao-Ming."

"Damn it...."

"Don't be mad at her. She was worried about you."

He sat down on the bed next to me, and I leaned against him. He put his arm around me and squeezed my shoulder.

"I heard about Jin," he said. "I'm sorry, Sam."

I didn't answer. I couldn't think about Jin.

"I'm sorry I worried you," I said instead.

"It's okay."

"And I wish those people hadn't jumped."

He nodded. "I saw the footage. It was pretty bad."

"The sound they made...." I shuddered, wishing I could bleach it from my mind.

"You going to be okay?"

"I will be, yeah." I shook my head. "Why did they do it?"

"Sometimes people believe things so strongly, they're willing to go to extreme lengths."

"I guess." I reached across my chest, and put my hand on his. "Aren't you going to ask me why I went?"

"No, I know why." He curled his lips, not quite a smile. "Nice video, by the way."

"Oh," I said, sheepish. "You saw that, huh?"

"Oh, I think it's safe to say all of Hangfei's seen it by now."

"How'd you know it was me?"

"I raised you, Sam. You think I don't recognize the outline of my own kid?"

"So you're really not mad?"

"Sam, it's like this," he said. "I don't like it when you're in harm's way. I'm never going to like that, and that's just the way it is. Maybe I don't say it enough, but my life really changed when I met you. Having you around made me realize the kind of man I wanted to be. So when you're in trouble, or hurt, I don't like it."

I'd been expecting a fight, and found myself at a complete loss. Dragan almost never said things like that. It came as such a surprise I had no idea what to say.

"I . . . me too," I managed.

"But," he said, "you're not the little girl I found out in the rim anymore. You're a grown woman, now, and you've shown how strong you can be. I know that better than anyone. I wouldn't be here if it wasn't for you. And don't forget, I'm the one who tracked the burn to the haan. I saw what went on down in Shiliuyuán. I don't trust them, either, Sam. Not anymore."

"Maybe it's pointless. I just . . . feel like I have to do something, you know? I feel like maybe time's running out."

He looked at me, real serious. He made sure no one else was close by, then lowered his voice a little.

"Sam, I've asked this before," he said. "What did you see down there? When you found me in Shiliuyuán Station . . . what did you see?"

"Sillith . . ." I started, but the words didn't come.

"You've never been the same," he said. "Not since that day. What did you see?"

"You won't believe me. No one will."

"I know you saw something that shook you hard," he said. "I believe that much already."

There were all kinds of things that kept me from talking about it. Prior to that moment I hadn't planned to tell him. I wished I could forget it myself. I never planned to tell him, but the next thing I knew, the words were coming.

"Sillith didn't just want the burn," I said, my voice almost a whisper. "She meant to double-cross Hwong."

He narrowed his eyes a little.

"How?"

"She'd been experimenting down there. All those bodies? She'd been working hard on something totally different from the burn virus, and she'd figured it out, too. She even infected me with it."

"With what?"

"It grows inside you," I told him. "It eats you from the inside out, and then it takes your place. If Ava hadn't removed it in time . . ."

I looked in his eyes for some kind of sign of what he might be thinking, but I couldn't tell. He still looked serious.

"It takes your place," he said. "What takes your place?"

"A haan," I said. "I think the scaleflies are spreading it. I think they're turning people into haan." When he didn't say anything, I grabbed his arm and stammered, "It's true, I know it sounds crazy but it's true."

"If Ava removed it," he said, "then how—"

"The little girl you rescued," I told him. "And the old man you dropped her off with. They were both haanyŏng."

"Cocoons," he said, sounding out the Mandarin. "For the haan?"

"All these disappearances," I said. "These people that have gone missing . . . it has to be them."

"According to security, the mass disappearances aren't a real thing, Sam."

"But they are."

"If they are, someone high up is keeping it out of the official records. The numbers are statistically a little higher than some years, but not enough to call it a mass disappearance."

"But all the signs, the posters of missing people . . ."

"People disappear in Hangfei every year," he said, his voice low. "Besides, you just said these haan take the place of people. The people you're talking about are missing—"

"The new haan are off the grid, Dragan."

"So?"

"So they have to eat something."

"They—" He stopped, and for a second he looked at me like I might be crazy. He didn't say it, and he tried not to show it, but not before I saw. He saw me see, and the look faded just as fast as it appeared. He sighed, and grew thoughtful.

"I never found that girl. I looked, but . . . I was never able to find her. She didn't go back to the Pan-Slav Emirates, and she wasn't processed at any detention center. Same goes for the guy I left her with . . . it's like they both vanished."

"I'm telling you she's here, in the city," I said, lowering my voice to a whisper. "Her and the old man both."

He looked at me, his eyes serious, but uncertain.

"You've seen them?"

"I . . ."

There were a few times, now, when I thought I'd seen the girl, glimpsed that bush of blond ringlets so out of place on the Hangfei streets from out of the corner of my eye. I thought I'd seen her, maybe.

When I didn't answer, he patted my shoulder a little. Not to make fun of me, but to let me know it was okay. He gestured at the TV, which still showed footage of the Xinzhongzi protests. More had come to join the people that had held their ground during the riot, and it looked like the crowd had doubled. They filled the square, bleeding out to cover every sidewalk and fill every alley while walls of officers with shields tried to contain them. A forest of handmade signs stuck up over the expanse of heads and waving arms while security aircars hovered low, monitoring the crowd.

"It's only a matter of time before something else sets them off," he said. "It's getting ugly out there. If they knew half of what you and I know, it would be much worse."

"Do you believe me?"

He stared at the screen.

"I know what the haan are capable of," he said, not looking at me. "I knew that back before I even met you."

"But do you believe me?"

"You know that footage you showed last night, when you said the haan were buying people from meat farms—"

"Dao-Ming is the one who—"

"I know, she told me," he said. "And she's right."

"Really?"

"I knew it, too. Way back, that night when I found you in the processing plant, I saw one of them."

"A haan?"

He nodded. "I think it must have been Sillith. I saw her buy three kids. On my way in, I stumbled on them, but I was so preoccupied with finding you . . ."

"Oh."

"I knew it, and I just let it go," he said, still watching the TV. "She told the butchers she was buying their freedom."

"She didn't save them," I said.

He nodded. "I know what she did."

"Dragan, I—"

"Do you have a plan?" he asked. "Don't say what it is for now. Just tell me yes or no."

"I think so."

"Yeah?"

"It's something big."

"It would have to be. We'll talk about it later. Okay?"

I nodded. On the feed, the mob screamed and shook their fists. "Gohan really doesn't see what's going on out there, does he?"

"He doesn't care. He's a fanatic, that's what worries me." He frowned at the footage. "He's the one stirring that pot. One man. He's dangerous. If Alexei—"

"Alexei will come around," I said. "I couldn't have been in much better shape when you took me in."

"I'd have worried about you, too, if you'd fallen in with a cult," he said. "You were vulnerable, then. He's vulnerable, now. The way Gohan has latched onto him . . . I don't know what his game is, but something's not right there. He's playing at something, and he's dragging Alexei, and all those protesters, and even the haan into it."

"What are you going to do?"

He didn't answer. The footage on the screen changed to display the foreign military buildup offshore, which seemed much closer these days. Even with the haan defense screen active those warships and the submarines lurking beneath them had enough missiles on board, both nuclear and conventional, that no one could be comfortable of the outcome should they up and attack. If they did that, the haan ship, safe behind its force field, might be the only thing left standing, defense shield or no.

"All haan might pay the price for what some haan have done," he said instead.

"Huh?"

"You told me once that Nix said that to you, before he died." He looked tired as he watched the foreign ships on the screen.

"They're coming," I said, pointing toward the TV, "because the haan can't influence them from so far away. They can see."

Dragan looked down at me, meeting my eye.

"I'll help you."

"Really?"

"Yes."

"Then you believe me?"

"I believe in you."

It was close enough. I hugged him, and he squeezed my shoulders. A scalefly flitted between us, and he waved it away.

"I'm still on duty," he said. "I have to go. Vamp's waiting in the lobby, he'll take you home."

"Cool."

"Get some rest, and take it easy for a while. Don't say anything else about this until you talk to me, okay?"

"Okay."

He gave me one last squeeze, then got up and headed for the exit.

"See you, Sam."

"See you."

When he opened the door, I could see down the hall where Dao-Ming stood. As Dragan began to approach her, she noticed me, and gave me a wave over his shoulder before the door closed again. I sat there on the bed a while longer, after he'd left, and thought about what he'd said.

"All haan might pay the price for what one haan has done. . . ."

I looked in the 3i tray, and the list of contacts there. I'd kept Nix's. I don't know why, but I hadn't been able to bring myself to delete it. It stayed gray, as always, but it reminded me of him. He'd always been the one haan I could look at and say, for absolute sure, that they had at least some good in them. Even with all the lies, and the manipulation, and the back room deals, the haan had some good in them.

All haan might pay. . . .

"Sam, you ready?"

I looked over and saw Vamp standing in the doorway. I hopped down off the bed, got my things from the bed stand and headed over.

"He kick your ass?" he asked.

"No."

"Really?"

"He's going to help us."

Vamp looked a little skeptical about that. "He might change his mind once he hears your little idea. Come on, I've got something I want to run by you."

"What is it?"

"We'll talk in the car."

"About what?" I asked. He looked back and smiled.

"Finding out what's real," he said.

Chapter Six

Vamp had come to pick me up in his new-slash-used beater aircar, a piece of shit that he loved and which I did too even though I made fun of it all the time. The outside was a mix of faded black and rust, glossed over with flickering light-paint that formed a snakelike, long-whiskered dragon on either side. The ashtray didn't look like another butt would fit in it, and every time he took a corner too fast, which was always, ash tipped out and sprinkled down onto the floor mat.

"What was Dao-Ming doing there?" I asked him.

"I don't know. She came with Dragan," he said.

"Oh." That surprised me a little. Dragan had met Dao-Ming, and I knew they got along, but I didn't expect to see them together. "So . . . how's she doing?"

"She's calmed down since last night," Vamp said, "but she's still talking crazy. She asked Dragan for a gun."

"Maybe she's onto something," I said. "This could get dangerous."

"He said no. The last thing she needs is a gun."

"Not her," I said. "Us."

He glanced sideways at me.

"We don't need guns, Sam."

"We might, before this is over."

He shook his head. "If we get pinched, it'll be by security. You go pointing a gun at them, you'll just get killed. Besides, the last time you used one you didn't like it so much, re-member?"

"I guess."

"Anyway," he said, jumping up into the skylane above us. A horn blared, and someone yelled at us while Vamp stuck his middle finger out the window. "I've been thinking about what you said last night."

"Which part?" I asked.

"The part about cutting off the power grid."

"Oh."

Pieces of the dream from the night before still lingered in my mind, faint, but there.

"... bring down the force field...."

"Is that really something we could do? Black out the whole city?"

Vamp nodded. "We can do it."

That surprised me a little, even though it had been my idea. I think I'd expected it to get shot down.

"Are you being serious?"

He nodded. "Hangfei's power grid is pretty open to at-tack, to be honest. A lot of that equipment predates the haan. Years back, an old friend of mine, Shuang Po, came up with the idea to dick around with the supply data. I'd manipulate the consumption figures, which would drive the price up and down. Then she'd make rigged trades online and cash in. An-other guy, Chen Chong, worked as an engineer inside Liàng-zǐchuán Relay and Power and helped us get access in return for a cut. It turned out to be more trouble and risk than it was really worth. By then the Channel X site was bringing in three times the money for almost no effort, but we were to-tally tapped into the grid. Once you had your hooks in there, you could destabilize the system, too, if you wanted."

"Really?"

"Yeah."

"I figured something like that would be super secure."

"You'd be surprised. Those systems were created a long

time ago. You'd shit if you knew how open to attack some of the transportation systems are. The power company even knows they're vulnerable, and they just haven't wanted to spend the money or time to update their security."

I thought about that. Hacking around for celebrity 3i pictures or online passwords was one thing. The penalty for that kind of thing was bad enough, but this . . . now that I thought about it, it scared me a little.

"You really think you can get in?" I asked him.

"I know I can," he said. "I contacted Shuang and Chong last night, and they're up for giving it a go again."

"Do they know why?"

"No. Turns out Chong got fired a couple years back and he's pissed at Liàngzǐchuán so I didn't have to twist his arm too hard."

"What about the other one?" I asked.

He made a little shrug. "Shuang . . . she's got her own reasons."

"But you trust them?"

"They'd be in this as deep as we would be."

"So does this mean you believe what I said? Last night?"

"It means I want to see whatever it was you saw."

He changed lanes again, dropping down into the one below as he closed in on the exit up ahead.

"So . . . how would we be able to actually kill the power?" I asked. "You can hack in and just shut it off?"

"No," he said. "There's no off switch. We'd be causing what they call a cascading failure. They've happened before just from faulty equipment and caused minor, regional blackouts throughout the city. Basically, the way it works is electrical power is stored in different nodes on the grid, and each node has a certain capacity it can store. If a node fails, the stored power is offloaded to surrounding nodes until it can be repaired. If that extra, offloaded power tips a surrounding node over capacity then it will trip and fail as well, offloading its load to the surrounding nodes, and so on. If one or more of those nodes fails you get a localized power cut. If we can trick one or more key nodes into believing they've been overloaded, then they'll shut down and offload their charges, and if we can disable certain fail-safes, then the failures should cascade out of control."

"And that will black out Hangfei?"

"If the failure's bad enough, yes."

"And we'll see what's really going on in Hangfei," I said. "Everyone will."

"It might kill their force field, too," Vamp said. "Could mean trouble for them. You okay with that?"

"The haan can defend themselves. I just want to know what's real, for better or worse."

"Could be worse."

"Then it'll be worse," I said. "At least it'll be true."

"And if nothing happens at all?" he asked.

He said it casual-like, but braced a little for the spark of anger, or maybe just self-doubt that I felt. The anger did rise in my chest, but in the face of what he was offering it couldn't pick up much steam.

"Then nothing happens," I said. I watched him a minute, his eyes full of . . . something that his voice didn't let on. He'd already waded out pretty far on this one. I lowered my voice, and added, "You'd seriously do that for me?"

"Yeah, Sam. I would."

I leaned over and kissed him, causing him to swerve. A horn behind us blared.

"You are the best."

I could have jumped him, right there. For the first time in as long as I could remember, the fear I walked around with eased off, just a little. For the first time since my life got turned upside down months back, I felt like there was something I could actually do.

"How long would it take?" I asked him. "To do it?"

"I'll need to scope it out," he said. "But a lot of the work's been done. It could happen fast."

"How fast?"

"Weeks," he said. "If that. Unless they did some massive upgrade since the last time we poked around in there. Hang on."

He dropped down out of the skylane so suddenly my butt came up off the seat, then whipped between two buildings before dipping down just above the strip's canopy of street signs. I could hear them huffing by underneath us as he accelerated, then banked down a side street to approach my apartment. Haan constructs skittered along crisscrossing power lines, their little clusters of pinprick, glowing eyes watching us as we cruised by. As we descended, the graviton stream disturbed a passing swarm of scaleflies and they flit past the windshield like big flakes of disturbed ash.

I released my grip on the door handle, my heart still thumping. He took us down to street level and double-parked near the front entrance. As vehicles inched past us, he popped the passenger door open.

"Oh, one last thing," he said. He fished out his Escher tablet. "Sync up with mine—I set up a plan with a shared space to use while this is going on."

I touched my tablet's screen to his, and Vamp tapped at the controls on the back of it for a minute.

"Okay, open it up," he said.

I opened the field on my tablet, and saw that a different space appeared behind it.

"Where's all my stuff?"

"It's still there, you can toggle between the storage spaces, but if we need to get something to each other fast . . ."

He shook a cigarette from his pack, and dropped it into his tablet's field. While I watched, the smoke plopped down in the space in front of me. I reached in and took it.

"Cool," I said, fitting the cigarette behind my ear.

"Put ice on that," he said, nodding at my forehead. "Get some rest, and we'll talk more later. Okay?"

"Okay." I kissed him again.

He touched my cheek, and I could see he wanted more than kisses. He wanted a lot more than kisses. He'd been patient, too, but the hunger in his eyes said he might not be patient much longer. I worried that soon he'd make me decide whether I ever intended to be with him or not.

Not today, though. He eased back, and I saw him let it go.

"Is it okay to bring Dragan in on this?" he asked. "All of it?"

"Not yet. I'll do it."

"Okay. I'll see you soon."

I stepped out onto the street, and hot air puffed around my pant legs as he fired the emitters back up.

"Thanks again," I called back.

He winked. "Anything for you."

The door thumped shut, and his aircar lurched back up off the street. He turned it around ninety degrees, then shot back up into the air, and was gone.

I watched his car become a small silhouette, then heard the distant blare of horns as he reentered the skyway.

A flash in the corner of the 3i tray caught my attention, and I looked in time to see a gray icon turn red.

NIX

The little heart began to beat as I stared, caught completely off guard. By the time I picked it from the tray, it had turned gray again.

Nix? Nix, are you there?

The icon stayed gray. The messages bounced back, unread.

Nix?

Nothing. Had I imagined it?

I crossed the street and saw a gonzo shrine set up at the edge of my building, next to the alley. A man in white robes knelt in front of it, eyes closed as he faced the spinning wax apple. The wind blew, causing bright embers to glow at the ends of the incense sticks beneath it and threads of smoke to spill over him.

"You've got to be kidding me," I said.

The gonzo opened his eyes and looked over at me.

"I'm sorry?" he asked.

"It isn't bad enough you've sucked my brother into your stupid bullshit and gotten my father written up over it? You've got to stake out my place now too?"

The gonzo stood and brushed his robe off with both hands. "I'm not staking out your place."

"You can't solicit here," I told him. "I'm calling security."

"I'm not soliciting, and anyway, this, over here, where I am, is technically public property so I'm allowed to be here."

"Just stay away from my brother," I said. "Can't you just stay away from him?"

"This has nothing to do with him. I've been waiting for you."

A red flag went up at that. The gonzo had a strange look in his eye as he watched me.

"Me?"

"Yes. Gohan instructed me to place a shrine here, and await your arrival."

"Why?"

The gonzo reached into his robes and I tensed for a moment, but all he drew out was a paper envelope, sealed with a fancy gold sticker. He held it out to me.

"What's in it?" I asked him.

"If I had to guess? A letter."

"What kind of letter?"

"Open it and find out."

"What if I don't want it?"

"Then don't take it," he said.

I snatched the envelope out of his hand, and turned it over. The envelope formed a perfect square, and the paper had a faint pink tint to it. On the front, beautiful calligraphy spelled my given name, Xiao-Xing. "You know, your boss is an asshole," I told the gonzo.

"He's not my boss," he said. "He's the leader of our church, and he sees through the veil to gaze on secrets few can imagine."

"Whatever. He's still an asshole."

"He is a compassionate, illuminated man who you do not even know."

"I know he crashed his aircar because he was drunk, and killed a guy and his kid. Everybody knows that, and about how his rich father got him off."

The gonzo bristled a little, at that, but kept his cool.

"That happened decades ago."

"Oh, okay. I guess it doesn't matter then."

"Gohan has paid—"

"He didn't pay shit; his dad even got him out of that."

"You don't believe he suffered for that? That the memory of it causes him suffering?"

"Give me a break. He gets driven around in a fancy aircar, eating fancy food and wearing fancy clothes like some posh celebrity."

"That accident changed his life, forever."

"The people he hit, too."

"You know," the gonzo said, dropping his ethereal tone a little, "your father didn't get in trouble with his superiors because his life is unfair, he got in trouble with his superiors because he harassed a religious official."

"Are you kidding me? The only people who think he's that are the gonzos."

"Reunification church members."

"Whatever."

"No matter what you believe, Gohan Sòng is still a private citizen and security can't target him for harassment."

"Is that a joke? They target people for harassment all the time," I said. "They just can't do it to Gohan because he's rich."

"Whatever," he mocked. "He doesn't have to tolerate it, and he won't. Alexei chose the church."

"No one finds religion at nine without help," I said. "And I'm telling you, if Dragan thinks you're threatening his family, then you're not going to like it."

"Sounds like you're the one making the threats."

"It's not a threat."

"Look, my job is to deliver the envelope. Just open it, read whatever he wants you to read, and I can leave. Okay?"

I turned the envelope over in my hands. The calligraphy characters displayed the meaning of my name.

Little Star.

I detected a faint, sweet smell, and sniffed the paper. It had been perfumed.

"That isn't creepy," I muttered, but in spite of all the shit I'd just given the gonzo I had to admit to being a little curious. I tore the gold sticker, and opened the envelope that contained a single square card with no fold. Gohan had written on it in columns of little, precise characters.

> *Xiao-Xing Shao,*
> *I wish to invite you as my special guest to the new haan colony of Xinzhongzi in anticipation of its grand opening. There is an important matter I would like very much to discuss with you, and so I sincerely hope you will consider my invitation in spite of any issues I may have had with your family in the past. I look forward to your reply.*
>
> *All the best,*
> *Gohan Sòng.*

"Unreal," I said. I used my phone to scan the coded seal he'd stamped in the corner, then texted the number that it pulled.

Eat me.

I slipped the card back in its envelope and flicked it at the gonzo, who recoiled as it bounced off his chest. Twenty people dive bomb onto the street right outside the gate just last night, and he wants to invite me to the illegal colony's "grand opening"?

"Fine," I said. "You delivered it. Now beat it."

His phone buzzed in his pocket, and he removed it. The screen lit up and he read something there, and then he put the phone away again. He looked to his left, then whistled with his finger and thumb.

As soon as he did, the doors of a vehicle parked nearby sprang open and two more men in robes got out. They started heading toward me.

"What the hell is this?" I asked.

When I turned back, the gonzo by the shrine grabbed my shirt and pulled me off balance. I almost fell to the sidewalk, but managed to get my legs back under me as he continued to pull.

"Hey!"

My shirt got hiked up under my tits as I got spun around and fell back, my heels dragging fast on the pavement. In seconds the mouth of the alley had fallen away in front of me, along with anyone who might be able to help me.

"Let go!" I screamed, trying to twist around as the two other gonzos entered the alley and ran to join the first. The guy who had me was strong, far too strong for me to stop. He whipped me around, and then shoved me away toward the brick wall next to a big trash bin.

"Wait," I said, holding up my hands. "Just wait . . ."

The gonzo from the shrine hit me in the side and knocked the breath out of me. I fell down onto one knee, and when I tried to suck in air a sharp pain jabbed into my ribs. Before I could recover, a cloth bag came down over my head.

"Just hold on," I said, blood leaking from my nose. "You don't have to do this. . . ."

"We tried it the easy way," I heard the man say. "You had your chance."

He tightened the bag around my neck so tight that I choked, and spots swam in the darkness as I struggled to draw a breath. One of them kicked the back of my knees and sent me crashing down onto the ground.

"Sorry," a voice said into my ear through the bag. "But he wants you there for Rapture, one way or the other."

"Hey!" A man's voice shouted from back toward the street. "Hey, let her go!"

The pulling stopped for a moment, as the people around me hesitated. I sensed they weren't sure what to do.

"Security!" the man yelled. "I said let her go!"

Boots tromped on the pavement as someone began to approach. The man who held me dropped his guard, and loosened his grip. When he did, I got up and barreled into him, blind, with one shoulder.

He stumbled back. He didn't fall, but with a witness approaching the three decided they'd better get lost. They took off down the alley, and I pulled the bag off. There were two officers. One flew past me and took off after the gonzos, while the other stopped in front of me.

"Are you okay?" he asked.

"Yeah, I'm okay."

He looked at my face, holding my chin and angling it toward the light.

"You don't look okay."

"They didn't do that," I told him. "It happened last night."

He raised his eyebrows, amused. "Sounds like this isn't your week."

"Tell me about it."

I handed him the cloth bag and he took it.

"You want to make a statement?" he asked.

"No," I said. The guys were long gone. "My father's in security, too. I'll call him."

The officer nodded. "If you're sure."

"If your buddy catches them, though, I'd like to know."

"Will do."

"This is my apartment right here. I'll be fine. Thanks."

He nodded, and headed off after his partner.

I leaned against the concrete wall for a minute, to catch my breath. The pink envelope sat on the pavement near the alleyway with its corner in a puddle and a boot print squashed over it.

When I had my wind back, I limped back toward the street. As I went, I took my phone out and texted Gohan's number again.

Nice try, asshole. Next time come after me yourself.

I headed up the stairs and into the building. When I got halfway to the elevators, my phone buzzed. I checked it, and saw my message had gotten a response.

Next time, it said, *perhaps I will.*

Chapter Seven

Snow drifted down around me as I knelt on a patch of cold pavement, watching the flakes melt as they touched down. I heard footsteps approaching, and looked up to see a pair of pink, glowing eyes approaching from out of the fog. His suit jacket fluttered behind him as the wind blew and sent snow swirling down a broken street flanked by abandoned buildings.

He walked right up to me, and then knelt down to join me on the ground.

"Hello, Sam."

He'd eaten recently, I could feel the heat still coming off from him.

"You're warm," I told him. "Come closer."

He did, taking some of the chill away.

"I've been looking for you," he said. "I need to find you, soon."

"I moved," I told him. "I live in Chenngong complex now. Or you could find me up on Ginzho tower. I still wash windows there."

"Maybe I will do that."

I remembered how his 3i icon had turned red the other day, and how it made my heart jump. My throat tightened. "Are you really still alive?"

"I am looking for you."

"Are you alive? I thought I saw your 3i contact go active the other night but I'm not sure. I hope . . ."

"Something terrible . . ."

". . . is going to happen," I finished with him. "I know. You told me. What? Who causes it?"

"You plan to bring down the power grid." he said. I jumped, a little, in surprise.

"How do you know about that?"

"That could be very dangerous."

"I know that." My voice had begun to shake. "But they're everywhere, Nix. I . . ."

Over the past week or so, the flashes, or hallucinations, or whatever they were had gotten even worse. The strange movements seemed to appear in the corners of my eyes at every turn. I'd become afraid to use the eyebot app, for fear of what I'd see.

"I can't be afraid anymore," I told him. "I have to do something—I have to."

"I have knowledge you don't," Nix said. "My people have constructed a second—"

The snow stopped falling suddenly, and Nix froze. Static crackled, and a voice cut in.

"... if you should receive this message, we are going to attempt a surgical strike. Bring down the force field if you can. Should the force field fail we are prepared with ..."

The snow began to fall again. Nix lowered his head, looking down at my hands.

"A second what?" I asked him, but he seemed to have forgotten about whatever he'd been saying.

"You have beautiful hands," he said instead.

"Nix, you were saying something. The haan developed a second . . . what?"

I followed his gaze down and saw my right hand adorned with a sleek black opera glove that hadn't been there before. In my palm, a dead scalefly lay with its hooked legs sticking up.

"Be very careful," Nix said.

My head lolled and I jerked awake.

For a second, panic welled up inside me as I sensed movement all around. A rush of light and sound left me disoriented, then began to resolve into the familiar surge of city streets.

A ceramic pipe smoldered in my hand as I sat at the Gong Street bar stand, little more than a wooden booth with a couple of rickety chairs propped in front. The old man behind the bar stood like a statue, the light from his phone's screen playing on the deep wrinkles of his face as he watched it through the slits of his eyes. Next to him, a poster for a missing boy fluttered in the breeze.

I stared at the pipe, letting the chocolate mint smoke tickle my nose. The opiates that smoldered in the bowl were stronger than the typical store-bought stuff. One puff is all it would take to steady the thin thread of smoke that trickled up from it, squiggling in time with the shaking of my hand.

My cheeks flushed with shame. I hadn't done it, not yet, but I'd come this far, and I wanted to so badly. The edges of my life had begun to unravel. I'd taken to avoiding Dragan so I wouldn't have to tell him what kind of trouble I meant to cause, and Vamp . . . he'd been preoccupied. It worried me. I felt lost. The gonzos hadn't tried to approach me again, but something told me they would, sooner or later.

"Smoke it or don't," the old man said without looking up. "Either way, no refunds."

I wanted to. I really wanted to. Everything had begun to pile up, crushing me like a bug under someone's heel. I wanted to be fuzzy again, to not feel the way I did anymore, more than anything. It had driven me here, looking over the brink and ready to jump.

Behind me, a steady flow of people trundled past, coats and briefcases brushing me from time to time. I couldn't look at them. I sensed some of them glancing my way as they went by, maybe wondering what my problem was, but all I could do was look down at the pipe in my hand and try to slow the rhythm of my heart. How many were imposters? How many of the people passing right behind me were only pretending to be human?

I watched the smoke drift from the pipe and laughed, even as tears welled in my eyes.

I'm cracking up.

I checked the 3i tray and saw that Vamp still hadn't responded to my messages, but some new ones had appeared.

> HangfeiFriendshipHospital: URGENT. Please contact us at your earliest convenience regarding your recently rejected insurance claim, to discuss how this will affect your unpaid balance.
> DraganShao: Sam, what gives? Stop avoiding me. Swing by this weekend and take a day trip with me to Render's Strip like old times.
> DMing: Sam, I have a proposition for you. Call me.
> SultrexBOTxx1: R UR TITZ 2 SMALL? Let us FIX U.
> AlexeiShao: Sam where r u? I'm waiting.
> AlexeiShao: Sam?
> AlexeiShao: r u coming?

Shit. Alexei. I was supposed to pick him up at his language tutor's, and I'd completely forgotten. I started to try to figure out some kind of recovery . . . to figure out how fast I could get to him when I saw Dao-Ming's message:

> DMing: I have picked up Alexei, as you have failed to do so. He is with me. I understand you have a lot going on, but so do we all. He needs you. Pay more attention.

I took out my phone and called him, but he didn't pick up. When I tried to get him on the 3i, he signed off.

He's pissed. I didn't blame him.

I felt like I'd begun to fall apart. I decided to call Vamp, instead, and stared at the flashing sign across the street as his phone rang.

BOTHERED BY SCALEFLIES?

The characters lit up in sequence, then went out and started over in a loop. They were selling something that would presumably help, but the store window still had flies on it, and chemical strips covered in them blew in the breeze from the awning. Underneath, a little haan construct used a tube to suck up any fallen insects.

Vamp's phone rang so many times I thought I'd get bumped into voice mail, but then he finally picked up.

"Sam," he said. I could hear music in the background. "What's up?"

"Not much. What are you up to?"

"I've kind of had my head down, working with Shuang."

"Oh," I said, my heart sinking a little. "How's it going?"

"Great," he said. "It's going to work."

He shifted the phone, like he was changing positions or maybe leaving the room. The music turned quieter, and I realized then that he sounded a little bit drunk. I gnawed on my lip.

"You don't say."

"Yeah," he said. "We've already got the bots deployed, and they'll establish the hooks for us to tap into the system. Once we figure out the best way to trigger the failure, we can go in and ..."

He kept going, but he got more and more technical, and the more technical he got, the less I understood. Since he'd gotten back together with his old friends, something had begun to bother me, and I realized then what it was. For the first time in a very long time, I felt like an outsider in Vamp's world. He'd always had smart friends ... techno-wizards who were all pirates—coders and hackers or whatever—but even when we hung out in a group he always made it clear that I held top spot in his book. We were a package deal. I was never on the outside looking in, but that's how I'd begun to feel lately.

"So, yeah," he said. "It's going to work."

He had definitely been drinking, I could tell for sure by then. The whole thing had him excited. He'd dabbled in the illegal before, sure. If he ever got busted for his piracy he'd be in trouble, and eyebot was more than a little subversive, but breaking copyright and maybe bending privacy laws were one thing. This was something else altogether. I thought that maybe for the first time he really felt like the person he'd always pretended to be. It charged him up in a way nothing else had in all the time I'd known him.

"How long?" I asked.

"We'll be ready for a test run soon," he said. "Another night or so."

"Test run?"

"The Zun-Zhe district loses power all the time," he said. "No one will think it's weird if it goes out again. Before we go for the whole thing, I want to make sure we can cause a controlled, localized failure. We need to see if everything will behave like we projected, so we can make adjustments before—"

"Hey," I said, changing the subject. "If you can get some time away, I thought maybe we could go out tonight. Just me and you."

He paused and in that little pause I felt my heart drop. Vamp didn't pause when I asked to see him. He never paused.

"I'm a little bogged down," he said. "Can we do it another time?"

"Yeah," I said. "Sure."

"Sorry," he said. "There's just a lot to cover."

"It's okay; I know there's a lot going on," I said.

Just then another voice, a woman's voice, called from somewhere on the other end of the phone.

"Vamp, is it okay to smoke in here?" I thought I heard her ask. If Vamp answered her, he just nodded or something. I thought he hoped maybe I didn't hear her. My face began to burn.

"Well, I'll let you get to it then," I heard myself say.

"Thanks, Sam. Maybe tomorrow?"

"Sure," I said, and hung up.

I stared at my phone for a while, feeling worse with every second. The voice had been Shuang's, I was sure of it. She was with him right now and maybe there was some coding going on, but there was also smoking, drinking, and music. The screen grew blurry in front of my eyes; then the call icon winked out.

I flicked the screen with my thumb, and brought up the picture of the woman, the picture of Shuang Po I'd trolled off the wire from her profile on Channel X. I hated that I'd done it, and I hated even more how goddamned pretty she turned out to be. She wore a neo-punk style, with twin wet drives sprouting from behind a half-shaved head. She had high cheekbones, gorgeous eyes, and a much better body than mine. I stared at her image, hating this woman I'd never met, then wiped her off the screen.

He's hooking up with her, I thought, and even as hurt and anger started to twist around in my chest, I realized the unfairness of it but that just made me feel even worse. Vamp had made his feelings toward me pretty clear, but I'd always kept him at a distance. I kept him just close enough to keep him from leaving me altogether, just enough to leave that door open, and no more. He'd been really patient for a long time, but I found myself really afraid that his patience had run out.

I stared down at the pipe. Ash covered the top but it still had two good hits in it. I stared, and tried to push the idea out of my mind. So what if it was Shuang? He'd just finished telling me he'd been working with her, it didn't mean anything. He wanted to run the blackout test soon, so it made sense they'd be working together tonight. He was doing all this for me. . . .

She asked if she could smoke, though, so they had to be at his place.

On the screen behind the counter, I saw more footage of Ava from the other night. Her and LeiFang, together, shaking hands. The ticker that scrolled underneath them advertised the upcoming ceremony, and the old man in the booth scowled.

"Too soon," he muttered.

Some old instinct flared up, almost prompting me to remind the guy it had been over fifty years, and that the haan weren't going anywhere. They were citizens by default, no matter whether some fancy ceremony got held. They were part of our world, now, and they couldn't leave if they wanted to, which they probably did.

I didn't say any of it. I just watched the two on the screen. They cut a great picture, the two of them. LeiFang looked regal in her full uniform, strong, while Ava looked like some ethereal princess from a far-off land. They kept their hands clasped, their faces close so that the glow from Ava's eyes bathed LeiFang's face.

. . . and something flickered there, just for a second, some electronic glitch. A flash of static gray near LeiFang's head.

I looked at the man behind the stall. He hadn't seemed to notice. I leaned a little closer, waiting to see if it would happen again.

I sensed her before I saw her, a figure that broke from the sidewalk's flow and began to drift my way. Her crisp, clean clothes stood out from the sea of damp colors and sweaty skin around her. She wore black slacks and a stylish paisley blouse, and her black hair hung down around her shoulders. She looked different enough that it took me a moment to realize it was Qian, the nurse who'd taken care of me in the hospital. Her heels rapped as she approached, and when she saw me she smiled and waved.

I found myself glad for the distraction, and the thread of

smoke stopped jittering quite so much as she sat down in the seat next to me.

"Wow, you clean up nice," I said.

"Thank you."

"Qian, right?"

"I'm flattered you remember. Hello, Sam."

"What are you doing in this dump?" The old man threw me a look.

"Heading home. I saw you, and thought I'd join you for a moment if that's all right with you."

"Knock yourself out."

She ordered a drink, some kind of hot tea that I got the sense the old man had served to her before. She lifted the drink to her full lips, and sipped.

"Sam," she said. "Is that a European name?"

"Kind of. My real name is Xiao-Xing. Everyone just calls me Sam."

"Should I as well?"

"Sure."

"You know, opiates, even the synthetic ones, can cause long-term health problems."

I looked down at the pipe, which had almost gone out. "Yeah, I know."

"Sorry," she said. "I worry. It's in my nature, but it's none of my business."

"It's okay."

"How are your friends? The ones who visited you?"

"Fine."

She looked me over.

"You look upset, is something bothering you?"

"It's nothing."

She leaned in. "Boy troubles?"

I laughed, and it turned to a snort. "Boy troubles? Really?"

"Well," she said, still smiling, "if it involves the young man who you asked for that night in the hospital, I think it fair to say you have him in the palm of your hand."

"You don't know the situation."

"Maybe not . . . but I've been around a few years longer than you have. I know men."

"Well, thanks," I said. I watched the pipe fizzle out. Ten yuan up in smoke and me just as close to the edge as before, but I felt a small relief, a small victory, just the same. "He told me you said I remind you of your daughter."

"That's true."

"I hope she's not as much of a mess as me."

Something in her expression changed, some emotion that bubbled up and was hidden just as fast.

"Don't be so hard on yourself," she said.

"I'll try."

"So . . . what have you and your friend been up to, since we last saw each other."

"Not much." I looked at her warily. That weird expression appeared on her face again, and then disappeared. A moment later, I felt a jab of pain in my temples.

"Are you okay?" she asked, noticing.

"I'm fine," I said, rubbing my forehead. A scalefly flitted in front of my face, and I waved it away.

Her eyes moved to the poster for the missing boy, and turned sad. The kid couldn't be any older than Alexei.

"It's too bad," she said.

"Yeah."

"I hope they find him."

"They won't," I told her. The old man shot me another look.

"You don't think so?" Qian asked.

"Not where he's gone."

Qian shifted in her seat, curious.

"And where do you think that is?"

I turned back to her, and felt that shooting pain behind my eyes again. I felt like just saying it, just blurting it out to anyone who would listen. Something about her made me want to say what I thought, but I stopped short of doing it.

"The haan know," I said instead.

I thought she'd question me on that, but she didn't. She just sipped her tea.

"You know the haan have a proverb," she said. "'When you can eat a problem, you solve two.'"

She smiled, and her face flickered. Just for a second, but long enough. I felt my stomach begin to drop.

"Look, I've got to go," I told her. I started to get up, and she put one hand on my wrist to stop me.

"You know, you really do remind me of my daughter," she said.

"You said that."

"It makes me feel a connection to you. I can't seem to help it."

Something appeared on the front of her blouse, a stain that I felt sure hadn't been there a second ago. When she moved, it seemed to almost hover in front of the material, a red splotch, a squiggle surrounded by five frantic drops. It was the blood stain, the same one that had been on her uniform's lapel in the hospital.

"I've got to go."

She curled her fingers around my forearm, her grip gentle, but insistent. When I tried to pull away, she squeezed tighter, and leaned forward to speak into my ear. As she did, I caught movement from the corners of my eyes, something wet, and black, ropy strands of something that peeled away from her body, moving with a life of their own.

"I know you can see," she said.

The world seemed to slow down around me, and the sweat on my neck turned cold. I tried to pull away again, and again she stopped me. Her grip had become like iron.

"What?" I asked.

"Please," she said, and it felt so sincere, so genuine, that it stopped me. The alien movement flickered and disappeared. She returned to normal and I watched, still stunned, as she ran the tip of one finger over the bond band tattoo on my left arm. She traced the hanzi that spelled out Nix's name.

"He's looking for you, you know."

My eyes widened.

"How do you know ... ?" She didn't answer. She just smiled. "He can't be. He's dead."

"He's alive."

"Alive?" I managed.

She couldn't know. She couldn't even know about Nix at all, but if she did, she'd know he was dead. I'd seen him die. I'd passed through Sillith's gate, landing in some cold, snow-dusted Pan-Slav alley. When I turned and looked back through the portal, I saw him plain as day. The facility in Shiliuyuán Station got fire bombed. Whatever they pumped down there burned white hot even after consuming the breathable air. He'd barely been able to get Vamp and Dragan through the second gate he'd opened when the blast took him. He'd been engulfed in seconds. Not even a haan could survive something like that.

"He ... couldn't have survived," I said. "How can you even ..."

I tried to pull away and knocked over the ceramic pipe, tipping ash onto the counter. My hand had begun to shake again. Qian took it, and curled her fingers, still warm from the tea cup, around mine. She stroked the back with one finger.

A scalefly lit on my knuckles, then crawled across from my hand to hers. Through the mite cluster, I felt a short pulse of signal.

"Let me go."

"I know what you and your friends talked about that night," she said, her smile still fixed. "And I've learned much more since."

"Let go."

"I know what it is you're planning. You, and your friend Vamp."

Terror pricked through my brain, and I felt my heart begin to beat faster. My mouth went dry.

"I don't know what you're talking about," I said, but even in my own ears my voice sounded uncertain.

"I will give you this one warning," she said. "I will tell you the same thing your friend Nix will say, if he ever finds you. You are making a serious mistake."

"I don't know what you're—"

"We have come too far," she said. She gestured to the screen inside the booth, where Ava and LeiFang waved to the crowd. "Things are going well. Better than we dared hope. Your species is on the cusp of something great. I won't let you ruin this, not for us, and not for them."

I pulled my hand away again, and she let go.

"I have to go," I told her. I reached for my cash card, and she held up one hand.

"My treat."

I stood, and she rose with me so that she could speak close to my ear.

"Sam, I worry for you," she said. "Please choose your course very carefully."

"Get away from me."

"I don't wish to see any harm come to you."

I stumbled back, away from the stand. "I said I don't know what you're talking about. Leave me alone."

"I will tolerate ideas," she said, following. "Not action. Do you understand? If you force my hand, you will not be able to protect yourself from me. Not you, or your friends, or your family. Do you understand me?"

I slipped into the flow of the crowd, and let it carry me away. When I reached the street corner, I let out a pent-up breath. My hands still shook as I took out my phone and flipped through my contacts.

I called Dragan, but he didn't pick up. I brought up Vamp's number next and was about to try him, when I remembered Shuang.

"Shit," I muttered. I looked back, through the moving streams of people. Qian still sat with her tea, watching Lei-Fang and Ava on the TV screen.

After a minute, I punched up another contact, and waited by a lamppost while the phone rang.

"Hello?" Dao-Ming asked when she picked up.

"Dao-Ming, it's Sam."

"Sam," she snipped. "I can't believe you left a nine-year-old boy alone in—"

"Just listen," I told her. "They know."

That stopped her. She didn't ask what I meant.

"Who knows?"

"The haan. They know."

"The haan? Are you sure?"

I slipped around the corner, ducking into the shadows of an unused alley. I pressed my back to the brick wall behind me, and stared up past fire escapes and power lines to where a tarp fluttered between two buildings high above. I struggled to decide how much I should tell her.

"The nurse, the one from the hospital, she ratted us out," I told her. "I don't know how, but she knows. She knows everything."

Even though I hadn't taken a hit off the pipe, I felt dry-mouthed and dizzy. Somehow, even though it felt like I'd barely just thought of it myself, news of what I'd planned to do had gotten to the very ones we were trying to expose.

"They're all coming at me," I said, retreating farther into the shadows and staring out at the crowds of people moving down the strip.

"What?"

"The gonzos, the haan . . ."

"Why did you call me?" she asked.

"Dragan is on patrol," I said. "He—"

"But why me?"

"Because . . ."

Part of me knew why. She had something about her, something that made you gravitate toward her when things began to go wrong, but there was more to it than that.

"Because what?"

"I need to feel safe."

"You need to feel safe?"

"I need to protect myself."

I could almost sense her smile on the other end of the line, a smug, self-satisfied smile as one of us finally came over to her way of thinking.

"My offer still stands," she said. "If you can provide the connection, I will pay for whatever—"

"Dao-Ming, this is just for protection."

"Of course," she said. "But you'll understand that I will also require protection?"

I didn't answer. Already, the whole thing had started to feel like a bad idea.

"Sam?"

"What happened to Jin," I said, "you can't do anything about—"

"I know that."

"I'm just saying, he wouldn't want you to—"

"Don't talk to me about Jin," she interrupted, and her tone didn't leave any room for argument. "I'm not stupid enough to try going after the officer who shot him. I didn't even see who did it. You're going to have to trust me. Now, will you do it, or not?"

"Let me think about it," I said.

"Sam, if what you say is true, you may have to defend yourself. Like it or not, things have changed."

"I told you, I don't want—"

"You may have to defend someone you care about. What will you do if they come for Vamp, or Alexei? What will you do then?"

"Dragan can—"

"Dragan can't be with you all the time," she said. "Like

it or not, we're all in danger now. Not everyone believes that but I know that you do."

"You don't believe me any more than—"

"We may not agree on everything, but regardless of the details we both know that the rulers of Hangfei and the haan are working together, and we are all in danger." She paused. "I know you know where to get what we need."

"And why would I know that?"

"Because you've done it before," she said. "Dragan told me the story of how you managed to find him, back then. Don't lie to me, Sam. Set it up, and I'll provide you with whatever cash you need."

I thought about it. I didn't like the idea of feeding her like this, and there'd be fallout from it. I didn't even want to think about how Dragan would react, but the way things were headed . . .

"I'll see what I can do," I said. I felt a little calmer. "Just don't tell—"

"Believe me, Dragan will never know."

A message appeared in the 3i tray, and I brought it up to scan it. Dao-Ming had sent me a list. She'd already had a list ready of the pistol and ammunition she wanted.

"Set it up. Then call me."

She cut the line. I hung up and squeezed my hands together, trying to stop them from quivering.

I turned and looked back toward the stall where I'd been sitting, a little afraid to see if Qian was watching me.

The stall's chairs both sat empty.

Chapter Eight

I hadn't planned on ever returning to the Row after what happened there before the festival two years back, but then, I hadn't planned on returning then, either. As ugly and as dangerous a place as it could be, though, it had offered the closest thing to safety I'd known as a kid in the form of a little shithole named Wei's Hotel. The owner, Wei, let me work for a room and spare change. At the time, a roof over my head and even a little cash on the side had seemed like a godsend. It marked the end of begging, stealing, or, should all else fail and starvation creep too close, catering to men in return for the promise of scraps. I'd seen things in the Row I wouldn't want Alexei to see, and I'd been taken from the Row, too, almost dying on a butcher's block, but when things got dicey, it seemed like something always brought me back there.

Things had gotten dicey enough. Citizens weren't supposed to own guns, but if there's one thing my time in the Row taught me it was that underneath Hangfei's ordered exterior flowed a current of illegal food, water, and weapons. I'd seen more than my fair share of guns flow through Wei's Hotel.

When I reached the corner, I saw that Vamp had finally responded to my messages.

Sorry, he'd sent. *I'm back.*

I grabbed his contact icon from the 3i tray and messaged him.

Yo.

Hey, Sam.

What's up? Where have you been?

Sorry. We've been working on that thing.

You and Shuang?

And Chong. We're making some real progress. We hope to have something before too long. I think we can do the test run in Zun-Zhe as early as tomorrow.

That soon?

That soon. I mean, this is just one section of Hangfei, but if it works, then we'll be ready to go ahead maybe even the night after.

That's good.

Good?

It's great.

Awesome is the word you're looking for.

Fine, awesome, dipshit. A smile crept onto my face. *Hey, were you able to get that info on Qian I asked about?*

The nurse? Yeah. I've got it here. He paused for a minute. *Qian Cho. She's on the grid, thirty-five years old, divorced, and works as a registered nurse at—*

The daughter?

It's true, she had a daughter named Pei Cho.

Had? Is she dead?

Probably. According to the records she got abducted.

She's one of the people who went missing?

No, this happened a while back. They never found her. Probably meat farmers grabbed her. He veered quickly off the topic. *Anyway, her story checks out. You really think she's a haan?*

Now you believe me?

I believed you before. I'm the one who noticed the original footage of that little girl, remember? I know something changed.

You just think they look like us. You don't believe what I saw when—

Hey, I checked Qian out for you, didn't I? He'd begun to get annoyed. *I'm ready to go pretty far out on a limb for you, Sam. I'm always ready to—*

I know. I'm sorry, Vamp. I know.

He went quiet for a minute.

I don't want to fight, he said.

I don't either.

So, what are you up to?

I passed a streetlamp where a man in shabby clothes stood, rifling through a woman's purse. He tossed away a tube of lipstick, a compact and a pack of tissues looking for something valuable.

Not much. You want to get together later?

Actually this is going to go late. Tomorrow? No, wait. Shit, the test run. The night after?

You mean it this time?

Yeah, I mean it. Of course I mean it. We'll set something up. You okay?

Yeah, I'm okay. Talk to you later.

Stay safe.

You, too.

The streets of the Row were steamy and rain-slicked as I made my way down the sidewalk, past shuttered up shops and ramshackle homes. A jiangshi puppet still hung from a power line overhead, left over from the last Fangwenzhe festival, its trailing whiskers waving in the humid breeze where swarms of scaleflies buzzed like drifting parade confetti.

As I passed an alley, I sensed several pairs of eyes peering out at me but I didn't look to see who they belonged to. I just kept walking, which is what you do when you find yourself in the Row. I'd learned that a long time ago, as a child, the hard way, but from the corner of my eye I saw what the group of men had. An empty pair of pants lay plastered to the ground between them, and one held up a wet, wrinkled shirt.

I swallowed, my throat dry, and hustled past. Up ahead I spotted the sign of Wei's Hotel, and felt a pang in my chest for the old man. Between the time I'd lost my real dad and found Dragan, Wei had been the closest thing to a father I'd had. Whoever ran the place now had kept the name, at least for now, but Wei had met a violent and bloody end some time ago trying to save me.

I gritted my teeth, refusing to let any tears appear. They'd only cause me trouble here, and nothing would change what had happened. When I remembered his face, though, and the look in his eyes when I'd first come back, it hurt. He, like Dragan after him, gave more of himself to me than my real father ever had. He'd sheltered me, let me feed myself, and when the time came, he'd protected me, or tried to.

I headed down the concrete steps and pulled open the metal door. Flyers and posters covered the hallway on the other side, some looking for lost loved ones, but most advertising girly shows, street meat, and other even less savory offerings. A guy in rags sat in the corner at the end, looking dead except for the constant twitching of his chapped lips. I followed the hallway left, and when I passed by him I smelled shine fumes and urine.

"It's the end," he slurred.

A force field emitted a dim glow ahead, covering the opening into what Wei used to call "the foyer," the tiny room where he checked people in and out. Sillith had punched her way through the bulletproof glass that used to be there and the new owner had ripped the broken pane out without bothering to replace it. I stepped up to it and looked inside. It didn't look much different from the way it had when Wei ran the place. Stacks of junk still covered every surface, leaving almost no room to move around. The only notable difference was the lack of Wei's signature ashtray, and its payload of spit-soaked cigar butts. Three fly strips hung inside now, as well, each of them covered top to bottom.

I didn't see anyone inside, which was strange. Wei had almost never left it. He couldn't without someone sneaking in or robbing the place. Except for the guy in the corner, though, I didn't see or hear anyone at all.

I headed down the rows of rooms to the stairwell, and made my way down to the basement level. Another dreg lay huddled in the empty space where an ice dispenser had once sat, one cheek pressed to the filthy floor. I saw him breathing, but scaleflies made lazy circles in the air above him like they were waiting for him to die or something. He didn't move at all, even when I passed right by him.

The place had gone downhill, and given what a pit it had been before, that was almost impressive. The overhead lights flickered as I passed underneath them, making the place look even dirtier and creepier than it already had been, and the hallway was strangely quiet.

I passed by a door that hung partway open, and looked inside to find an empty room. Clothes lay strewn over the bed, and the air had a sour sweat smell. Someone had been there, but they'd gone and left their things with the door hanging open.

Something wasn't right. I checked the room number on my 3i, and hurried my way to the door marked 39B. I gave it a knock that triggered a flurry of activity on the other side. Someone got up, and knocked something over. Stuff clattered to the floor as someone else cursed. There were overlapping footsteps as things were hidden and stashed. Then someone approached the door and pulled it open a crack.

A dirty, pockmarked face glared down at me with a frown that formed pits in his hollow cheeks. I could see his pupils were dilated, and his eyes jittered in their sockets. Whatever he was on, he looked crazy with it. A bead of sweat trickled down the side of his face, and the barrel of a gun poked out from the gloom to point at my chest.

"Who the fuck are you?" he asked.

"What do you mean, 'who the fuck am I'?" I asked back, trying not to let on how nervous the gun made me. "I'm Sam. We talked on the phone."

"You alone?"

"You see anyone with me?"

The creep glared at me a minute longer before glancing up and down the hall and conceding that no, he didn't. The door opened just enough to let me in.

"Can't be too careful," he said. "Ain't safe these days."

"Safe from what?" I asked as I stepped inside.

"They knock," he said. "Always knock. Not here. We dangerous here."

As a kid, I'd lived in Wei's Hotel and I'd worked for him, cleaning the rooms. I knew the layout of each one, but I'd never seen anything like what I saw when I stepped inside. The walls were almost hidden behind stacks of boxes of all different sizes, and the floor had accumulated a visible layer of dust and grime. The bed had a metal footlocker stuffed underneath it and several automatic rifles had been propped in a row against the wall next to it. The end table's surface was piled with empty shine bottles, shot glasses, and several ashtrays that were all full. One had fallen on the floor and lay facedown in a scattered pile of butts and ash. The overhead light had been covered in red cellophane, giving the whole room a crimson tint.

It smelled as bad as it looked. The pockmarked guy stepped back, kicking a stray empty bottle by mistake and sending it spinning into a pile of boxes. The toilet's privacy curtain flew open, and a second guy, a shorter, uglier man with long, stringy hair and a United Defense Force tattoo on his neck, stepped out. A bent cigarette dangled from one corner of his mouth, sending a stream of smoke up toward the ceiling. He looked like he'd taken a double dose of whatever his friend had taken. His eyes looked ready to jump out of his head.

"You Sam?" he asked.

"Yeah. You got the stuff we talked about?"

"I got it," he said. "You got the money?"

"Yeah."

"Let's see it."

"Let's see the stuff."

He smiled, exposing yellow teeth and causing cigarette ash to sprinkle down the front of his shirt. He turned to the footlocker and hauled it out into the middle of the floor, then unlatched it and opened the top. When we both leaned over it, I could smell some chemical stink on his breath, and in his sweat.

Inside, several pistols had been arranged, along with boxes of ammunition. There were grenades, knives, and other, nastier stuff like flechette pistols and single-round shotguns with flesh-eating bullets. Part of the trunk had been devoted to more high-tech toys. I spotted a few Escher Field tablets, a graviton gun, canisters of the muscle paralyzer Red Light, and a haan nutrient reclamation wand capable of reducing a human being to a blob of edible jelly in seconds.

He took out two pistols, and began stacking boxes of ammo on the floor next to them, one, two, then three.

"Where's mine?" I asked him.

The guy took a palm pistol from the locker and handed it to me.

"Fucking peashooter," he said.

The last time I used a gun, which was also pretty much the first time I used a gun, I'd had to shoot a man in the chest. It wasn't like he didn't deserve it, and it wasn't like I had much of a choice, but I never forgot the way the blood burbled up from out of that hole, and the way the life had gone out of his eyes. I didn't want to shoot anyone else.

"What if you have to defend yourself? What if you have to defend Alexei?"

I took the pistol, feeling the weight of it in my palm. He laughed as I slipped it into my pocket.

I didn't ask him where he got the stuff. I didn't have to. Some of the stuff they could get from other arms dealers, and some, like the Escher Fields, were probably just stolen. Some of it, though, like the graviton gun and the canisters of Red Light, was security issue only. The nutrient reclamation wand they could have only gotten from a haan. It meant these two either killed security officers or else they'd actually made a deal with them. Either way, they weren't people I wanted my name coming back to.

"You're pretty sweet," he said near my ear. I turned with a start, and swatted his hand away as he brushed my hair.

"Hands off, asshole."

"Tell you what," he said, smoke drifting from his mouth. "I can't float all of it but go behind the curtain with me and suck my dick, you can have the gun for free."

His friend laughed behind me.

"Let's just get this over with."

I took my Escher tablet from my pocket and activated the field, which jumped forward into the air in front of me to reveal an empty storage space on the other side. I put the guns and the ammo in, keeping the palm pistol in my pocket.

I grabbed Dao-Ming's cash card, ready to settle up when the guy dropped another box down between us. The cardboard container, a squat rectangle the size of a cinder block, had been sealed with packing tape.

I pointed at the box. "What's that?"

"What do you mean, 'what's that'?" the guy asked. "It's the rest of your stuff."

"I didn't order anything else."

"Yeah, well, your friend did," he said. "And I got it for you so you'd better be planning on fucking paying for it."

I crooked my neck, bringing up the 3i tray, and brought up Dao-Ming's contact icon. She answered right away.

What the hell, Dao-Ming?

Sam, don't get upset. The box is for me. The extra cash is on the card, and there won't be any—

How the hell did you get in touch with them?

It isn't important.

Yeah, Dao-Ming, it kind of is. How the fuck—

"Hey," the guy with the cigarette snapped. "Quit jerking us around and pay up."

This isn't over, I told her.

My mind raced. For her to have known how to contact them, she had to have somehow monitored me, spied on me. How? Half of the setup had been word of mouth, talking to street contacts. How did she—

"I said pay up," the guy with the cigarette said.

He took out his cash reader, and I slipped the card into it. Sure enough, the extra had been covered. I watched the account drop down to zero.

"See anything else you like?" the guy asked.

I started to make a snide remark when a pair of devices resting in the trunk's corner did catch my eye—two palm-sized oval remote controls, each fashioned of shiny white plastic or metal. I recognized them. I'd seen Nix use one before.

"Holy shit, are those free-standing gate remotes?"

The guy smiled and plucked one out. He held it up and turned it under the red light so I could see. It had a button in the center, another button to activate a holodisplay, and dials on either edge. Even two years ago they had been on the restricted tech list. The haan made them part of the last package, but only for security personnel, and even then only for the heavies.

"These don't come cheap," he said.

"How much?" I asked. Not even Dragan had one of these. Something like this could be handy for quick escapes, especially if I wasn't paying for it.

"Hundred thousand," the man said.

He chuckled when he saw my face fall. His friend laughed again.

"That gonna mean a lot of dick sucking," he said.

One hundred thousand was high, but the truth was that Dao-Ming was funding this little shopping trip and Dao-Ming was pretty loaded. I figured it didn't hurt to ask.

"How do I know it even works?" I asked.

Still chuckling, the guy took the remote from me and aimed it at the wall behind him. He activated the holo-screen, and a bright point of white light appeared there. He messed with the dial, and a hole opened that looked directly into the adjoining room.

I crossed in front of him and peered through the opening. I pushed my head through, feeling the familiar lag of gate travel as I did, and then it came out on the other side. I looked to my right and saw an ugly, sweaty man sitting naked on the bunk there, looking up at the ceiling with a cigar sticking up from his lips like a smokestack. A topless woman with her silver stretch skirt hiked up over her bony hips bounced up and down in his lap with a blank, distant expression on her face. I could see the track marks on her arms as she gripped his freckled shoulders.

I quickly retreated, and he closed the gate.

"Satisfied?" the guy asked.

"Thrilled," I said, making a face.

"Her card's reading zero," the pockmarked guy said. "Quit wasting time."

"I'll give you fifty thousand for it," I told cigarette guy.

"Fuck you. One hundred thousand."

"Seventy," I said. "One hundred is bullshit."

He rolled the cigarette between his lips.

"Ninety."

"Eighty," I told him. "That's as high as I can go."

"She's broke," Pockmarks said. "Would you quit fucking around?"

"You get me eighty," he said, "it's yours. If you're pulling my chain, though, you're gonna wish you didn't."

"Hang on," I said. I got Dao-Ming back on the chat.

They've got a gate remote, I told her. *Could come in handy.*

What does it do?

They can open free-standing gates. You can store end-points, too. They're good for getting around in a pinch.

She thought for a minute.

How much do they want for it?

80K.

The pockmarked guy had started to chuckle along with the other one, when the cash reader, still holding my card, beeped. The number flipped from zero to eighty thousand.

"Holy shit," the one with the cigarette said under his breath, leaning closer to the screen as if making sure he hadn't hallucinated it.

"That cover it?" I asked him.

They both looked from the screen to me, and their eyes had turned predatory. Without saying anything to each other, I could see they'd both come to the same idea that if I had that much money at my disposal, how much more might they be able to squeeze from me.

The guy with the cigarette accepted the cash, knocking the balance back down to zero. I took the remote, and slipped it into my pocket.

The two looked at each other in a way that I didn't like. I grabbed Dao-Ming's container, which was heavier than it looked, and slipped it through the Escher field.

"Nice doing business with you," I said. The guy with the cigarette nodded, but his partner had eased himself behind me, standing between me and the door in the cramped space.

"How'd a stray like you get so much cash?" Cigarette man asked.

"How'd you get your hands on a gate remote?" I asked. He took the cigarette from his mouth, and dropped it on the floor where he used the toe of his shoe to grind it out.

"I killed a haan," he said, "and took it."

He didn't kill any haan. No haan would wander around in the Row and if one had and this guy jumped him, he probably wouldn't be standing in front of me now.

"Where'd you get the fucking money?" his friend asked. "You someone important?"

"Not really."

"You got a rich daddy or something?"

They hadn't expected me to pay what they asked. Too late, I saw that neither of them expected anything like that much money, and the smell of it had turned them dangerous.

"We keep her," Pockmarks said, "and we keep the cash and the remote, plus the money for selling her off."

"Try it," I said, trying to push past the guy. "Nice doing business with you, asshole—"

He never telegraphed the punch even a little bit. One second he stood with his hands by his sides, one open and one holding the gun. The next his free hand jerked out and creamed me right in the cheek hard enough to knock me back. I staggered, and fell back onto my butt.

"Motherfucker . . ." I muttered. Blood ran from my nose, and trickled down over my lips and chin. They both laughed.

"Grab her," Cigarette guy said. The one who hit me reached down to haul me back up, and I whipped the palm pistol around, snapping the butt down on his gun hand as hard as I could.

He barked out a cry of pain and the gun fell onto the floor with a clunk as he pulled back, holding his wounded hand out in front of him. His index and middle fingers both jutted out at odd angles, broken between the first two knuckles.

"You fucking bitch!"

I stood, sticking the pistol up toward his face and he backed away as I started toward him. His back had thumped into the door, when I heard the click behind my right ear. The cold metal of a gun barrel pressed against the back of my head.

"Take it easy," Cigarette guy said.

"Tell him to take it easy," I said, still pointing the gun.

"Drop the piece, and I won't blow your brains out."

I could feel the barrel shake as it dug into my head. He'd was so amped one bad shake might make him fire without even meaning to. I lowered the gun, pointing it at the ground.

Something hit me in the ribs, and I fell to the floor next to the trunk.

"Grab her, you useless piece of shit!"

The guy with the gun lunged. His heel came down and I rolled to avoid it, knocking over a stack of boxes. One of them popped open and sent loose bullets scattering all over the floor around me. I still had the pistol in my hand and jammed the barrel down on the guy's foot where he'd tried to stomp me. Before he could move it, I pulled the trigger.

At first he didn't react, but a beat later blood began to pool around his shoe and it registered in his drug-fried brain. I aimed the pistol toward him, afraid he'd shoot, but he didn't even try. His mouth dropped open, and he fell to the floor. He pushed his palm over the hole to try to stop the blood coming out.

His friend moved toward me as I scrambled to my feet and stuck the barrel against the side of the other one's head. He held up one hand, the one with the gun, while he kept the other on his wounded foot.

"Drop it," I told him. He let the gun fall to the floor, and I took it. I dropped it in the Escher tablet with the rest of the stuff.

I backed away, moving the pistol from one of them to the other as I made my way to the door. The one with the broken fingers glared after me while his friend kicked his shoe off. His drenched sock left prints across the floor as he limped toward a stack of boxes. Before he could reach them, I slipped out, and took off back down the hallway the way I'd come.

"Thanks a lot, Dao-Ming," I said under my breath, heading for the stairwell.

"You're welcome," the guy on the floor slurred, face still pressed to the tiles.

Chapter Nine

I left the hotel, more worried the dealers would come after me than I was the cops ever showing up. Neither one made an appearance as I joined the flow of foot traffic and took the first gate out of there. I kept my Escher tablet deep in my side pocket, and moved as fast as I could through the crowd. When I felt sure no one had followed me out, I relaxed a little, but not much.

How had she known? The thought kept nagging at me. Somehow, Dao-Ming had snuck some kind of tracer on me ... something on the 3i? Something through eyebot, maybe? Something let her pull the contact info for those dealers after I set everything up, because no one else but me had it. She'd followed up with them, and promised them more cash, a lot more cash, for bigger stakes. She'd sent me in there blind, knowing damned well what would happen, and if anything went wrong and we got caught, I'd be left holding the bag.

Sam?

The message flashed in front of me, the 3i's chat window floating over the back of the man in front of me.

Screw you, Dao-Ming.

I'm sorry. I wasn't sure you'd go along if—

You're goddamned right I wouldn't.

At least hear me out.

No. I don't want to hear you out. I don't want to know. Stop talking over the 3i.

You might not see it now but we have to be realistic about things. If you really want to change things, we're going to need to—

We're not doing anything. You're not getting your hands on any of it.

Sam—

I mean it. Don't contact me again.

Sam, I'm warning you, don't you dare cut me off.

"Excuse me."

I heard the man's voice from behind me a beat before I felt his hand on my shoulder. I turned, and my stomach dropped as I found myself face-to-face with a security guard. Eyebot painted his face, and began spitting out information about him as he looked down at me.

Sam, Dao-Ming sent. *Answer me.*

Don't contact me again, I sent, and blocked her.

"Excuse me," the guard said again.

"Is something wrong?" I asked him.

"You tell me." When I just gaped at him, he touched my chin, and angled my face so he could see the side the dealer had punched. "Someone hit you?"

"No," I said.

"No?"

"I'm fine."

The Escher tablet felt like lead in my pocket, and I felt the urge to do something, anything to cover it up or get rid of it but I made myself stay still. The Escher tablets the haan used couldn't be scanned, at least not by us, but when they shared the tech with us one of the conditions the government had was that they be fitted with security overrides. Any guard, including this one, could look inside it and see what I had in there if he got it in his head to do it. He had no reason, but they didn't always need a reason. If he scanned me, he'd pick it up, and if he did that he'd look inside for sure. He'd—

"You don't look fine," he said.

"No?"

"You look scared."

"Sorry," I said. "It's really not as bad as it looks. I'm fine."

"You sure?"

"Yes. I'm sorry. I have a sitter watching my brother. . . . Can I please go?"

He watched me a moment longer, not looking suspicious so much as concerned. He just wanted to know who beat me up. He didn't suspect me, at least not yet. In the end, while he didn't look convinced, he gestured for me to go on my way.

"If someone's bothering you," he said, "flag one of us down. That's why we're here."

"I will."

"Take care."

I turned and made myself keep a steady pace, heading toward the nearest jump gate I could find. The jump put the Row miles across town, and left no way for anyone there to track me. I took two more jumps to Tùzi-wō just in case, then made my way up to my apartment.

At my apartment door, I flashed my keycard at the scanner but when I went to open it one of the inside bolts held it shut. I thumped on it with one fist, annoyed.

"Yun, Alexei, unlock the damned door," I called. I heard stirring on the other side. After a minute, I thumped the door again, harder. "Guys, it's me, let me in!"

I heard the bolt turn, and then the door opened and I saw Yun standing in the doorway looking a little flustered.

"What the hell, Yun?"

"Sorry." She looked at my face where the guy had decked me. "Shit, Sam, what happened?"

"Nothing," I said. "It's a long story. Did something happen? Why'd you have the door locked?"

"Someone came by," she said. "He spooked Alexei. Me, too, a little."

"Who came by?"

"I don't know. Some guy. Wanted to talk to you. I shut off the TV and pretended we weren't here but he said he knew you were in here. He hung around for a while, and then he left."

"Oh."

"Do you know who he was?"

"No," I said. "Don't worry about it. Thanks again for watching him."

She looked back over her shoulder, then back at me. "He's getting really bent. Getting shuffled around like this."

"I know."

"He thinks neither Dragan nor you has time for him. He ditches him with you. Then you turn around and ditch him with me. He just—"

"I know," I said. My face hurt like hell, and I felt worn down, and tired. "No one's ditching him . . . he has to work, you know? I have to work. We're doing the best we can."

"He's nine though, he doesn't get that—"

"I'll talk to him."

"Because he—"

"I said I'll talk to him."

She shrugged, looking like she might say something else, but didn't.

"He's in bed," she said instead. "See you, Sam."

She left, and I headed inside. I locked the bolts behind me, and headed back toward my bedroom. I'd almost stepped through the doorway, when I heard Alexei's voice.

"Sam?"

I stopped, turning toward the sound. Alexei had been waiting for me. He'd gotten out of bed, and stood in the doorway of the room I'd set up for him.

"It's late, Alexei," I told him.

"I know. I—"

"You should be in bed, you have school tomorrow."

"I know." He looked at my face. "What happened to—"

"Nothing, I'm fine."

Who hit you? The message came over the 3i, through the translator.

"No one," I said. "Just . . . go to bed."

My face throbbed. My ribs ached, and my head felt ready to split. I wiped at my nose, and felt a little blood there.

"I—"

"Alexei, I said go to bed," I said. As soon as I did, I realized how curt my voice sounded. I turned to apologize to him, to try to calm down so I could deal with him, but I looked over in time to see his door slam shut.

Great.

I trudged down the hall to my bedroom and shut the door behind me. I plopped down on my bed, then took the Escher tablet from my pocket and turned it over in my hand.

"I didn't order anything else."

"Yeah, well, your friend did. . . ."

I waved my finger across the screen, causing the blank, metallic screen to flicker as the field opened, expanding as it jumped up into the air in front of me. I reached in and removed the heavy, cinder-block-shaped box from inside it.

The box had no markings. I peeled the tape away, and pulled the lid up. Inside, three rectangular gray bricks had been packed, side by side.

I felt pretty sure I knew what they were even before I scanned the codes on the edges of the bricks. They were explosives. Dao-Ming had me buy, and transport, ten pounds of plastic explosives that had been smuggled into Hangfei from who knew where.

"You didn't," I whispered, but she had, and now they were sitting in my apartment, right in my lap. The guns, if we got caught, would mean prison for sure. That box would mean death for whoever sold it, and whoever bought it.

I closed the box tight. After a minute, I hauled it over to my closet and pushed the racks of clothes aside. I used my twistkey to open the black hole gate in back, and carried the box inside.

The light from my room cast a dim glow through the hidden room, so dim that even the small concrete space trailed off into shadow. I took the flashlight from next to the opening, and turned it on.

There was plenty of room for the box among the other things I had hidden there, but somehow even the black hole itself didn't seem like a big enough barrier between it and the rest of Hangfei. I cast the flashlight ahead and carried it farther into the darkness.

Down the dark, grimy hall I saw the rusted green door. I made my way over to it, and looked through the gap and the bottom left corner. It led into another open space.

I pushed against the door, heaving until it moved with a scrape and a squeal against the metal jamb and concrete floor and I could push the box inside and then crawl through after it.

The door opened into a big, dark cavernous room whose ceiling looked ready to cave in. As I cast the flashlight beam around, I saw wires and sections of metal grid work that hung down above an area filled with large, heavy shapes.

"A factory," I whispered. It must have been demolished, buried under the rubble of the Impact.

The underground facility covered a huge, wide open area where rusted pylons stretched from the stained concrete floor to an exposed ceiling of metal beams and crisscrossing pipes. The hulks of old machinery rested under dust-covered tarps, and huge metal hooks hung from the rafters here and there, covered in grease and grime. They dangled from thick cable that wound around great mechanical pulleys that loomed in the shadows above. From somewhere far up above, I could hear the faint moan of wind coming from the Impact rim.

It would do. I put the box against the wall next to a pile of crumbled cinderblock, along with the guns and ammo. If the whole place collapsed at some point, all the better.

I headed back, through the door, down the dingy hallway

and back through my closet where I shut down the gate field and hid it behind my clothes again. I heard Alexei stir in his room, but he didn't get out of bed again. When I checked his 3i icon, it had gone gray.

I sat back down on my bed, my mind racing, and wished I'd never called Dao-Ming.

Chapter Ten

Sam, it's Vamp. The message popped up on the chat in front of me as I headed down the hallway of Dragan's apartment complex. *I've got the info you asked about.*

Nice.

You were right. I scanned your 3i client and found a little piece of spyware had hooked into it. I got rid of it.

How'd it get in there?

It could have ridden in on anything you were sent, or that you scanned recently. You've got to watch for that stuff.

Dao-Ming's list. She'd sent me a list of the type of pistol and ammo she wanted specifically, along with her cash-card code — and the spy bot.

I figured. Okay, thanks, Vamp.

Checked out the apartment security footage too, for your mysterious visitor last night. This guy look familiar?

He sent an image of a man, dressed in white gonzo robes, caught midframe as he moved down the hall with his hands clasped in front of him.

I don't recognize him, but he's a gonzo. I know why he came.

For Alexei?

No, for me.

Why you?

I don't know. Gohan's a freak. Look, I'm at Dragan's, can I call you back?

Sure. Why Dragan's?

We're doing the daddy-daughter thing. He's been bugging me for a day trip so we're going to Render's Strip.

Okay. Talk to you later.

When I knocked on Dragan's door he didn't answer right away, which was weird, because when I checked my phone I saw I was a little late and that usually bugged him. I knocked again, a little louder.

"Yo, Dragan," I called.

I heard something stir inside; then his heavy footsteps approached. When he opened the door, I noticed that while his clothes were clean and pressed as always, his hair had been a little mussed.

"Sorry," he said, smoothing it back.

"Where's Alexei?" I asked, looking past him, into the apartment.

"At school. He give you any trouble the other night?"

"No, he was fine."

"Yeah?"

I shrugged. "I think he's still a little mad at me. I had to hand him off to Yun for a couple hours."

"I thought he liked Yun."

"He does, but between getting juggled from you to me, and from me to her, I think he's getting pissed."

"Yeah, I know," he said. He looked tired. "Why'd you have to leave him with Yun?"

"I had an errand I had to run."

"That where you got the bruise?"

He moved to take a closer look at the spot where the dealer had hit me, and I turned my head. I noticed, then, that in addition to the mussed hair, I noticed a red mark, too, on his lower lip.

"What the hell happened to you, did you get in a fight or something?"

"Don't change the subject."

I tried to peek past him and he maneuvered to sort of block me, keeping the door partway shut.

"What's with you?" I asked, but then I realized what was wrong with his lip. I reached up, and wiped it with my thumb. "Is that lipstick?"

Behind him, I saw Dao-Ming step out from his bedroom wearing a thin robe, and nothing else. Her hair, mussed, had come straight from the pillow.

She glanced back at me, her expression cold, and our eyes met. She was furious, still, that I'd stashed her purchase and wouldn't give it over. The look in her eyes unnerved me a little, but I didn't look away.

You owe me something, she sent over the 3i.

I've got no idea what you mean.

The other day—

Never happened.

With her normally straight hair tangled and mussed, the intensity of her stare made her look wild. Her makeup, usually so carefully applied, had also faded, leaving her looking almost like a different person. Why was she . . .

A beat later, the pieces fell into place. Dao-Ming had come out of Dragan's bedroom, wearing nothing but a robe, hair tousled and makeup wiped away. My blood began to boil, and she must have seen it because a glint of amusement flashed over the anger in her eyes.

We'll see, she sent.

As she turned toward the bathroom, the robe fell open and before she pulled it closed again I saw an ugly white scar underneath her rib cage, surrounded by what looked like circular burn scars.

"Oh my God," I said. My rising anger deflated, just a little, at seeing them. She walked into the bathroom, and closed the door without looking back.

"Sorry," Dragan said.

"Holy shit . . ." I said. I looked at the thumb I'd used to wipe Dragan's face. "It is lipstick."

"I . . ." he stammered. "Look, I just . . ."

"You were . . ."

His face turned red, which under other circumstances might have been cute. I looked toward the bathroom door, then back to him.

"It just kind of happened," he said.

"Hey, it's cool," I said, holding up my hands. My brain was having trouble processing it. "You're a man . . . she's a woman. . . ."

"You seemed a little upset there for a minute."

I looked toward the bathroom door, imagining her on the other side, standing still and waiting for us to leave. Vamp and I used to joke she had a screw loose, but I realized now that it wasn't a joke.

She was never the same, after the incident in the rim, Jin had said.

I had to tell Dragan. Didn't I? But what would he do with that information? What Vamp and I had planned, that was one thing. It would make a mess, sure, but turning off the lights was a far cry from blowing stuff up. He'd be duty bound to turn her in, but would he? Especially once he knew she'd involved me. Did I want him to know that?

I decided I didn't. I absolutely didn't. Not that.

"It's . . . not my business," I stammered. I managed to swallow the idea of the two of them together, and to smile at least a little. "Come on, never mind that. I'm cool with it."

"You sure?"

"Yeah."

The thought nagged at me though—you didn't go to the trouble and expense of getting your hands on explosives unless you had something you meant to blow up. Dao-Ming knew how to get in touch with those guys now, and even if she didn't go back to them, they were a direct link straight back to us if they ever got busted.

"Maybe we should just keep our sex lives to ourselves," I said.

"Agreed. She's going to stay and wait for Alexei. You ready?"

"Lead the way."

The crowded streets of Render's Strip were hot and even in late afternoon the temperature gauge read one hundred and three degrees, and it felt even worse than that. Scaleflies, thriving in the sticky heat, drifted through the mob like weightless, buzzing rain.

We wove through throngs of people passing money and goods back and forth, dodging pedestrians and cyclists as we passed underneath the shade of the rippling tarps that had been stretched from building to building two stories up. Ahead, a tall glass window next to a row of hanging paper lanterns looked into a closet-sized booth. Inside, a stripper sat on her bare bottom, eating a scalefly wafer and reading from a tablet. The sign for Fang's Café blazed as a pink column of block characters, sporting a white tab and an orange one, indicating that in addition to redeeming ration tickets he also sold booze, and smokes.

As we headed in, Dragan took out his phone and frowned at something he saw on the screen.

"What's up?" I asked.

"Alexei never came home," he said. "Dao-Ming doesn't know where he is."

"Is he okay?"

"He messaged her to say he had to do something, but didn't say what." He shook his head, and dropped the phone back in his pocket.

The muscle in his jaw flexed. He'd begun to get really attached to Alexei over the months since they were thrust together, and Alexei liked Dragan, too, I knew that, but the kid pushed him sometimes.

"I was a pain in the ass, too," I reminded him.

He nodded, rubbing his forehead. "Cool off by the fan. I'll wait in line."

He got in line, a sweat stain painted down the middle of his back, and waved off a few scaleflies that buzzed around the crowd's heads. With not much sleep under my belt, just keeping my eyes open turned out to be an effort as I positioned myself under a ceiling fan and leaned against the wall. I fiddled with my keychain as I brought up the 3i and found Alexei's contact lit up.

Alexei, I sent. He didn't answer.

On one of the feed screens mounted above the crowded tables, footage of the Xinzhongzi protest ran. Soundless panic erupted in the square, surging in the strobe of flashing security blues and floodlights. In one window of the screen, a pair of men held reporters back from Gohan Sòng, hanzi underneath saying he still had no comment about the jumpers. Another window showed a snippet of the recording we'd played. The ticker underneath that window said that security had ruled out a foreign cyberattack, and were currently working to trace the source of the pirate signal.

Worry stirred in my belly. The text scrolling past said they already felt confident the feed had been hijacked by someone inside of Hangfei. How had they figured that out so fast?

I tried Alexei again. *Yo, Alexei.*

Leave me alone.

The message sat there in the chat window floating behind my closed eyes. He was angry. He seemed angry a lot of the time these days, but in spite of what he'd said his little candy red heart icon beat impatiently on the 3i's tray, waiting for me to answer.

No can do, kid.

Why not?

I'm your sister, that's why.

You're not my real sister.

Hey—

And Dragan's not my real father.

I leaned my head back, and felt a drop of sweat wander down to the divot between my collar bones.

Yeah, well, we're the best you've got. You don't have to be such a dick about it.

You don't care about me.

That's not true, and you know it Alexei.

You forgot to pick me up, before. Even when I come over you can't wait to leave me with Yun.

I'm sorry, Alexei. Okay? I'm sorry. I've got shit going on.

So do I.

I rubbed my eyes. He was nine. Fucking nine. I felt like snapping at him, reminding him that there were things more important than his little world.

Instead I said: *I said I'm sorry.*

I wanted to tell you something last night.

I started to get mad again, when I remembered that he actually had tried to tell me something. He'd wanted to talk to me, and I'd brushed him off.

Someone jostled me as he squeezed past, making his way toward the counter. Fang's was one of the oldest ration marts in Render's Strip and it both looked and smelled that way. The last weekend of the month had it packed full, and I could feel the people all around me like a single, enveloping organism that murmured, chewed, and smoked. Spiced smoke, licorice and clove scented, tickled my nose with the promise of nicotine, tetraz, and opiate.

I know. I'm sorry, Alexei. What did you want to tell me?

Never mind.

"When they gonna just gas those protesters already?" someone muttered.

"You believe LeiFang is going to make that freak a citizen?" another voice grumbled back. The first man snorted.

"Citizen. They should be locked in cages."

The image on the feed screen changed, and a flicker of gore registered, catching my eye. I turned and saw footage of a security officer's helmet feed, looking down into a room that part of my brain recognized right away.

Look, will you just go home, please? Dragan and Dao-Ming are worried about you.

You're not.

I am, too, I said, but I'd been distracted by the footage on the screen.

That's one of Wei's rooms, I realized. The camera scanned back and forth across the filthy floor, lingering on a trunk of weapons and a few expended shells. Against the far wall next to the room's bunk, several automatic rifles were propped against the wall. My mouth dropped. It was the room the arms dealers worked out of, the same room where I'd gotten the guns, and the explosives.

The camera followed a wandering trail of blood that joined up with a large pool near the toilet's privacy screen. A bloodless hand peeked out from under the plastic, fingers curled like a dead bug. A cloud of scaleflies swarmed behind the curtain.

"Shit," I said under my breath.

When they moved the curtain I saw the guy, the one that smoked, with a bullet hole where his left eye had been and half his head blown off. A deal gone wrong, it looked like.

My first thought, that at least I didn't have to worry about them identifying me now, wasn't my most charitable. My second, that at least I hadn't been there when it happened, wasn't much better. Still, I couldn't say it upset me too much the men were out of the picture.

That must have happened last night, I thought. *Last night or early this morning. Who could have—*

"Race traitors!" a voice shouted from somewhere down the street, cracking as it rose over the general din of the place. I huffed through my nose.

Just stay out of it, Alexei said.

No. When you pull this shit he worries, and so do I.

The heart beat some more while the rattle of Fang's ancient air-conditioner played in the background, competing with the chatter from several of the wall-mounted television sets. I watched the wobbly ceiling fan spin overhead while I waited for him to answer. He didn't respond, but he didn't disconnect either. He had something to say, I thought.

The gonzos are trouble these days, I told him. *I just don't want to see you get sucked in.*

No, they aren't.

Alexei—

They didn't try and kidnap you, I know you're making that up! I can take care of myself!

"You're all a bunch of race traitors!" the distant voice screamed again.

I turned and peered out through the window shutter behind me. Down the crowded street at the main intersection I could make out some kind of assembly, a band of Reunification gonzos it looked like. They had signs, and yellow incense smoke from one of their little shrines drifted up from out of the crowd.

Yeah, they've got a group in Render's Strip right now, not causing trouble.

Leave them alone, okay?

What if I don't?

A wiry guy in a pastel green tank top was standing silhouetted against the blue field in the distance, making a fist at the gonzo crowd. Way off down the street behind them I could see the shimmering haan force-field dome and the shadow of the massive structure underneath it. At the surrounding wall, long turret barrels jutted up into the air like giant spikes and I could see the one of the two-story black balls sticking out from behind a building there, one of the graviton lenses ready to wash the site in a field strong enough to squeeze everything inside into slag.

"Go back to Shangzho, haan lovers!"

Just leave me alone.

The words floated there in front of the scene through the window, but again his little icon pulsed, waiting.

You got something you need to say? I asked him. Cheers surged from one of the TV sets nearby as the icon continued to beat. Down the street, the man tried to grab the gonzo's sign from him.

Alexei, if you have something to say, say it, I told him. I let the heart beat ten more times, then got fed up and disconnected.

Pain in the ass.

My mood shifted from bad to worse. My stomach growled as the smell of opened ration bars seeped through the miasma of smoke, bad breath, and sweat, and I swallowed saliva.

"Sam, it's us," Dragan called. "We're up."

At the counter, Dragan stood in front of Fang, looking back my way and trying to see out the window.

I felt a jab at my neck and slapped my hand down over it, causing a couple of tired faces to turn in my direction. I looked into my palm and frowned at the smear there, a broken black shell in a gob of red- and plaque-colored guts. The scalefly's compound eye stared back at me over a needle-sharp stinger.

"Stupid bloodsucker." I scraped it off under the edge of the counter beneath the TV.

"Hey," Fang called over. "People eat in here."

"They eat scalefly."

"Processed scalefly. What are you, a barbarian?"

"Yeah, yeah."

I squeezed my way over to join them around the dangling fly strip that hung over the register. The strip swayed a little in the current of the overhead fan, specks of amber glue peeking through the coating of black bodies, wings, and legs. Behind Fang, several flyers hung. More faces, more contact info, and more offers of reward for anyone who could help find the missing who, according to security, didn't exist.

"Gonzo, you look like shit," Fang said. I smiled, but still gave him the finger.

I winced as a stray signal jabbed in through the mite cluster . . . It was close, probably just outside passing by. A pang of hunger slithered down deeper into my belly, and I caught a whiff of a haan's stinky, fermented tofu breath as the signal faded and cut.

"You okay?" he asked.

"Yeah." I rubbed my forehead.

"Phase six in three weeks," Fang said. "It's going to be good this time."

"You going to genetically double your dick size?"

"If I can afford it," he said without missing a beat. I figured he'd come back with a crack about my flat chest but he didn't.

"So, except for looking like shit how you been?"

"Okay."

"How's your friend, the guy with the tattoos?" Dragan gave him a little head shake.

"Vamp," I muttered.

"What's the matter, you don't like him no more?"

I bristled. "Stay out of—"

"Okay, okay," Fang said, putting up his hands. "I get it. What about your haan friend? The one who helped you when you—"

"Nix," I said.

Dragan seemed to decide that maybe the time had come to get me out of there and pushed three pink tickets across the counter toward Fang. "Can you take these?"

Fang peered down at the tickets, peeling them off the counter and looking them over.

"Security's treating you guys well."

"Got any left?"

"Yeah, I got some left. You know the phase six rations are supposed to be even better."

I snorted through my nose.

"Pinch me."

Fang reached under the counter and rustled around in a box before placing three fat bars in plastic wrappers marked with the Shangzho haan district's official seal. One of the men in the crowded room glanced over from his table, and watched Dragan drop the bars in a plastic bag. After a decade of powdered kelp, krill, and scalefly cake, the new rations bought the haan more points than probably anything else they'd done so far. At least among the people who could afford them, which in Hangfei, were the people who mattered.

I looked down at the bars. They were processed and wrapped behind the force-field dome with no human intervention, but the wrappers were stylized, with elaborate hanzi characters. Except for the haan seal, they could have rolled off a Hangfei assembly line. They were learning how to market to us, how to make their gifts feel more like products with brand names, and logos.

No ingredient list, though, I thought as I closed the bag. Sometimes, especially with the haan, it was best not to dig too deep.

"All right flykiller," Dragan chided. "Let's go."

I squirmed out from under his hand and he tossed the bag of rations playfully against my chest so I had to grab it before he headed for the exit.

"Hey, let me get that for you."

I wrapped the bag into a bundle and looped the handle around one wrist. Dragan wove through the throng of bodies toward the door, waving back to Fang over his shoulder as he went.

Fang waved back, taking one of the smokes out of the jar as the little bell jingled. With Dragan outside, he flicked the cigarillo toward me and I caught it out of the air.

"See you later, little dragon."

I blew him a kiss, and tucked the smoke in my pocket as I turned to follow Dragan.

Outside, the district's main drag was a mass of bumper-to-bumper traffic surrounded by flows of people on foot, and on bicycles. Thumping music blended into electronic mish-mash as people leaned out of car windows to talk to vendors, and catcall women. The shiny, smoke-colored domes of haan heads bobbed among the mass of human ones, eyes blazing and the occasional shifting movement under their scalps visible even from a distance.

Dragan lingered in the more or less clear patch of black-top tucked to the side of Fang's entryway, where a group of wiry boys stood in a tight circle drinking cans of whiskey soda and adding to the overall babble. He looked down the street at the commotion with the gonzos.

"Don't start with them," I told Dragan, tugging his sleeve.

"I'm not," he said. "Dao-Ming made me promise I'd leave them alone."

"She made you promise? Are you kidding me? She thinks they should all be lined up and shot."

"She was very insistent about it."

"Since when is she about not starting trouble?"

From the top of Fang's steps I could see over the heads of the crowd to the main intersection in the distance. More people had gathered around the group, and while I couldn't make out what they were saying I could see trouble wasn't far behind. Someone snatched a handful of fliers away from one of the gonzo women and threw them across the pavement. When a tall gonzo with a bullhorn tried to step in, someone else tried to take his poster-board sign that read PREPARE FOR SECOND IMPACT.

I shook my head. You could see the damned ship from the intersection. Some people living in the area were old enough to remember the first Impact firsthand. After seeing a quarter of a million people get wiped out they didn't want to hear about how great a Second Impact was going to be.

Someone was going to get punched. Pretty soon, by the look of it.

"Dragan, come on," I said, turning back. "Never mind them."

When I looked back, though, I could see he'd tensed. His eyes had changed, angry now, and when I followed his gaze to the gonzos my heart sank. Alexei stood with them, near another small group of younger boys and girls. That little shitbag had been chatting me from right down the street.

I squeezed back past the group of boys and grabbed Dragan's arm before he started plowing his way toward the intersection.

"Dragan, wait."

Alexei, I sent over the 3i. *Answer me.*

"He knows today's the day I redeem our tickets," he said. "He knows this is where I come, and when. This is deliberate."

I moved in front of him to block his path, but he didn't move toward them. He didn't even really seem mad, or maybe he just didn't have the strength for it. He glared over my head toward the assembly.

"Come on," I said, my voice getting drowned out for a second as an aircar horn blared above us. "Go home. I'll talk to him."

"He won't listen to you."

"He'll listen to me before he listens to you."

The second I said it I felt bad, but it was true, and Dragan didn't seem as wounded by it as I thought he might be. He just stared down the street at Alexei.

"I couldn't save his mother," he said. "If I could have, I would have. I cared about that woman."

"He knows."

"I promised her. . . ." He drifted off.

Alexei, I sent. *Answer me, so help me, I saw you over there.*

He didn't answer, but his icon pulsed away. He'd gotten my messages, he was just ignoring them. I scanned the crowd to try to get his attention, but I'd lost track of him. I couldn't see where he'd gone.

"I'll talk to him," I said again. "I promise. You're already in enough trouble with the gonzos. If you go over there now, you'll just make it worse. Okay?"

He frowned, trying to spot Alexei again as another aircar horn went off above us.

"Okay?"

More horns honked overhead, emitters whining as the neat rows of moving shadows broke apart suddenly. I looked up and saw a procession of slick white aircars heading toward the gonzo gathering. One of them had broken from the pack and come cutting down through three lanes of traffic, nearly clipping a convertible before cruising in really low. People edged out of the way, clearing a hole as it came down toward the pavement, ready or not. It vented hot air, and the people around it shielded their faces as it kicked up clouds of grit.

"Hey, watch it asshole!" I yelled over, but at least Dragan's attention had moved off of Alexei. He watched the vehicle as it thumped down halfway in a no parking zone. One of the tinted back windows slid down partway, and a hand snuck out to wave someone over.

"You!" a voice called. "Yeah, you!" I realized that he was calling Dragan. Over the crowd, the rest of the procession had reached the street gathering and the gonzos had begun to clear spots for them to land.

"Dragan, never mind them," I said, but he had already begun making his way over. By the time I caught up, he was standing by the rear door, peering in the crack in the window. "Dragan just go home. I'll talk to Alexei and meet you—"

"What do you want?" he asked the guy in the car.

I looked at the driver but he just sat there with one hand

on the control stick. He had the divider behind him closed, so I couldn't see into the back.

"Dragan . . ." I warned.

The back door opened. Dragan looked in, and seemed to recognize the person inside.

I moved in next to him and saw three guys back there, all wearing suits. Two were big, tattooed guys and the third was an older guy but I couldn't see his face. He gestured for Dragan to get in with one bony hand.

"Dragan . . ."

"It's okay," he said. "Wait out here."

I tugged at his shirt, but he was doing it—he was getting in. He slid into the plush backseat and one of the suits grabbed the door to close it. Before he could, I slipped in and plopped down next to Dragan. We were facing a second seat that was under the divider. The older guy sat in the middle of it, his legs crossed like a woman, with the two tough guys sitting on either side of him.

The inside of the car smelled amazing . . . someone had been eating back there and the smell of food, real food, not rations, lingered heavy enough to make my mouth water.

"Sam, I told you to—"

The doors locked.

"It's okay," the older guy said.

It wasn't until then that I saw the guy's face and realized who he was. His picture was all over the TV and street posters around town. It was Gohan Sòng, the king gonzo himself, slumming it in Render's Strip.

He's making an appearance at the Second Impact rally, I realized. That's what the procession was all about. He'd shown up to give some wing-nut speech or something, and spotted Dragan and me as he came in to land.

"Hello, Little Star," he said to me.

I'd always thought it was makeup and photo retouching that made him look like some kind of weird, living mannequin but he kind of looked that way in person, too. He watched us, his eyes intense under a pair of carefully plucked eyebrows. One eye peered out from under a heavy, drooped lid that made one half of his face look asleep. His black hair looked like shiny, molded plastic.

I started to say something, but Dragan signaled for me to be quiet. Gohan looked at me, then down at my hands, which made him grin, then back over to Dragan. He stared at him, like he'd just seen the most amazing thing he'd ever seen.

"How are you feeling, Officer Shao?" Gohan asked. His lips curled a little more, and Dragan scowled.

"What do you want, Sòng?"

"I wanted to talk to you both face-to-face," Gohan said. "In private."

"Why?"

He looked at Dragan with an odd expression, and then tapped at a series of contacts on the tabletop without looking. A hidden panel popped open and cold air misted out, swirling as he reached inside and plucked out a piece of fruit . . . real fruit. I recognized it as an apple, like the ones from the gonzo shrines, but this one wasn't made of wax.

He bit into the fruit's flesh with a crunch and held it in his mouth while he snatched a bottle filled with some kind of orange liquid from the minifridge. He pushed the panel door closed in a puff of mist, then bit off a big piece of the apple while he popped the bottle top with his thumb. He glugged down half of the orange stuff with the apple still in his cheek, and then chewed so that a little bit of juice leaked from one corner of his mouth.

"Sòng, what the hell do you want?" Dragan asked, his voice hardening.

Gohan swallowed and his lips curled into a little smirk, like he knew something the rest of us didn't. He stared at Dragan a long time, until it started to get weird.

"You seem different to me, somehow. More . . . enlightened, maybe?"

"Is that so?"

Gohan nodded. "I have an eye for these things. I wondered if maybe you hadn't reconsidered your position regarding the church."

I hadn't told Dragan about Gohan's little grab attempt he'd made outside my apartment. If I had, he might have decked Gohan right there. As it stood, a vein in his forehead stood out and he looked to the goons to see if they had any idea what Gohan was on about. If they did, they didn't show it.

"Well, I haven't," Dragan said.

Gohan bit off another piece of apple and as he chewed, his smirk grew another couple of notches.

"Are you sure?" he asked around a mouthful of pulp.

"Yes, I'm sure. What the hell is wrong with you?"

Gohan's face held its look of amusement, even as he sighed.

Whatever was happening, I didn't like where it was heading. People were milling past the aircar, not able to see inside and unaware of what was going on. One girl even used the reflective surface to check her hair as she passed. As Gohan slurped his way through the rest of his apple, I tugged at Dragan's shirt.

"Hey, you're not supposed to be talking to him," I said.

"You're so precocious," Gohan said, the plastic smile still on his face. "I could eat you up."

"Watch it," Dragan said, pointing his finger in Gohan's face. "The Sòng name is only going to take you so far with me. I don't care who your father is—"

"Well, you should," Gohan said, his voice calm. "My father is the reason Governess LeiFang holds her office, and you answer to her."

"I don't answer to anyone. Let go of her."

"Dragan," I said. "It's okay."

"That's very dramatic," Gohan said, "but you do answer to someone, you really do. Hangfei is still under martial law, and everyone answers to the governess. Especially you."

"Dragan, don't," I said.

"This stops now," Dragan said.

Gohan leaned closer to Dragan and lowered his voice a little. "He is a lost soul, your Alexei. . . . I'll tell you, I don't know what it is that happened to him, or what he saw, but whatever it was has left him obsessed with the haan."

"He hates the haan," Dragan said, "and I don't blame him."

Gohan shook his head.

"No . . . I don't think that's true. That's not what I see."

"You don't know him."

"Maybe it's you who doesn't know him."

Dragan's hackles went up, and I put one hand on his arm to try to calm him a little.

"I don't know what your obsession is with him, or any of us," he said, "but find someone else to fixate on or I promise you you'll wish you had."

"It's really not your choice to make," Gohan said. "Alexei is with us, now."

"No, he's not. They can put me on a short leash, but believe me I will make your life difficult."

"The days of Governor Hwong are over," Gohan said, "and I promise you the governess is well aware of who was most instrumental in getting her where she is. I can do whatever I want. You watch."

He turned his attention back to me. He put down the apple and took my right hand in his two cold ones, all sticky with juice. I gaped, not expecting it. Dragan's hackles went up another notch, and he leaned forward in his seat. I tried to pull my hand away, but he held it fast.

"Take me up on my invitation," he said. "Come by our headquarters in Xinzhongzi . . . both of you come. I promise to make it worth your while."

He smiled, and then he leaned forward and planted a

kiss on the knuckles of my right hand. He let the kiss linger, until I felt his tongue, still cold from the apple, slither between my index and middle finger where it began to probe.

Dragan moved before even I could, his hand clamping down on Gohan's wrist. He twisted the arm, making Gohan break the kiss and squirm in his seat.

"Dragan, don't —"

"You think you're being clever," Dragan said, leaning close. Gohan's hand was turning purple, the veins bulging out as Dragan squeezed. "You're not."

Gohan was staring at him, his mouth a little open almost like he was in some kind of trance.

"Such passion," he breathed.

Dragan let him go, shoving his hand away.

"You're quite strong," Gohan said, nursing his hurt wrist. His weird smile had returned.

"Dragan," I whispered, "he's got a screw loose, just ignore —"

"Keep pushing me," Dragan said to him, violence edging into his voice.

I'm sorry, Sam.

The words popped up in Alexei's 3i chat. They floated there in the little translucent window between me and Dragan. He didn't say anything else, just that. Just "I'm sorry, Sam." I turned in my seat, looking through the back window to try to spot him again but I couldn't see through the crowd.

Sorry for what? I sent back. Sorry for blowing Dragan off? For what he'd said earlier . . . or something else? He didn't answer. He just repeated his message again.

I'm sorry.

Could he see us, now? Did he know his little stunt may have caused our run-in with Gohan?

Dragan gestured for me to snap out of it, and get out of the car.

"Sam, go."

You should be, you selfish piece of shit—

A boom crashed down the street, so big and so loud that I felt the aircar shake. Everyone in the car turned to look as a collective gasp filled the air outside, people stopping to stare as a black cloud of smoke still bubbling with orange flame rose up from the middle of the intersection where the gonzos, and Alexei, had just been standing.

Chapter Eleven

With the noise from the explosion still rolling down the block, the street fell into complete chaos. A cloud of smoke billowed up between the buildings, while people surged away in a frantic, expanding circle from the blast site. The wave backed up against the mob of people surrounding it, and in seconds the strip was a tangle of shoving, screaming bodies. A sick feeling grew in my stomach as I realized Alexei's 3i icon had gone from shiny red to idle gray.

The driver unlocked the car doors but there were too many people pressed against it and I couldn't push it open. Dragan managed to muscle his side open and I followed him out, sticking close while people swarmed around us. As soon as we were clear, the door slammed shut behind us and I heard the aircar's emitters wind up. Hot air ruffled my clothes as it whooshed up into the air behind me amid the racket of blaring horns.

Dragan pulled his gun, pointing it toward the sky as he looped his badge around his neck and began shoving his way through the stunned crowd, back toward the blast. After a beat, I snapped out of it and took off after him.

"Alexei!" he shouted. "Alexei!"

I wove through the mass of bodies in the wake Dragan created, hammering Alexei's 3i with message requests. Tears welled in my eyes even as I fought to push my way through the panicked crowd.

You selfish piece of shit. It was all I could think. *You selfish piece of shit.* That couldn't be the last thing I ever said to him.

"Security!" Dragan yelled, wrestling past a group of men clogging the sidewalk. "Out of the way! Now!"

The wall of bodies was too cramped for me to see between them and I was too short to see over them. All I could see was Dragan's back, and the tangle of arms and legs that surrounded him.

"Everyone, out of the way!"

I ducked a swinging elbow at the last second and stumbled into a man who shoved me away into the wall of the building next to me. I hit hard, and almost went down onto the ground before I managed to get my footing back.

I wasn't going to make it. There were too many people, and the crowd had turned violent. It was all I could do to not get pulled under and trampled. Sticking close to the side of the building, I looked through the mob where people clambered over and around the vehicles gridlocked at the intersection. Above them was a fire escape, the ladder collapsed against the second-floor grate.

A man on a bicycle crashed down on the sidewalk in front of me as another man collided with him. The opening they made was small, but big enough for me. I darted forward and jumped over them, slipping through the people on the other side, and then following the shop fronts until I got to the intersection. I climbed onto the hood of the nearest car, and then up the windshield and onto the roof.

"Hey!"

I lunged for the fire escape ladder and just managed to grab one of the rungs before I fell. It didn't come down like I hoped, though, and for a second I hung there like a spider looking down at the people who surged below. I brought my legs up, and managed to scramble over the side where people inside the building were watching through the windows.

I pushed off one foot and ran the length of the escape, which took me all the way to the opposite side of the building. I stopped at the rail and looked down at the chaos.

Up ahead, I could see that the gonzo assembly had been wiped out. Bodies lay strewn across the street around a circle of twisted metal and spitting flames. Several cars had been thrown over onto their sides amid smoking shrapnel, broken glass, and concrete rubble.

Alexei, answer me. Please answer me.

Off to the side I could see Dragan as he muscled his way toward the blast site, but he still had a ways to go. I climbed over the rail, and hung there gauging the distance to the truck below me. I dangled at arm's length, and then dropped down onto the roof with a hollow thump followed by the blare of a horn.

"Off the truck asshole!"

I jumped down and took off at an angle toward the street. Foot traffic had thinned close to the explosion, and I could see bodies and flapping, bloody clothes through the crisscrossing streams of people.

Alexei, please, answer me.

I pushed through the last of the mob, and stumbled out the other side to the edge of the blast site. As I approached, the wind shifted, and through the stink of exhaust and body funk I caught a blast of acrid smoke and burned meat. Dragan pushed his way through the last of the crowd and ran to me. He grabbed my elbow, but I pulled away.

The street was a mess. Two of the gonzo procession cars lay on their sides, showing jagged edges of blackened metal and broken glass. The nearest car's shattered windshield had been splashed with blood, and I could see a shapeless mass of black and red inside. Dark trickles wandered across the blacktop, creeping toward a sewer grate.

"Sam, stop," Dragan said. He grabbed my arm again, and again I pulled away.

I lurched farther into the wreckage, looking for Alexei.

The remains of the gonzos were strewn among their ruined shrine where somehow the floating wax apple wobbled but still spun. An armless body lay several meters away, one of its missing limbs on the curb nearby. Others who had been even closer to the blast fared far worse. With some I couldn't even tell what part was what, it was all just blood, bone, and guts.

The Pan-Slavs had bombed Render's Strip before, it had to be them, but for a minute all I could think about was Dao-Ming's box of explosives. That this, this mess in front of me, was the type of mess she meant to cause if given half the chance. Her hatred of the government, the haan, and the gonzos, this is where it would lead.

And where will you lead us? The voice nagged from within. *When the lights do go out, where will we find ourselves then?*

Blobs of red were splattered across the remains of a bus stop shelter, and several glass flytraps had shattered around clumps of chemical-soaked flies. Down at my feet lay the remains of the gonzo sign, painted partly over with a big swatch of blood. Black and red lines bled from lettering on the wet cardboard.

PREPARE FOR SECOND IMPACT

It felt like some kind of dream. Everything had grown distant, and even the sounds and smells around me faded to the distant static of white noise. My stomach tingled, threatening to throw up the little bit that was down there as I grew dizzy. Far off up ahead, the towering haan ship seemed to tilt behind its shimmering dome.

What if this actually was Dao-Ming? The thought buzzed in my ear. I didn't want to believe it, but part of me had already begun to think it could be true. Pan-Slavs went after distribution centers for food and water, but this had targeted the gonzos. Dao-Ming hated the gonzos, maybe even more than the rest of them. I remembered her words at the protest:

"That man has sold out his own race to gain favor with the haan. One of these days, he'll pay for that. . . . Cut off the head, and the rest will die."

She couldn't have, I thought. *I never delivered the box. The dealers are dead. She couldn't have. She—*

Sam?

I perked up as Alexei's heart icon pulsed. It had turned from gray back to red, and right then it felt to me like a flat line had just blipped. He might be hurt, may be hurt bad, but he was alive.

"Alexei!" Dragan shouted, his voice rising over the din as the first siren chirped from somewhere up above us.

"I got him," I called back. I looked around, trying to spot where he may be.

"Where?"

"I'm not sure. Close, though. He's alive."

I couldn't see him in the crowd but he couldn't be far. I used the 3i's locater to home in on him, and a spot on the map flashed from somewhere just across the street.

The siren chirped again and I looked up to see the underbellies of aircars slowing down in the skylane to get a better look. Sun shone down between them, where another dark shape moved into view, making a tight circle. The vehicles overhead began to part carefully, sneaking past one another to let the security vehicle descend down to the street. As it lowered through the hole, two more cruisers darted out from between the buildings to join it.

I waved to Dragan, tapping my forehead with one finger. He saw it, and on the 3i his heart icon turned from gray to red.

I got him, I told him. *You take care of this. I'll bring him to my place.*

He—

He's a Pan-Slav; you don't want him to get sucked into this.

Dragan paused, then nodded as the first security ship

came down, heat ripples pouring off the undercarriage as the coolant pumps whined to keep up. People in the crowded street began to shield their faces as the graviton emitters kicked up dead flies and bits of debris, sending them swirling on a huff of warm air.

After a moment, Dragan tossed something to me and I caught it. It was his security twistkey.

There's a security gate one block over, he said, pointing. *Get him out of here.*

I nodded and crossed the street to the smoke shop on the other side. There were people crowded around the door and window but they stepped back to let me in when I approached. Inside people were talking to each other in hushed voices, some of them crying while a TV set displayed an overhead view of the scene outside.

I turned away, moving farther into the shop down one of the aisles where cartons of tightly packed cigars were displayed in and among exotic additives, powders, herbs, and oils. A soft, shuddering breath came from up ahead.

When I got to the end of the aisle, I saw Alexei sitting on the floor. He had his back to the wall, hugging his knees with tears in his eyes.

"Hey," I said. He didn't look up. I thought he might be in shock.

I walked over and knelt down next to him, then took him by one arm and pulled him toward me. He resisted at first, but then leaned over and put his head to my chest.

"I'm sorry," he said.

"You're okay," I told him.

"I'm sorry."

He let out a pent-up breath, sagging farther into my arms, and I felt him shake. I hugged him, looking him over as I stroked his hair. There wasn't a scratch on him. He couldn't have been there when the bomb went off, even though he'd been standing with the other gonzos only a minute before.

"How did you—"

"I was on my way over here," he said. "I was going to get gum for you . . . the kind that helps you stop smoking. I didn't mean what I said. . . ."

Back outside the first security ship landed with a heavy thud, and I peeked down the aisle out the shop window in time to see its doors spring open and four officers step out. Dragan joined them and they started to secure the perimeter.

"I know," I said, and hugged him a little tighter. "Me neither. You just dodged a bullet, kid."

"I never got the gum."

"That's okay."

"Is Gohan dead?" he asked.

Anger flared, but I just sighed, and stroked his hair.

"I don't think so."

As I watched the guards, Vamp's app bubbled up again. It locked on to each officer's security transponder, then captured their faces and ID numbers. Eyebot had them flagged as toughs with records of violence. They meant the first response to crack down hard.

"Come on," I told Alexei, standing up and helping him to his feet. "They're going to lock this place down; we have to get out of here."

Alexei nodded, still looking down at the floor. Back outside, I saw one of the officers pointing toward the shop while another got on his phone.

"Is there a back way out of here?" I called over to the woman behind the counter. She pointed, and I took Alexei's hand. "Come on."

I led him along after me, heading toward the back of the store and through a door that led to an alley outside.

Back on the street, people had seen the writing on the wall and made themselves scarce as the security perimeter closed in. Eyebot's data, compiled from the thousands of eyes who ran the app, showed security troops in a net that covered several blocks around the blast site. They'd already closed it, and were moving in fast. None of the people running was going to get through. The only way out would be the security gate.

Someone shoved past us and bolted down the sidewalk as we came out of the alley. I spotted the security gate off to my right and pulled Alexei's sleeve.

"This way."

He trailed after me as I made a fast clip toward the set of concrete steps at the street corner. We climbed down to the landing, a graffiti-covered cinder-block box where the metal gate frame was mounted. More people stormed past on the sidewalk above us as I took Dragan's twistkey and slipped it into the frame's socket. When I turned it, the air in front of the concrete wall shimmered, and was suddenly replaced by what looked like the inside of an office. A woman in a pantsuit who was standing near the gate when it opened nearly jumped out of her skin and dropped her electronic tablet down onto the tiled floor in front of her with a crash.

I turned the key again, then again until the doorway looked out onto a street I recognized. It was off in Jangbong somewhere, far away from all of this.

"There," I said. "Come on, let's go—"

A man came barreling down the steps toward us, with several others close behind him. They'd seen that the gate was open and that they had a way to duck the security net. The man clipped me with his shoulder and spun me into the wall as he ran through. The others didn't slow down as they closed in.

I grabbed Alexei around the waist, turned, and dragged him through the portal with me. There was that moment, that strange feeling of stepping into deep, dark water that froze us both in place. I could feel Alexei next to me, a solid, living presence, but for that instant he was as still as a statue.

As suddenly as it started, it ended and my foot came

down on the pavement halfway across Hangfei. As soon as I felt solid ground again I grabbed Alexei and hauled him out of the way, taking refuge against the wall to our right as the people behind us stormed through. Two more made it before the gate's timer wound down and the field collapsed. The chaos of Render's Strip disappeared from the doorway, replaced by a cinder-block wall.

I got to my feet. We'd managed to get away, and the sooner I could get us back to my place the better, but I found myself just standing there, staring down the neon-lit streets.

"Sam?" Alexei asked.

Dao-Ming, I sent over the 3i. Her little heart pulsed in the tray, lit up red, but she didn't answer.

"Sam?"

Just tell me, I sent. *Did you have anything to do with this?*

"*. . . blood will come next.*" That's what she'd said.

Did you have anything to do—

Anything to do with what? she answered.

You know what I'm talking about.

I have no idea what you're talking about.

Alexei was there, I sent. *He was right there. He could have gotten killed with the rest of them—*

Whatever you're talking about, I wasn't involved. I've been at Dragan's, you stupid child, you saw me there yourself. I called him in Render's Strip, from his apartment, most likely while you were standing right there. Now, tell me what happened. Is Alexei okay?

I paused, confused. That was true, wasn't it? Dragan had taken a call from her as we arrived at Fang's. She'd spent the night with him, so she couldn't have . . .

Dao-Ming, I—

Never mind, she sent. *I'll contact Dragan. Get your facts straight next time, before you go throwing accusations around.*

Wait—

She disconnected.

"Sam?" Alexei asked again, and tugged my shirt. I looked down at him. His face had been smeared with soot, and his eyes were wide, and frightened.

"Come on," I said to him. "We've got to hustle."

He nodded, and followed as I started down the quickest route home.

Chapter Twelve

By the time we got back to downtown Tùzi-wō, every alert screen on every building and signpost showed footage of the blast while news tickers scrolled messages about the attack. They showed the wrecked distribution centers that got caught in the blast, and images of mangled bodies with their scattered gonzo signs.

"...appears to not have been the work of Pan-Slav terrorists, who typically target food and water supplies," a voice reported as I passed one of the feeds. "Early speculation is that the Reunification Church members themselves may have been the target of the attack, which may have been carried out by the same mysterious dissident responsible for the propaganda cyberattack during the recent incident at Xinzhongzi."

I glanced over in surprise and saw an image of my head in silhouette, a screen capture of the video we'd made.

What the hell? I thought, but I could see it for myself.

They're blaming me.

I picked up the pace, Alexei running to keep up while I messaged Vamp to let him know what happened. The bomb had stirred things up. If he still meant to run his test on the power grid tonight, there could be more heat than he expected.

"Sam," Alexei said, tugging my sleeve. Vamp didn't pick up so I tried again, then settled on leaving a message.

"Sam . . ."

"What?"

I looked ahead at my apartment complex, and saw what Alexei had already seen. Through the lobby window I could see three security guys and I stopped short, pulling Alexei off to one side with me to check them out from across the street. Two watched something on the video screen mounted in the corner while the third one tried to flirt with a woman who looked like she was waiting for someone else.

"Shit," I muttered. "Shit!"

It couldn't be coincidence. Had they managed to trace the Xinzhongzi feed already? Did they know it had been me on the video, and the media just hadn't found out yet?

"We can't go in," I said.

"Where, then?"

"Hold on."

I pinged Dragan on the 3i.

Dragan, security's staked out at my place. Any idea why?

No, but stand by.

His little heart icon beat for what seemed like forever while he checked into it. I began to get antsy, watching the officers in the lobby while Alexei fidgeted next to me.

Sam, they're there for you.

What do they want?

Looks like a tip came in about a possible connection to the Xinzhongzi recording.

A tip from who?

It doesn't say. Look, they're not there to arrest you so that means they don't know for sure. You're just a person of interest for right now. Get out of there for now, and we'll deal with it.

Where should I go?

Don't go to my place; it's the first place they'll look. Vamp's been flagged too, so don't go there. I sent him a warning and it looks like he's not there anyway.

Then where?

Find someplace to hunker down and lie low. Grab a room somewhere. Can you do that?

Yeah, I think so. Thanks, Dragan.

Be careful, Sam.

I will.

"So we aren't going in?" Alexei asked. I looked back at my apartment, and the security men waiting there.

"No."

We had to go somewhere no one would think to look. I thought about Wei's Hotel but after what happened with the dealers I thought I'd better not chance it. On the 3i, I brought up the Hangfei map and looked for someplace else, the kind of place most people would leave as a last resort. Anyplace else would be filling up already anyway. As I sifted through my limited options, one name in particular jumped out.

"I've got it." I told him. "I know where to go."

"Where?"

"Baishan Park. We can rent a tube there."

"Where's that?"

"It's going to be a haul, but if they turn the gates back on we can ..."

That's when I realized that I didn't have my Escher tablet with me. I'd left it on the dresser in my bedroom. It had my cash card inside of it. Not only that, but the gate remote, and ...

"Shit."

"What's wrong?"

"Nothing."

The tablet also contained the twistkey to the black hole gate in my closet. The space where I'd stashed my computer tablet, full of evidence, as well as the guns, and Dao-Ming's explosives.

"Sam ... ?"

I couldn't leave without it. If they suspected I might be involved in the incident at Xinzhongzi, they'd bust in there and search the place for sure if they hadn't already. They'd find the tablet, override the field, and they'd find everything. I couldn't leave it.

"Okay, Alexei, change of plan."

I fished my keys out of my pocket, then pulled my work twistkey off the ring and handed it to Alexei.

"This won't work on the regular gate system," I told him as he took it. "It's keyed to the maintenance gate at Ginzho tower. We use them to get to the washer rigging, for work. Do you remember where you and Dragan met me that time for lunch? The access gate?"

He nodded.

"Go there," I told him. "It's not part of the regular gate network so it should still work. Take the gate up to the rigging, and wait there for me. No one will find you there."

"You said don't go off on my own."

"I know, but this is an emergency. Go straight there. Don't talk to anyone. Understand?"

He looked down at the twistkey, and then slipped it in his pocket. "Okay."

"If I don't show up or contact you in an hour, then go to Dao-Ming's. Got it?"

He nodded, and took off. When he'd disappeared into the crowd, I crossed the street, and slipped around the apartment building to the side entrance. I used my badge to open it, and then headed down the hall toward the elevators. As I approached, I could hear the TV blaring in the lobby, along with the voices of the security men.

I stepped through the doorway and banked left toward the elevators, wondering if I shouldn't keep walking and just take the stairs, when a voice called from behind.

"Xiao-Xing?"

I turned to see a fourth security guy, who must have been sent to keep an eye on the side entrance I'd just used. He started toward me.

I glanced toward the doorway I'd just come through, but

knew I'd never make it. The man rested his hand on his stunner, but didn't draw it.

"Xiao-Xing?" he asked again.

I'd already turned at the sound of my name, and he'd seen it. He knew it was me.

"Look, I—"

"Into the lobby," he said, gesturing toward the door.

"I—"

"Now."

Part of me wanted to run, but I knew my best bet was to stay cool. I did like he said, and he moved in behind me while I headed into the lobby.

All three of the security guys there looked over at us when we came through. In between them was a little twig of a woman I hadn't seen when I first came in, her skirt flared out around skinny legs in striped stockings.

"Yun?" She didn't look away. She raised her finger, and pointed at me as one of the guards patted her back.

"Well, well," Casanova called over. "You must be Xiao-Xing Shao?" The woman next to him looked relieved to have his focus somewhere else.

"Yun?" I called, but the guard said something to her, and she left the lobby. On the sidewalk outside, she glanced back once as she headed down the street.

"We've been waiting for you," Casanova said.

"My Dad's still pulling security over in Render's Strip," I said, looking back to them.

"Are you Xiao-Xing Shao?" he asked again.

Yun had turned me in. My goddamned babysitter had turned me in. Why? How much did she know?

"Yeah," I said. "That's me. What's the problem?"

"We need to ask you some questions," he said. "Come with us."

"Why?" I asked. "What's this about?"

Casanova's hand drifted down toward his stun gun as he took another step toward me.

"We going to have a problem?" he asked.

"No," I said. "Look, my Dad's in security and—"

"Did I ask you if your father was in security?"

"No, I'm just saying. I know the drill. Don't get your dick in a knot."

His eyes narrowed, and he popped the latch off the holster where the stunner sat. I held up my hands.

"Kidding," I said, trying to think fast. I had to get into my apartment. If I could manage that then I could grab the gate remote and I'd at least have a chance to get away.

"Let's go."

"I can't," I said. The officer unclipped the stun gun from his belt and started toward me. "No, I mean . . . I just have to go to my apartment first."

"Why?"

"I've got a surrogate haan up there that needs to be fed, like, ten minutes ago. That was my sitter who just left. Let me go up and take care of him."

"You're in the surrogate program?"

I wasn't, not anymore, though I had been for a long time. If he checked I'd be busted, but if he didn't, then it just might work. I fumbled in my wallet and dug up the old card, holding it up just long enough for him to see.

"He could die," I said. "You want that on your record?"

That did stop him. He looked at the screen for a minute, then back at his buddies, then back at me. His eyes went out of focus for a second and I could tell he was looking me up, checking my story. After a minute, he snapped back. He didn't look happy.

"Mei," he said over his shoulder. "Go with her."

"Thank you," I said, hustling past them. One of the three other men broke rank and followed me as I headed to the elevators.

"She gives you any trouble, shock and hood her," Casanova called after us. "We got a schedule to keep."

The officer moved in close behind me as I jabbed the

elevator button. When the door opened, he got on with me and stood rigid while we rode up.

"You want to tell me what's going on?" I asked him.

"We'll explain at the detention center."

"Dandruff," the ad box said, the A.I. icon appearing on the screen. "Embarrassing dandruff—"

Mei used his security card to override the box and the A.I. flickered out.

He didn't say anything else the whole ride up. How much did he know? Could they have already found and tracked the intrusion back to us? I tried to calm down, to tell myself that if they did know, if they were sure, then I wouldn't be headed up to my apartment right now. I'd be arrested, and on my way to prison.

I went to contact Vamp on the 3i, but the transmitter had been taken offline. The officers had used the security back channel to shut it down.

Damn it.

"Just tell me—"

"I told you we'll explain at the detention center."

When we reached my floor, Mei followed me as I hustled down the hall, hooking a left at the hallway T toward my unit. My badge shook in my hand as I touched it to the reader, and when I pushed open the door I crossed the room on the other side before I heard it clunk shut behind me. I glanced back and saw the officer unclip his radio, keeping his eyes on me as he spoke into it.

"We're here," he said. "She's going to feed the little maggot now. We'll be down shortly."

"Grab a drink if you want," I told him. "I have shine. Check the cabinet."

He didn't move. He just stood in the doorway blocking the way out.

"Suit yourself."

I headed into my bedroom where I'd once kept the crib, and heard him follow me not far behind. As soon as he looked inside, he'd know I'd been bluffing. I didn't have many options left.

I slipped through the door and closed it behind me.

"Hey, open the door," he called.

"Other people make him nervous," I called back. "Just give me three minutes."

I turned the bolt just as he turned the knob and tried to push open the door.

"Open the goddamned door, right now."

"Three minutes!"

He wasn't giving me three minutes. He tried the door again, and then I heard him radio down.

"She's locked herself in her room," he said. "Get up here and bring the pry."

"What about the surrogate?" a voice came back.

"I don't think she's got one; I think it's bullshit."

"On our way."

I didn't have long. I grabbed my Escher tablet from my dresser and opened the field. I found the black hole twist-key, then threw open the closet door and jammed it into the gate's socket. I turned it, and as soon as the portal opened I scrambled through into the factory ruins. The sounds of the guard shouting and banging on my door echoed through the hall behind me as I sprinted to the rusted door.

I squeezed through, and made to grab the box of explosives along with the pistols and ammo, when on impulse, I stopped.

Once I was gone I wouldn't be going back to the apartment, not now. Assuming I could get away, they'd stake the place out. That meant I wouldn't be able to get back to the black hole drop, unless . . .

I found the gate remote inside the tablet and switched it on. The interface lit up in the air in front of me, and I waved my finger through the options until I found where to set up an endpoint. I pointed the remote onto one grimy wall of the factory, and locked the endpoint in.

The box would be safer out in the rim. Chances are they wouldn't find the drop, and wouldn't have the twistkey if they did. My tablet could be searched, but not the drop. I took the pistols and ammo and fed them into my tablet's Escher field, but left the box behind as I ran back as fast as I could.

By the time I crawled back through the gate, the guard had reached the end of his patience. I shut down the gate, tossed the twistkey into my tablet, and stowed the whole thing in my pocket. I shut the closet door behind me and looked around the room for anything else that might be useful. I noticed, then, that my computer sat idling when it had been off before I'd left. A lightwire connector hung from one port, draping over the edge of the desk.

Yun, the little shit, had been in my system. She'd been listening to me talk on the phone, overhearing things, and putting things together. She must have searched my computer the night before, and then turned me in.

I struggled to remember what if anything might have been sitting in e-mails and chat logs on my system. How much did she know? How much did they know? I moved to the keyboard, and began sifting through the info she'd pulled up. She'd found clips from the Xinzhongzi pirate video, chats with Vamp and Dao-Ming about it, and worse.

Something hit the bedroom door, hard enough to split the wood trim and skew the bolt housing. I jumped, spinning around to see that Mei had decided not to wait for his partners to show up before grabbing me. His second kick pulled two of the screws loose; then his third caused the door to crash open.

"Move away from the computer," he said.

He must have decided I'd locked him out so I could destroy evidence, which I hadn't even thought of. I backed away as he moved into the room.

"Please, you don't understand—"

"I knew you were full of shit," he said.

I glanced at his belt, and came up with the only plan I could think of. Before he could unclip his stun gun, I gestured back at the computer screen.

"You're too late," I told him. "Everything's already getting fried."

He turned to look, leaning over the keyboard to see if there might be some way to stop whatever I'd supposedly kicked off. As he did, I reached for his belt and popped the safety snap on the canister of Red Light. He turned, but by then I'd already plucked it out and flipped the cap.

He was lunging when I spritzed him right in the eyes. The chemicals spiked through the mucous membranes and went right for the brain. By the time he grabbed my throat, they'd already begun switching off his motor functions.

His grip loosened, and he dropped like a stone. He tipped back, and thumped over onto his side on the floor, completely paralyzed except for his involuntary muscle systems. When I was sure he couldn't move, I let out a pent-up breath.

This is bad. This is very bad.

I stepped over him and headed back to the kitchen and grabbed the rations I'd picked up at Fang's. I stowed them in my Escher tablet, and headed back to my room.

The Red Light would last for the next five to ten minutes. I wouldn't get to Ginzho by then, but I could be long gone before they figured out what happened. I reached into his pocket and fished for his scanner.

"Sorry," I muttered. My fingers found the remote and I pulled it out, then synced it to my 3i and reactivated the transmitter before tossing it on the floor.

Vamp? I sent.

This time he answered right away: *Sam, I—*

Vamp, they know.

I know, Dragan told me.

Yun's been spying on us. She broke into my system and called security. They know.

Are you sure—

Vamp, security is here right now.

Where?

In my apartment. Based on what Yun found on my computer, I'd say assume they're coming for you, too.

I know; I'm lying low at Shuang's for now.

I bristled a little at that, but there wasn't time to worry about it.

What about the plan?

The test is on for tonight, he said.

Still?

Sounds like if we're doing this, we better do it quick. If all goes okay, we'll do the full run tomorrow.

Okay. I have to run. Contact the others and warn them?

I already did.

Thanks, Vamp.

I left the apartment, and took the stairs before the other officers arrived. I took three flights down, then got out and took the elevator down past the front lobby to the basement level. From there I made my way through the boiler room to the maintenance door on the opposite side. A set of stairs took me back to the first floor on the other side of the building from the lobby where the officers had been waiting for me. None of them was there.

I headed out the rear entrance, and hustled across the street to an alley where hutong vendors had gathered to see what was going on. I squeezed past them and down the narrow row of little shop fronts. An old man who sat under a fluttering cloth sign for old-world remedies scowled as I passed. At the far end, I scooted around a rack of bicycles and looked back to see the apartment door lock flash red as a security boot was applied. Through the lobby window, I saw rows of badge readers along the unit doors cascade red down the hall. On the street, the LCD panels over the front entrance flickered to display a lockdown warning.

I turned, and took off toward Ginzho.

Chapter Thirteen

The bombing had the streets buzzing big time, and now people had gathered on the sidewalks around the apartment to try to see what the lockdown was all about. A small mob at the intersection had backed up into the street, and cars honked as they edged around them. I crossed the street and joined the flow of foot traffic, squeezing around knots of people who were hanging around the shop fronts to watch the LCD panels show footage of the Render's Strip blast. As I passed them I saw officers in bomb gear picking through the aftermath, bagging up shrapnel and body parts to try to deconstruct the explosion.

Alexei, I'm on my way, I sent. After a pause, he answered.

Okay.

Did you make it there okay?

Yes.

Sit tight. I'm coming.

I wove through clusters of people gathered around apartment stoops, drinking and smoking in the summer heat while venting to each other about the lack of response from LeiFang. I wove through a buzz of angry muttering around bar stalls and on street corners when a call came in from Dragan on the 3i.

Sam?

I'm here.

Are you okay?

I'm okay. I just left—

Don't tell me where you are. A warrant just went out for your arrest.

"Fuck," I muttered. I figured it would happen, but that didn't make it any easier. With a warrant they'd be gunning for me big time. A few people looked over as I stomped the sidewalk in front of me. "Fuck!"

Anyone else? I asked.

Vamp is flagged as a person of interest, along with Dao-Ming. No other warrants yet, but they know something.

My sitter hacked my computer. Little bitch turned me in.

I made a fist, and cursed again under my breath. We hadn't even gotten out of the gate, and already everything had started to come crashing down.

Dragan, I'm sorry.

Don't worry about that. Flush your phone and 3i logs and shut everything down after this conversation. Is Alexei with you?

Yes. A half lie. He would be soon.

Have him do the same. They want to talk to him about the bombing and the less they can latch onto the better.

Okay.

Through the crowd, I spotted the lights of a gate hub up ahead and saw the network had been reactivated. I veered left and quickly squeezed into the proper line. Through the free-standing metal doorway I could see the front of Ginzho tower, a close-up of the same tower lit up off in the distance miles down the main strip.

Lie low for tonight, Dragan said. *Contact me tomorrow to let me know you're safe and I should know more then.*

I will.

My turn at the gate came up and I passed through. When the hiccup passed, my foot came down on solid pavement again as the grand entrance of Ginzho tower appeared in front of me. All at once the subdued lights of Tùzi-wō were replaced with the bright blaze of Ginzho in full swing, streams of vibrant electric color painting the square and flowing down all five strips of the traffic star as far as the eye could see. The tower blazed from across the street, looming over the heads of the men and women mobbed at the Ginzho gate hub, which was the largest in Hangfei. Past the queues, throngs of people flowed down the sidewalks, edging between the bumper-to-bumper traffic that converged on the star, inching around the huge statue of former Military Governor Jianguo Hwong, Hangfei's illustrious murderer, across four lanes like cogs in a giant machine.

I headed for the closest walkway and rode it to the arch, then crossed over looking down on the vast circles of traffic below while vendors barked at me from the tight rows of carts assembled along either rail. Most were selling souvenirs, junk jewelry and knock-off haan tech to any suckers they could reel in, but some were selling clothes, gate passes, art, and music someone might actually be halfway interested in.

As I started down the end of the bridge, the big screen over the tower's main entrance began displaying an ad where a haan female with an impossibly beautiful face smiled at the crowd below. She wore a skintight black dress that hugged her large breasts into mounds of smoke gray cleavage while she held a haan ration bar in front of the swell, the unwrapped end pointed up at her chin like a human phallus. As I gazed over the crowd, I saw men staring, like they were in a trance. It didn't matter that you could see through her skin, or that she wasn't even human. It didn't even matter that, as far as anyone knew, the only haan female alive was Ava and since that wasn't her, she was most likely a virtual construct. They stared anyway.

Are we that easy to sway? I wanted to chalk it up to men being men, but when I'd first met Nix, as an adult, anyway, hadn't I found him handsome in his own way? Hadn't his looks and his clothes bought him some slack? Didn't they still?

Below, the Shangzho haan seal floated among other haan symbols that were interleaved with nutritional information and other, fuzzier promises like better memory retention and enhanced sex life. The haan remained perfectly still, her perfect doll's face molded into a static smile.

When the ad faded, a new face faded in right behind it, one with narrow black eyes and shiny, plastic hair. I curled one hand into a fist as he smiled that weird smile of his.

Most of the men's heads turned as they realized the cleavage had gone away and wasn't coming back, but I found myself watching him. Underneath Gohan's face, words faded into view and as they did, his grin twitched a little broader.

ARE YOU PREPARED?

Some people booed, while others laughed it off. Most just shook their heads and went back to their business, even when Gohan's calm, sure voice came from the speakers like the low chant of an ancient wise man.

"The little star has crossed Fangwenzhe," he said. "The Reunification is at hand. Join—"

The screen flickered, and the image was covered by a security override. When it blinked away, the face had been replaced by a picture of the Pingi whiskey soda logo.

I moved through the crowds in Ginzho square, around the side of the tower where a set of concrete stairs led down to a fenced-off maintenance gate. A few people glanced over as I opened the chain-link gate and slipped through, pulling it closed behind me and fishing my key chain out of my pocket. I shook out Dragan's security twistkey and slipped it into the socket on the gate frame.

"Override accepted," the A.I. said.

The field crackled when I turned the key and the cinder-block wall behind it disappeared. A second later the doorway looked straight down the side of the tower, a floor of dark glass windows stretching off into the distance toward the busy streets below. I slipped through, and stepped out onto the sheet of hexagonal graviton plating on the other side. I stood between the rows of dark windows, looking down at my own reflection in freshly clean glass that was already starting to speckle with scalefly biocide again.

I took a minute to let my brain adjust to the new perspective. Above my head, instead of the sky I saw the face of the building across the street from Ginzho tower where a line of haan constructs skittered along the length of a rain gutter, looking for leaks. Ahead, eighty stories in the distance and past the hanging washer rig platform and layers of aircars, was the blazing lights of the city square like a living wall that went on forever in every direction. Headlights and flashing vehicle lightpaint coursed through the streets like electric blood through arteries and veins while the columns and spires of smaller towers reached back toward me. I watched it for a moment, listening to the far away street noises, then turned around and faced the starry night sky.

Alexei sat a few floors away with his back to me and his reflection cast in the window next to him. I could see his profile staring down at his shoes as I approached.

"Got room for two?" I asked. He started when I spoke, but nodded.

"Sure," he said.

I sat down next to him. With my back toward the streets below, I fished out the cigarillo Fang had snuck me earlier. Before I could change my mind, I pinched off the sticky, opiate-infused end and flicked it away. It went out of range of the graviton field and flitted down toward the street. The paper tasted like clove when I clamped my lips around the end and found my lighter. I flicked it and held the end of the smoke to the dancing flame, shielding it against the breeze as I sucked until the fibers crackled bright red.

You shouldn't smoke, Alexei sent.

I know.

I drew in a thick mouthful of bittersweet smoke and inhaled deeply. The hit carried a chemical undertone, a speck of the opiate oil I'd missed, but just a speck. I let myself have it, holding it in until my eyelids drooped and my muscles relaxed just a notch. When I couldn't hold it any longer I blew it away from Alexei in a long blue-gray stream that swirled away into the night air.

You're in trouble, aren't you? he asked.

"When am I not?"

I took another drag off the smoke, and blew out a plume that swirled back over our heads on a downdraft. Alexei picked at the toe of his shoe, looking miserable with his chin on one knee.

Will you get fired? For us coming up here? he asked.

It was the least of my worries at the moment, but I would get in trouble for it. I'd get flak for using the company gate after hours, but I didn't think they'd fire me over it. Assuming I wasn't already in a detention center by then.

"No, I'll tell them I forgot my phone on the rigging and went up to get it."

He nodded, picking at his shoe again. I nudged him with my shoulder.

I'm sorry I called you a selfish piece of shit.

"Whatever."

You're just a regular piece of shit.

He nudged me back with his shoulder.

You're a regular piece of shit, he said, but I saw the hint of a smile on his face.

You should talk out loud more. Your Mandarin is getting not half bad. I can almost stand to listen to it now, I told him.

"Ha, ha."

I slipped my free arm around his neck and squeezed him in a gentle headlock.

I'm really glad you didn't get blown up.

"Get off," he complained, trying to squirm loose. I pulled him closer, and planted a kiss on his cheek just before he got away.

"Blech," he muttered, wiping the spot.

We've got to lie low for a while, I told him.

I expected him to argue, but he didn't. He nodded, staring off toward the sky like an intense, mini-Dragan.

"I know."

I'm going to finish this smoke, and then we've got to go, okay?

"Yeah," he said, still wiping his cheek.

We sat in silence for a while. Him staring, and me smoking.

Look, I told him. *I know things haven't always been so great. You lost your home, and now it feels like you're getting shuffled around.*

He blew air through his nose.

I am getting shuffled around, he said.

I admit it's not perfect, but we care about you. I know we've both been distracted, but we both really care about you. Try and understand.

You act like you don't want me here.

I saw his eyes shimmer a bit, and took his small hand in mine.

I'm sorry if we made you feel that way, Alexei, but it's not true. Things will calm down, and you'll see. Give us a chance.

Alexei shrugged, looking down at our hands, clasped together. *We want you to be happy,* I told him.

He started to say something, and then stopped. I could see the frustration on his face.

I'm . . . He paused. *I want to be. I'm trying, but . . .*

He shook his head, and sighed, pressing his forehead to his knees.

Let us help you, I told him. *Not the gonzos. I know you're into them right now, but—*

They care about me.

Maybe, but you don't know Hangfei well enough to be at a rally like that one in Render's Strip.

I can take care of myself.

I sighed, blowing smoke through my nose, watching the cigarillo cherry reflected in the glass window in front of me. I held the cigarillo tucked in the corner of my mouth, and stroked his hair with my free hand.

I know you can, Alexei, but there's a history there. A quarter million people died within spitting distance of that rally today. Some of the old folks in Render's Strip lived through the Impact. You can't just show up there and tell people it's going to happen again.

Alexei's cheeks flushed red. His eyes were defiant, but he didn't say anything.

Seriously, I said. *You rile up that many people that bad and what do you expect to happen?*

"Do you think that's why the bomb went off?" Alexei asked, his voice cautious.

"Huh?"

"You think it was someone mad at the church?"

"I don't know."

"Does Dragan think that?"

"I don't know, Alexei."

I could tell there was more on his mind, but he was still rattled, and he didn't say it. He'd almost died today. Even dodging that bullet, there was a moment where he thought he'd lost Dragan, or me, or both.

Never mind. It doesn't matter, I told him. *It wasn't your fault, okay?*

I scooted a little closer to him, letting our shoulders touch. After a minute, he reached out and put one hand on my arm, and leaned against me a little. We sat like that for a while, before he piped up again. When he did, he sounded distant, and unhappy.

"Gohan wants me to tell you to go see him."

"He does, huh?"

"Yes. But don't."

"Did he say why?"

He shook his head.

"Sam, I want to tell you something."

"Sure, Alexei."

"Before, in Render's Strip, I . . ."

"You what?"

"I was . . ."

He never finished. Suddenly, I felt him slump. It wasn't in a tired or defeated way either, all the life went out of him all at once.

"Alexei?"

His head lolled, and then he crumpled. He slid off my shoulder and fell down onto his back with a thump.

"Alexei!"

I spun around, crouching over him. He was still breathing, I could see that, but his body had gone limp, with one cheek pressed to the glass of the office window next to him.

"Hey," I said, giving him a shake. When he still didn't move, panic welled up in my chest. "Hey, what's wrong with you?"

I shook him again, harder.

"Alexei, wake—"

"He's fine," a voice said. "Don't worry."

I turned back toward the starry sky and saw that two large points of light phased into view, standing out from the speckled background. They floated there like coals, and I realized that they weren't actually part of the starscape but right in front of me. They'd appeared in a patch of darkness that blended in with the night sky, a freestanding gate that had opened silently only a few meters away.

The lights were a pair of haan eyes. Instead of the normal red, orange, or yellow, they were a pretty shade of sunset pink, and my breath caught.

Nix.

"He's only asleep," he said, the light on his voice box flickering in the dark. "I didn't want to startle him."

He stepped through the gate. His movements were jerky, and he shook a little like he had some kind of tremors, but it was him, I had no doubt. His suit trailed behind him, rippling in the summer breeze, and as he approached I saw his heart as it pulsed in his chest. His face looked exactly the same, handsome without being overly so, with the frozen expression of a mannequin, but something wasn't right. I could feel it, and it grew worse the closer he came.

"I've been looking for you," he croaked. I just stared.

"You are alive," I whispered. "It's really true."

His head lolled as he closed the distance between us, and he held up one shaking hand to point down at me as his voice box flickered, and his voice sifted through like gravel.

"I've come to warn you, Sam," he said. "Something terrible is going to happen."

Chapter Fourteen

For a minute, I forgot all about Alexei. I stood, stunned, as Nix reached for me, but before his elegant fingers could touch my cheek I took a step back. His signal came in strong, cut by hesitant stops like he couldn't control it, which felt strange because he'd always been cool, and a little distant. This felt intense. It left me staring, with the cigarillo dangling from between my parted lips.

"I thought you were dead," I said. "All this time."

"No. Not yet."

Nix approached again, his boots clacking on the graviton plating. The closer he got, the stronger the feeling grew. It felt as though he had something bottled up inside, some pressure building that he didn't know how to release. Up close, it made me a little nervous. It felt like, at any moment, he might snap.

"Nix, what's wrong with you?"

A gust of wind blew his smell over me, a dank, sour smell that tingled in my nose. I felt his hunger, even as he fought to control it, and the pulses of desperation that bled through in the wake of it. Beneath it all, I felt his fear.

"Nix," I said. "Hey . . ."

His footsteps rapped to a stop on the plating and he stood, his draping suit fluttering in the wind like a cape while his sunset pink eyes watched me.

"I'm sorry I couldn't come before now," he said. "I've been cut off."

I didn't know what he meant, but I could see something had gone wrong.

"It's okay." I waved him closer. "Sit down."

He did, but still his body trembled. I sat down in front of him, and took one of his hands. I could feel it shaking.

"Nix how are you alive? Where have you been?"

Behind the serene glow of his saucer eyes the main mass of his brain shifted, pushing the smaller one underneath back deeper.

"I've been on the ship."

"No," I said. "You couldn't have been. I looked back through the gate, and I saw you get caught in the fire."

"When I began to burn, I was gated back to the ship," he said. "The interior of the structure contains an advanced form of perfluorocarbon, an oxygen-rich liquid which we breathe while inside."

I remembered, after gating back with Sillith's remains, waking up to the blackness inside the ship. I remembered the terror I'd felt when I first drew the cold fluid into my lungs.

"I very nearly died, but it kept me alive until I could regenerate," he said, his voice box flickering in the dark.

"You told me they'd exiled you, because you didn't kill me like they wanted. You said they'd kill you."

"I believed they would. However, when they examined my memories and saw the true extent of my newfound individuality, they decided to study me, rather than send me back to the vats."

"Study you? Why?"

"We aren't like you," he said. "We are much closer to what you might describe as a hive society. We share all info, all concerns, burdens, and workloads. I am a deviation from a long-established norm. Your influence has changed me in a way they hoped, I think, might be used as a bridge between our species. I cannot be certain, but I think they even considered me for the position of female."

"But you said . . . " I trailed off as what he'd said registered. "Wait. What?"

"When our population reaches a certain threshold, we divide the populace into two distinct regions, and create a new female for the new group," he said. "We've never reached that point on your planet, and so you have only ever witnessed a single female. Typically the need is anticipated and the female is grown, but any male can take the role of female, once the right trigger is administered."

I ran my fingers through my hair, wondering how the day could get any weirder. "I don't think I can get my head around you being a female," I said.

"If they ever truly considered it, then they decided against it."

"So then they let you go?"

"No," he said. "She kept me in stasis for a time, until they could reach a consensus regarding how to handle me."

"Who did?"

"The current haan female, Ava, and—"

"Ava?" That surprised me. "But she helped you. She helped all of us when Sillith came."

"It is not personal," he said. "When I didn't cooperate, it constituted a significant breach in our way of doing things. I presented her with a difficult challenge."

"I guess." I watched him shake. The thin stream of terror that still bubbled over through the cluster told me that personal or not, he'd been shaken bad. Even when Hwong had tortured him, I'd never felt anything like it. "She seems different, now, I guess. Even on TV."

"Ava had not, at the time, taken her place as the new haan female. Once Sillith died, she did. She has merged, since then. Her perceptions are not what they once were."

"Merged? Merged with what?"

"She has all of the memories of every haan female to precede her. They are present in her consciousness as virtual personality sums."

"Even Sillith?"

"Every female. She is, but is not, the Ava you knew. The benefit of so much history and experience comes at a cost. She is well aware now of all the evils both men and haan alike have done. She knows what Sillith and Hwong tried to do, that they conspired to wipe out the Pan-Slav Emirates. It colors her perception of your race."

"Then she knows what Sillith did, too, before she died."

I wondered if he would deny it. He paused, and I watched his brains shift in their soup as he struggled with it for a bit.

"Yes," he said. "She knows. She knows that humans are being converted."

"Nix, tell me — was that the plan all along?"

"No."

"Sillith had to have been working on that for ages. You're telling me no one else knew?"

"What Sillith did was not part of some greater plan," he insisted. "She acted alone."

I looked at him warily. He seemed to be telling the truth, but he'd lied to me before.

"We do not intend to change you," Nix said. "We would never try to make you something other than what you are."

"I wonder sometimes if you know what that is, Nix," I said.

"You have the potential to change us more so than we do you," he said. "When the time came, Ava did not package my memories for distribution throughout the hive, but they were shared among a select group. When they realized my bond with the humans had altered my perception, they decided to explore my memories in greater detail."

"Explore them?"

"By extracting them, and, most likely, growing clones to run simulations on—"

"So they did plan to kill you?"

"Eventually. I knew I had to escape, if I was to avoid that."

"I thought none of you was afraid to die," I said.

"As I said, my perceptions have been altered. When I felt my life begin to slip away, I discovered that I was afraid. I didn't know what to do. I panicked, and killed the scientists in charge of my handling. I killed . . . many more as I fled the ship."

As he recounted the story, I could sense a renewed surge of anxiety from him. Anxiety and guilt bled through, flaring up through an undercurrent of misery.

"Hey . . . it's okay, Nix."

He reached out and touched my arm, and when he did I jumped.

"Let me see," he said, gesturing at my left arm. He'd spotted the bond tattoo there.

"Wake up Alexei."

"Not yet. Let me see."

I let him take my arm, and felt the warmth coming off of him as he scooted closer, until our legs were touching. I held it out next to my right where the bond bands for Dragan, Vamp, and Alexei ringed my biceps. He compared the band on the left side to them, tracing the name with one long finger.

"That's my name," he said.

I pulled my arm back and looked at him, crossing my arm over my knees and resting my chin there.

"I didn't intend to get attached to you," he said, "but I did."

"Me, too." In spite of it all, I realized that I'd missed him. He stared back at me, shivering in the summer heat. "Wake up Alexei."

"I have to tell you something," he said. "I know what you're planning to do."

"How can you know—"

"One of Sillith's creations, what you call the haanyŏng, has learned. In tracking you down, I obtained the information via a scalefly-transmitted memory payload."

I felt my eyes go wide. "Do all of the haan know?"

"No," he said. "Not yet. The new haan still retain their human identities, at least for a while. They often don't understand how to forge a symbiosis with the scaleflies at first. Those that do, however, have the potential to receive these memories. They will learn who you are, and what you intend to do."

"And what about what the haan intend to do?" I asked.

"My people are aware of what Sillith started, and what will happen if it is found out before we can stop it."

"Can you stop it?"

"We will try—"

"But you don't know if you can."

His eyes flickered.

"I've come to try to make you see reason," he said. "I promise you that a worst-case scenario has been studied, and a response prepared. Whatever it is—"

Something boomed from across the city, loud like a crack of thunder. I turned, and saw a fading flash in the distance.

"What was that?" Nix asked.

Another bright flash came, and then another followed a beat later by two more loud booms.

Transformers, I thought. *Blown power transformers. The test . . . Vamp's power cut. It's started. . . .*

I looked around, trying to spot the Zun-Zhe district, when the first flicker of light drew my eye. I watched as a whole block went out, then another. The rest rolled fast after that, the blackness spreading out until the brilliant lights of Hangfei had a single dark patch off in the distance.

Even with all that had happened, I felt a smile creep onto my face. It had worked. Vamp had somehow wormed his way into the system, and his cascading failure idea worked. He'd shut off the power to hundreds of thousands.

Not for long, and in an area where there wouldn't be any haan, but he'd done it.

For me.

"Sam," Nix called, "what have you done?"

"It's just that one spot," I told him. "It's just a test to see if—"

Another boom sounded, and then more lights flickered somewhere else, somewhere outside of Zun-Zhe. The Gong district, maybe? Another dark patch appeared in the sea of lights, a city block gone black. Some of the lights dimmed, then several more blocks went out.

"What was that?" I asked under my breath. "Was that supposed to happen?"

Vamp, I called. *Vamp, are you there?*

The 3i connection dropped. Then, like a tidal wave, the darkness began to spread out from the two blacked-out sections.

Even as more booms rolled through the city, a strange sound began to swell. A low hum rose in pitch, then became an angry electric buzz. It broke into overlapping tones, a shrieking, dissonant chord that drowned out everything else.

The darkness moved across Hangfei, winding between lit sections in patterns that looked random. I could still make out the distant movement of cars, pinprick headlights streaming through the dark as it picked up speed, and began to rush toward Ginzho.

"Something's wrong," I whispered. "This isn't supposed to happen like this. We have to get off the building. Now."

The electric screech continued as one by one the surrounding blocks went dark, cascading all the way to Ginzho until the buildings around the tower winked out one by one. Streams of traffic slowed as they suddenly lost connection to the airway guides.

I turned back toward Nix as a wave of dizziness came over me and sent me staggering to one side.

"Sam, get on the rigging. . . ." I heard Nix shout, but his voice seemed far away and his voice box was cutting in and out.

The last of Ginzho's lights blinked out. I had never seen the city dark like that before in my life, and the sight of it scared me.

Dizziness turned to nausea that made me double over, hugging Alexei close. I struggled to see as bile crept up in my throat. The lights were still on in some parts of the city, but far away. In Ginzho, only the tower and the buildings surrounding it still had power.

"Sam," I heard Nix shout, "get on the—"

His voice cut out, overlapped by a low, raspy whisper. The sound was deep, resonating in my head along with a series of clicks like the creeping legs of an insect.

Haan speech. I remembered the sound from Shiliuyuán Station, when Sillith had crept closer to me in the darkness of the tunnel. The sound came from Nix. I could hear Nix's true voice.

The blackout . . . the field is failing. . . .

The lights directly ahead flickered, and the tower, having held out as long as it could, went dark. As soon as it did, my body began to feel lighter. My feet began to come up off the ground underneath me. I felt Alexei's body begin to peel away from the wall and start a slow slide away from me.

The graviton plating. With the power gone, the field had scattered. We were going to fall.

I pushed myself back up onto my feet as true gravity took over and the whole world flipped. I spotted the washer rigging ahead to my left, a direction quickly dropping away to become one story below. I lurched forward and grabbed Alexei's arm, hauling him up as he began to stir.

As the last of the power drained from the plates, I hooked one arm around Alexei's waist and ran for it, stumbling as the floor underneath me dropped away and turned back into the wall that it was. As I pushed off with one foot and the sole peeled free, the cigarillo came loose from my mouth and began tumbling down the building face end over end.

I lunged, feet peddling in the air as the last of the graviton emissions faded. Alexei panicked and began to flail as we fell down toward the street eighty stories below. I managed to keep my arm around him as the momentum of my leap sent us sailing down onto the washer rigging, and I struck the metal railing that surrounded the platform. My stomach hit the bar, forcing the air out of me as my head pitched down toward the deck and I went ass over end to crash down on my back next to Alexei. A bucket of cleanser and squeegees toppled over and went sailing down toward the street below.

I rolled over, pain pulsing through my ribs as I crawled across the platform to Alexei. Off to the side, something big and dark whooshed past, one limb cracking against the rig's railing before it sailed by.

"Nix!"

I looked over the railing in time to see a dark shadow in front of a honeycomb flash of light, like a sunspot, before Nix plunged into the gate he'd created and was gone. I blinked, and the light disappeared.

"Alexei," I hissed in his ear, still seeing the afterimage of the gate as I shook him. His eyes swam, and blood trickled from his nose. "Alexei, are you okay?"

"I'm okay," he moaned, waving me away.

The electric racket stopped, its echo rumbling off into the night sky. Through the railing I could see the dark city blocks sprawled out in front of me far below. The grid hadn't failed, and the haan ship still had power, but big sections of the city had been completely knocked off the grid. I looked out over the dark section, and saw one island of light off in the distance in the middle of it.

My GPS was off but I didn't need it to know where that was. I could see the big central tower, and the electric lanterns from the protesters at the outskirts. The light came from Xinzhongzi. The tower, where the gonzos had set up shop, still blazed with bright electric light.

I looked and saw that the 3i connection had come back up. I used eyebot to take a snapshot, and sent it to Vamp, along with a message.

Vamp, what happened?

I don't know.

What do you mean you don't know; I thought this was supposed to be just a test?

It was. This shouldn't have happened. Our calculations couldn't have been this far off.

It spread all the way to Ginzho. You have to shut it off.

We're trying. It's cascading out of control.

Xinzhongzi still has power.

Xinzhongzi? They shouldn't.

Check the picture I just sent you.

I stood, leaning against the rail for a better shot, when something moved down below. Something big. I saw it more in the way that it covered the lights of the traffic streams below than I saw it directly, a long, undulating shadow that cruised over the streets below about twenty stories down. I squinted, straining to see in the dark but before I could make out anything more it snaked around the corner of Ginzho tower and disappeared out of view.

"What in the hell . . . ?"

"What?" Alexei said. He sat up, wiping the blood out from under his nose.

"Did you see that?" I asked.

"See what?"

Another wave of nausea hit and I doubled over. The air rippled in front of me for a second, growing stronger until I clenched my teeth, and swallowed bile back down.

The rippling stopped. The nausea stopped too, just as abruptly, and I found myself staring down at the rigging's deck.

"See what?" Alexei asked again.

"Nothing." I looked back down over the city.

Light flickered and one of the city blocks got its lights back. The towers lit up again, and then one by one the blocks surrounding it came back to life. Within seconds the cascade reached Ginzho, and the district blazed back into brilliant, bright color. The graviton plates hummed back to life, tugging the edge of a stray rag in one of the rig's buckets toward it.

Vamp, the power's back on.

I see it. We don't have full control yet, though. Get off the street and get inside.

"What happened?" Alexei asked, his eyes wide. "What was that?"

I didn't answer him. I just stared out over the city, watching as it came back to life. The sound of overlapping horns and squealing car alarms drifted up for a minute, before easing off, and shifting back toward the reassuring blanket of urban white noise that was only marred by the odd siren.

"Come on," I said.

"What?" Alexei asked. "Back on the wall?"

The power's back. We can't stay up here all night.

He nodded. I gave him a few moments, then opened the gate in the railing and stepped out onto the plates on the other side. I closed my eyes as my center of gravity changed again, feeling a nervousness as I crouched there that I hadn't felt in years. When the shift was complete, I stood, and waved for him to come out with me.

"Come on," I said. "Let's go."

I took his hand, and coaxed him back out onto the plating. He squeezed my hand tightly as I guided him back toward the gate, and the chaos down on the ground below.

Chapter Fifteen

Back down on the street, things had gotten tense. Several aircars had hit each other during the blackout, and while no one crashed a lot of people were pissed off and the street cops had already called in backup. Fallout from the collisions had rained down onto the crowd and a section of bumper had crashed through the middle of a street vendor's cart. Sirens filled the air, and as Vamp's app reinitialized I could see red markers popping up all through the district like someone had knocked down a hornet's nest.

"Come on," I said to Alexei. "We have to get off the street."

"Are we still going to Baishan Park?"

"Yes."

The streets were gridlocked. The gate hub was clogged, people piling up at the portals while others wove between the crowds looking for news on shop-front LCDs. At the gate, we were already looking at a twenty-minute wait, and it was getting worse by the minute.

"... did you see it?" I heard someone ask as we passed, but when I turned to find the source, I couldn't figure out who'd said it, but I then realized that quite a few people looked rattled, even scared.

They saw, I realized. When the power dropped, some of them saw something, just for a minute. Not long, but long enough to scare them.

The chatter on the street had gotten tense, and confused. Several people pointed up, shouting about something. From down the street, I heard a woman scream.

"What's happening?" Alexei asked.

"Nothing. Come on."

I took Alexei by the hand, and he followed as I scooted down the nearest side street. A moving walkway hummed on the other side that would at least get us out of the central square and we hopped it. We nestled in between two groups of clubbers and watched the mobs on the sidewalk stream by, riding the conveyer past the bridge to the nearest metro station. It was as clogged as the gate hub. People were backed up onto the street.

Just then the screens lit up along the shop fronts all flipped from running ads and logos to display a security alert. Governess LeiFang appeared on the screen, her face calm.

"Due to an unforeseen emergency," she said, "a curfew has been imposed, effective immediately. Citizens will be allotted an hour's grace period to return to their homes, so for your protection and ours, proceed there immediately by order of Hangfei security."

I snorted, looking at the mob blocking the metro stairs. An hour was a joke. There wasn't time for anyone to get home. They'd be lucky to find a room to bunk in.

We started down the next alley over, heading off the main streets and into the maze of the inner-block sprawl. I followed the GPS route to the first turn and met with a chain-link fence that spanned the narrow gap between the two buildings. On the other side, past a long row of old bicycles down by a big metal trash bin, I could see a group of people facing several security officers who held them back.

"What's happening?" a man screamed, his voice cracking. "What's happening to us?"

One of the security men grabbed his arm, and the man

tried to pull away, still screaming as scaleflies drifted around the fray.

"Calm down!" the officer ordered.

"I saw it above the skylane! I saw it! It—"

The officer jammed his stunner into the man's ribs, sending him sprawling down onto the sidewalk.

Next to them, a square-jawed woman turned and looked right at me. I saw the recognition on her face, even as she raised her finger to point.

"Hey!"

"Sam . . ." Alexei said in a low voice, pulling my hand back the way we'd come.

The officer began to march down the narrow alley, her black poncho slapping against the row of bicycles as she passed.

"You are wanted by Hangfei security!" The woman yelled. Several other officers broke from the pack and began to follow her. Eyebot painted each of their faces in the display, and as information began to scroll under each of them several orange blips appeared on the tracker heat map.

"Sam, let's go . . ." Alexei said.

I backed away, ushering Alexei behind me as they approached us. We darted back out of alley and farther in between the clusters of buildings, ducking around the corner as they scaled the fence to come after us.

"Shut off your phone," I told Alexei. "Now. Hurry up."

He did like I said and I did the same as we scrambled down the narrow alley between rows of trash bins as the footsteps approached behind us.

I spotted a series of boarded basement windows at the base of the sidewalk ahead and ducked behind one of the trash bins to kneel in front of one. I sat back and knocked the panel loose with my feet, then ushered Alexei inside as the board clattered onto the ground.

He went, and I slipped in after him, landing hard on the concrete floor then hugging the wall beneath the window as the officers stormed past outside.

The single open panel didn't provide much light, but I could see a bunch of furniture arranged in rows around us, covered over with dusty tarps. Far across the room I could make out a sliver of light that might have peeked through the edge of another boarded window.

I took Alexei's hand and we made our way carefully between the rows of old furniture. As we got closer to the light, I felt something squish under my shoe and grimaced, not sure I wanted to know what it was.

Something smells, Alexei said. It was true. The air had begun to develop a musky, sweaty kind of smell.

I forged on to the sliver of light and sure enough, another basement window had been covered with a wooden panel. I managed to pull it loose, and electric light shined in from outside.

"Look," Alexei said.

I turned, and saw the floor had been covered in some kind of mostly dried muck. An empty shirt had been strewn there, along with a discarded pair of pants. They lay in the approximate shape of whoever had worn them.

Why are they there? Alexei asked.

I followed the outfit toward the opposite side of the room and saw another shirt, and another. More pants, shoes, and stockings lying atop one another in the gloom. Something had been feeding down here.

"I don't know," I told him. "Come on, we're leaving here. Right now."

I boosted him out of the window and crawled out after him. With security off of our trail, we ran away from the Ginzho glitz until the streets grew narrow underneath a canopy of faded plastic blister signs in a mishmash of Hanzi, English, and Pan-Slav. Vendors stood outside shops and hawked their wares under canvas tarps that flapped in the humid breeze.

It took twenty minutes to get there while avoiding eye-bot's security markers, but by the time we did I felt confident we'd lost them. When I spotted the arch of cheap filament bulbs over the grimy plastic sign I recognized it right away. It looked like the site of a demolished building, an empty, building-shaped patch of relatively fresh blacktop in the middle of a tight cluster of towers.

The gate was open, coiled razor wire bordering a rusted sign that read BAISHAN PARK. A few kids played jianzi in a patch of flickering neon next to the check-in station, the shuttle's colored feathers bouncing between them while the guard watched something on his phone. Past the station were stacks of sleep tubes, coffin-shaped pods arranged in rows, and topped with sheet metal.

Long ago, I'd lived there for years with my mother and father, one of the many families that rented a pod week to week. I thought I'd forgotten most everything about it, but it hadn't changed much at all and I found myself slowing down, not quite sure I wanted to walk under that arch again.

"Is this okay?" Alexei asked, a little unsure.

"Yeah." I pulled him along, thinking that in another few years I wouldn't be able to get away with that. He would be bigger than me before long. I approached the check-in station and slapped my cash card down on the counter in front of a long-haired guy with bad teeth and bad breath. He slid it through the reader and studied the screen in front of him, peering down through a pair of cheap wireframe glasses that sat on the end of his beaky nose.

"How many?" he asked.

"Two."

He punched in the fee and slid my card back to me along with a magnetic key.

"Unit sixty-seven."

"Thanks."

It felt strange, being back there. I'd walked the route more times than I could count on my way back from school, but that had been in another time, and another life. The residents had mostly changed, I thought. I didn't see Mr. Chen's bicycle and lawn chairs, or Ping's card table—but they'd been old men. I wondered if maybe they hadn't died. A group of younger men hung out just outside the range of one of the flood lamps, smoking and talking in low voices. They stopped, and watched us as we passed.

Alexei followed, sticking close as we headed down the first narrow row of crash tubes that were stacked five high. They'd arranged them in a mazelike pattern to maximize the use of space, but the route through had been hardwired in my brain. Dirty people in dirty clothes watched us from some of the open tubes as we moved down the rows, none of them familiar.

I don't like this place, Alexei said.

We'll be okay, trust me. Don't worry.

I took him around two tight corners and down another row until we got to the sixties where I noticed the old woman's paper lantern. I'd never known her name as a kid, and I'd forgotten that lantern until just then, but a strange, bittersweet feeling rode in on the memory. She'd been a tiny, bent old thing who used to sit on the edge of the open tube and watch TV on her phone. She'd held the screen right in front of her face, but would wave every time I came through, and I'd wave back. The lantern swayed in the breeze, bumping against the closed hatch of the tube as we passed.

I found the stack in the middle of a crowded block. One of the bottom tubes hung open there, where an old woman hung laundry on a rack. I counted up, and spotted unit sixty-seven halfway up the stack.

"Okay," I said, handing him the key. "Up. Let's go."

Alexei climbed up the ladder and opened the lock, pushing the unit's hatch open with one arm and holding it while

I scrambled past him. As we crawled into the cramped space, a light stick flickered on along the length of the ceiling.

Inside the tube was a single mattress with sheets that looked more or less clean except for a permanent yellowish stain that looked as old as the bedding itself. The far side of the unit was molded into a shelf where you could put your stuff, and Alexei tossed the surrogate kit down onto it with a hollow thud.

I crawled back to the end of the tube where the pillow was, and threw it over at Alexei, hitting him in the face. He acted annoyed, but I saw him smile a little.

"Take it," I said. He tossed it back.

"You take it."

"Thanks." I put it in the corner and patted it down. "You okay?"

"Yeah."

He sighed, looking down at the bedding between us.

"You sure?"

I've seen people get blown up before, he said.

"Oh," I said. His eyes looked harder, and more resilient than any young boy's should. It made me sad to see. "I didn't know that. In Lobnya?"

He nodded.

People died all the time there. When they pushed us out, they sent tanks. My father, my real father, put a bomb in the street to blow them up, but it went off when he tried to set it.

He'd never talked about his time in Lobnya to me before. He may have to Dragan, but if he did, Dragan never told me about it. He didn't cry, or even get teary. I would have felt better, I think, if he had. Instead he just sat there with this sort of bitter resignation on his face.

I'm sorry, Alexei.

We die all the time, he said. *My father, my uncle, my brother. Even my mother. Everyone dies. I didn't know those people in Render's Strip.*

"Alexei . . ."

I pulled him closer, and he let me do it but he no longer seemed to need, or want to be comforted.

Dragan couldn't help her, he said.

He looked down at the flattened bedding between us, and there, just for a moment, his eyes shone. Then he pulled away and nestled himself at the opposite end of the tube so that we're feet to feet. I pulled the hatch down hard enough to make the bolt snap into place.

"He tried to save her," I said.

He pulled the sheet tighter under his chin.

Don't talk about my mother. You weren't there.

That's true, but I saw the whole thing.

I caught the glint of his eyes as they opened in the dim light. I waited to see if he'd shut me down, and when he didn't, I continued.

When I tracked you guys down, I found the security re-cording on Dragan's wet drive. It's how I knew where to look.

I'd never talked with him about it before, but I'd never been able to get that recording out of my mind. It wasn't just because of the way she died, the way her head splashed apart like an egg, it was Alexei's reaction. He saw it happen, and even though I didn't know him yet, the look on his face had always stayed with me. He'd called for her, it was all he'd said, but through the shock I could see in his eyes that he'd understood. He'd understood that the thing he'd loved most in this world, needed most in this world, had been squashed out in a second, without even a chance for good-byes.

Let Dragan in, I said. *Trust me. When he pulled me out of the butcher's pen I'd been on the street for years, and I was a total wreck. I didn't trust him either at first. I used to piss him off so bad, I thought he'd blow a gasket. I hit him and scratched him, ran away, came back wrecked. . . .*

That got Alexei's interest, a little. He didn't sit up, but he turned his head to look at me.

You scratched Dragan?

Hell, the very first time I saw him, I stabbed him in the face with a piece of wire. It's how he got that scar.

Why did you?

Because I was scared, and I didn't realize who he was. I thought he'd come to hurt me.

But he helped you.

Yeah, he did, I said. *You know it's funny. For a long time, it was just me and him. When I first heard about you I was actually pretty pissed.*

He didn't answer at first, then, in a quiet voice, "Why?"

I was jealous, I guess. When I heard he'd latched onto some other kid, it bugged me. Like, a lot. When I found you, I was going to just turn you over to security.

I saw him start to get angry at that, and cut him off before he could respond.

I'm glad I didn't, I said. *I'm glad Dragan found you, and took you in, and I'm glad you stayed. You mean a lot to me, you know.*

He opened his mouth to say something, but whatever it was, it didn't quite make it out. His face flushed, and he shrugged.

I like you, he said. *But I don't like it here.*

Give it a chance.

This is not my home.

Dragan loved your mother. He wanted us to be a family. Just try and give it a chance.

He didn't look so sure, but he nodded.

I will try.

Good.

He lay there, not saying anything for a while, then asked, *Do you think Dragan will marry Dao-Ming?*

I laughed, but then I saw he was serious.

I don't know, Alexei.

Does he like her?

Yeah, he likes her.

He nodded. He looked at me a moment longer, then turned back over on his side and faced the wall. I turned and nestled in as best I could before reaching back to slap the light contact behind me.

"Good night, shitsplat."

The overhead flickered once, then went dark.

Chapter Sixteen

". . . anyone receiving this message, this is an attempt to by-pass the . . ."

The voice whistled through a whine of static as I stood on the side of Ginzho tower, my feet planted on the graviton plating. The rows of air traffic far ahead of me were frozen over the streets below them.

Everything was frozen, even the ground traffic, and the mobs of people on the sidewalks. The LCD screens displayed static images, advertisements stuck midstream and clusters of brightly lit signs frozen in midflash. The quiet made me nervous. There were no street sounds, no voices . . . just nothing at all.

Static whined again. I couldn't tell where it was coming from.

". . . we are being invaded. You will be hesitant to believe this but we have scientific proof of . . ."

The voice cut out again, echoing between the buildings before fading to nothing. I looked around again, across the reflective surface of the glass windows to either side of me, then turned to look toward the tower's spires and the night sky beyond. There was no one there.

"Hello?" I called. No one answered. The static ended in a loud pop, and a whine of feedback.

Something groaned behind me and I spun back around to face the wall of city streets ahead. The cars were all still frozen, but something, a large, long shape, slunk past the corner of the base of the building that loomed above me.

"Who's there?" I called.

I felt heat between the knuckles of my right hand and looked down to see a lit cigarillo, the cherry burned down to the crook of my fingers. I flicked it away.

"Hey, who's there?"

"*. . . the alien spread must not be allowed to . . .*" The radio voice crackled. "*. . . if it does we may never be able to shut down the field that keeps you . . .*"

Something struck the building face up ahead of me, down toward the street. Something big, that caused the plating to vibrate under my feet. The weird shadow moved again, and I saw it slink along on the other side of the grids of frozen aircar traffic. The shape crept closer to the tower; then the building vibrated again as it connected somewhere near the tenth floor.

"*. . . field, which continues to expand at a rate of . . .*"

"Hey," I called, "what—"

The vibrations got stronger as the shape moved toward me. Being oriented on the graviton plating, it seemed to be moving across the ground toward me but it actually climbed straight up the side of the tower. Whatever it was, it was big, and it moved fast.

I stepped back as the thing picked up speed. It moved through the glow of aircar headlights, some kind of massive worm the size of a metro train. Its spindly legs undulated in waves along either side as they carried it toward me, faster and faster.

My breath caught in my throat as the thing closed the distance between us in a sudden burst of speed. Something inside me urged me to run, but my legs wouldn't work. I just stood, and stared, as the thing crept right up to where I stood, then stopped.

It loomed over me. In the light of the building's huge neon sign I could see that the rows of legs were actually haan arms, each ending in a haan hand with five delicate fingers. There were thousands of them. They connected to the main body just under a ridge of shell that capped each of the long train of body segments. What looked like clothing, partially rendered, flapped from the shoulders of each arm.

It surged toward me again, just a little, and I stepped back with my hands out in front of me.

"Stop," I said. "Just wait. . . ."

It stopped, and then leaned closer, its giant head blotting out the lights of the street behind it. I could make out enormous, glassy black domes formed into clusters on the surface of its face. Where its mouth might have been, there was a writhing curtain of more haan arms, fingers working in the air as they reached toward me.

"What are you?" I whispered.

One of the black eye domes flickered, and light began to grow behind it. It began as a faint, reddish glow and quickly swelled into an intense, fiery orange that formed the saucer-like circle of a single, enormous haan eye. I froze as it stared down at me.

"THE MESSAGES YOU HEAR ARE AN ILLUSION," the thing said, its voice so low it put my teeth on edge. "THEY ARE THE RESULT OF ELECTRICAL EXCITATIONS IN YOUR CEREBRAL CORTEX DURING YOUR SLEEP CYCLE. THEY ARE NOT REAL. NONE OF THIS IS REAL."

"What are you?"

"*. . . an attempt to trigger the graviton lenses which surround the ship and . . .*"

The worm shivered, vibrations pouring off of it, and the foreign signal faded away to silence. It leaned in again, and the curtain of mouth parts began to paw in the air, reaching toward me.

"THERE ARE NO FOREIGN MESSAGES. THIS IS ALL A DREAM, AND NOTHING MORE. NONE OF THIS IS REAL."

"I heard them," I told it, my voice shaking.

"No. NONE OF THIS IS REAL."

A low, raspy sound drowned out the radio voice, so loud I could feel it rattling in my chest as the writhing haan arms parted and a blast of steamy, hot air ruffled through my hair and clothes. I felt the strength go out of my legs, and sank down onto my knees as underneath the deep rumble, a rhythmic, insectlike clicking began to resonate. . . .

I awoke with a start, cracking the back of my head on the cheap plastic molding behind me. It had gotten hot in the cramped tube over the night, and I was covered in a film of sweat. The air smelled like armpits and morning breath, and my stomach felt painfully hollow. I rolled over on my back, and rubbed my eyes.

"Shit."

The memory of the dream churned for a while, leaving me on edge. They were getting stranger, and that weird signal . . . it kept getting stronger. I remembered the other surrogate, the one I'd met at Dao-Ming's apartment building, and the fear in her voice.

"Do you hear the message, too?"

It's not just a dream, I thought. I'm not the only one who had heard it. Were the foreigners really trying to reach us? Had the thing in the dream just now been some kind of haan response to it?

I rubbed my eyes, and nudged the sheets at the other end of the tube with my foot. "Alexei, wake up."

When he didn't stir, I tried to poke him with my toe but he wasn't there.

"Son of a bitch . . ."

I tried to call him, but he didn't answer. He didn't respond to a 3i message, either, but I saw there were a couple other texts that had arrived during the night.

DraganShao: Yun provided chat logs that implicate you but nothing specific. The clips from the pirate

broadcast could have been downloaded after-the-fact.
I'm going to try to defuse this. Lie low.
Vamp: Figured out what happened. Call me.

I pulled Vamp up on the chat.
Vamp, what's up?
Okay, I had Chong, the guy that used to work at the power company, do some digging, and it looks like Xinzhongzi has a substation that went up less than a year ago. They're using it to power something with a massive draw inside the colony. To get a cascading failure means figuring the capacity of each station in the grid. The presence of this extra one has the failure moving out of control.
But we want the blackout, so can't we just let the failure go?
I don't think we'll get a total failure with the Xinzhongzi station there. It has a ridiculously high storage capacity so it keeps soaking up the excess, and things stabilize before we can get anything but a localized outage.
You can't take it down?
We can't access it at all. Unlike the rest of Hangfei's power grid, this station is brand new and locked down tight. We haven't been able to get past their security. I'm sorry, Sam.
No, I sent. *No way. We aren't getting shut down because of Gohan Sòng's gonzo bullshit.*
Sam, we have a limited window to get in there. Liàng-zǐchuán is going to get a handle on this failure before too long, and that will be that.
Then we take it down.
Take it down how? It's inside Xinzhongzi, on the other side of the security wall. On the other side of about fifty thousand protesters and security troops. Even if we could get in to the colony, the station itself is going to have security.

I fumed inside the sweltering tube, wanting to scream. It had worked. The whole thing had worked, and now, at the last minute, the whole thing was going to get derailed. It couldn't all be for nothing.

Sam?

Vamp was right, though . . . we'd never get at that power station. We'd never get into any of them, let alone that one. If Vamp couldn't sneak in remotely, then there was no way to . . .

Sam?

There is a way, I sent.

How?

I fished out the gate remote, and turned it over in my hand. One of the endpoints had been set to the black hole drop, but I could set another one.

Does Chong know where the new power station is? Does he know where exactly inside Xinzhongzi it is?

If he doesn't, he can find out.

Good. Tell him to contact me. I have an idea.

And what's that?

I balked at telling him. I knew what he'd say.

Just have him contact me.

Sam, what are you going to do?

Please?

His heart icon pulsed for a bit.

I'll tell him.

Thanks.

He signed off, and I rubbed my temples.

"New power station . . ." I muttered.

A new station to power something with a massive draw . . . Gohan had bought up Xinzhongzi, cleared it out, then built . . . something. Something for the haan who would live there.

But what?

I took a deep breath, trying to get my footing. The hunger I felt grew worse, so bad that for a moment it frightened me a little. I always felt a little hungry, but it had gotten worse than I should have let it. I found the bag of rations I'd taken from my apartment and looked inside. Alexei had taken one, leaving me with five. I unwrapped one of the bars, and bit it in half, chewing as I pulled the tube's latch. I pushed the door up to let in sunlight, and a wave of humid heat rushed in along with a few scaleflies. Outside, residents had begun to stir and some of the ones lucky enough to have bottom units had set lawn chairs out on the blacktop. An old man across the way stood in front of his open tube, wearing only boxer shorts and sandals as he washed himself with a facecloth. A tinny voice carried from someone's tablet nearby.

". . . has residents beginning to ask questions about the strange sightings, which more and more citizens are coming forward to insist that they saw . . ."

When I swung out onto the ladder, I saw a figure below, huddled against the side of the bottom tube. He sat hugging his knees, the material of his suit draped down onto the blacktop around him while the sun glinted off the glassy dome of his skull.

"Nix?"

I climbed down, then knelt for a closer look. His eyes were dim, but the flickering light had a sunset pink hue. His head had slumped forward, his forehead almost touching his knees.

"Hey, Nix," I said, giving him a gentle shake.

His eyes flashed, and the glow intensified in each as he lifted his head. When he did, the hunger I felt grew much worse, so bad it made me feel weak, and sick. Through the surrogate cluster I could feel the hollowness inside of him, as it threatened to drag him under.

"Nix?"

His pupils did a slow revolution, focusing on me.

"Sam?"

"Were you out here all night?"

He looked around, and I felt a faint thread of confusion through the mite cluster. He didn't seem to know where he was, or how he had even gotten there.

"Yes," he said, but he didn't sound sure.

"Nix, you're starving," I said. "You need help."

"You need to cease your attack. . . ." He drifted off.

I didn't respond to that. I couldn't stop the cascade now even if I wanted to. The best I could do was let it go until they could fix it, but I couldn't do that.

I glanced up and down the row. The old man still scrubbed himself with the cloth, but his attention had turned toward us.

"Nix, can you make it up there?" I pointed to the crash tube I'd rented, and he nodded.

He climbed up, and went inside. I followed, crawling in with him and sat cross-legged as I pulled the door shut. The overhead flickered back on.

"Please," he said. "Stop what you're—"

"Nix, no."

"Please."

I pressed my palms to my eyelids, wanting to scream. "We're not attacking you, Nix. We're not coming at you with guns or bombs. I just want people to see what's really going on. Don't we deserve that much?"

"They will see it as an attack."

"Why, Nix? If you guys have nothing to hide, then why is this such a big deal? What if the power went out because of an accident? Would they retaliate then?"

"This won't be an accident, and they will know that."

"You're just afraid people will see what you don't want them to see."

"No," he said. "It will bring down the force field, as well. If the foreign forces see the opportunity, they will attack."

"And why would they do that, Nix? What is it they see that would make them do something like that?"

"Please, trust me."

My free hand had curled into a fist. The signal pouring off Nix felt like fear, or dread, and I felt for him but what he was asking wasn't fair.

"It's just the truth, Nix," I said. "People have a right to make their decisions based on the truth, not a lie."

He blew air from his feeding vents, ending in a low rattle.

"How many of them are out there?" I asked him. "How many people have changed?"

"I don't know."

"Bullshit you don't know. You can see them. How many?"

He looked down at the mattress between us, not speaking for a long time. He tried to keep how conflicted he felt from bleeding through, but he couldn't. Not from me.

"The truth," he said finally. "Here is the truth—the foreigners observing from the outside have noticed the . . . fallout from Sillith's final act. That much I know. They don't understand, and are frightened. If they see an opening, a chance to attack, they will take it but I am more worried about the reaction here in Hangfei. If the people of this city are allowed to see the truth, they will assume that we have broken our agreement and they will destroy the ship, even if the foreigners don't."

"What agreement?"

He didn't answer that. "Such an attempt will put humans and haan in direct conflict."

"And what does that mean?"

His two brains quivered underneath the dome of his skull, the smaller one retreating beneath the larger one like it did whenever he got really upset.

"You believed in us, once."

I sighed, and took his hand. I laced my fingers through his, on the mattress between us.

"I still believe in you, Nix."

"Is that true?"

"I don't think the haan are all bad," I said. "I don't think you're all evil, and believe it or not I do think you mean to come through on your promises, but it can't all be just on your own terms."

"We will help you," he said. "We will help you all but believe me Sam, you should be concerned about this. The ship, Shiliuyuán, is a research center and contains technologies you can't yet imagine—"

"I don't care, Nix."

"You should care."

"Well, I don't," I clipped. "You guys have lied about everything from the start, and our government is helping you do it. This has gone on for over fifty years. No more secrets."

"There is more to this than you realize. . . . What Sillith did should not have happened. Give us time to make things right again—"

The hum of an aircar made the tube rattle as it passed overhead, and I waved at Nix to be quiet.

"Shh!"

"What is it?"

The aircar began to descend, heading toward the clear patch of blacktop near the entryway. I'd heard the sound a hundred times growing up. No one who could afford an aircar stayed in Baishan Park. The only time aircars ever showed up was when someone called security.

I slid the little plastic panel away from the hatch's tiny window and peeked out. Sure enough, two marked vehicles had begun making their way toward the park's only good landing spot.

"Damn it," I hissed, sliding the window shut.

Outside the tube, a siren chirped. Someone shouted something, and then I heard the unmistakable sound of aircar doors popping open.

"Nix, we have to run. Are you up to it?"

"Yes."

"Then we've got to hustle. Come on."

I pushed open the tube door and jumped as a figure appeared on the other side. The afternoon sun shone bright on her white sundress, the ghost bloodstain still visible on the right breast as she crouched on the tube rail, her skirt flapping in the breeze that came in off the shore.

I pushed back, away from her, and went for my pistol but never reached it. Something cold slithered around my wrist, and stopped me cold. It smashed my hand back against the wall behind me and pinned me. Behind her, I saw a group of three security officers marching down the row of tubes toward us.

"Qian, wait. . . ."

She climbed into the tube with us, and I felt something grab my other wrist. I fell back as she pinned it to the wall, too, stretching my arms taut as she leaned in close.

"I'm sorry, Sam," she said.

The security guards were closing in fast. One spoke into his radio as the other two drew stun batons. I decided to try a different tact.

"Qian, security's coming, they'll—"

"They will be too late." Her tone had shifted. All at once, the promise of violence began to bleed through the mite cluster. "I'm sorry. I did warn you."

Something slithered across my ankle; then all at once her unseen tentacles began to coil around my legs, my arms, even my neck.

Nix lunged, then, grabbing her. Her eyes widened, and though I saw her lean back and grip her throat, my wrists stayed pinned by some part of her I couldn't see. I heard a crunch and she gasped; then the coils around me loosened.

Qian turned her attention to Nix, and my arms fell free by my sides as she grabbed his arm with one hand while clamping down on his shoulder with the other. I felt a sharp bolt of pain through the cluster.

"Wait!" I shouted.

Qian pulled, twisting the arm until the bones splintered

and it popped from its socket. Pain flooded through his signal as the limb tore away completely.

I stared in shock as warmth spritzed my face. Blood dripped from her hands as she cast the arm away behind her, and I saw it split into two distinct limbs before falling away. Two bangs followed as each one gated back to the ship. It struck me that she had felt nothing at all while she'd done this. The signal I'd felt from her as she tore the arm free felt as detached as if she'd been crumpling and discarding an unwanted wrapper.

"You . . ." I gasped. Nothing else would come out. I pulled the palm pistol from inside the Escher field and shot her three times, but she just put her hand on my chest and hurled me back into the tube. My head struck the shelf, and I bounced off onto the mattress.

Nix lunged, and I saw his missing arm had returned. His hand clamped down on her face in the second before she was torn away from the tube rail. The impact sent her flying through the air, across the row to crash into the stack of tubes opposite ours. She hit so hard that the plastic door cracked down its center and one half broke free to spin away and crash down onto the pavement. The stack rocked, like it might actually tip over, but righted itself as Qian's body tumbled down onto the ground in a heap.

"Run," Nix said to me. He started to leave the tube, when I grabbed his arm.

"Wait."

I pulled the tube door shut again, latching it and triggering the lock.

"That will not keep them out long," Nix said.

"It won't have to."

Outside, someone began clambering up the ladder toward our unit as I found the gate remote. I triggered the holodisplay and selected the endpoint for the black hole drop, then aimed it toward the back wall of the tube and pushed the button.

A white point of light appeared, which dilated out into a circle. On the other side, I saw only darkness.

"Come on," I said, pointing. "In."

Nix slipped through. When he did, I saw electric light flicker on from above as he triggered a motion sensor. He stepped away out of view on the other side, and I stuck my own legs through.

Someone tried to open the tube door, but it jammed against the magnetic bolt. A fist thumped on the other side, and a man's muffled voice came through.

"Give it up," he barked. "You're trapped. Open the damned—"

I grabbed the bag of rations off of the mattress and jumped through the gate. After a short hitch, I came out onto the factory floor. I turned back as the gate collapsed, and saw a metal pry forced under the door seam just before the portal shrank to a point of light, then faded.

Chapter Seventeen

"Shit," I breathed. I took out my phone and pulled up the flashlight app. In the dim light, my eyes began to adjust and I looked around. I laughed a little. "Holy shit, it worked."

"Where are we?" Nix asked, looking down the row of rusted machines.

"Out in the rim somewhere," I told him. "It's where I hide things."

He nodded, not asking for any further explanation. "How do we get out?"

"This way."

I led him back to the green door, past the box I'd stashed, and squeezed through the gap. He followed, slipping into the corridor in a single, fluid motion while I retrieved the twistkey from my tablet.

"Let me go first," I told him. "Security is probably watching the place from the outside to see if I come back, but they could have someone waiting inside."

I put the key in the gate's socket and turned it. The concrete wall shimmered, and then disappeared to reveal the inside of my closet. My stuff had been disturbed, a shoebox of pictures dumped out onto the floor and my duffel bag emptied, but it didn't look like they'd found the gate. I pushed the hanging clothes aside and crept through, moving into the closet and then stopping with my ear toward the door. I didn't hear anyone on the other side.

I turned the knob, and opened the door a crack so I could peek in. I didn't see anyone. The apartment sounded empty.

"Okay," I whispered back to Nix. "Come on."

I opened the door and stepped into my bedroom. As Nix came in behind me, I crossed to the opposite door and tiptoed out into the hall to check the other rooms.

"We're alone," I told him. "For now. Come on, over here."

I patted the sofa, and Nix shambled over, his hunger pangs seeming to grow worse by the second. He dropped down onto it, sounding heavier than he looked.

"Lie down," I told him, crouching beside him so I could ease him onto his back. When he'd gotten comfortable, I removed one of the rations from the bag.

Has anyone seen or heard from Alexei? I sent out over the 3i. *I had him with me in Baishan Park last night, but he ditched some time before I woke up.*

Nothing, Vamp sent back. *Sorry. I can scan the eyebot data and look for any hits on him.*

I haven't heard from him, Dragan said. *How long's he been gone?*

I'm not sure what time of night he bailed, but—

He's with me, Dao-Ming sent.

Dragan, I asked, *can you pick him up? Or should I—*

I think this is the safest place for him, Dao-Ming said. *For the time being.*

They've got me stationed in Xinzhongzi, Dragan said. *Dao-Ming can watch him.*

I didn't say anything. There wasn't much I could say without spilling everything. I didn't like the idea of Alexei being with Dao-Ming anymore, but at least he was off the street. Whatever else she might be, she wouldn't let anything happen to him.

Is that okay? Dragan asked.

Yeah, I said. *Of course. Thanks, Dao-Ming.*

You're very welcome, Sam.

I disconnected.

"It appears that security has found you out," Nix said, watching me from the sofa. "You should stop what you're doing."

"Quiet," I told him, tearing the ration's wrapper.

"Sam, you—"

"Come on, Little Demon, eat."

I propped up his head, and aimed the ration toward his mouth. The lower part of his face dissolved into smoke, and I felt it connect with the feeding tube. A rush of pleasure, and relief flooded in through the cluster as Nix devoured the bar in seconds. I grabbed a second, and fed him that one as well. He ate the second, and then a third before I felt him relax. As the nutrients flooded through his body, I felt his aches and pains begin to leave him. The hollowness in him filled, and his strength began to return. I stroked his forehead, which had begun to grow warm under my fingertips.

"This feels familiar," I said.

"Yes."

I sighed, putting one hand to his cheek.

"I should be afraid to even touch you," I told him.

"Your brain is hardwired to recognize faces. You interpret the face you can see, not the one you can't, and my face has already formed an association in your mind that you cannot help."

"But I know it isn't true. In my mind, I know it isn't true."

"You know it as an abstract concept. Your brain is wired to believe the sensory input it receives."

"Are we so easy to fool?"

"Your brains are very well adapted for your world, but they contain many exploits."

"Exploits," I said, annoyed. "So I'm right then. It really is all a lie."

Nix considered that. The three pupils in each of his eyes revolved slowly in the pink light.

"Your race is very visual," he said. "You are programmed, from an evolutionary standpoint, to react to things outside your experience. To become alarmed by them, to a degree we didn't initially understand. When we realized the extent of it, we knew your people would have to be eased into accepting us as we are."

"It's been over fifty years. Give us some credit."

He put his hand on mine. His delicate fingers curled around them, warming them.

"Please," he said. "Consider what you're doing."

"I have."

"The haan from the park—"

"Used to be human." Nix didn't answer. "Didn't she?"

"In the ways that matter, she still is."

"Don't bullshit me, Nix. Sillith's virus changed her, right?"

"Yes."

"Her and how many others?"

He didn't answer that.

"Nix, are they eating us?"

"I don't know."

"I think you do."

"Sam, she knows," he said, changing the subject. "And if she knows, then others will know. There will be more. Once she learns to utilize the scalefly memory transfer efficiently, all haan will know."

"Then we'd better move fast."

"Revealing the truth now will cause pain, and upheaval."

"Working through things does, sometimes."

"But—"

"Nix, you won't talk me out of this. No more secrets. At this point, I'm thinking that if we can't figure this thing out with all the cards on the table, then it's because our interests don't line up."

"You truly believe that?"

"Yeah. I do."

"Even if it means bloodshed, on both sides?"

I straightened the lapels of his suit, smoothing them down with my palm before putting my hand over the pulsing mass of his heart. I could feel it beat, strong and steady against my palm.

"You know, in fifty years you've gotten most of the country to love you guys. Those protesters outside Xinzhongzi? They're still a pretty small minority, and even they wouldn't be out there if Gohan hadn't tried to do an end run around LeiFang. Thanks to you guys, we're the one shining star left in a world that's gone to shit and on some level everybody knows that, even the ones who complain. But the thing is, Nix, is that they only see the positive side. It's all they're allowed to see. Things like the ability to wipe out an entire continent, or convert people into a totally different species, those things get hidden. If someone does manage to see through it, people like Governor Hwong or Sillith make sure they disappear. Those people out there love you guys, but you can't love someone if you don't know what they really are."

I thought about that for a second, then let out a small laugh.

"What?" Nix asked.

"Nothing," I said. "I just realized that's the same reason I'm blowing it with Vamp. I always thought that Vamp wanted me, but that he wouldn't if he knew the truth about me. Here I am, willing to tip the whole city on end, but I can't just tell him the truth, and let him decide."

"It may not be too late."

I shrugged.

"I don't know." I patted his arm, and stood up. "There're more rations in the bag, and I'll leave the twistkey for you in case you need it. Stay as long as you need, then find me again?"

"I will. Where are you going?"

I headed toward the factory exit, lining up the quickest route to Chong's meeting point on the 3i. I checked the endpoint, and his note, and raised my eyebrows.

"You don't want to know," I said.

Chapter Eighteen

The sun beat down as I approached Chong's marker on the 3i map. His directions had taken me down to the south side of Jangbong, where the crowds of people seemed to grow dirtier and skinnier with each block. The destination seemed to be an aircar electrical charge station at the street corner up ahead, and as I walked along a rusted chain-link fence, I spotted Chong across a lot of cracked asphalt.

I assumed it had to be him, anyway. He dressed like Vamp, and looked totally out of place, leaning against the back wall of the station's run-down minimart while puffing a cigarette to life. He flicked his lighter closed, and blew smoke. When he saw me approach, he met my eye and waved.

"You must be Sam," he said. He held out his hand, and I shook it.

"And you must be Chong."

"That's me."

He waved a fly away, and it buzzed back to join the cloud that hung around the mart's trash bin. Off in the distance, I heard the "pop" of a gun going off. A second later, two more sounded.

"Lots of security," Chong said. "Something's got people stirred up."

"Something."

"You hear the news?" he asked. "What they're saying about the blackouts?"

"No."

"They're blaming it on an American cyberattack," he said, grinning. "Pretty rich, huh?"

"Better them than us."

He looked me up and down.

"Vamp said you were cute," he said. "He wasn't kidding."

"Vamp said that?"

He shrugged his shoulders. "He mentioned it." He took a last drag off his smoke, then tossed it, only half-finished.

"So, you ready to go?" he asked.

"Go where, Chong?"

He used the station's restroom key, attached to a big metal plate, to unlock a grimy metal door and then pulled it open. As soon as he did, a wave of stink hit me, a hot cloud of urine, shit, and cigarette smoke that made me want to gag.

"Ugh," I said. "What the hell, Chong?"

"You want to get into the Xinzhongzi station?"

"Yeah, but how—"

"And you've got a gate remote?"

"Yeah . . ."

He handed me the key, and gestured for me to go inside.

"This better be for real," I said, taking the key and stashing it in my pocket. I stepped inside, where the smell somehow got even worse. I waved a fly from my face and wrinkled my nose. "This place is terrible."

The walls had been covered in overlapping scribbled hanzi announcing everything from gang names to sexual conquests. A sink mounted on the right-hand wall looked like it hadn't been used or cleaned in years, and the filthy plastic mirror over it was missing the bottom left corner. Against the far wall, two paces from the door leading in, sat a squat-style toilet surrounded by urine stains. An ashtray next to it overflowed with so many butts it looked like some kind of carcinogenic flower.

"We can access the sewer from here," Chong said, pointing toward the stall. "From there, we can reach the station."

"You're sure it will take us there?" I asked him.

"One of the tunnels goes right under it."

I stood in front of a grimy toilet, boxed in on all sides by bathroom graffiti. The cramped stall left almost no room to move around so I perched on the toilet lid, facing the door where Chong stood, and slipped my Escher tablet out of my pocket. I traced the pass code with my finger and the metallic screen dissolved to reveal a pocket of impossible space inside. Among the stacks of weapons and supplies, I spotted the little remote in the corner where I'd left it.

When I moved my palm over it, the field jumped forward, expanding so that I could reach inside. I pulled the remote device out of my pack, then leaned forward on the toilet and aimed the lens at the tip of the controller down toward the grimy, tiled floor.

"How do you know how to use that thing?" Chong asked.

"I read the directions."

I pushed the button. A thin, almost invisible laser made a dot in the middle of the floor, and a holodisplay adapted for the human visible spectrum appeared in front of me above the surface of the remote. It displayed a sort of X-ray of the floor, and I could see wiring, support beams, and pipes down there. I eased the right wheel down with one finger, and the image dove deeper while numbers ticked past to indicate the depth in meters. A red warning icon hovered over all of it, letting me know it hadn't found a space big enough to gate into yet.

I moved the wheel a little more, and the icon turned yellow, then finally green. On the holoscreen, I could see a drop below me, then a fuzzy tunnel floor at the bottom.

"You see it?" he asked.

"Yeah, I got it."

I eased the depth down just a little more, then released the button, and clicked it once.

A point of white light appeared on the floor, like a bright little LED that lit up the inside of the bathroom. I dialed the wheel on the remote's left side, and the point of light opened to form the thin hexagonal outline. Through it, I could see the sewer tunnel below. I dialed it open a little more, then a little more, just enough for us to slip through. When I had it ready, I pushed the button a second time to store the location for our return trip.

"Where does it lead?" I asked him. He sent the sewer map over the 3i, with the destination marked off. It would be a bit of a haul, but he was right, the tunnels did pass right underneath Xinzhongzi.

"You ready?"

"I don't really need an escort, Chong."

"What are you going to do if you run into trouble?"

"And what are you going to do if I do?"

"You need me to show you where to set the endpoint," he said.

I really didn't want him along, because once I got into the station I didn't think he would like what came next. It would be better, I thought, if he just didn't know.

"Just tell me where to put it."

"It's better if I show you."

I thought about ditching him, just jumping through and closing the gate behind me, but he looked so damned earnest and he was right, really. Having some backup couldn't hurt.

"After you," I told him. He removed a small flashlight from inside his jacket and handed it to me.

"Ladies first."

I grabbed the light, then gave him the finger, took a deep breath, and jumped through.

Dropping through the gate felt like plunging into thick mud. I fell straight through into darkness, and then met sudden resistance that slowed and stopped me almost immediately. For a couple of seconds I hung there, stuck, with no sense of space. Then, before I could even try to get oriented, I came out the other side in free fall.

I dropped only a few feet before landing on the concrete floor of the tunnel with a shallow splash. I stumbled, then lost my footing and fell down on my back as Chong looked through the gate from above. I could still hear the street noise leaking through, and echoing down the tunnel.

"You okay?" he called. I winced, and rolled over in the shallow muck.

"Yeah, I'm great."

I turned on the flashlight as he splashed down next to me, almost tumbling over, and above us the gate shrank to a point of light and disappeared. I aimed the beam down the tunnel first one way, then the other. Something moved, skittering away in the distance and I froze.

"It's just a rat or something," Chong said. "Take it easy."

"You take it easy." I brought up the sewer map on my 3i, and shined the light across the tunnel wall until I found a sign indicating the junction. Something else moved in the tunnel, and I jumped.

"There's someone down here," I said.

"There's no one down here. I checked it all out. There's no scheduled maintenance. You'll be able to set an endpoint to sneak into the station later. Then all we have to do is figure out how to shut it down from the inside."

"I know how to shut it down," I said.

"Yeah? And how's that?"

I headed down the tunnel, following the map as the rumble of traffic rushed overhead, washed out by the occasional rumble of a metro car.

"Hey, how do you think you're going to shut it down?" he called, coming after me. "You're going to need me to—"

"Let me worry about that. Just get me inside."

He let it drop, following along with me in silence for a bit.

"So, what's up with you and Vamp?" he asked. I glanced back at him, frowning.

"Why?"

"Because if you guys aren't a thing, then I figured I might see if you want to go out some time. Hit a club or something."

I stopped, and turned back toward him.

"Me and Vamp are complicated, okay?"

"So, you're a thing?"

"I don't know what we are," I said.

"Okay, okay," he said, putting up his hands. "I just thought maybe he and Shuang were back together, so—"

He almost ran into me as I stopped short.

"Back together?" I asked. He saw the look on my face, and began to stammer a little.

"Well . . . yeah," he said. "He never mentioned her?"

I shook my head. "No."

"Hey, it's ancient history," he said, trying to backpedal. "Don't worry about it."

"You just said you thought they were back together."

"I . . . did just say that," he agreed. "Hey, what do I know though?"

"Are they?" I asked. He shrugged.

"Only thing I ever talk to Shuang about are schematics from the power grid when she was coding the virus."

"Did Vamp say anything?"

He started to protest again, then stopped, and let out a sigh.

"I'll put it this way," he said. "I figure the only reason Shuang is in on this, is because of Vamp. Back then, she called it off. He took it hard. She's back because she wants another shot. That's the only reason."

"Does Vamp know that?"

"If he isn't blind he does."

An underground train passed by somewhere below, and as the roar faded back to silence I heard the skittering sound again, and brought my flashlight around.

"There's nothing down here," Chong said, when something froze in the beam.

The thing was small, and low to the ground. I thought it might actually be a rat or something but then I saw the pinprick, glowing lights. Several long, spindly legs pawed at the floor ahead, uncertain; then the little haan construct scrambled away. When it reached the corner, it startled a couple more and then took off after them.

"You were saying?"

"Huh," he said. "What the heck are they doing down here?"

"No idea."

"Should we squash them, just in case?"

"Good luck catching one of those things," I told him. "Besides, they don't care that we're here."

"Security will."

"The constructs don't record visual data."

"Says who?"

"The haan."

"And we know they never lie."

"Let's just get this over with before the station attendant comes back looking for his key, okay?"

"Fine."

We headed down the tunnel, trying to stay out of the muck until we reached the junction and the tunnel widened. A concrete platform appeared, jutting from the right side to allow maintenance workers to make their way through. We climbed up onto it and followed rows of thick, black wiring that powered the tunnel lights, which were currently dark except for the faint glow of green power LEDs.

Following the map, we navigated the maze of sewers until according to the overlay I'd traveled several city blocks. By then, the air felt thick and heavy, and I found it harder and harder to breathe. With nothing but blackness behind us and ahead, I lost all sense of where I was and even my footsteps echoed and overlapped so that I wouldn't know if someone snuck up behind me until it was too late. I picked up my pace, following the hanging wires down the platform with Chong in tow until the beam of my flashlight caught something up ahead.

"Shit." My voice echoed as I slowed to a stop in front of a metal gate. It went floor to ceiling, a series of thick metal bars and when I pulled on the door I found it locked tight with an electronic lock. I shone my light through, and could see the next junction ahead.

"Um . . . according to the map, that shouldn't be there," Chong said.

"Well, it is there, Chong."

"I can see that."

The gate looked new, its paint clean and fresh in the dank surroundings.

"Can we go around?" I asked.

"No, the tunnels don't meet up anywhere else. According to the map, the only way to get under the power station is through there."

I shined my flashlight over the gate. The bars covered the whole of the tunnel, with no place to squeak past. A metal sign had been posted above the gate, displaying a Hangfei security seal.

TOP LEVEL SECURITY ACCESS ONLY BY ORDER OF THE MILITARY GOVERNESS.

"Governess," I whispered.

"This went up after Hwong's death, then," Chong said. "It's less than a year old."

"That's why it isn't on the map."

She knows, then, I thought. If LeiFang had gone to the trouble to not just surround Xinzhongzi with security but even choke off access from the sewers, then she must want whatever is in there kept secret, too. Was that why she hadn't come down on the protests yet? Was she using the protesters as a distraction, and so that she didn't appear to be too much in favor of the colony?

Standing close to the bars, I gauged the gap between them. Designed to let water through, they were wide enough apart to not get clogged with random flotsam. The space between them was still pretty small, but then again, so was I.

I angled myself sideways, then snuck my arm and leg through between two of the bars. As scrawny as I might be it turned out to still be a hell of a squeeze, but I managed to scrape through.

"Hey," Chong said, moving up to the bars that were now between us. He'd never fit through to come after me, and he knew it.

"Sorry," I told him.

"Come on, gate me through."

Something chirped to my left and I jumped. A haan construct had perched on the wall there, its bulbous eye stuck out toward me on the end of its little eyestalk. It dropped to the floor and scuttled away down the tunnel.

"Just tell me where to go," I said.

"Sam, quit messing around and gate me through."

"Tell me where to go."

He thought about it for a moment, and I could see he wasn't in love with the idea but he didn't have much choice. "Son of a bitch," he muttered. "Follow the map to the marker, and when you get there call me on the 3i and I'll walk you through where to set up the endpoint."

"Thanks," I said, and started down the tunnel.

"And what the hell am I supposed to do in the meantime?" he called after me.

"Keep watch," I called back.

"Keep watch . . ." he muttered.

I gave him a wave as I walked away. In minutes, he was lost in the darkness behind me, and I was alone.

I followed the map, sweeping the tunnel with my flashlight as I went. The walls of the tunnel turned darker ahead, and as I got closer I saw that they had been covered with shiny, black hexagonal plates that interlocked like honeycomb. They were smooth, like glass, and warm to the touch.

I'd seen similar scales inside the haan colony of Shangzho, where they'd covered the faces of entire buildings in some spots.

Something skittered farther down the tunnel again, and I shined the light in its direction in time to see a big shadow move past. My breath caught in my chest.

That was no construct.

I struggled to stay calm. The shape looked man-sized. There wasn't supposed to be anyone down here but you couldn't account for everything. There might have been some kind of emergency, or something unexpected that made them send a team down—

Something else rustled from that direction, and a scraping footstep echoed in the tunnel.

I strained my eyes in the dim light. On the heels of whatever it was, a many-legged shadow crept past, low to the ground, and I saw it had something. The construct dragged something behind it, a pile of wet cloth, it looked like, but I didn't get a good look before it had moved past the opening and out of sight.

Distant footsteps slapped across concrete, this time back from the way I'd come. They were unmistakable.

"Who's down here?" I asked the construct. It hopped down, and scurried away from me as another shadow moved from somewhere around the corner.

Don't panic. Just keep moving.

I picked up the pace, moving as fast as I dared in the dark until I reached the final junction. The tunnel walls there had been completely covered in the haan scales. They glinted in the flashlight beam all the way down the tunnel to an open doorway at the top of three brick steps.

A strange smell lingered in the tunnel at the junction, and whatever caused it made my eyes water. It came from the adjoining tunnel, getting weaker as I headed in the opposite direction, then up the steps to the doorway to look through.

I'd studied pictures of the stations, but this one had even

less room inside than the ones I'd seen. The interior of the large room had been packed full of big metal boxes arranged in a grid. They were covered in haan characters, and lights along the sides flashed in and out of the visible spectrum. At the top of each, a pylon stuck into the high ceiling. A revolving, coiled ring floated around each pylon where forking arcs of soft light flickered.

I crooked my neck to bring up the 3i display, then pinged Chong.

Okay, I'm here.

Good. Use your GPS to find north, face that wall. Then find a spot on the ceiling as far left as you can go.

I turned around, following the GPS direction marker until I faced the far wall at a slight angle. From there, I followed the ceiling until I came to the left-hand corner.

Okay, got it.

Place the point there. That will guarantee the gate will open inside the facility itself.

Where?

You're right under it, anywhere in that room should get you in.

I aimed the remote at the ceiling, and brought up the holodisplay. The scan began to push into the concrete as I eased the dial with my thumb, heading toward the surface, and hopefully the inside of the substation.

How far up? I asked him.

Just keep going until it detects open space.

I turned the dial, slowly, until the red light flickered to green. The way didn't exactly look clear, but it opened into somewhere.

Okay, I got it.

I stored the endpoint, then headed back out into the tunnel. As I headed down the concrete steps I caught another whiff of the strange smell and stopped, wrinkling my nose. It smelled sickly sweet, managing to overpower the sewer's stink.

I shined the flashlight toward the source and something moved in the light ahead. When I focused the beam, I saw the wet scrap of cloth the construct had carried by earlier. It lay plastered in the muck, something near the end glinting back at me from down the tunnel.

What is that?

I stepped closer, covering my nose, and saw it move again. It was a shirtsleeve. When it moved, the shiny button flashed in the flashlight beam.

Leaning over the platform I saw the shirt had begun to disappear through a hole in the tunnel floor and I hustled toward it, hopping off the walkway to get a better look.

The sleeve slipped over the edge of a wide circular pit just as I reached it, and I heard a soft splash.

Leaning closer, I shone the flashlight into the opening, triggering more movement below. The hole had filled with water, and I saw that some sort of spines or bristles lined the inside of the tunnel. The shirt sank slowly between them, billowing in a gentle current.

I've seen this before, I thought. When I'd visited the haan colony to drop off my surrogate, I'd seen a pit like that inside one of the buildings they'd occupied.

My beam found a pile of gently swaying clothes near the bottom. There had to be hundreds of shirts, pants, shoes, belts . . . all of it dumped down there . . .

Chong, it looks like the constructs are dumping something down here.

Never mind the constructs. Come on.

They're dumping clothes, it looks like.

Leave them. We need to get back.

Below, a shadow swam past the flashlight beam and I gasped. The pile disappeared, leaving only a single stocking that swirled in its wake as whatever it was moved down some branching tunnel.

Chong . . .

A rumble filled the tunnel as a metro train cruised past

somewhere underground. The floor shook, and the flashlight sent shadows moving through the base of the hole. I
put one hand on the slimy concrete to try to see if I could
spot anything else down there, but what I'd thought was
water turned out to be something cold and jellylike. As it
squelched between my fingers I felt squirmy movement inside it. I jerked my hand away, trailing goo, and wiped it on
my pant leg. It felt like millions of tiny little worms were
wriggling around in the stuff, but when I shined the light I
didn't see anything. Just a clear, runny liquid.

Chong . . . I sent again. He didn't answer.

Okay, I told myself. *Never mind it. Do what you came to
do, and get out of here.*

I scraped my hand on the edge of the platform until the
feeling stopped, then took out my phone and snapped a few
pictures before aiming the gate remote at a spot on the tunnel wall. I dialed up the endpoint for the black hole drop
and opened a portal.

A point of white light expanded, revealing the darkness
of the underground factory. I shined my light through, passing it over the machinery to the collapsed wall where I'd
stashed the box.

I stepped inside, the muted street noise and metro rum-
bles disappearing in favor of the low whisper of the rim's
endless storm. I hurried over to the box, and scooped it up.
Before I could change my mind, I carried it back to the
portal and into the tunnel.

I closed the gate behind me, and knelt down on the tunnel floor. My hands shook a little as I opened the box, to
reveal the three bricks inside. When I saw them, in front of
me like that, I hesitated. Just one should be enough to bring
the station down, and I had to bring the station down,
but . . .

I'll do it in the middle of the night, I told myself. *I'll do it
when no one is there. No one will get hurt if I do it when no
one is there. I'll just—*

"It's a form of perfluorocarbon," a voice said near my ear. A hand touched my shoulder, and I screamed.

I whirled around to see Nix standing there in the tunnel with me. He had to have gated in, and the train noise covered the sound of the portal opening.

"Shit, Nix."

"Sorry."

"You almost gave me a heart attack."

He pointed at the liquid pooled on the floor, the strange liquid I'd been looking at earlier.

"It's a form of perfluorocarbon," he said. "The liquid breathing medium used inside Shiliuyuán."

"What's it doing here?"

"I'm not sure, but it didn't come from the ship. They must be using it for some reason inside the Xinzhongzi colony."

"Why?"

"Humans can breathe it . . . in fact you did some years ago when you were gated to the ship. More likely, though, it is being used by haan."

"But the colony hasn't been opened yet."

"Regardless, at least some haan are inside."

"Great."

If LeiFang thought the protesters were getting out of hand now, just wait until Hangfei got wind that haan had already started to move in.

"I've seen tunnels like that one before," I said. "Why is it here?"

"We use tunnels extensively in our habitats," he said. "The bristles assist movement through the perfluorocarbon—"

"How deep do they go?" I asked. "How many tunnels are there down there?"

Instead of answering, he gestured toward the bricks that he'd seen inside the box. "What are those?" he asked.

"Nothing, Nix, I—"

"Detonating an explosive device doesn't sound like something you would do."

The way he said it made me feel angry and ashamed all at the same time. A sense of dismay, of disappointment, trickled in through the surrogate cluster.

"I need to shut down the colony power station," I said, my voice rising.

"But like this?"

"I'll do it after hours. No one will get hurt."

"That is naïve."

My face grew hot, as I turned back to the box. I reached in and pulled one of the bricks free.

"I'll make sure. . . ."

My words trailed off as I saw the brick in the light.

"What is wrong?" Nix asked.

The bricks had the same weight as before, and the wrapper around the one in my hand was the same as before, but the insides had changed. The solid claylike gray brick had been replaced with what looked like a piece of drywall.

"Sam, what's wrong?" Nix asked again.

I dumped the other bricks out. They'd all been swapped, and the detonators were gone.

I stared at them on the sewer floor. Had they been fakes all along? Did I get ripped off? Or had Dao-Ming somehow managed to swap them out without my knowing?

Could she have done that, though? The only way to access them would have been with the remote, or through the black hole gate.

"Alexei has a key to my place," I said.

"What?"

"She must have gotten it from him," I said. That meant Dao-Ming had her explosives, and the detonators, and might have had them all along. She had set off the bomb in Render's Strip.

"I knew it," I said under my breath. "I fucking knew it!"

I threw the box away, and stood back up. I put the remote back into my Escher tablet, and dropped it into my pocket.

Chong, I'm coming back. I've got a haan with me so don't freak out. I know him.

The message sat, unanswered, in the 3i chat pane.

Chong?

"He's not answering," I muttered.

"Who?"

"Chong, the guy I came down here with. Come on, we need to get back."

"I can gate us out."

"We can't just leave him down here, come on."

Something boomed from down the tunnel, and echoed into the distance. Two more followed right after.

"Gunshots," I said. "Chong's in trouble, come on."

Three more shots went off as I drew my palm pistol and sprinted back the way I'd come. Nix followed, our feet splashing through the shallow water until we finally reached the junction. I turned the corner, and saw a muzzle flash in the dim light up ahead as Chong fired another shot.

"Chong!"

Something white stood out in the gloom, and I spotted Qian, back in her white uniform, standing only a few paces from Chong. As she passed by a fallen electric lantern, her shadow changed, just for a second. Just for a second she cast a shadow too large for her small frame, and right before she moved out of the light I saw something begin to uncoil from either side of it.

Her hands were still by her sides but Chong seized as if he'd been grabbed. His right arm went rigid, and began to turn purple as something invisible coiled around it. He tried to fire his gun again but something peeled his fingers off the grip. Two of them snapped and were peeled away as the pistol thumped onto the concrete floor.

"Shoot her!" he screamed. He stared bug-eyed at the spot where his fingers had been as blood ran freely from the ragged hole left behind.

I took aim, but they were so close together and I didn't

have a lot of experience with guns. I wasn't sure I could hit either one of them from that distance, and I could easily end up hitting Chong instead.

"Shoot her!"

The coil around his arm tightened and his arm snapped. He screamed as his forearm bent ninety degrees and a splinter of bone tore through the skin.

"Qian!" I shouted.

She turned and saw me, as well as the bars that separated us. Chong's screams became muffled as if something had moved to cover his mouth. Then she turned, and disappeared with him down the tunnel.

"Qian!"

I approached the bars and slipped through. Nix followed, and I shined my flashlight down the tunnel but saw no sign of Chong or Qian. Even his muffled screams had faded.

"Chong?" I called. My voice echoed down the tunnel.

"Sam, there," Nix said, pointing.

I shined my light onto the tunnel floor, where Chong's phone lay on the bare concrete, just on the other side of the bars.

"Shit." I reached through and picked it up. Three red dots, still sticky to the touch, had spotted the screen where a message still sat.

Chong: Gohan, we might have a problem.
Gohan: What is it?
Chong: She's starting to figure it out. I don't know where she's getting her information from, but she knows the new station is powering something. She suspects the existence of the device.
Gohan: Just stall her a little longer.
Chong: I'll try, but

The messages ended there. I started at the screen.

"He's a gonzo," I said.

Gohan must have either met him at his father's company before he turned gonzo, or got to him after Chong got fired and recruited him then. Either way, when Vamp approached Chong the night I was in the hospital, he must have taken it straight to Gohan.

I cycled back through his message log and saw three other conversations stored there.

Chong: There might be another issue. It seems that Sam has had contact with one of the changelings. She also has been in contact with a haan named Nix.
Gohan: The haan can't know about this. Did either of them indicate specifically that they knew?
Chong: Yes. They know, but not about our involvement.
Gohan: Is the plan still in effect, then? Are we still on schedule?
Chong: Yes.
Gohan: And the others don't know about you?
Chong: No.
Gohan: Continue as we planned. I'll try and find a way to take the haan who know out of circulation.

The next conversation had taken place later, after the first attempt when Ginzho had lost power.

Chong: Gohan, we have a problem.
Gohan: What sort of problem?
Chong: The Xinzhongzi substation that powers the project is interfering with our attempt to trigger the cascade failure.
Gohan: Are you certain? I saw the power fail.
Chong: Isolated failures. All of the work we'd done on this didn't account for the extra power storage capacity. I can't guarantee we'll see a full failure while it's online.

Gohan: I can't just take it offline, it will look too suspicious.

Chong: Sam seems to think she can manage it if I can get her into the station.

Gohan: How?

Chong: I'm not sure, but she seems pretty confident.

Gohan: Let her take her shot then. Just stall her long enough for us to store a charge that can power Rapture once the blackout is under way. And make sure this doesn't come back to us.

"Rapture," I said under my breath. "Nix, any idea what he means?"

"His reference seems to indicate some kind of device, with Rapture being its designation."

"You said before that the haan had developed some kind of failsafe," I said. "Something they could bargain with if they were threatened. Could that be it?"

"Perhaps."

The messages ended there. Anything older than that in the message logs had been erased.

I turned to Nix. "Why does Gohan want this?"

"I don't know."

"He didn't just turn a blind eye ... he wanted Chong to help us take down his father's company."

"It would appear so."

"But this hurts the haan. Gohan worships them." It didn't make sense. We'd missed something. Had this all been an act on Gohan's part? Could he have been planning to undermine the haan all along? "Okay, first things first. Let's get out of here."

I opened my Escher tablet to grab the remote, but I didn't see it. "Damn it...."

I widened the field so I could see better into the space, and that's when I realized. I'd dropped the remote into the shared space, not my personal one. It wasn't in there anymore. In its place, I saw the bin had been spotted with blood.

Chong. Chong had taken it. He must have been hoping for a quick escape when Qian showed up, but he didn't get the chance. Qian took him, and the gate remote with him.

"*Damn it!*"

I called Vamp, and as soon as he picked up, I spoke.

"Vamp, you need to hear this right now," I said. "Chong is missing, a haan grabbed him."

"A haan?"

"It was a haan, Vamp, I saw the whole thing. The thing is, I found his phone after the attack and found out he's been in direct contact with Gohan Sòng, probably this whole time. I'm putting his phone in the Escher space so you can see for yourself."

"Wait. If Gohan knew, then why wouldn't he report it?" Vamp asked. "He could have had us all arrested by now."

I dropped the phone into the field, and then closed it.

"I just dropped his phone into our shared tablet space," I told him. "He wants us to succeed, for some reason, I have no idea why. Just let the others know. I've got to go, security is looking for me. I'm going to try to lie low until we can get that power station offline."

"Understood. . . . I've got Chong's phone. He said you thought you had a way to do it?"

"I can't. My idea won't work, we need to think of something else."

"Come and meet me," he said. "I know someplace you can stay off the radar, and we can figure it out. Can you use the gate?"

"Not the remote. Chong had it when he got grabbed. It might be gone for good."

"They're looking for you, Sam, big time. Don't go back into the city right now. Just lie low until tonight, then meet me at a club called Phage Panic. I'll send the location to you."

"Then what?"

"I know where you can stay. We'll hide out there until we can figure this out."

"You're the best."

"Okay," I told Nix. "Looks like we've got some time to kill. Can you get us back up onto the street?"

"Yes."

"We need to grab a room, somewhere they won't ask questions. At sundown, we'll head out and meet with Vamp."

"What about your friend?"

Qian had warned me. She'd told me that I wouldn't be able to protect myself from her, or my family, or friends. It looked like she'd begun to make good on that promise.

"I don't know. We can't stay down here. If anyone can help us track him down, it's Vamp."

I looked down the darkened tunnel, though, and feared that there might not be anything left to track.

Chapter Nineteen

Phage Panic turned out to be in the blue district in the lower level of the Guanghuan mall. Under cover of darkness and the bustle of the night crowd, Nix and I managed to skirt security long enough to grab a bus to the Gong district. I gripped one of the rubber straps and stood with my chin tucked against my elbow, trying to keep my face at least somewhat hidden. Through the sliver of window I could see, I watched the city go by and tried to figure out what to do next.

Dao-Ming, are you there? The message floated in front of the window for a while, but she answered.

I'm here, Sam.

I know about the explosives, I told her.

She disconnected.

She'd bombed the gonzo rally. If I wasn't sure before, I was now. She'd bombed the rally to try to kill Gohan, and almost blew up Alexei instead. All those people, a lot of them not even gonzos, and she killed them all.

Weren't you about to do the same thing, though? A voice nagged.

It wasn't the same, I thought, but I wasn't so sure. Part of me was glad I didn't get the chance to find out.

I thought about Chong's texts, instead, trying to make them fit somehow.

Chong: There might be another issue. It seems that
Sam has had contact with one of the changelings. She
also has been in contact with a haan named Nix.
Gohan: The haan can't know about this. Did either of
them indicate specifically that they knew?
Chong: Yes. They know, but not about our involvement.

Whatever he was up to, the haan weren't in on it. They
didn't know, and Gohan didn't want them knowing. Could
his love of the haan all be an act? Could he have been getting close to them for some reason, just to strike when the
opportunity presented itself? It didn't seem possible. If he
planned to turn on them, he'd put up one hell of an act for
an awful long time.

I squeezed my eyes shut. *Think....* What sort of device
could he mean?

If he wanted the haan cut off from the power grid, then
Gohan wanted to expose them too. According to Chong's
messages, he wanted this to happen without his involvement being known—not by Hangfei security, but especially
not by the haan. What was he playing at?

"I'm sorry about your friend," Nix said. I glanced over at
him.

"I didn't really know him," I said. "But . . . yeah, me too."

My brain still struggled to wrap around the fact that
Chong was not only probably dead but that he'd been
working with Gohan this whole time. I remembered how
he'd flirted with me down in the tunnel, and how, in a way,
I'd kind of liked it.

"I just don't get what the hell Gohan stands to gain by
helping us."

I brought up Nix's contact on the 3i and pinged him.

*Nix, what will the haan do when they're exposed, and if
the force field goes down? How far would they go?*

*The haan would not think along those lines, as in, if you
try and destroy us we will in turn destroy you. Destroying us*

would be relatively easy. We don't have the capacity to destroy you all.

Hangfei, maybe?

All of our colonies are located in Hangfei and would be destroyed as well. Since they would be the only islands left of our species if Shiluyuán were destroyed, I don't think they would do that.

Then what?

He considered that for a moment, before venting air with a low rattle.

Individuals like Sillith will resort to strategic, direct violence to achieve an end, but taken as a whole our way is to find more sustainable solutions. Sillith's virus, the force field dome, and fostering a culture of dependency in your species. I don't have any direct information, but I think it's safe to assume my people's contingency will fall more along these lines.

The defense shield, maybe?

They will most likely use it to defend Shiluyuán should it come under attack, but as powerful as it is it would eventually fall.

"What, then?" I hissed.

Between Nix's back and the guys crowded behind him, I could see through a sliver of window as a dingy housing project swept by. Rows and rows of rust-colored walls flashed past, with little boxlike windows crowded around shallow balconies where laundry flapped like damp flags. The squiggles of graffiti eventually gave way to a lookout over Shin Park, streams of air traffic whizzing past in front of the skyline behind it. Then shadow, and flitting lights as we dove into the tunnel.

The train slowed and we all leaned into each other, holding on to the bar as it stopped with a hiss, and the doors slid open.

"Come on," I said.

"Are you reconsidering your position?" Nix asked. "To stop what you've started?"

"I'm still thinking about it."

A vendor fair in the Guanghuan Mall tube stop had the platform packed with carts selling everything from 3i plug-ins to sneakers. We followed the line of people off the train car and into the mob, edging between the queues where money and merchandise changed hands in a flurry. One guy sat with his shirt off next to a makeshift ink parlor while a bald woman with the bridge of her nose pierced worked on his back with a buzzing needle. At least half the merchandise looked like bootleg stuff but none of the station guards looked like they cared. Some of them were shopping, too.

I followed the crowd through the big glass doors and caught a nice rush of canned air as I passed under a blower. Nix stepped through and joined me on the first of four parallel walkways that whisked us down the yellow line toward the mall's club section.

When we reached the transfer, we hopped off the track and headed down the wide corridor out into the club plaza where a domed glass ceiling looked up toward the towering tips of skyscrapers.

I didn't go to the Guanghuan Plaza often, and I didn't think Vamp did either. He'd never even mentioned the Phage Panic Club, and while I'd heard of it, I'd never been there. The plaza always seemed a little high pitch for me, when I preferred a place you could zone out. Even the outside of the club was full of spastic activity, where a huge mob lingered waiting to get in. The queue formed a rave of its own, dancing to music being piped through to the outside, and ordering drinks and smokes from women on roller skates wearing shiny short shorts. Above them, a huge sign in blazing block hanzi announced the name of the club while hanging over the masses like some kind of mega-awning.

". . . use the defense shield to wipe out the fucking Americans," I heard someone say as I passed. There were some nods.

"I know what I saw," another man said.

"You were tripping."

"Fuck you, I'm telling you I know what I saw. . . ."

As I made my way through, I signaled one of the roller-girls and she glided over. She made a neat little spin in front of me, stopping on a dime without disrupting the wares in the wooden box she held in one hand. Inside the box were compartments tightly packed with various smoke offerings. I picked out a squat black-papered little drug-free smoke, thick but no longer than my thumb. She cocked one hip at me, presenting the cash card reader she had clipped there, but I paid her in cash, figuring it would be safer. She smiled and offered me a light.

I puffed the smoke alight, catching a mouthful of heavy, sweet smoke that tasted like chocolate and peppermint but no bitter chem aftertaste. She snapped the lighter shut, and floated backward into the crowd as I continued on in.

Yo, Vamp, I'm here.

Great, give the booth ID to the hostess, and she'll let you in.

Inside I got stopped by the bouncers, but when I flashed the booth ID and the hostess looked up the reservation they parted to let me and Nix through, just like Vamp said.

Everyone inside looked like they were loaded, and not just with booze. Everywhere I looked I saw expensive clothes, fancy haircuts, and plastic surgery. I followed the signs along a catwalk that looked down over a huge dance floor that had become a carpet of bobbing heads and pumping fists, jerking crazily in time with the heavy techno throbbing. I headed down to a row of sliding doors, each covered in elaborate woven designs and found Vamp's boot at the end behind the twisted face of a jiangshi. I tapped the booth access card to the electronic contact mounted on the side of the door's track.

The door slid open, and I slipped through the crack into the large booth, which was dominated by a rectangular sunken table. When I closed the panel behind me the sound screen kicked in and the racket outside became a faint rumble of white noise. The booth became a pocket of calm quiet, and smelled like a pleasant mix of sweet alcohol and scented smoke.

Vamp leaned back in the booth with a tall, empty glass in front of him. He stared at the tabletop in a way that made me think he was zoning on his 3i. He wasn't alone. I recognized the woman with him from her Channel X profile that I'd dug up from the wire. She was Shuang Po. Vamp's ex. She had half her head shaved with a braided wet drive lanyard dangling from behind each ear. Spray-on black jeans and a skintight green top showed off a killer body, and she had a lot of tattoos and piercings.

Vamp glanced up and when he saw me he scrunched his brow. Then he saw Nix and his eyes went wide for a second as we approached. He waved with his free hand for us to come over and sit down. He caught me staring at Shuang, and took my wrist to guide me into the booth.

"You brought a haan?" Shuang asked.

Vamp stood, staring, and moved closer. "Sam?"

He looked at me like I'd gone nuts for a minute. For a minute, he looked at me with the same accusing look Shuang did.

"Unbelievable," I said. Vamp looked confused.

"I just don't get—"

You don't even recognize him, do you? I sent over the 3i.

He looked over at Nix, then back to me. He didn't, and I could see him get uncomfortable.

He saved your life? I sent.

I saw it click, then, and Vamp's eyes widened as he looked back to Nix.

"Nix?"

"Yes, Vamp." His head bobbed on his neck a little. "I am glad to see you."

Vamp approached him, and shook his hand.

"Nix, I am so sorry . . . I thought you were dead."

"I understand."

"Vamp, what the hell?" Shuang demanded.

"It's okay, Shuang," Vamp said. "You can trust him."

She wrinkled her nose a little. "It's a haan."

"I wouldn't be here if it wasn't for him. I'm telling you, you can trust him."

"But it's a haan."

"I owe him my life," he said. He glanced over at me. "I owe him more than that."

Shuang turned to me. "Why did you bring it?"

"Him." I ignored her, and spoke to Vamp. "He's in trouble. He needs our help."

"Of course," Vamp said. "Anything he needs. Anything you need, Nix."

"Thank you."

Vamp saw Shuang and me eyeing each other again, and moved to get between us.

"Sam, this is Shuang Po," he said. "She's the one who's been helping with the grid intrusion."

Shuang held out her hand, and I shook it. She had a firm grip, and her hand felt ice-cold.

"You run into any trouble?" Vamp asked, as I sat down next to him.

"No," I said, resisting the urge to look back at Shuang.

"You want anything to drink?" he asked.

"Um . . . just a bottle of shine."

"Just straight shine?" Shuang blurted. The way she said it made me a little self-conscious.

"Yeah."

"It's what she wants," Vamp said. Shuang shook her head.

"Coming right up."

She waved her hand over a section of the table and the lacquered wood surface disappeared to reveal a touch screen. She punched the order in, her nimble fingers dancing over the contacts, then flashed her cash card at it. The screen chirped, then faded and the wood surface returned as Vamp turned his attention back to me.

"You're hurt," he said, pointing to his forehead.

I touched the spot above my right temple and my fingertips came away bloody.

Shuang wrinkled her nose again.

"Yeah, you're leaking, sister."

"I'm fine," I said. I grabbed a napkin from the table and dabbed the blood away.

Vamp, I sent over the 3i. *Any idea why Chong was helping Gohan?*

Vamp looked a little sheepish. *No.*

Do you think he's been a gonzo all along, even back when you knew him before?

I doubt it. I think it happened later, and he just took advantage when I got back in touch with him.

Chong was going to help us take down the Xinzhongzi substation. Why does Gohan want us to succeed so bad?

I don't know.

He just handed the haan the biggest piece of real estate they've ever gotten. Why would he do anything to threaten them?

Shuang had turned her eyes back to us, and I could see she'd started getting a little annoyed at our private conversation but I didn't care.

Maybe he wants the haan to strike back at us, Vamp said.

That would only hurt the haan, though. Even they know that.

So what do you want to do?

Can the attack be stopped, if we had to?

Vamp shook his head. *It's out of control. This was just supposed to be the test run, remember? The station in Xinzhongzi should prevent a full blackout, though, until they can fix it. The defense screen and the force field should both stay up.*

If Gohan doesn't figure out a way to shut it down without implicating himself.

Both those things are out of our control, now, Sam. I'm sorry. You're going to have to just keep your head down until this plays out. Shuang is off their radar, so you can stay with her for now. No one will look for you there.

I hated the idea of staying with Shuang, and I could see in his eyes that he felt bad even suggesting it but we didn't have many options.

"Guys?" Shuang asked. I turned to say something, and Vamp stopped me.

"Sorry," he said.

A light on the wall flashed, providing a distraction Vamp seemed grateful for. He slid open the booth's door, and let a waitress in a supertight dress lean in. She put a tall, clear drink in front of Shuang that had a long, black wooden pick dropped into it, the submerged end speared through a large scalefly. She placed a small bottle of high-end shine on the table in front of me, along with a little shot glass.

Shuang sipped her drink and scooted a little closer to Vamp, turning toward him and smiling. "How many of these things did we go through, back in the day?"

Vamp smiled, but made sure he didn't smile too much.

"A few," he said. Shuang took the pick out of her drink and tapped the booze off of the candied scalefly. She turned to Nix and made a face.

"I still don't think it should be here," she said, crunching her teeth down on the fly.

"He," I said.

"Whatever." She flicked one lanyard back over her shoulder. "Word on the street is, people have been seeing some pretty strange shit since the power started to fail. It's all over the wire. People are starting to get nervous, to not trust them. I never trusted them."

"I know him better than I know you," I said.

"I don't know either of you," she said, her voice cool.

Vamp leaned in to get a better look at my forehead. "Sam, you probably want to go deal with that."

"Yeah, yeah."

He reached for my face and I squirmed away.

"Hold still," he said.

I thought Shuang might get jealous, but his concern for someone else seemed to have the opposite effect on her. When he turned back to look at her, she smiled up at him like she was warming herself at a fire.

"What?" he asked.

She leaned over and kissed him on the mouth. She let the kiss linger, too, and the longer it went the hotter my cheeks got. I looked away, keeping my eyes cast down on the table, not wanting to be as hurt as I was and definitely not wanting to show it. I hoped he'd stop her, but he didn't.

"I'll be back," I said, and got up from the recessed booth. As soon as I did, Vamp flashed me a guilty look. He still had some of her gloss on his lips when he tried to break away, and held out his hand.

"Hold on," he said. "I'll—"

"I think I can deal by myself, thanks," I said, opening the sliding door and shouldering through the people on the other side.

Vamp moved to follow me out of the booth, and I slammed the door shut between us.

Chapter Twenty

I marched away from the booth and through the crowd, heading toward the restroom. When I lost myself in the mob it was a relief, and I slowed my pace so I could weave through the ravers.

You don't have time to worry about this now, I told myself. *There's too much going on. Just put it out of your mind and worry about it later.*

I did worry, though. I worried that there might not be a later. Whatever was forming between Vamp and Shuang was happening now. If I didn't say or do something soon, I might not get a chance to worry about it later. For all I knew, it might already be too late.

As I approached the restrooms, I spotted a woman in a white gonzo robe standing against the wall off to my right. Her eyes followed me as I approached and I looked away.

Here? Are you kidding me? What the hell are they doing here?

When I glanced back a moment later, I saw that she'd begun to follow me.

"Oh, goddamn it, not now . . ."

I kept walking. When I got to the restroom I banged a right to head into the women's room, but before I could open the door I felt a cold hand on my wrist.

"Wait."

I turned and saw the gonzo had a twitchy, scared expression on her face. She tightened her grip, and guided me toward the wall with her, out of the flow of foot traffic.

"Look, I'm not interested," I told her. "Shouldn't you be hassling people in a gate terminal somewhere?"

"I know who you are," she said, keeping her voice low. "Your father is that security officer."

That gave me a start. I realized then that she didn't act like a typical gonzo. Usually they seemed kind of out of it, like they were in some kind of trance or something. They were always calm, no matter what you said or did. When I looked at this woman, I saw real fear in her eyes.

"Who the hell are you? Have you been following me?"

She took out a gonzo pamphlet and handed it to me.

"No," I said. "Keep your pamphlet because I'm not joining—"

"I don't want you to join the reunification movement," she said. "I want you to stop him."

"Stop who?" I asked her. "What do you mean?"

"Gohan is insane," she said.

"Yeah, no shit."

"He's going to do something crazy."

"He's always doing something crazy."

She gripped my arm harder, hard enough to make me wince, and pulled me a little closer.

"I mean it," she hissed. "I don't know for sure what, but he's going to do something bad. He's working with the haan."

"What does that mean?"

"Just listen—he wants you in the new colony. You might have a chance to—"

She jumped as a man grabbed her arm from out of the crowd. Two other gonzos had caught up with her, and neither of them looked happy. The woman's eyes widened in terror for a moment, but she forced a smile.

"Only He can move the stars," she told me.

The man who had her arm pulled her away, and I

snatched the pamphlet out of her hand as they herded her back into the crowd, toward the club's exit.

"Wait!"

I started to go after her, but before I could get halfway to them they'd taken her back out into the plaza. I watched through gaps in the crowd as they hopped a walkway and were carried away, passing two security guards as they went. I turned back before they could see me, and slipped into the bathroom.

Inside I headed down the row of women touching up makeup in the mirror and took the first empty stall where I sat down. I folded a length of toilet paper, and pressed it to my forehead, wincing as the blood soaked through to my fingertips.

I dropped it into the toilet and applied a fresh one, then checked out the pamphlet the gonzo gave me.

ONLY HE CAN MOVE THE STARS.

Underneath, there were two images of the planet, eclipsing one another, with the gonzo symbol over the spot where they overlapped.

I opened it and found more pictures inside, along with blocks of text. I didn't read any of it, but the illustrations showed the Earth with a dot on it where the Impact had occurred. The pictures that followed showed a ring expanding out from the dot, growing until it split the globe into two halves, then all the way around to make another dot on the other side.

That surprised me. They'd depicted the Impact, but not the Impact as most people believed it. The diagram suggested the event Sillith described to me, one planet being consumed by another. The haan home world being replaced with ours, leaving only Shiliuyuán. I remembered the gonzo protesters in Xinzhongzi, the ones who jumped.

"... *you are being lied to*.... *They have lied about the haan, and they have lied about the Impact*...."

"*Look at my face. This is the face of belief*...."

The image of Shuang locking lips with Vamp bubbled up, in spite of everything and I clenched my fists, trying to scrub it out of my brain. The sad thing was that Shuang, in a lot of ways, was probably a better match for Vamp and not just because of her looks. Vamp liked me, sure. Maybe it was true and I was his first choice, but that woman connected with him on a level I never could.

The screen on the inside of the stall door flickered.

"You look like you could use some male companionship," the A.I. said.

"I'm fine," I growled.

"Desirable, powerful men are available right now for discreet—"

I dropped a coin into the ad box slot to opt out, and the A.I. retreated so that a TV feed could take its place. A news stream began to play, showing footage of the Render's Strip bombing. It looked like the bodies had been cleaned up, but the area had been cordoned off. Groups of officers moved through the square, setting markers and taking samples from the rubble.

I opened the pamphlet and saw more gonzo propaganda . . . how the haan are superior, how they are more deserving of the planet, and how we should aspire to remake ourselves in their image.

"You guys have no idea. . . ." I said to myself.

Down near the bottom of the pamphlet, under a photo of Gohan, I spotted a small block of neat handwriting.

> *The cathedral houses something he calls Rapture.
> All I know is it will let the haan wipe us out. I be-
> lieve it. So does Gohan. I know your father was
> UDF. You must convince him to destroy the cathe-
> dral before it's too late.*

It was true, then. Gohan had built something, some kind of weapon or something, and given them the means to power it with the new substation. If the gonzo had pinned her hopes on Dragan, though, she'd overestimated him. Dragan couldn't just destroy the cathedral. Best case he might be able to bring a team in there to check it out, but even that was a stretch, given his history with Gohan.

Rapture.

He'd picked a Western word, an English word. It had to have some significance. When I ran it through the translator the closest match came back as kuángxǐ, or ecstasy, but a little more digging revealed it also referred to a religious event. I brought up the first link I could find on it. From what I could tell, it seemed to be some kind of end-of-the-world deal. The second coming of a Christian god, maybe? I remembered the gonzo with the bullhorn, in Xinzhongzi.

"The haan will return. . . . Rapture will see the return of the haan to their rightful place. . . ."

"The return of the haan," I said to myself. What did it mean?

An image on the feed distracted me, and I looked up to see the inside of the smoke shop where I'd found Alexei after the bombing, the place swarming with officers. One talked to the shop owner while others had collected around a spot at the end of one of the aisles.

I recognized it. They were grouped around the same spot where I'd found Alexei, sitting in a ball by the magazine rack.

One of the men reached behind a stack of magazines there, and with one gloved hand he removed a device. He held it up so the camera could see—it was cylindrical, with an antenna at the bottom, and a button on top.

The captioning said that security had recovered the detonator. The device was the detonator that had been used to set off the bomb outside.

The words kept scrolling by, but they seemed to suddenly get smaller, and more distant as my stomach dropped.

For a minute, I forgot about Gohan, and the colony, and everything else.

It had to be a mistake. Alexei wouldn't do a thing like that. He was only nine years old; there was no way he would do a thing like that.

Yet all of a sudden, things he had done and said seemed different to me when I replayed them in my mind. I remembered his message, just before the explosion. *I'm sorry, Sam.* I'd assumed he meant he was sorry for baiting Dragan, but what if I'd been wrong? What if he meant he was sorry not for something he'd done but for something he was about to do?

I'd found him in the back of the smoke shop, right next to the magazine rack. I'd assumed he was just in shock because of what happened, because it was such a near miss. The way he shook in my arms, the look on his face.

I didn't know those people in Render's Strip.

I shook my head. If he did do it, he couldn't have done it alone. He'd have no idea how to set something like that up.

"Dao-Ming," I whispered.

She couldn't have gotten to the explosives herself. She didn't even know about the black hole drop, but Alexei did. Alexei had his own key to my place. If she'd told him to find where I might have hidden them, he could have figured it out. He could have found them, delivered them to her and replaced them with fakes she provided. He loved Dao-Ming. With his own mother dead, he'd latched onto her hard, and he spent a lot of time with her. She could have convinced him.

Alexei, I messaged. He didn't respond.

Alexei, please answer me.

Over the mix of running water, chitchat, and tinkling I heard a woman begin to cry outside my stall. She hitched for a minute, sobbing, but no one asked her if she was okay. After a while she managed to contain it, and I heard the sink on the other side of the door blast on for a couple of seconds before the valve squealed shut again.

I leaned forward and peeked through the crack along the side of the stall door. I could see the woman's back as she leaned toward the mirror, dabbing at her face with a paper towel. It was Shuang.

I felt a bitter little surge of glee that brought a grin to my face before being followed by another, more complicated feeling that I didn't expect. I felt a little sorry for her, sure, but the thought that popped into my head was that I wondered what the hell Vamp had said or done to make her cry like that. It made me a little mad at him, and I didn't even like Shuang.

"Shit," she muttered, tossing the wadded-up paper in the trash. Other women clipped past her, finished primping, and curtly left the bathroom without so much as glancing at her. Not even when she began to cry again.

Goddamn it. . . .

I flushed the bloody tissue, and stepped out of the stall. When Shuang saw me, she froze and went wide-eyed like she'd just been caught stealing.

"It's okay," I said, putting up my hands. "I didn't see anything. You came in, peed, and left."

That made her smile, a little, but it didn't stick around long before twisting back into a frown.

"Thanks. And I'm sorry about back there. I just—"

"Look," I said, "don't take this the wrong way but I've got bigger things on my mind right now."

"I know," she said, her voice small.

I sighed. "You okay?"

She shrugged. "I just . . . thought things might be different this time," she sniffed.

"So . . . you two were serious?"

She nodded. "I dumped him," she said. "I don't know why. Things started moving fast, and I got nervous I guess. I started to feel . . ."

"Trapped?"

"Yeah." She tried to smile, failed, and wiped her eye again. "I regretted it later, but by then it was too late. He didn't want to talk to me. When he called me the other day out of the blue I thought maybe he'd changed his mind, or that the hack was just a pretext to get back in touch, but I don't think it is."

"You sure about that?"

"I can tell," she said, and I could see it really bothered her. I found myself relieved, and put off at the same time.

"You've known him a long time, right, Sam?"

"Yeah."

"Is there someone else, do you know?"

"Did he say there's someone else?"

"No, but ... I feel like there's someone else, someone he's got his eye on," she said, like she hadn't heard me. "Vamp's not a player. He acts like he is, but when he settles on someone, he just ..."

"Falls in love easily," I said. "He doesn't worry about what might happen later."

She looked back at me, and I saw her eyes go from startled to understanding.

"Oh God, it's you."

"Huh?" I said. "Wait. I—"

"It is, isn't it? It's you."

Heads up. The message popped up from Vamp, scatter shot to both of us. *We've got a problem. Stay where you are.*

A beat later, the LCD that ran along the bathroom wall up over the mirrors flashed a security warning. Something was going down.

"What's happening?" Shuang asked.

"Vamp's in trouble," I said. "Come on."

"He said stay where we are—"

"I know what he said."

Vamp, I'm coming back.

Sam, don't—

The message stopped short, and his contact icon turned gray.

"Sam, he said—"

I stiff-armed the bathroom door open, and started making my way back toward the booth.

Chapter Twenty-One

"Sam, wait," Shuang called as she followed me out. I pushed my way through the crowd, back the way I'd come. When I could see the row of booths, I saw that the door to ours hung open but I couldn't make out anyone inside. "Sam!"

She grabbed my arm but I pulled away, squeezing between two clubbers as just then, something trickled in through the mite cluster. A low signal, not Nix, but familiar.

"She's here," I said.

"Who?"

"A haan. She's here," I said.

"I know," Shuang said. "I was sitting right across from the creepy—"

"Not that one."

I reached the booth and looked in to see Qian, still dressed in her black slacks and paisley. She had been looking down at Vamp and Nix, but turned to face me when I approached.

Her signal carried regret, genuine regret, but it hummed over an undercurrent of resolve.

"I have warned you about pursuing this line of action," she said.

"Qian, just hold up," I told her.

"Get inside the booth," she said.

"Qian—"

"Both of you, get inside the booth or I will kill them."

"Who the hell is that?" Shuang asked near my ear, but I waved a hand to shush her.

"You know I can do it," Qian told me.

"Nix will stop you."

"Not before I kill your male companion."

"Sam, who the hell is she?" Shuang asked.

"Do what she says," I told her.

"Who is—"

"Just do what she says!"

I stepped inside the booth and went to Vamp. Shuang followed, still looking at Qian, not seeing a knife or a gun, and not convinced she posed any real threat. Qian reached over, and slid the door shut behind us.

"As you know by now, I have your friend," she said.

"He's not our friend," Vamp spat.

"If you don't cease the attack on the power grid, I will kill him."

"Like I said, he's no friend of ours."

"Wait," I told her, holding up one hand. "Wait . . . don't hurt him."

"Then stop the attack on the power grid."

"I can't."

"You've seen what I can do. I will pick you all apart, piece by piece."

Shuang turned pale. She looked to Vamp.

"What does she mean?"

"I truly do regret this," Qian said, her voice quiet.

"What would Pei think of this?" I asked, taking a chance and dropping Qian's—the real Qian's—daughter's name. Her eyes flicked toward me.

"How do you know that name?" she asked.

"You told me I reminded you of her."

She let up her grip on Vamp a little. Her gaze turned distant.

"We had been at the mall," she said. "This mall. We were shopping together. We'd separated, just for a minute. I was shopping for clothes, and she wanted to visit a music store. I let her go. She was eighteen, and it was a public place. I didn't think anything of it, but when she didn't return, I . . ."

Tears formed in her eyes, real tears, and one began to roll down her cheek as her pretty face contorted. She wiped the tear with her thumb, but another came right behind it.

"Do you know what you are?" I asked her. She nodded. "I'm Qian Cho."

Her tears stopped, and she swallowed hard. Her eyes grew determined again.

"I'm Qian Cho," she said again.

She moved toward me, and Vamp lunged. He grabbed her wrist, and twisted her arm but it just seemed to roll in its socket. Her hand flickered, and when the flicker passed it was still in the same position as before, like the twist never happened.

"Vamp, no!"

Vamp let out a grunt of pain as he released her hand. I couldn't see what had him but I could make out the impressions of something coiled around his arm from wrist to elbow, constricting hard enough to cause the skin to turn dark and veins to pop out. Before I could even draw the pistol, Vamp screamed.

Nix moved as I managed to free the pistol from my pocket. Something struck Qian, and then the pressure on Vamp's arm let up. Her arm fell, bouncing off the booth's chair and rolling under the table, but when I looked back, it had returned.

"What the hell?" Shuang shrieked. "What the—"

Qian went for me again as I raised the pistol and fired five times, as fast as I could pull the trigger.

Her head jerked back as the first bullet hit her in the cheek. Vamp pushed away farther into the booth while he pulled a butterfly knife from his jacket. Qian shielded her face and the rest of the bullets either struck her arm, or missed and punched through the ceiling above her.

She recovered and I scrambled out of the way just as she lashed out. Something hit the table where I'd been sitting a second before and pulverized the bottles and glasses there, snapping the end off of the table in a shower of splinters and broken glass.

I fired again, hitting her in the chest even as I felt something slither around my ankle. By now the whole club had started screaming and yelling, and I could hear people surging outside the booth in an attempt to get the hell out of there. The grip on my ankle tightened, dragging me toward Qian as I fired three more shots into her. The shot to her face didn't show—the skin stayed as smooth as ever, and completely unharmed—but the shots to her chest were being rendered. Blood bloomed through the white fabric around the powder-burned holes.

Vamp whipped his blade around and stabbed her in the side so hard it might have killed her, had she been human. Instead she turned to him and grabbed him by the neck, hauling him toward her and shoving him down onto his knees. The LCD marquee near the ceiling blinked on, and displayed a security alert. Someone had just triggered the alarm, but by the time anyone got there it would be over for sure. I aimed for her head again and fired three more times. Her head snapped back, and a chunk of something flew away from it.

That seemed to do it. She hadn't expected the gun, and decided she'd taken too much damage. She let go of me and Vamp, who fell back, gasping. She turned and crashed straight through the booth's sliding door. With the noise screen broken, the screams on the other side jumped in volume.

I grabbed Vamp by the arm and helped him up.

"We've got to go, now," I said. "Is there a back way?"

He nodded.

"Come on," he said. "Follow me. Nix, help Shuang."

We stepped through the wreckage of the door and I saw

Qian pulling herself free from the smashed door across from ours where she'd barreled through. The club had flown into complete chaos as everyone tried to get out at once. As we struggled to fight our way through the current, Qian stood and turned toward us. The clubbers piled up behind her, building until one of them got impatient and shoved her. Without turning around, she threw back one shoulder and blood sprayed from the guy's broken nose as he went down.

"Come on!" I said, pulling at Vamp's shirt. I ducked as something whooshed over my head and crashed into the wall next to me. People swarmed in behind us, running for the exits and cutting Qian off from us. In the bar area, something crashed but I couldn't see what had caused the commotion. It sounded like it had been close but outside people surged every which way, scrambling for the exits.

"This is a security lockdown," a voice boomed over an amplifier. "Everyone return to your seats and await further instructions. Do not attempt to leave the premises."

We followed a line of sweaty people through the blanketing fuzz of bass and the electronic crowing that wailed above it to the bar area, which sat on a raised platform. We clambered up the set of stairs, and I looked over the rail to a sea of silhouetted arms waving and pumping in the air while people shouted. Men in black ponchos and helmets herded the crowd back, keeping their rifles pointed toward the ceiling for the moment.

Qian tried to plow through the crowd toward us. As she passed a pair of security men, one of them stepped out to block her. She hit the officer hard enough to knock his helmet off and send him sprawling down onto the ground. The second one unclipped the graviton gun from his belt and took aim.

She had sprinted three paces toward us when the beam washed over her body, causing it to become ten times its original weight. She crashed down onto the floor, and struggled as the officer approached. "Come on," Vamp said.

He led us past the bar, and shoved open a door there. Someone shouted behind us as we filed through, and before we'd even gotten halfway down the corridor, I saw the shadow of a security officer on the far wall and heard the crackle of a radio.

We scooted through a doorway just as the officer turned the corner, and we raced around the corner to a fire door.

Vamp slammed it open, and an alarm began to sound as we headed out into the plaza. People began pouring out behind us, shoving to be first out the door.

"Sam, Shuang, come on!"

Through the tangle of arms around me, I spotted Qian's paisley shirt, then heard a scream. Blood splashed against the metal door as something hit it; then an arm severed at the elbow flopped down onto the pavement.

Several shots were fired inside the club, and the crowd surged again, piling up at the door. Someone pitched down onto the ground and the others just trampled over her. Qian spotted me, and started shoving her way toward us.

"Back!" an officer shouted. "Back! Everyone get back against the wall!"

Behind them, the last few people wrestled through the door and it slammed shut behind them.

"Come on," Vamp said. "Never mind them, go!"

Police blues and reds formed an overlapping strobe in the chaos of the club plaza as armed officers cruised in on one-man air transports. Others tromped through the mob to try to surround the club. As we darted toward the walkway on the other side, I heard another shout.

"Secure those exits!" a man barked. "Cut them off!"

The lights along the moving walkways winked out, and they wound down. People shouted as they slowed, then stopped.

I took another step and slammed headlong into what felt

like a wall, caroming off and staggering back before falling on my butt. Ahead, I saw Vamp skid to a stop in front of a faint blue force field that had appeared in front of us.

"Shit . . ." I got back onto my feet, wiping blood out from under my nose with my forearm. Shuang looked around, and spotted a break in the crowd.

"That way!"

"Freeze!" a man barked from behind us.

We turned, Nix parting the way in front of us, but got only as far as an outdoor café before another field lit up in front of us.

"Shit!"

We were stuck. There was no way out. I turned back and saw Qian appear in the crowd back the way we'd come. To our left and right, two of the men who had come through the dome were moving in fast.

"Sam . . ."

Security moved in behind her. She stared at me, meeting my eye for a moment, and then seemed to decide that she'd missed her opportunity. She turned and disappeared into the crowd.

"Stop where you are!"

I turned to see at least two black-helmeted guards had moved in from our side of the field. When a third one joined them, Vamp rushed them.

"Hey!"

He plowed into them, knocking one down. He made a hole, big enough to get through, but one of them had him and the other two were back on their feet before he could even twist free.

The guard that had taken the brunt of the impact unclipped his nightstick from his belt and slammed Vamp square in the gut with the butt of it. Vamp doubled over, falling to his knees in front of the guard. The other two went for Nix. They both hit him with the prods and pumped enough juice into him to send a visible arc squirming between the cells of his rib cage. His body went rigid as they held the stunners to him, and the first guard crossed behind Vamp to grab one wrist and twist it, pushing the arm down so that Vamp was forced onto his chest. I bolted toward the guards, ducking some flailing chick with a bush of peroxide-white hair as I closed in on the brawl. My intention was that I would use the nearest table as a launching pad and jump the guard, but it turned out the table had a single, central support. As soon as my foot came down on the table's edge it tipped over and fell away leaving me in midair with almost no momentum. I did manage to at least hook my fingers through the guard's collar as I fell, and he choked as he staggered back, then fell in a heap on top of me.

"Let go!" he grunted, reaching back as I squirmed free and tried to get my arms around his neck. He managed to roll over onto his knees, and then from there he hauled himself to his feet with me hanging off him.

When one of the guards zapping Nix went to help him, he waved him off. "Keep on it! I got this!"

I leaned back so that all my weight was on his neck, but he had a thick neck and I didn't weigh much. I almost made him tip back and lose his footing, almost. Instead he leaned forward, reaching back with both hands and grabbing me.

Before I knew what was happening he'd peeled me off and flipped me over his shoulder. I came down on the floor on my back hard enough to knock the wind out of me for a minute, and before I could get back up he had his knee on my chest. He leaned forward until I thought he was going to crack a rib, then stopped.

"Let her go!" Vamp yelled. I couldn't see him but I could hear him struggling. "Let her go, asshole!"

"Shut up!" one of them barked.

"Get off her!" he grunted as one of the men grappled with him. "Get off her or I swear I'll—"

As I squirmed under the guard's knee I caught a flash of

light, Vamp's voice cut out as I heard the rapid popping of a stunner.

"Oh, come on," one of them said as Vamp's legs folded and he fell to the floor. "Now we'll never know what he'd do." A couple of others laughed.

"Zip him and hood him," the one holding me down said. The crackle of electricity coming from Nix finally sizzled out and I heard him collapse with a heavy thud.

"What about the haan?" someone asked.

"Put a shock pin in him. They want that one back in Shiliuyuán."

Nix's eyes flashed bright, at that. He began to stir.

The knee came up off my chest and I gasped in a breath as the guard's big hand grabbed my arm and flipped me over.

"Hands behind your back," he said. "You know the drill."

I did what he said, craning my neck so I could see Vamp. He was still woozy, but he was moving as they tied his wrists behind his back with a plastic zip tie. When he was secure, one of them pulled a hood over his head and jerked the strap tight under his chin.

"What is this about?" I asked as the guard tied my hands behind my back, pulling until the plastic tie dug into my wrists.

"You know what this is about."

He hauled me to my feet, and shoved me toward Vamp who had begun to stir on the floor. A crowd had formed around us, a wide circle of faces that looked in on us, phones held out to snap pictures and video.

"Not the ship . . ." Nix said, his voice faint.

"Huh?" one of the officers grunted.

Nix stirred again, placing his palms on the floor and trying to push himself up. "Not Shiliuyuán . . ."

A thread of fear, mixed with a rising sense of violence, began to stream in through the mite cluster. It grew more intense the more he struggled.

Nix, don't, I sent over the 3i.

"Just tell me what's going on? What's this about?"

"Shut up," he snapped. He waved at Shuang, who hovered near the edge of the crowd. "You, over here with the rest. Don't make me come get you."

Shuang looked pale as she stepped away from the others, and approached us. One of the other guards approached Nix.

"I can't go back," he said, his voice box flickering very faint.

"Nix, it'll be okay," I told him.

The guard jammed a shock pin into Nix's chest. He activated it, and Nix's body went limp.

"My guardian is in security," I told him as he grabbed Shuang's arm and shoved her toward us.

"Good for him."

"Just call him, he can—"

"One more word," he growled in my ear, "and you get the stunner, got me?"

"Just—"

The guard whipped back around, his stunner out.

He wasn't bluffing.

Chapter Twenty-Two

I couldn't see where we went, but back through the mall and then through a door somewhere to the outside. The sounds of the metro faded and were replaced by the bustle of street noise. There was a lot of reverb, like we were in one of the garages, and then we got marched up a couple of flights of stairs to the outside. The guard pushed me along, and then heavy doors ahead of me groaned open. I bumped onto a metal step, banging my shin before I managed to get one foot up on it.

"Watch your step," the guy next to me said before putting one hand on my ass and shoving me forward. I fell down into the back of what had to be a prison transport, the metal deck drumming underneath me as my shoulder hit. Vamp and Nix followed, and then the guards tromped in after us. The doors squealed closed again with a heavy thud, and I felt the engine whine to life through the floor.

"All right, up," a voice said. Someone hauled me up and shoved me back into a chair, then undid the hood strap and pulled it off. The first thing I saw was Vamp, sitting across from me. His hood was off now too, his face red, and angry. He glared at me as the guards hauled Nix's unconscious body past us and shackled him down in the rear of the transport.

"What the hell was that?" he asked.

"What was what?"

"You jump on the guard?"

"What was I supposed to do?"

"Run! I was creating a distraction so you could get away!"

"Both of you, shut up," one of the guards warned.

"What's the matter? No smart-ass comeback?" Vamp asked.

I shrugged.

"I should have known. I should have known that instead of getting away like a smart person, you'd dive right into the middle of an armed security—"

"Hey, I said be quiet," the guard said. I felt my gut drop as the graviton emitters wound up and the vehicle sprang up into the air. Outside, a horn honked as we veered and then began to accelerate.

"If the table hadn't slipped—" I started.

"Oh, yeah, if only the table hadn't slipped. I had it under control."

"Yeah, you had it totally under control."

"It was under control."

"Yeah, facedown on the floor with the goon squad Tasering your asshole. . . ."

"Hey!" the guard barked, drawing his nightstick. That shut both of us up. When he had our attention, he pointed the end at me, then Vamp, then back to me.

"First off," he said, "We have names. I have a goddamned name. It's Li. Second, if both of you don't shut up right now the hoods are going back on, and if that doesn't work things are going to go downhill from there. You understand?"

"Can I ask where we're going?" I asked.

"You cannot."

"Sam, just can it," Vamp said under his breath.

"You can it."

"No, you can it. Shit, you just don't know when to—"

"No, *you* can it!" I shoved his knee again with my foot and the guard banged his nightstick against the wall of the transport.

"That's it!"

He grabbed the hoods and pulled one down over Vamp's head, then the other over mine.

"You just don't know when to quit, do you?" I heard Vamp say.

I tried to call Dragan, but my 3i transmitter had been switched off. He'd know, though. I'm sure he'd be keeping a close eye on our warrant status. He'd do something. We just had to be cool.

"Hey," one of them said. "It just came over the wire—looks like a security camera picked up the Pan-Slav kid over in Tai Po district, near Ping Xi."

I perked up at that. Ping Xi . . . that meant he'd left Dao-Ming's place and not too long ago. Where the hell was he going?

"They catch him yet?" someone else asked.

"No, but they'll get him."

"Where to first?" a voice crackled over the radio.

"Shangzho," the man, Li, said. "They've got a team there ready to take this one back to Shiliuyuán. Then we'll take the rest in."

"Shangzho's out of the way," the voice crackled back.

"No shit. Just do it."

"It'll take an hour to process the paperwork," the radio voice said.

"Listen to me," Li said, keeping his voice low. "The haan want the maggot back. LeiFang says it's a top priority, so that's the situation. Take us to—"

The vehicle bucked suddenly, my gut dropping as we dipped in the air. Something thumped against us and I turned my head, but the hood had me in pitch darkness.

"What the hell was that?" Li spat.

The vehicle dipped again, as outside several horns began to blare. I felt us slow down, and then stop.

"Hey!" Li said, thumping his fist on the back of the hold. "What the hell's going on up there?"

The vehicle dipped a third time as something boomed through the air outside. It sounded like thunder, almost, followed by the sizzle of a huge, far-off electrical arc. Li pounded the wall again.

"Talk to me!"

". . . electrical disturbance," the radio voice crackled through static.

"What?" There was more static as the sound outside swelled, turning from an angry buzz to a long, electric moan that made my hair stand on end.

"disturbance . . . lanes are cutting out . . . 'nother black . . ."

Something cracked outside so loud I jumped, and a second later all the icons in my 3i tray flickered from gray to pulsing pink.

The security field had just dropped. I pinged Vamp, and he picked up immediately.

Vamp, what the hell?

I'm on it.

The vehicle wobbled hard enough to toss me in the seat, and then the driver seemed like he decided to abandon the magnetic lane and just freestyle it. I sank into the chair as we shot up into the air amid the blaring of horns. The vehicle bucked, and I heard everyone stumble.

"Damn it, get back on the goddamned skyway!" Li yelled.

"The magnetic lanes are failing . . . bunch of goddamned idiot commuters are all on autonav and everyone's drifting all over the goddamned place, it's safer—"

Something clipped us, and I heard glass break as everyone got thrown.

Vamp, what's happening?

It's another partial blackout. The whole district's dropping off. We're going to lose—

All the icons went gray again as the 3i network went dark.

". . . outage is localized . . ." The radio voice skipped. ". . . if I can make it to the gate . . ."

I managed to scoot my zip-tied wrists under my butt and in the confusion no one tried to stop me. I reached into my pocket as far as I could, looking for anything that might help. I didn't have my pocket knife with me, but I did feel something metal, something vaguely sharp.

The restroom key, I realized. From that charging-station toilet. I'd never returned it.

It would have to do. I managed to slip it out, but knew I'd never get through the plastic tie with it. I decided to go for the hood instead, using the edge to poke through the canvas in front of my face.

Another crash boomed from somewhere below us, and an explosion of glass that faded as we peeled away from it. It sounded as though, with the field gone, one of the cars had drifted out of its lane and hit a building. I was jerked to one side as the transport stopped almost on a dime and then dropped suddenly as a horn wailed off into the distance above us.

"Damn it!" Li barked. One of the guards fell to the deck as the vehicle righted itself.

"Are you okay, sir?" someone asked.

"I'm fine, I . . ." He trailed off.

"Sir?"

"What in the hell . . ."

His voice had changed. The anger and frustration had gone out of it and he sounded almost awed.

"What is that thing?" he said.

"What thing?" another voice asked.

"There . . . out the back . . . in between the buildings . . ."

I managed to tear a small hole in the hood before I dropped the key and heard it skitter across the deck. Through the space, I saw officers crowded around the back window, looking out at something.

Then I heard a low rumble, something I almost heard in my head more than my ears. I could feel it in my chest a little, and as it changed in pitch something like several different whispers began to overlap. Through it all, a deliberate clicking sound began to trickle through that sent a shiver down my spine. On the far wall, I saw part of Nix's shadow as it began to unravel into a shivering, writhing mass.

Li turned, and his face turned ashen.

"Holy—" he gasped, but then everyone began yelling at once and I sensed a lot of movement all around me. I struggled, trying to squirm my hands out of the zip tie but he'd tied it too tight. Even when I felt blood trickle down my palm I couldn't get even one hand out.

"Don't shoot!" Li screamed at someone I couldn't see. "You'll blow out the—"

I cringed, ducking my head down as a burst of gunfire sounded in the small space. With my ears still ringing, muffled panicked voices yelling over each other, another three-shot burst went off so close that I felt the heat against my shoulder. Glass popped, and air began to whistle into the back of the transport.

An alarm went off as something in the engine sputtered, and the whine of the graviton emitters lowered in pitch. Butterflies fluttered in my stomach as the whole ship spun on its axis, throwing me back against the wall behind me. As the spin turned violent someone crashed back into the transport's rear doors. The centrifugal force pushed me harder against the wall as metal pinged. Then the cabin filled with the roar of wind and street noise, a scream fading through it as someone flew out the open back.

The ship bobbed, righting itself, started to spin again, then steadied. Something crashed against the wall next to me, and warm fluid splashed my left shoulder and neck.

"Stop shooting, you idiot!" Two more single shots went off. "We're going to ..."

"The gate still has power, I can get us through!" the pilot called. "They have power at the remote side, we can get back on the skyway!"

I turned, trying to get oriented through the hole in the hood. I spotted the doorway that led into the cockpit, and through it, the windshield that looked out onto the city. A sky gate floated there, with vehicles queued up to go through.

"Hold on!" the pilot shouted.

He skipped up over the grid of vehicles waiting for the gate, then dropped back down on the other side, accelerating even as the ship began to spin out of control again.

"Hold on!"

The gate began to flicker just as we crashed into it and the chaos around me froze.

For a long moment, time seemed to stop. I'm not sure how long it went on. Long enough for me to realize something had gone wrong with the jump. Then, all at once, cold air bloomed through the cabin as time and space returned. Weight returned to my body and my stomach dipped as the airship continued its spin.

I turned toward the source of the wind, and through the hole in my hood I saw that the transport had been clipped neatly in half. The skygate we'd just passed through had gone down before we made it all the way through, and several officers who had been sucked out tumbled end over end through the air.

Voices shouted over one another, the panicked jumble barely rising above the shrieking wind. Through the open back of the transport, Hangfei spun.

"We're going down!" the pilot screamed. The seat lurched underneath me as he opened up what emitters were still active.

I pushed myself back into my seat, and leaned forward with my hands over my head, waiting for impact.

Chapter Twenty-Three

Wind whistled, huffing across an open space to momentarily drown out the rumble of distant machinery and vehicles. Nearby, someone groaned. Shuang, I thought.

I opened my eyes, and saw a red light flashing through the opening in my hood. I rolled over onto my hands and knees, and managed to find the nearest guard, who looked to be either out cold or dead. I used his field knife to cut my zip tie, and then the strap on my hood so I could pull it off.

I found myself staring down a slope at the opposite side of the transport where Vamp sat, still shackled.

"Vamp?" I called. He stirred, and I went to him. I cut his hands free, and got his hood off.

"Shit, you're bleeding," he said, squinting into the light.

I looked around, wincing as I turned my head. Nix and Shuang looked rattled, and bruised but otherwise okay. The rear of the transport had been neatly chopped off. The back end had crashed, I figured, across town at the other side of the gate. Four of the six guards had gone with it. I tried to spot the other two.

One lay facedown near the back, blood pooled around his head. I couldn't tell if he was dead, or just knocked out. The guard named Li stood, leaning against one of the seats. He thumped his fist against the wall beneath the hatch that lead to the cab.

"Pilot, what's your status?" he called.

The little window slid open, and a voice called back.

"I'm okay."

The guard unclipped his own radio from his belt, and was about to speak into it when I lunged on impulse and looped one arm over his throat. I squeezed, and he dropped the radio as he reached back to try to knock me off.

"Goddamn it," he grunted.

I managed to twist around, and jam his Adam's apple into the crook of my elbow as I pulled him off balance. We fell down onto the floor toward the cockpit door, and I struggled to pull us closer to Nix, who sat slumped in his seat with the shock pin still sticking up from his chest.

Li was too big, I couldn't drag him. I let him go and scrambled toward Nix. Li flipped over and grabbed my ankle, but I managed to get one hand around the pin. I jerked it free, and saw the pink light swell in his eyes as I went facedown onto the deck.

When I rolled over I saw Li had unclipped his stun gun and brought it around to fire. I jammed the shock pin down in the middle of his thigh and he went rigid, his scream cut off as the muscles in his body seized. The stun gun clattered to the floor.

"Nix, don't let the pilot call out!" I yelled.

Without hesitation, Nix slipped through the cockpit door and I heard a crash.

"Don't kill him!" I called.

"What the hell happened?" Vamp asked, going to Shuang. He pulled her hood off and her eyelids fluttered open.

"Gate went down while we were still going through," I said.

"You okay?" Vamp asked Shuang as he cut through her ties. She nodded, throwing her arms around him and hugging him as Nix came back into the rear of the cabin.

With the security field down, the 3i had begun to pick up a lot of chatter over the wire. The most recent power cut had resulted in even more sightings, which were becoming harder and harder to explain away. Over the rush of the wind, I could hear people shouting in the streets, and the blaring of car horns. Sirens had begun to swell in the distance.

Alexei, I called. *Pick up.* When he didn't respond, I tried again.

Alexei, answer me.

His icon went gray.

"Goddamn it . . ." I turned to the others. "These guys are going to snap out of it soon. Security will be sending another car, too. Let's be gone when that happens."

"Gone where?" Shuang asked.

I climbed to the edge of the severed vehicle with shaky legs and jumped down onto the pavement outside, the others right behind me. Smoke was still drifting lazily off the outer skin of the ship, and through the fog I saw many staring faces crowded on a transport platform. Rows of phones were pointed down at us, recording everything. It wouldn't be long before security got tipped to where we were.

When we were all out, everyone stood on the narrow tarmac to catch their breath for a moment. I looked down the runway, between the bordering chain-link fences, and saw a long scar dug in the blacktop where we'd come down. The people on the platform stared at the wreckage that had been strewn out behind us. Glass and metal littered the strip, along with a pair of seats that lay on their sides. Past that, a body lay crumpled in a pool of blood.

Vamp glanced at me as if to ask what our next move was. Everyone was taking our pictures now, and two men in transport security uniforms had begun marching in our direction. We had to get away from the platform.

"Go," I said. "Come on, let's go."

I sprinted to the fence bordering the tarmac and climbed over it, dropping down on the other side. The others followed as the security men began shouting at us, and we made a break for the street. I bolted across four lanes of stop-and-go traffic, horns blaring as I went, then stumbled down a side street on the opposite side. When we were a few twists and turns in, I stopped in an alley and the others piled up behind me.

"Shit," Shuang gasped, dancing like she had to pee. "What do we do? What do we do?"

"Hold on," I panted.

I went to message Dragan, when I noticed a text message had just dropped into the 3i tray. When I brought it up, I saw it had come from Chong.

"Chong just messaged me," I told them. "He's alive."

I brought up the message.

All clear. I'm at an endpoint inside the rim. Need help.

I fished out my tablet and opened the field. The gate remote had been returned, with a dried, bloody thumbprint on one side of it.

"Yes," I whispered. Finally, some luck. I removed the remote and held it up so Vamp could see. "Here's our way out."

"What about Alexei?" Vamp asked.

"I'm going back for him," I said, pointing the remote at the brick wall opposite me. I trigged it, and opened a gate. Through the portal, I could see the grime and shadows of the abandoned factory. "You guys go, and lie low until I can find him. Then we'll figure a way out of Hangfei."

"Sam, with the gates he could be anywhere by now," Vamp said.

"I'll find him," I said. "I know the route he takes from Dragan's to Dao-Ming's. You guys go ahead and wait for me. I'll—"

"No way," Vamp said. "I'm coming with you."

Shuang's face fell a little, at that.

"Vamp . . ."

"Vamp, go with Shuang," I told him. "I've got this."

"No."

Before I could protest again, he turned to Nix.

"Nix, go with Shuang."

Shuang's face fell the rest of the way. "What?"

"I know you can keep her safe," he told Nix. "Make sure nothing happens to her."

"I understand," Nix said.

"Vamp, don't send me off—"

"Once you're there," he told her, "they won't find you. Use your connections to try to work around the Xinzhongzi substation."

"I don't know, Vamp," she said.

"Please."

He kissed her, and I saw her resist for a second but then she gave in. She kissed him back, and smiled even though her eyes were teary.

"Please," he said again. She still didn't look too sure, actually taking a step back when Nix approached her, but Vamp took her by the arm, gently, and spoke in her ear.

"I trust him," he told her. "He saved my life, once. You can trust him too."

"But—"

"Go."

I started off, and Vamp followed. When I looked back over my shoulder, I saw Shuang still standing there, watching him leave with me. Her eyes looked hurt, or betrayed, as Nix took her elbow and led her through the gate. Nix turned back to me, and I could feel his worry, his fear for me. Then the gate closed behind them, and the signal cut out.

"We can catch a gate five blocks this way," Vamp said, pointing. "From there we can hit Ping Xi and retrace Alexei's route. With any luck we'll pick him up there."

I only half heard him, as I scanned up and down the street. Vehicles crowded every lane, and had parked up and down either side of the street. At the end of the block, I spotted the red and white of several taxis queued up at one of the stops.

"Sam, are you listening?"

Among the tight row of vehicles parked along either side of the street, one idled while a woman stood behind the open trunk, putting an armload of shopping bags into it. I started toward it, picking up speed.

"Sam!" Vamp called after me.

Before the woman even saw me, I slipped into the driver's seat and started the emitters up. I heard her shout something from behind as Vamp came around to the passenger side.

"Sam!" Vamp barked. "Shit, what the hell—"

"It's an emergency!" I snapped, shoving the passenger door open. "Get in!"

Vamp didn't look too sure but when I brought the car up off the pavement he climbed in. As soon as he did I took us up, the woman screaming after us.

"Watch it . . ." Vamp said as I zipped into the skylane. The city lights flickered around us for a few seconds, but they stayed on.

"You really think Shuang can work around the new power station?" I asked.

"If she has time."

At the intersection, I checked to make sure the way was clear, then did a full stop before rocketing straight up toward the skylane above. Vamp pushed against the dash as the streets below began to shrink.

"Sam, slow down."

I pulled the control stick and we leapt into the air, picking up speed as I took us over the rows of waiting vehicles. Horns began to honk, swelling and fading as we passed along with the curses of the other drivers.

"Sam!"

In the rearview mirror, I saw a single black security car jump up from somewhere across the street to pursue us. It circled over the traffic below, then began to close in fast.

"Hang on."

I accelerated, then banked at the last second and cut the line to the skyway, clipping the vehicle that had been next to go with a crunch and the squeal of metal. As I locked us into the first available lane the black car followed, flashing its blues as the damaged vehicle caused a backup behind it.

"Sam!"

I looked back out of the windshield where a set of tail-lights had appeared and I cut the stick, whipping into the other lane and sideswiping the car there before he braked. His horn blared behind us as I wove through traffic, picking up speed.

"Sam, there's too much traffic—get off the skyway," Vamp said. He pointed to the left, past the bridge.

"There, go there."

I banked across three lanes of air traffic, and heard two vehicles collide behind us as we flew out of the skyway and into open airspace. A siren began to wail, and the second we were clear, I dropped us like a stone down toward the streets below.

A hole opened in the crowd beneath us as the people there saw what looked like a runaway aircar headed straight for them, and they all ducked as I stopped our descent about one story off the ground then swooped off down a side street. A second siren joined the first; then a third chimed in as I whooshed out over an intersection and in between the buildings on the other side where something white and billowy appeared in the windshield.

"Watch it!" Vamp barked as I pulled up to clear a line of laundry strung between two windows on opposite ends of the street. I could still see the blue and red lights flashing against the building faces in the rearview mirror, but the sounds of the siren began to fade.

I slowed down a little, just enough to avoid too much additional attention, then disappeared into the sprawl.

Chapter Twenty-Four

". . . Reports of strange, often disturbing sightings continue to pour in," the woman on the radio said. "Governess Lei-Fang has ordered a curfew of six o'clock pending investigation, while authorities and scientists struggle to find the cause behind the mass hallucinations. Citizens are being urged not to panic, as localized instances of violence have already begun to tax resources. . . ."

I stared at the skyline, only half listening. The city below seemed static, like we weren't moving at all, even though I'd pegged it as almost twice the allowed speed. "Sam, come on." I could feel my hand shaking on the control stick when he put his own over it. "Put it on auto. You're not going to get us there any faster, you're just going to cause an accident."

He reached past me, toward the dash console, and I let him cut the controls over to autonav. The stick froze in my hand as the computer took over, and he gently eased my fingers off.

"Your hands are cold," he said.

He took my hands in his and I pulled them away.

"Sorry," he said, and I felt bad for letting him see the flinch. "Look, that thing with Shuang . . ."

"It's okay."

I took his hands, and let them warm mine. He sighed, and looked down at the seat between us.

"Seems like there's never a good time, huh?"

"That's my fault," I said.

"No, it isn't."

The truth was that Shuang managed it. She got involved with this, and put her whole life on hold. She did all that just to get another shot, the shot I'd been afraid to even take.

"Why didn't you stay with her?" I asked him.

"Look, I know you didn't want me to come—"

"I'm glad you came. Just . . . why didn't you go with her? She really cares about you."

"I know."

"Don't you care about her?"

I saw him struggle with an answer to that.

"Yeah," he said finally. "I do."

"Then why didn't you—"

"Because I wanted to be with you."

"But—" I managed to clamp down on it before I asked "but why?", but the thought lingered. She was tall, and I was short. She was gorgeous and I wasn't. She had great legs, great tits, full lips, all the things I didn't have. My throat burned.

"Sam . . . this isn't fair," he said.

"I know."

"You know you were my first choice."

"I know."

He sighed, and rubbed his eyes. "What happened between us happened a long time ago," he muttered.

"She seems like she's still thinking about it," I said.

"I know."

"Are you?"

"I did, for a long time."

"But not anymore."

"No. Not anymore."

He sidled closer, and put an arm around my shoulders.

"Come on," I said, shoving him a little with my elbow. "I'm filthy."

"So am I."

He was warm. Vamp's temperature always ran high. His hands were always warm, really warm, and I found myself settling against him despite what I'd said.

He held me, and after a while, as the adrenaline chill left me, I let my body relax. I rested my head against him, and put one hand on this chest. I could feel his heart beating there, heavy, and fast.

"I've missed you, Vamp," I said. It just kind of popped out.

When I looked up I saw him watching me, staring right into my eyes. He ran one thumb over my shoulder.

"Stop it," I said, but there wasn't much conviction there.

He leaned in and kissed me, full on the mouth. I started to push against his chest but somehow my hand ended up running up the side of his neck instead, until my palm was on his cheek. He ran his fingers through my hair, scattering rim grit down my back as he pulled me in closer. I parted my mouth and let his tongue touch mine.

When he felt me kiss him back he moved in, kissing me hard. The whole thing was insane. We were probably going to be arrested before the day was out. Even as I snaked one arm around his neck and his stubble ran rough across my cheek, images kept intruding . . . Shuang biting his lip, pressing against him . . . guards shocking them . . . Nix's face, back from the grave like a real life jiangshi, moving close to mine and telling me the things I thought were real were all lies . . . and somewhere in the middle of it all, Qian's almond eyes staring into mine.

"I will tolerate ideas, not action. Do you understand . . . ?"

Vamp's hand pressed warm against my ribs, his thumb just brushing the base of my breast, waiting for an invitation, desperate for an invitation.

I turned in the seat and let him ease me onto my back, pulling him in closer and kissing him back. Our lips mashed together and as his tongue moved against mine his hand moved to squeeze my breast, such as it was. My nipple turned hard as he rubbed it with his thumb, sending a shiver down the length of me. I locked my legs around him as he pressed himself against my crotch, grinding his hard bulge in, rubbing until he tripped the right spot for a second and I sucked a breath in through my nose.

The whole thing was nuts, but I didn't care. I didn't care about anything. Vamp's hand slipped under my shirt, touching my bare breast while his other one reached down to unbuckle my belt.

I thought if I was going to stop him, I'd better do it then, but I didn't. He unzipped my pants, pushing the flaps aside and slipping his fingertips down past the spay scars to the ruff of coarse hair.

I pulled him down, lying on my back with my hips still locked with his, my butt up off the seat. My phone slipped out of my pocket and thumped down onto the floor mat as he reached lower, fingers working me. Vamp was good with his hands. He was really good with his hands. I could feel my pulse pounding in my neck, my breath panting through my nose as he drove me closer and closer to the edge.

I reached down, fumbling with his belt, ignoring the horns that honked down below us and managing to get it undone as he continued working me slowly. I found his zipper, and pulled.

Something buzzed as I got the zipper halfway down. Then it snagged. I could feel him now, hot against my palm. I tried to get the zipper going again, when the buzz came again. It was my phone. My stupid phone was ringing.

I cracked one eye open and saw the glow from the screen as it buzzed on the floor down by the aircar's pedals. Vamp had his eyes open too, now, and had seen it.

Never mind the phone, I thought, squeezing him in my hand. *Never mind the goddamned . . .*

His hand stopped.

"Forget the phone," I gasped, breaking our kiss. "Just forget it."

I saw him think about doing that, I saw him seriously think about doing exactly that, but something stopped him. He was looking down at the phone, able to see the screen that I couldn't make out, and in spite of the heat pouring off him, his hand pulled away.

"Vamp—"

"It's Alexei," he said, breathing hard. His breath was hot on my neck and chest. He looked angry, and frustrated, but he was telling me anyway, knowing what it meant. "It's Alexei."

I jerked away from him, like he knew I would, and scrambled for the phone. I managed to get a hold of it, and pick up the call, still on my back, with Vamp hanging over me.

"Alexei," I breathed. "Alexei, where the fuck are you?"

"I'm in Xinzhongzi."

"What are you doing there?" I asked. "No, don't tell me. I'm coming to get you. Get out past the security gate, and I'll—"

"I can't. I have to do this. Tell Dragan I had to do this, and that I'm sorry."

"Alexei—"

"I just wanted to say that." He paused. "You mean a lot to me, too. I'm sorry."

"Alexei—"

"Good-bye, Sam."

The line dropped.

"Goddamn it!"

I punched the dash hard enough to hurt my hand. Vamp tried to take my arm, but I pulled it away. I stared out the windshield, fuming, scared, and still a little horny. Below, the suburban sprawl gave way to clusters of shanty shacks, and then finally piles of waste salt at the shore. Beyond them were towers of rust and greased metal pumping in seawater. At the shore, clouds of scaleflies swarmed with circling trash birds.

"He's in Xinzhongzi," I said.

"How the hell did he get in there?"

"I don't know. Vamp, I'm afraid he's going to try to do something stupid."

I disengaged the autonav, and took back the control stick.

"What are you doing?" Vamp asked.

"I'm going to go get him."

"How?"

"I don't know."

I leaned over and kissed him once more, on the mouth.

"Shit," Vamp hissed. He looked past me, and his face fell.

I heard it a second after Vamp did, the whine of emitters growing louder, and turned toward the passenger side window in time to see the aircar on the other side rush in, and fill it.

Chapter Twenty-Five

Vamp and I were thrown across the cab in an explosion of safety glass as the world through the windshield flipped end over end. I couldn't tell up from down as we rolled, spinning at the same time. Glass rained down the seat as the crumpled passenger door flipped up over my head, and I slid down, both legs shooting out the empty window to dangle in the air before I grabbed the control stick.

The A.I. kicked in and struggled to right the vehicle. Vamp, who had one hand clutching what remained of the door handle, reached down to pull me back as the car righted itself. Smoke drifted through the air between us as I struggled to see through the spiderweb cracks that covered the windshield.

"What happened?" I asked.

"Someone hit us."

I crawled over him and looked out the broken window. The other aircar, a heavier vehicle with a flatbed, had fared better than we had. Its grille had crumpled, and both headlights were smashed out, but the body and the emitters all looked intact.

"It wasn't an accident," I said. "They rammed us."

The other aircar took off like a shot, accelerating as it closed in again.

"Shit!"

I grabbed the control stick and pulled back on it, stomping on the accelerator. We lurched up, but not quite high enough before the vehicle reached us. It hit near the undercarriage, flipping us and sending us crashing over its hood. The A.I. righted us again, and we glided to a stop in a wake of smoke. Something had begun to burn, I could smell it.

"Get us out of here," Vamp yelled.

I spun us around, sending more glass tumbling through the cab, but I couldn't see anything through the wrecked windshield. Vamp leaned back in his seat and stomped on it with both feet until it popped free and went sailing down toward the streets below.

As the air came rushing in, I saw the other vehicle approach again and pulled the control stick but nothing happened. We didn't move.

"The emitters are overheating," Vamp said. "They must have damaged the casing."

That meant we were going down, one way or the other. The A.I. would keep us airborne as long as it could, but the altimeter showed we were already in a controlled descent. With the steering shot, we were sitting ducks.

"Shit . . ." I gasped, cringing in my seat as the vehicle closed in a third time.

It didn't hit us, though. Instead it slowed, and then stopped with our vehicles nose to nose. They matched our slow descent, still floating over the sprawl below, and the vehicle's doors popped open.

Vamp shielded his face against the wind blowing into the cab, trying to see. "What the hell are they doing?"

I spotted a woman I didn't recognize behind the wheel. She had three men with her, one in the passenger's seat and two in the back. All three began to climb out of the car. The first one out jumped onto the crumpled hood of their vehicle and began making his way toward us. As he did, something flickered, and I caught a glimpse of something black and wet begin to uncoil along one side of him, which then disappeared. "Vamp, they aren't human!" I yelled as the man approached, wind rippling through his clothing and hair. Vamp's butterfly knife flashed, and he held it out ready in front of him.

Qian, I thought. *She's learning to make contact with others of her kind. They know, and they're coming to stop us.* How did she know? How did she know where we'd be? How did she always manage to be one step ahead of me?

I dug out my pistol as the second man made it onto the hood.

The first guy lunged at Vamp but he managed to duck away and then stab him in the side of the neck. As he jerked the blade free, blood sprayed out, carried on the wind in a red mist. The man staggered back, but not for long before he recovered. He pulled his hand away from the wound, and I saw the dark hole there close up.

I shot the intruder twice, and he fell back. Half of him rolled out of the cab and the weight caused him to flip end over end, out into the open air where he fell like a stone.

One of the emitters on the driver's side failed, and the car tipped, dropping us into a forty-five-degree angle. The two haanyŏng on the hood tumbled, one falling off and the last managing to catch himself.

Another emitter failed, and the car dropped a full ninety degrees. I fell, and collided with the driver's side door, which popped open. I dropped through, clawing at the seat and grabbing on to the seat belt to stop myself before I could tumble out into the open sky. My legs dangled high above the city below, as my pistol dropped away spinning end over end.

Vamp had braced himself above me, one heel dug into the seat and the other wedged against the control stick. The city swayed beneath us as the car rocked.

We aren't going to make it. What can we do? What can we . . .

One of the haanyŏng landed on top of the passenger door above Vamp's head, and I saw him reach down.

No time, I thought. *No more time.*

I did the only thing I could think to do. I took the gate remote from my pocket, and used the controls to connect to the safe house endpoint.

"Vamp, look out!" I yelled.

He looked up as the man above him went to grab him and slashed his forearm with the knife. The haanyŏng pulled away, then hammered his fist down on Vamp's chest. The force of it knocked Vamp loose. His foot slipped, and he fell, crashing into me as he went.

The seat belt slipped from my hand and we both dropped out through the open door and into the air.

For a moment we both fell, high above Hangfei with nothing but the rush of wind in our ears. It didn't feel like falling, more like floating, with the city's approach feeling very slow, but just as certain. Then I aimed the remote below us, opened the portal wide, and pushed the button. The white point of light appeared, dilating open as it rushed toward us.

We plunged through, and the roar of the wind and aircar engines flattened into silence.

Chapter Twenty-Six

The momentum of the fall sent me flying through the air of the factory ruins in a horizontal cannonball, until I dropped and rolled across the grimy concrete with Vamp right on top of me. I picked myself up, wincing at the pain from where my hip had struck the floor.

I turned and saw the last haanyŏng looking down over the side of the aircar at me. He jumped, dropping straight for the gate.

The second he reached it, I closed the gate. The portal shrank to a pinprick of white light, closing on the man's ankle. The foot, severed clean, tumbled away into the darkness while the rest of him, I assumed, continued his fall toward the streets below. A beat later, the foot vanished with a sharp bang.

"Sam, are you okay?" Vamp called.

"Yeah. Where are Nix and Shuang?"

"I don't know."

A faint light blinked on as Vamp lit up the screen of his phone. I looked around, but didn't see either one of them.

"We missed him," I said. "We missed our chance to get Alexei back."

"We can still go back," Vamp said.

"How?"

"We can still go back to Xinzhongzi."

"How, Vamp? How the hell will we get in now?"

"Another car. We'll take my car."

I took out my phone, and called Dao-Ming. She picked up on the first ring.

"Sam," she said. "Is Alexei with you?"

"No," I told her. "Security picked him up on camera heading away from your place; where are you?"

"At Dragan's. I'd brought him here, but he left. He didn't say anything he just left—"

"Dao-Ming, listen up. Alexei went to your place, and then he went to Xinzhongzi."

That made her pause. The surprise in her voice sounded genuine.

"What?" Dao Ming asked.

The way she said it didn't sit right with me. I heard her concern for him, sure, but something else, too. Dread, maybe.

"Do you know something about this?" I asked her.

"No, I . . . I'm just worried for him."

"Worried for him?" I said, my voice rising. "Worried for him? You dragged him into the middle of something that almost got him killed!"

"Someone had to do it," she said, her voice flat.

"He's a kid, you lunatic!"

"It had to be him," she said. "Gohan is obsessed with Alexei, with all of you, he—"

"He's nine," I said. "Nine years old. He lost his whole family."

"It's why he hates them."

"So you twisted him to—"

"No, he saw how dangerous the haan are before he ever met me. He wanted to honor his mother's memory—"

"He is nine!" I barked.

"He doesn't have the luxury of being a child," she said. "Who is going to protect him? You? Dragan and I will prepare him for this world."

"Don't even try and tell me Dragan knows about this," I told her, and she fell quiet. No. Dragan didn't know. He didn't know, and she was afraid for him to find out. Not out of fear of what he'd do to her, but out of fear he'd abandon her.

"I care about your father, and your brother," she said. "And you, Sam, no matter what you think."

"Why would Alexei go back to Xinzhongzi?" I asked. "What did he need to get at your place before he went?" She didn't answer, but we both knew. Dao-Ming convinced Alexei that she needed Gohan dead. In his mind, he'd failed her and Dragan. He was going to try to fix it. He was going to try to take out Gohan.

"There may still be time to stop him," she said, her voice faint.

"Dao-Ming, I swear," I said in a low voice. "If anything happens to him . . ."

I petered off as something on the floor behind her caught my eye. A dark blotch had been smeared there. A haphazard series of dots trailed away from it, around the corner and into the shadows.

"Sam," she said. "Please believe—"

I hung up on her, still staring at the floor.

"Sam?" Vamp asked. I held up one hand, approaching the stain.

"Shh."

When I got closer, I could see it was blood. I grabbed the electric lantern from the floor and shined it ahead. The drops turned steadier, the farther they went.

"Someone else is here," I whispered.

"Where's your gun?"

"I lost it in the aircar; it's gone."

A faint sob echoed from somewhere in the darkness.

"Shuang," Vamp whispered. I nodded.

"Come on."

I stood, and followed the trail. It led down the empty factory floor, through one of the open doorways at the far end where a dim light now shined. I stepped through into what looked like a large, empty utility closet. Past a half-toppled section of shelving, I saw a man's leg, the shoe partway off and the trouser cuff hiked up. The light came from somewhere behind the shelving. I waved Vamp over, pointing to the foot, and he nodded. We crept around the corner, and looked.

Chong lay facedown on the floor, blood pooled around him while Qian knelt over him. She gazed down at the body in front of her with a calm expression on her face. Somewhere behind them, out of view, I heard Shuang begin to sob.

Chong's bugged, glassy eyes stared from his bloodless face. The back of his skull had been caved in and Qian's red hand still dangled just above the hole, drops of blood falling from her fingertips.

I ducked back before she could see me, and opened my tablet. I dropped the remote into the shared space, and contacted Dao-Ming again.

The first stored endpoint. There's a haan here. We're in trouble, I sent.

"I know you're there," Qian said.

Dao-Ming didn't answer me, but she had to have gotten the message. I had to just hope she'd do something, send help, maybe.

"I know you can hear me," Qian said. "Come here."

I came around the corner where she could see me, and Vamp followed. Qian had risen, standing over Chong's body, while behind her, Shuang shivered against the wall, hugging her knees. I saw no sign of Nix.

"Give me the gate remote," she said, taking a step toward us. "Or she dies."

Something invisible grabbed Shuang by the ankle, and she whimpered as her leg came up off the floor. She struggled as Qian dragged her across the concrete and then hoisted her up, dangling her as if she were on some invisible hook, so that they were face to face.

"Please," Shuang whispered. "Please, just do what she wants."

"Where's Nix?" I asked Qian.

"I had to send him away."

"Send him where?"

"To the other endpoint found in your gate remote," she said. "Now, give it back to me."

Other endpoint . . . assuming no one changed them, that could be either the power station in Xinzhongzi, or the charge station restroom in Jangbong.

"Then what?"

"Then you're going to make this attack on the power grid stop," she said. "Right now Hangfei has power, but that could change at any minute. I know that you came up with the idea to black out the power in Hangfei, and by extension, the thirty-two haan colonies. I know that with the help of these other humans you were able to turn that idea into a concrete plan, and that less than twenty-four hours ago you put that plan into effect. We are in immediate danger of being exposed. That makes you a threat to me, and to all haan."

"It's just the truth," I said. "I just want everyone to see the truth."

"You will be shown the truth in due time, but now is not that time."

"I say it is."

"Your government does not agree. They speak for you, do they not?"

"Not for me," I said. "No."

"You live in this country. You enjoy the quality of life it provides. If your interests aren't served by your leaders, you could always try and make your way somewhere else."

"Why don't you try and make your way somewhere else?"

"Because we can't," she said. "And as you now know, this world exists in our reality now. This may not be the planet we knew, but the solar system, the galaxy, and even the universe are all part of our reality now, not yours. It's been kept from you, to keep you calm until you are capable of understanding, but other parts of the world have, by now, discovered the small changes in physical laws, additional planets, the life forms on the satellite of what you called Jupiter. This could be a new era of discovery for you, and we will share with you all that we know—"

"When?" I asked.

"When we are ready," she said. "When you are ready."

"It's been fifty years, Qian."

"And yet still, you see how those outside our sphere of influence react. We need a solid, secure presence here. We need, to be honest, the protection of your world's great superpower. Do you think the only thing keeping them at bay is our defense shield? It's your vast army, air power, and nuclear arsenal. We need your protection. When we have it fully we will proceed, but I warn you, I will not let one small group of humans undo all of this. Compared to the future we offer, your lives are inconsequential."

"We can't shut it down," Vamp cut in. "The failure is cascading out of control, but it shouldn't—"

"That's not good enough. I want the attack stopped. If it isn't, I'll kill each one of you, starting with this one." She shook Shuang's dangling body.

"He's telling the truth," I said. "We can't stop it but the whole city won't lose power, there's a power station we didn't know about that's keeping it from tripping. The power company will figure out a way to fix it, and—"

Qian lunged, and clamped one hand around my throat, dragging me down onto my knees in front of her. I felt her steady calm falter through the cluster, and a pulse of frustration, and anger seeped through. The promise of violence flooded my mind, but unlike my encounters with Sillith years before I didn't sense the same perverse excitement that had accompanied her acts. Qian would commit violence, and lots of it, that much I could tell, but she wouldn't enjoy it. As far as she was concerned, she was defusing a bomb and we were nothing more than wires to be cut.

Vamp went for her, then. Out of the corner of my eye I caught the flash of his butterfly knife as he twirled it open in midstride; then the blade chirped through the air. The edge bit through what appeared to be Qian's throat, and opened a gash there. Warmth spurted down over my face and chest, dark, oozing red that felt like wriggling little worms. I tried to turn my face away but couldn't move as Vamp whipped around for another attack.

The blow never landed. Vamp's arm collided with some invisible part of Qian she'd raised to block him, and I saw a ghost image of a haan hand flick around his wrist before fading again. It twisted Vamp's arm back until he barked out, and the knife fell from his hand.

I stared in horror, sure that the next thing I'd see would be Vamp's hand being torn from his body, but Qian didn't do it. Once she'd disarmed Vamp, she hurled him away. I heard him hit the floor with a grunt, then roll into the wall with a thud.

"You shouldn't have done it," Qian said, her voice becoming softer as she moved her face close to mine. Another spurt of blood burbled out of the gash before it closed up, and disappeared. "You are correct. Sillith's virus has spread, and continues to spread. Invisible to you our numbers have grown, but this is not what we wanted. It shouldn't have happened, and we are trying to stop it. The other nations of your world, outside the scope of our influence, have seen what is happening and they are preparing to invade. If this comes to light now, we will never be able to reverse it."

"You're replacing us," I said. "You're wiping us out."

"No," she insisted. "We would never change you. We're trying to save you."

"Save us? You're supposed to fix the planet, not this. I've seen it. People are being changed."

"Their bodies have changed. We would never change who you are. I have all my memories, every joy, every sadness, all human. I am still me. I am still Qian Cho."

I tried to shake my head. "You say 'we.' 'We' would never change 'you.' You're not Qian Cho, not anymore."

I felt anger through the mites, defensive anger. She pulled me a little closer, and lowered her voice.

"You say we should fix the planet that you depleted?" she said. "This planet can't be fixed. Not now. Not anymore. If you're going to survive what's coming, then you need to evolve."

"You're eating us," I gasped.

"There weren't supposed to be so many, so soon," she said. "We weren't supposed to have to resort to this. Sillith's virus—"

"Even without it, once we've all changed we'd still have to eat," I said. "The planet can't feed humans; how are haan going to live on it?"

"Sam," a voice said. "There is some truth to what she says."

From the corner of my eye, I saw that Nix had returned. He stepped into the room, moving between Qian and me just a few paces back. He made no move to interfere with Qian's hold on me.

"Nix?" I managed.

"It isn't common knowledge," he said, "but it's true that your world as it is cannot be fixed. Our universe is very similar to your original one, but there are small, but fundamental, differences. Your world doesn't have much time. There is a reason for all of this, I promise."

"How did you get back here?" Qian asked.

Nix didn't answer, but wherever she'd gated him I guessed he used the gate system to reach my apartment and came in through the closet portal. Qian wouldn't have known about that.

"Nix, help me," I wheezed.

He didn't move. I could sense how conflicted he felt at that moment. On the one hand, the haan had abandoned him and his loyalty to me was real. On the other hand, he faced the extinction of his race. He couldn't reconcile it.

"He's not going to help you," Qian said. "He knows that I'm right even if he can't quite accept it. This is your last chance to do as I ask."

I struggled to stand my ground, but I found my resolve slip, just a little. I made myself remember Sillith, and how she'd almost killed millions of people. I remembered her victims, bound and mutilated down in the pit under Shiliuyuán. I remembered the little girl, smiling next to her own discarded skin and how afraid I'd become to walk the streets of the city that was my home. Nothing else that happened to me, not losing my mother, or ending up homeless, or even being taken by the meat farmers had made me scared to be in Hangfei. Only the haan had managed that.

"You hid the truth from the start," I gasped. "It's time for people to see. . . ."

Spots bloomed in front of my eyes as her grip closed my throat, and choked off the words. Still, Nix did not move.

I'm going to die, I thought. The time had come. I felt myself slipping, blacking out, and I knew that once I lost consciousness I would never awaken, not this time. Several scaleflies crept from her hand, their legs tickling as they crawled up my jawline and over my cheeks. I grabbed her, trying to peel her fingers away but she felt as hard and as strong as stone. Crushing me took no effort at all.

"You don't have any choice in the matter," Qian said. "The universe you find your world in now is rejecting you. The decay will be slow, but certain. All life on this world that does not evolve will die. Stop fighting. Let us save you."

A sound like water rushing filled my ears and as my eyes began to roll, I felt no fear. For once, I wasn't afraid at all. I felt a strange, disconnected calm and if anything, it came closer to relief than anything else.

It's over. . . .

A boom sounded from somewhere behind me, and the dark cloud scattered back into spots as my lungs pulled in a long, painful breath. I fell, landing hard on my back and looking up at the ceiling as a second boom went off. A shiny brass shell casing spun past me, and Qian dropped Shuang onto the floor in a heap.

Gasping, I rolled over and saw Dao-Ming, the gate remote in one hand and a pistol in the other. The gate she'd just stepped through shrank closed behind her as she fired three more times.

"Sam, get away from her!" she called.

My vision flickered, and the image of Qian shifted for a second. Wet, black coils unraveled down the front of her and snaked out across the floor toward us. One lashed out and grabbed Dao-Ming's wrist, pushing the gun away, toward the wall next to her even as she continued to fire. Another wound around her right leg just under the knee, then jerked her up into the air.

Dao-Ming landed hard on her back; then the gun flew from her hand and spun across the floor behind Qian. Dao-Ming struggled, the cords in her neck standing out as the grip on her leg tightened.

This wasn't going to end well. Even all together, we were no match for the haan and all the while the struggle had been going on Nix still stood there, stuck in a state of indecision. Even now, he just watched as Qian forced Dao-Ming to the floor and pinned her there.

Vamp closed in to try to free her, and Shuang, terrified, tried to run. Before she could reach the exit, something snagged her ankle and she went facedown onto the floor. Her body slid backward across the floor toward Qian, and I took the opportunity to dart back behind them, toward Dao-Ming's gun.

Something whipped through the air near my face and knocked my leg out from under me. I spilled onto the floor, but managed to grab the gun. I rolled over, and took aim at the back of Qian's skull.

Dao-Ming screamed, her face turning bloodred and shiny as her right leg came off at the knee. I fired, over and over, as fast as I could pull the trigger as blood began to jet from the stump. Pain bored through the mite cluster as the bullets punched into Qian, but while her wounds forced her to let go of the others, I could see they weren't going to stop her, not this time.

I heard the whip of one of her arms slash through the air and then felt it snake around the length of my arm. It squeezed, and I cried out, the gun falling to the floor.

That snapped Nix out of it. He turned, almost as if he'd noticed the things happening around him for the first time. He looked at Dao-Ming, still screaming as she stared at her missing leg, then me, seconds away from joining her, and he moved.

He sprang, and I heard something slash through the air. Qian loosened her grip on my arm and I fell back as the air warped in front of me. Two haan hands appeared from out of nowhere, each severed at the elbow. One hand still gripped my wrist while the other clutched my forearm, but the strength had gone from them. I shook them away and they fell to the floor before each blinked out of existence with a loud bang.

Shuang rolled away and climbed to her feet as Qian turned her attention on Nix, who had begun to shake. Waves of signal began to pour off of him as the conflict he felt inside peaked, and as the shaking grew worse I felt him tip over the edge.

A rage washed over me through the cluster that left me cold. Nix's back sprang apart, torn in two to expose the glassy spine underneath for a second before whatever controlled my interpretation of him filled in the blanks and presented him with much wider shoulders. His arms split down their center, turning rubbery and uncoiling before each half flickered and resolved into a completely separate arm. Two additional arms unfolded from out of nowhere, as his legs split apart.

"What are you doing?" Qian asked, and I felt genuine shock from her. Not because Nix had the ability to do what he'd done but that he'd broken some hard-wired taboo.

Nix's body grew, becoming a shivering mass of limbs, hands, and fingers that loomed over Qian. He grabbed her, the forest of hands clamping down on whatever part of her they could reach. Qian let out a burst of shock and pain as her flesh tore free in a spray of blood. Whatever controlled Nix's appearance adjusted and his body reverted to normal, but the hands were still there, crushing and tearing Qian's body in an uncontrolled fury. Parts of her flew back behind Nix, tumbling across the floor before blinking away while Qian struggled to fend him off.

A bright point of light appeared on the wall behind us, growing to allow a shaft of sunlight to shine through. I turned and saw Dao-Ming on one side next to a splash of vomit, still pointing the remote at the gate she'd opened. This one connected to an endpoint she must have set somewhere in the city, an alley, it looked like. She looked to me, her face ashen, and her mouth moved but nothing came out.

"Go!" I yelled to the others, who stared at the spectacle, stunned. "Now! Go!"

Dao-Ming's eyes rolled as Vamp scooped her up and began to head toward the gate. Shuang darted through ahead of them, and then I followed, the battle still raging behind me.

I stepped through, silence swallowing the racket of the struggle and replacing it with a blanket of street noise. Vamp laid Dao-Ming down on the blacktop, her face ashen and her eyes swimming. Shuang joined him as he removed his belt and pulled it tight around the stump.

"She's bleeding out," Vamp said. I hovered behind them,

with no idea what to do. Before I could shake myself out of it, Nix appeared in the alley and the portal collapsed behind him. He approached Dao-Ming, and gently pushed both Vamp and Shuang aside.

Kneeling in front of her, he removed the makeshift tourniquet and put his hands on the stump of her leg. The bleeding slowed, and then stopped altogether.

"What did you do?" I asked, stepping in behind him.

"I've knitted the flesh," he said. "It's stopped the bleeding, but if she doesn't get medical attention soon, she will die."

"I'll stay with her," Shuang said. Vamp protested.

"No, I'll—"

"You stay with Sam," she told him. Before he could protest again, she pushed him away. "Someone needs to call an EMT and stay with her."

I hung back and redialed, punching up Dragan's number. On the second ring, he answered.

"Sam," he said. "Thank God. Where are you? Where's Alexei?"

"Alexei called me not long ago. He's headed for Xinzhongzi."

"Xinzhongzi? Why?"

"It's a long story," I said, glancing at Dao-Ming. "The bottom line is I think he's going after Gohan, and he's in trouble. Can you get there?"

"The protests are going to make that difficult," he said. "But I'll manage it."

"Get a few guys you know you can trust and get ready to meet us there."

"Where are you going?"

"I'm going in after him, but I'm going to need help getting back out I think."

"Sam, you'll never get in to Xinzhongzi. The place is locked down; you'll get arrested the second you show your face there."

"I'll get in."

"Sam—"

"Just trust me. Get ready, and wait for my call. Please. I have to go."

I hung up before he could answer, and turned to Vamp and Nix.

"I have to go after Alexei," I told them. "I can't leave him there."

"You'll need help," Vamp said.

I felt like I should try to talk him out of it, but the truth was that I didn't want to. I kissed his cheek, and then brought up the number Gohan had included in his fancy little invitation.

"Who are you calling now?" Vamp asked. I held up my hand to shush him.

The phone rang twice before someone picked up.

"Hello, Xiao-Xing Shao. I was hoping you'd call, though I confess, I didn't think you would."

"Shut up. You still want me?"

"I would love to have you join me in Xinzhongzi."

"Okay then, you win. I'll come."

"I understand I am not your favorite person right now," he said calmly. "May I ask what changed your mind?"

"Honestly? I've got nowhere else to go."

"I see."

"I need to get off the radar, and I figure that inside Xinzhongzi should fit the bill."

"I agree."

"I need you to take two others, as well. One human, one haan."

"Done."

I'd expected him to balk at that, but he didn't, not even for a second.

"And I want you to tell me why you're so hot to get me over there in the first place."

"When we meet."

"Now."

"When we meet."

I gritted my teeth.

"Fine."

"I am sending you an address," he said. "There is a private metro access there. I will have someone waiting for you."

"Thanks. We're on our way."

"Excellent, and let me tell you just how pleased I am that—"

I hung up.

"We're in," I told them.

"In where?" Vamp asked.

"Xinzhongzi. We're getting Alexei. Then we're getting out of Hangfei."

Chapter Twenty-Seven

Gohan marked out a specific route for us to take, and we arrived at the first marker to find four robed gonzos waiting for us. The one woman in the group approached. She took my arm and herded me and the others into the middle of them.

"Keep your heads down," she said.

As we walked, I moved closer to Nix so I could talk to him without the gonzos hearing.

"What did you mean back there?" I asked him. The pupils in each of his eyes swam through the mellow light to fix on me.

"When?"

"You said that Qian was right."

"I said there is some truth to what she says."

"You said that our world doesn't have much time."

One of the gonzos glanced over at us, and Nix switched to the 3i chat.

Each universe has six potential fundamental forces, he said. *At least as far as we know. Your universe has four, and ours shares those four—gravitation, electromagnetic, strong, and weak force. The relationships between these forces are complex, but—*

Nix, just get to the point. What did you mean when you said "our world doesn't have much time"?

The four forces were nearly the same between our two

universes, but not identical. A small but important variation in the weak force mediated by particles your people call "weak bosons."

Nix . . .

The end result is that the natural radioactive decay occurs more quickly here than in the universe you came from. Over the past fifty years, the levels of radiation on this planet have increased. It hasn't become problematic, not yet, but it will. It is only a matter of time before your planet can no longer support plant and animal life in its current form.

I didn't exactly understand what he'd said, and it annoyed me that I couldn't really verify it, but I got the gist.

If that's true, I said, *then how was there life on your planet?*

Because it evolved in that universe. Everything that did was well suited for it.

And we're not.

He nodded.

I'm sorry, he said. *But as I said before, there is some truth to what Qian told you.*

So you . . . changing us—this was the plan all along?

Not because we wanted to. You have to understand—unlike your world, ours never suffered any mass extinction. We've had millions of years to evolve, to even take control of and perfect our own evolution. We had achieved resonance hundreds of thousands of years ago with a perfectly functioning ecosystem. That luxury doesn't exist here. You will not adapt, or evolve, to this new environment. Without some kind of external push, eventually you will die.

He noticed that I'd begun to back away, and turned. When he made to take me by the arm, I pulled away.

I don't believe you, I said.

I can sense you, he said, *as you sense me. On some level, you know what I'm telling you is true.*

Shut up.

By the time we arrived at the next marker, another six

robed men and women waited and as we continued more and more joined the group, each carrying picket signs. By the time we'd reached the halfway point, we were completely surrounded by a procession of worshippers, their bodies and signs forming a shield around us that concealed us from any security officers or cameras.

I drifted back from Nix, not sure whether or not to believe him but feeling anxious at the thought of it. Could it be true? Could the haan, and even Sillith herself, have had our interests in mind all along?

I took Vamp's hand and squeezed it as we walked. He glanced down, uneasy, and I shared that unease. The gonzos provided an excellent cover, and no one bothered us at all during the trip, but the fact that Gohan had gone to such lengths worried me.

"This feel like a trap to you?" he asked.

"We don't have much of a choice at this point," I said, then messaged him, privately.

Dragan is coming. We'll be okay.

The procession stayed with us the whole time, ignoring Vamp and me for the most part in favor of fawning over Nix, who seemed willing to put up with them as they touched him like some kind of good luck charm. When we reached a keyed metro tunnel, they followed us down and the first woman we'd met stepped from the group to meet a lone gonzo standing by the platform's glass door. As she approached, he spoke into his phone.

". . . Three of them. They've arrived," he said. He hung up and then slipped the phone back into his robe.

"Here they are," the woman said.

"Thank you," he responded.

She bowed, and smiled. "Only He can move the stars."

The procession then retreated, heading back up the stairs in a crowd of white robes.

"They're expecting you," the man at the door said. A key card appeared in his hand from his sleeve like some kind of magic trick. He touched it to the turnstile's scanner and the door unlocked with a metallic click. "You should get off the street."

He went back to meditating or whatever it was he was doing as one by one we passed through the turnstile to a set of stairs that led down to a semiprivate monorail platform, shared by key members of Hangfei's upper crust. I'd seen the entrances around town, but I'd never been in one of them before. There was no graffiti, not a single piece of trash, and instead of a dirty concrete floor the platform was covered in shiny ceramic tiles that were colored red and gold.

"There they are," Nix said.

I looked down the platform and saw two men heading toward us, their shiny black shoes rapping on the tiles as they came. These guys weren't wearing robes, they were wearing suits, and they didn't look like your run-of-the-mill, doped-out gonzos, they looked like they might be dangerous. When they stepped under one of the overhead lights and I got a good look at them, I realized I actually recognized them. They were the same two thugs Gohan had with him in the aircar when he set Dragan up.

"Watch these guys," I said under my breath.

"Both men are armed," Nix said.

"It's okay," I said, "just stay cool."

As the men approached us, one of them spoke into his cell phone but his words were swallowed by the low clack and rumble of an approaching train. The rush grew louder as a light appeared from down the tunnel; then a short, three-car bullet train whooshed up to the platform and stopped with a loud, hydraulic hiss that made the two goons' pant legs ruffle.

They split up as we met on the platform next to the train, one approaching me while the other approached Vamp and Nix. He motioned for them to move away from me as the doors on two of the train's cars opened with a soft chime.

"Hold still," the one in front of me said. He held some kind of tablet up between us, and used it to scan me up and down. While he watched the screen, the other one checked out Vamp and Nix.

"Let's have the pistol," the one in front of me said. I took it from my pocket where I'd stowed it, and handed it over to him.

"They're clean," the other goon said. He'd begun to herd them back, away from me.

"Hey," I said. "They come too. That was the deal."

The guard with me dialed, then spoke into his phone again. "We've got them," he said. "We're bringing them on now."

He nodded toward his partner, who signaled to Vamp and Nix.

"You two," he said, "rear car."

I took a step toward them and the other guard grabbed my arm.

"Not you. You're up front."

I jerked my arm away from him.

"Bullshit. Why?"

"Because that's how it is," he said, his voice turning hard. "Is there going to be a problem?"

"It's okay," Vamp said.

"We stay together," I told the two men. The one with me shook his head.

"No," he said. "Gohan's only taking them because he wants you. They ride in back or not at all."

"Sam, it's okay," Vamp said. "We can take care of ourselves. We'll see you in Xinzhongzi."

The guard took my arm again, and again I pulled away.

"Fine," I said, glaring. He motioned toward the train.

"Front car."

Vamp gave a wave as the other guard ushered him and Nix into the rear car, and I stepped through the doorway into the front.

The inside was posh, I had to admit. Shiny clean, crisp canned air, and big, plush seats. The car sat only six total, and all the seats were empty at the moment. A fancy bar booth had been set up at the far end of the cab, a round glass table in front of a plush, curved seat made of faux leather.

Sitting at the table was Gohan himself. He didn't look at me when I came in, in fact he wasn't really looking at anything. He sat with his hands folded in front of him, staring blankly at the tabletop like he was in a trance.

I turned to ask the goon if the old guy was okay, but he hadn't followed me in. The door slid shut, leaving me alone with Gohan as the train started to move. Through the windows I saw the big dragon mural streak past; then the overhead light flickered on as we headed into the tunnel.

"Hello?" I called, creeping toward him between the rows of seats.

He looked up at the sound of my voice, and I saw he looked even more tired and strung out than he had in the aircar the day before. There were dark circles under his eyes like he hadn't slept in a couple of nights, and his face was covered in graying stubble. Even his plastic hair had shifted a little out of place, wiry strands sticking out here and there.

The weirdest thing, though, had to be the expression on his face. That strange smile of his appeared, but his eyes weren't in on the smile. They seemed to be operating on a completely different wavelength.

"Hello there," he said, patting the seat next to him. "Please, sit down."

I didn't sit right next to him like he wanted, but I took a seat at the table with him.

"Okay," I said. "I'm here."

"Yes. Good. Did my people give you any trouble?"

"No," I said. "They were fine."

He leaned back in the booth, and let out a long sigh.

"You're in an awful lot of trouble, Xiao-Xing Shao."

"Yeah, well . . . I thought I would be when I started this."

"I suppose a complete loss of power isn't in anyone's best interest," he said. "Except yours."

"And yours."

He grinned a little, and nodded.

"I imagine you have questions."

"I know Chong was working for you."

"Is he alive?"

"No," I said. "Why was he working for you, Gohan? Why did you try to help us?"

He reached across the table, and took my right hand in his. He ran his thumb over the back of it, and I pulled it away.

"Are you hungry?" he asked.

"I want answers, Gohan."

"I'm hungry."

His fingers wandered across a row of contacts built into the table's surface and a panel on the wall between us popped open. Cold air puffed out of a little fridge on the other side, causing goose bumps to prick up on my arm.

"Doesn't it bother you to live like you do while everyone else starves?"

"Not everyone else."

The cold air made its way to my nose and immediately my mouth started watering as I breathed in smells both savory and sweet. I blinked, everything else forgotten for a moment as I stared at the shelf inside. Three ceramic bowls had been arranged there, along with a single square ceramic plate. The bowls each contained shiny fruit of different shapes and colors. The plate had four items on it: oblong molds of what I thought might be rice. Sitting on top of each one was a strip of something pale white, and shiny.

"Take it," he said.

"No," I said, but I couldn't stop staring at the offering.

"Enjoy what fruits the world has left," Gohan said. "You never know when they may be gone."

I wanted to say no, but I hadn't eaten since Baishan Park, and the smell of food seemed to fill the whole car. Before I even knew what I was doing I'd reached toward it, stopping myself before I'd actually touched anything.

"I . . . don't have much money," I said, still staring into the fridge. Gohan looked amused.

"You are my guest."

"I can have anything?"

His creepy grin curled wider. "Anything."

I leaned closer to get a better look at the white flesh draped over the rice.

"What is that?"

"Fish," he said. "On rice."

I looked at him, eyebrows raised.

"Fish," I said. "Like from the ocean? I don't think so." Fishing had been outlawed decades ago, before I'd even been born. I'd heard about it, but it wasn't done anymore. Most species went extinct a long time ago, the ones worth eating anyway. The ocean supported the feedlots now, and provided water, after desalination. Not fish.

"No," Gohan said. "Not from the ocean. I clone them."

"Where did you get the material to clone from?"

"It's out there, for the right price."

I decided I'd better go for the fruit first, not exactly sure about the cloned fish. I knew what fruit was, of course, but I'd never actually eaten any. I reached for the most recognizable piece—the shiny red gonzo apple. It fit neatly in my hand, firm and cold.

My teeth broke through the thin skin, and into the crisp flesh underneath as sweet juice flooded into my mouth. It ran down over my tongue, forcing my lips into a smile before I could even close my mouth. I chomped down on the piece I'd bitten off and more juice gushed out, dribbling down the back of my throat and leaking from the corners of my mouth. I was still chewing when I took another greedy mouthful, packing it in with the rest.

"Good?" Gohan asked.

I nodded, unable to speak without spraying juice. The fruit tasted better, hands down, than anything else I'd ever eaten in my life, ever. I couldn't believe how much of the sweet liquid it contained . . . like a food and water ration all in one, except the food wasn't bitter, crunchy scalefly and the water tasted sweet and tangy, instead of flat and metallic.

I swallowed hard, forcing the first mouthful down toward my stomach, which was already antsy with anticipation. As soon as the way was clear I went in again, biting into the soft, white fruit. I wiped my mouth on the back of one forearm, smearing sticky juice across one cheek.

"Look," I said. "You can bribe me all you want but I still want answers."

I had to admit, though, that at least for the moment the bribe was kind of working. I'd seen the replicas of apples at their shrines all the time but had no idea that they, or anything for that matter, could ever taste so good.

"You'll get your answers," Gohan said. "Do you feel better?"

I nodded.

"Yes." I swallowed, then added, "Thank you, Gohan."

"You're welcome."

He took one of the fish and rice bundles, and popped it in his mouth. He licked his greasy lips, then leaned back in his chair and chewed with one cheek bulging. When he caught me looking at his droopy eyelid, he raised one finger to point toward it.

"Do you know why I suffer from partial paralysis in my face?" he asked.

"Is that what it is?"

"Yes. My face wasn't always this way. It happened when, at twenty-seven years old, I was involved in an aircar accident that resulted in significant head trauma. Facial reconstruction was quite successful, though the nerve damage was too severe to completely repair and left me with the lazy eyelid."

"That's interesting, Gohan, but what does it have to do with what's going on now?"

"It has everything to do with what's going on now. To understand, you need to know the whole story." He pointed to his lazy eye again. "It all comes down to this."

"It all comes down to your eye."

"In a manner of speaking."

I threw my hands up, then put them down on the table.

"Okay," I said. "Let's have it."

"You know about the accident."

"I read about it. I didn't realize you were so badly hurt."

"I was very badly hurt, Sam, but as you probably also know I was quite drunk at the time, and the other driver did not survive. Nor did his child. If not for my father's considerable connections, I would be in prison."

He caught me a little aback, there. I'd been ready to throw that in his face, and he'd just offered it up. He looked sincere, too.

"It helps having friends in high places," I said.

"Yes."

He grabbed another of the fish treats, and I decided to try one too. The rice felt sticky, and when I sniffed it my nose filled with a faint salty smell, along with a tang and something sharp.

"Go ahead," he urged.

I stuffed the whole thing in my mouth and chewed until the sticky, slightly tangy rice mixed with the soft, oily, salty fish. As the flavor flooded my mouth, I felt my whole body shiver and I reached for the last one. I stuffed it in with the first one and worked it into my cheeks, sucking the tasty oil from my thumbs. I felt embarrassed by my lack of control. I felt like I should apologize, but Gohan seemed amused to watch me eat.

"That accident was the defining moment of my life," Gohan continued. "Though not for the reasons you might think. You see, in addition to the superficial damage, I also suffered damage to my right parietal lobe. It caused a condition known as unilateral neglect, which is to say I do not see objects on my left side. It's why I no longer drive myself, and it makes navigation on foot through Hangfei very difficult."

I sighed. "Look, Gohan, I'm sorry about that, really, but like you said . . . the other guy and his kid won't ever be navigating through Hangfei again, right? Meanwhile you get flown around eating better than just about anyone in the city."

"Don't say you're sorry," he said. "You're not, and neither am I."

When there was room in my mouth, I took a small, oval piece of green fruit from a small cluster of them. When I bit down on it, it popped into a payload of soft flesh and sweet liquid.

This is heaven, I thought, tapping my feet on the floor. The whole thing was intoxicating. It seemed unreal to me that Gohan got to eat like this all the time. He watched me chew for a while longer, then tapped another contact and a second panel next to the fridge hissed open to six plastic bottles, all full of liquor.

I started to reach for one of the bottles, but then thought better of it.

"I think I'd better keep a clear head," I told him. "Thanks. You know how to live, though. I'll give you that."

"It must disgust you, on some level," he said. It did, but I didn't say. I'd have felt like a hypocrite, at the moment. "Still, these pleasures, they aren't what's important. The accident made me see that."

"Yeah?"

"You see," he said, "the injury to my brain carried an additional side effect."

"And what's that?"

"I can see the haan."

I almost choked on the mouthful of food I'd been working, spraying juice across the table. Gohan's strange grin widened, still not touching his eyes, but I could see he'd gotten the reaction he'd been hoping for.

"What do you mean, see—"

"You know exactly what I mean," he said. "Chong was in constant contact with me, remember? I know what you saw in the ruins underneath Shiliuyuán. I know that, while you can no longer see through their illusion, you know the truth about them. It's why you sought to find a way to cut the haan off from Hangfei's power grid in the first place, so everyone may see. Chong was a natural place to start since he'd worked inside Liàngzǐchuán Relay and Power and had already attempted an intrusion into their systems before. Since I convinced him to see the light back then and to not attempt to steal from my father, when he was approached for a second attempt he came to me with it."

"So why didn't you turn us in? Were you just giving us enough rope to hang ourselves with?"

"No. I want you to succeed."

"But why? I thought you worshipped the haan."

He waved his hand again, that dismissive gesture that I'd already begun to hate.

"Worship isn't really the right word," he said. "I've been able to see the haan for what they really are for eighteen years now, almost as long as you've been alive. At first, it was difficult. I wasn't sure it was real, or some hallucination brought on by my injury. I even entertained the idea that it was punishment for what I'd done. As time passed, and I realized the truth of what I was seeing, I thought I might lose my grip on my sanity."

I think that ship might have sailed, I thought, but just nodded.

"Eventually, I came to see the beauty of them," he continued. "They really are quite remarkable, much more so than the sanitized form they've chosen would imply. They can assume almost any shape. They can, and sometimes do, combine several together to create larger forms that they sometimes maintain for years. They are physically quite different from us, but there is no question which race is superior. They've achieved a level of evolution that without them we would probably never reach."

"Without them," I said. "You mean Sillith's virus." He nodded.

"Oh, yes. I know about that too, of course. I saw the first human change almost half a year ago, and since then I have seen more and more of them on the streets of Hangfei. It's funny . . . they often don't even realize the change has taken place. They sometimes cling to their old identities for weeks, even months, before they realize what they've become."

"That's funny all right," I said. He ignored my sarcasm, and smiled. "You know they're eating us, right?"

"Oh, they're eating us, of course," he said. "They're multiplying, and they have to eat something. Xinzhongzi was meant to be a safe place where they could do that, until things get back under control."

"So LeiFang does know."

"Of course. This is all part of an agreement with the haan, to help defuse the situation Sillith created. This progression, this transformation needs to happen much more slowly so that we don't end up falling upon one another."

"But even if it happens slowly, and we all end up as haan—"

"A form of haan," Gohan corrected.

"That would still be millions of haan, all with huge calorie requirements. They'd need to eat something."

"Yes," Gohan said, "but the foreigners. Not each other."

I just stared at him. His eyes twinkled.

"You can't be serious."

"It's an elegant solution," he said. "Humans would evolve, and the overpopulation problem, over time, would be solved as well. The haan could spread out, expanding their field as they went, evolving the best specimens and eating the rest. Eventually the planet would return to sustainability."

"When you can eat a problem, you solve two," I said.

Gohan clapped his hands together. "Exactly right."

"You're crazy."

"Well, it's not as though there's much choice," he said. "The accelerated radioactive decay of this universe will kill us all within a few hundred years anyway, if we don't do something."

"It's true, then?" I asked.

"Oh, yes. They've been preparing for it for years now. The haan alterations were planned to extend to certain humans, animals and plants in a sort of 'ark' moving forward, though of course Sillith's actions threw that plan for a loop."

"The world is going to die?" I asked. I wasn't even really asking him. I was just trying to get my head around it.

"Well," he said, drawing the word out. "That's what the haan insist, anyway. I haven't been able to prove it one way or the other."

"So it might all be bullshit?"

He threw up his hands in mock dismay. "Who knows? It certainly could be true, but then, you know how the haan can be sometimes."

I sighed. "Yeah, I do."

"Don't worry," he said, licking juice from his palm. "Either way, it won't matter anymore. You are right, you know, in that the foreigners who are outside the haan's field of influence can see the haan, and what you call the haanyŏng, the duplicates or changelings, as they truly are. The rate of their spread frightens them, and they won't let it continue much longer, defense shield or no."

"Then how does exposing the haan in Hangfei help them? Won't that make it worse?"

"It will make things much worse for the haan," he said.

"I need things to get much worse for them. Without letting them, or LeiFang know, I need them to become so threatened, so frightened, that they will do something they otherwise wouldn't attempt."

I opened my mouth to ask what, when it clicked into place, and I felt the color drain from my face.

The cathedral houses Rapture. All I know is it will let the haan wipe us out. I believe it. So does Gohan.

"What? What is he going to do?"

"I don't know for sure, just that it's bad, and he needs the haan to help him do it."

Rapture, the weapon. Rapture, which meant the second coming of a god. A machine that had come from Shiliuyuán, the haan facility that had attempted to open a gate to our world from theirs, and pulled us through.

"*. . . prepare for Second Impact.*"

And I understood, then. I finally understood.

"You're going to cause another Impact."

Gohan smiled, broadly that time, pleased.

"Yes. You see, as elegant as the haan's solution is, I don't believe they should have to sacrifice themselves in that way."

"Sacrifice themselves?" I said. "What about us?"

"They'd go extinct, more or less. The form of haan that remained would be a sort of hybrid, a shadow of the original, and we'd be gone too, either way. They don't deserve that, so I'm going to give them a little push toward a different alternative."

"Rapture," I said.

"They wouldn't be so foolish as to leave control of such a device in the hands of a human," he said. "I'm not going to cause the Impact myself. They are. Once they realize it's their only option."

"That's impossible," I said, my voice weak.

"Is it?"

Could it be true? Could Gohan have truly provided the

haan with the resources to build some kind of machine, some kind of gate, the same kind that had caused the first Impact?

Part of my mind rebelled against the idea, but at the same time, part of me believed it. All that money being moved into Xinzhongzi . . . the residents bought or forced out, and the security wall going up around it. The way the colony had stayed lit, even while the district surrounding it fell into blackout. The presence of a new electrical substation parked right next to the gonzo HQ . . .

"Their world is gone," I said. "You can't bring it back."

"No," he agreed, "but this one can be overwritten with one much more similar to the one they came from."

"That's bullshit."

"The possibilities are infinite. It's not bullshit at all."

I stood up, my legs a little unsure. When I spoke, I heard hysteria in my own voice.

"But you're talking about wiping out—"

"What? This world? All of its glorious accomplishments?" he asked, leaning back in his chair. "A long history of violence, oppression, and brutality that looked like it might one day produce an enlightened society but never quite did? What they lost . . . it's what we failed to become. Wouldn't you rather be a part of that than this?"

"If all this is true," I asked, "then what do you want from me?"

"You are special," Gohan said. "You were touched by the haan in a way no other human has been, not even me. I want to know what you know, what you learned when they took you. I want you to be there in the one piece of our world that will remain when this is over, and I want you to be part of it when we, the chosen, are evolved to join them in their glory."

"You're nuts," I said. "You're completely nuts."

"I want to know why they chose you," he said. "I need to know how to get them to—"

The lights in the train car flickered, and went out.

The train slowed, continuing on through its own momentum for several seconds before stopping completely. Then, with a pop, the car doors squeaked open a hand's width.

"Another power failure," Gohan said in the dark. "Stay put, I'll get a flashlight."

I heard him move, groping around for a moment. Then a light blinked on, and I saw him, the glow creating deep shadows in the contours of his plastic face.

"There," he said. "Now I'm sure if we just—"

I snatched the flashlight from his hand, rising up out of my seat.

"Hey!"

I lunged for him, and pulled his badge from his belt. The clip popped free as he struggled to get out from behind the table, but by then I'd reached the nearest set of doors and pulled them the rest of the way open.

"Shit," Gohan hissed, then shouted, "Stop her!" I jumped out into the tunnel, shining the flashlight beam back toward the rear cars.

"Vamp! Nix! Come on, hurry!" I called.

Two cars down, I heard a struggle, then something clatter and turned the flashlight to see Vamp and Nix hopping down into the tunnel with me.

"That way," I said, pointing, "we just keep going in the direction the train was headed, the platform has to be somewhere up ahead."

"Hold it!" a man barked, and I turned to see the beam of a flashlight move inside the train car. It turned at the door, passing in over Nix and casting a shadow on the tunnel wall. For a second, the shadow appeared as a tall, shapeless heap as the field hitched; then the beam jerked away suddenly as the flashlight fell to the floor. A man, one of the two suited men who'd been with Gohan, flew through the open car door and smashed into the concrete wall. His body stuck there, legs dangling like he'd been pinned through the back. Then something I couldn't see moved away from him and he fell down onto the tracks.

Nix picked up the flashlight and stepped out into the tunnel. His eyes glowed softly in the dark but, I noticed, didn't seem to throw any light.

I knelt down and took the pistol from the man's hand. In the glow of the flashlight, I could see blood leaking from his mouth and nose but he looked to be still breathing. I reached down to check his pulse when a voice shouted from behind me.

"Wait!"

I spun around to see Gohan step off the train. He had taken a step toward me when Vamp threw a punch that knocked him down onto his knees. As he struggled to get up, Vamp jabbed him with a stun gun he must have taken off one of the guards. Gohan shook as the charge hit him, then flopped forward onto his chest.

"How many more are on the train?" I asked.

"I think just the one other guy," Vamp said. "I took care of him."

"Okay," I said. "Come on, we have to get to the Xinzhongzi tower. We need to get Alexei and get him out of there. Gohan's been playing us this whole time."

"Playing us how?"

"Nix, he implied he was going to try for a Second Impact. Could that be possible?"

I sensed uncertainty.

"Shiliuyuán is, essentially, the research facility where the original experiment took place," he said. "It is possible my people could duplicate the event. Given what happened the first time such a device was used, though, I doubt any haan would ever attempt it."

"Let's hope you're right, but assume you aren't," I said. "We need to make sure."

"How?" Nix asked.

"I don't know, but we can't do anything from here. Come on."

We headed down the tunnel, following it as fast as we dared in the dark. A few minutes in, lights in wire cages flickered on down the length of the tracks.

"There," I said, pointing. In the distance, I could make out a train platform that cast a dim glow into the tunnel. The metro had lost power, but at least parts of Xinzhongzi were still lit.

When we reached it, Vamp helped hoist me up and then he and Nix scrambled up after me. We headed down the length of the platform to a set of concrete stairs that led to street level.

From the sidewalk I could see the gonzo church across the street ... the entrance to the building was the one brightly lit thing on the whole block it looked like, and it had a sort of human glitz to it. While they'd left the windows blacked out the way the haan liked them, the entrance was a shiny, polished bronze affair at the top of black marble steps. Whatever the building had been before, it hadn't taken Gohan long to convert it. He must have spent a fortune.

The huge glass doors were flanked on either side by stylish bronze emblems similar to the one on the front of their pamphlets. They foyer was more glossy marble, and a big security desk blocked an elevator lobby at the far end. Over the sidewalk awning, a big sign cast a warm yellow glow like faint firelight, with brushed hanzi announcing THE REUNIFICATION CHURCH OF XINZHONGZI.

Vamp stared, but not at the church. I'd been inside a haan colony before, but Vamp hadn't. I saw the unease on his face as we stepped out onto the sidewalk, and followed his eyes up to the side of a building across the street where many sets of eyes burned flame red and mellow orange. In the glow, I could make out the movement of haan brains, shifting like jellyfish under their domed skulls. Feet and hands padded across the graviton plating as they crept past dark windows, moving closer to ground level to get a better look.

"I thought the colony wasn't occupied," Vamp said.

They were everywhere. In the twilight, the buildings looked as if they were smoldering and their constant movement across the blacked out windows created a hiss of glass-on-glass squeals that rose above the wind. Draping haan clothing flapped in the breeze, and their smell wafted down, filling my nose with the scent of fermented tofu. Above us, a series of little haan constructs, each shining with a single black-light blue bulb, went skittering down the length of a power line, their spindly legs ticking across the plastic shielding like cockroaches.

"It's okay," I told Vamp.

"Yeah," he said. "All right."

He couldn't feel them, at least. The flow of haan thoughts had found the mite cluster in my forehead and before we even reached the old, faded crosswalk they were trying to worm their way in all at once. I felt curiosity, mostly . . . they were interested in us, especially me. I got the sense they'd seen Gohan come and go before, but here were two novel humans, and another haan. A directed wave of interest make the mites tingle, but underneath that I felt a simmering hunger. I'd felt it every feeding time while in the surrogate program, but it was stronger with adults—it felt much more intense—and there were so many of them. An empty, almost painful feeling poured in and made my stomach clench so hard I stumbled.

"Hey," Vamp said. "You okay?"

"Yeah." His phone started to buzz; then mine did too. "Shut off your phone. That's the haan. They're trying to communicate."

"They're trying to brute force the 3i."

"Yeah, they'll do that, just block them. Come on, we have to hurry."

I headed across the street and they followed as I crossed to the entrance to the church and up the fancy steps. A red laser flicked down over us as we approached, and something beeped when it touched Gohan's ID. The heavy glass doors slid open silently, and we headed in.

The air inside was crisp and cool and with every step the soles of my sneakers squeaked, echoing around the vaulted ceiling above us. When I looked up, I saw the dome was black, with points of light like a planetarium. In the center, bright white lines traced the gonzo overlapping rings symbol. A few paces away, a security guard sat at a large station outfitted with an array of monitors.

Off to the right of the station, in a sitting area, I spotted a familiar figure. A boy, dressed in flowing gonzo robes, sat on a plush, black faux-leather sofa. His knapsack hung from his hands by one strap, dangling between his feet that didn't even quite touch the floor.

"Alexei," I called.

He looked up, and his eyes went wide for a second when he saw me rush toward him. I knelt down in front of his chair and hugged him.

"What are you doing here?" he asked, but he did hug me back a little. I let him go, and smoothed his hair back.

"Never mind what I'm doing here," I said. "What are you doing here? Are you okay?"

His hands wrung at the strap of his knapsack.

"You shouldn't have come," he said.

"Excuse me," the guard said. "Can I help you?"

"Gohan invited me here," I said, which wasn't exactly a lie. "You got a problem with that?"

"If you two were anyone else I'd throw you out, but since Gohan has standing orders not to mess with you then no, I guess I don't. Except for your friends here."

"Vamp and Nix are with me."

"They're not on the list. The haan can stay in Xinzhongzi if he wants, but he doesn't just get a free pass. As for you" — he pointed at Vamp — "you're going to need to leave."

"Gohan is expecting all of us," I said.

"He's not on the list," he said, drawing his stunner.

I turned, and pulled the gun on him, keeping it pointed at him as I walked him back toward the security desk.

"Sit," I told him. He did as he was told, sitting back down in his seat as I came around.

As I took his stunner and handed it to Vamp, I pulled up the 3i display and called Dragan.

Dragan, it's Sam. I found Alexei. Where are you?

I've got a vehicle and a couple guys we can trust. We'll be in the air shortly.

We're in the church tower lobby. Hang on.

"Where's the aircar port?" I asked the guard. When he stalled, I poked him with the barrel of my gun. "Where?"

"There's an underground lot —"

"The one up on the tower."

"Level ninety, east wing. Follow the signs."

We're heading to the aircar port up top — level ninety.

I'll find it.

Good. Listen — Gohan is planning to try to reproduce the Impact . . . never mind how, just trust me, it's not a bluff. He made it sound like the haan have to activate it. If Hangfei blacks out and exposes them, they might panic enough to do it but it sounds like he's using Xinzhongzi's power station to charge the machine. If you can take out that station, I think it's better to risk it before he can get this thing up and running.

Understood.

I'll message you again when we're at the aircar port.

I reached down and unclipped the canister of Red Light from the guard's belt.

"Sorry," I told him, and sprayed him in the face with it.

The guard's muscles switched off, and he slid down off the chair to crumple in a heap on the floor behind the desk.

"What are you doing?" Alexei asked.

"Do you want to see Gohan or not?"

He knew something was wrong, I could see that, but he'd gotten what he wanted. He glanced at the guard one last time.

"Okay," he said. He started to head for the elevators, and I grabbed his knapsack by the dangling strap.

"That stays here," I told him.

"It's mine."

"I don't care. It stays here or you aren't going anywhere, you got it? Let me worry about Gohan."

He hesitated. I thought he might actually make a run for it, but then he finally relented.

"Fine," he muttered. He walked over to the guard station and stuffed the pack underneath the desk there before heading back.

"Okay," I said. "Good. Let's go."

We followed him to the elevator lobby, where he pushed one of the buttons.

The serious look remained in his eyes as he watched the numbers descend.

Chapter Twenty-Eight

Inside the elevator car, a badge reader had been mounted next to the grid of floor buttons. I showed it Gohan's badge, and the A.I. screen lit up. The gonzo double planet icon appeared, and began to twirl.

"Greetings, Gohan Sòng," the A.I. said. "What is your destination?"

"Level ninety," I said. "The aircar port."

The A.I., apparently keying off the card alone, didn't seem to think anything strange about my drastically different appearance or voice.

"It would be my pleasure."

The car started up. Alexei had to have put it together at that point that I had Gohan's security badge, but he didn't call me on it. He barely seemed to notice me at all.

"Alexei, what's wrong?" He didn't answer, and I stooped down to meet his eye. "Alexei, please, tell me what's wrong."

He still didn't answer. He still didn't even look at me. I tried the 3i.

Alexei, did you kill those people in Render's Strip?

He looked over at me then, his eyes serious, but he still didn't answer. He just turned back to watch the floor numbers go up. He had begun muttering under his breath, something in Pan-Slav that I couldn't make out.

The floor shook a little, as vibrations made the console

panel rattle. The light flickered, and Vamp looked up at it nervously.

"The building's shaking."

"The vibrations are from a haan power conduit," Nix said. "I believe it converts power to charge the haan device located somewhere in this building."

"They're going to do it," I said. "They're going to try to re-create the original Impact, to bring back the haan home world."

"Our home world was destroyed. That cannot be undone."

"You think Gohan is lying, then?"

Nix thought for a minute.

"The original Impact was an accident," he said, "but we were able to gather a lot of data when it occurred. Our world is gone, along with your universe. However, there are likely other versions of this world in existence that are much closer if not almost identical to our original one. In theory it would be possible to repeat the experiment under controlled conditions, to collapse another universe while pulling through a more favorable version of this world. In a case such as that, everyone inside Xinzhongzi would remain, while the rest of the world is replaced."

"Xinzhongzi would become the new Shiliuyuán," I said.

"Yes. The inhabitants of the new world would believe nothing had changed—only that they experienced an Impact-like event, which caused the sudden appearance of the Xinzhongzi colony."

"If this device really does exist, and the haan are exposed, what are the chances they would actually trigger it?" I asked.

"I can't say," he said. "I believe they would only consider such an act as a last resort."

"But it's possible?"

"No one can be sure with any kind of certainty that such an attempt would succeed. It could result in nothing changing, a less desirable world, or the destruction of both universes. They would have to consider the alternative to be extinction before they would attempt it."

"Stop the elevator," I said. The car lurched to a stop.

"Sam, we don't have time for this," Vamp said.

"I've changed my mind," I told the A.I. "I want to visit Rapture, instead." Its icon twirled.

"Of course, sir."

The elevator started up again, and my stomach dropped as the car shot upward.

"Vamp, we have to try to stop it," I said. "I have Gohan's authority, maybe we can shut it down."

"Sam, they're right behind us."

"I know, but what if I'm right?"

Vamp shook his head, while Alexei continued to mutter to himself in Pan-Slav. I brought up the 3i's translator, trying to listen in.

"*. . . though I walk through the dark valley of death . . . I fear no harm . . .*"

A prayer, maybe? He spoke too softly to make everything out, but he seemed to be repeating something over and over.

A low hum grew louder as the elevator slowed, then stopped.

"Only He can move the stars," the A.I. said, and the doors opened.

We stepped out into the pristine lobby, a mixture of shiny marble and brass fixtures. The cream-colored walls were speckled with scaleflies though, and as we stepped out of the elevator car more of them flitted through the air in front of me.

"Look," Vamp said, pointing.

I waved flies away from my face as we approached a short corridor that extended off the lobby. At the end stood a set of heavy glass double doors with swarming black bodies clustered in the corners. A badge scanner had been mounted on the wall next to the entrance.

I headed toward them, disturbing more of the flies and sending them buzzing in a cloud, some bouncing off the walls and others flitting past in a stream before settling back down. I slapped my arm as one of them bit me, and wiped it on my pant leg.

Above me something sparked, and the tube bulbs there flickered, casting shifting shadows across the floor. Somewhere farther in, a machine began to wind up and the vibrations grew, rattling the doors in their frames.

"Hold up," Vamp said, pointing.

Through the doors a pair of shadows moved, and I heard footsteps following them. I waved for the others to get down and we crouched, waiting for them to pass.

Something slammed, and I heard the footsteps of many people sprinting away in the distance.

"... this is it," a man's voice echoed from somewhere down the corridor. "It's really happening ... Gohan help us. ..."

"Sam," Vamp said, grabbing me by the shoulders. "Gohan's going to have every one of his guys looking for us. We came here to get Alexei, and we got him. We need to get out of here."

"Vamp, if this thing is real, we can't just leave it."

"We won't," Vamp said. "We'll come back—"

"We're not ever getting back in here," I said. "Once they figure out how you and Shuang got into the grid, they'll plug the holes and you won't ever get back in there, either. We have to do this now."

I crossed through a cloud of flies down to the corridor bend. Turning the way the others had come from, we headed farther in to an area where the walls were covered in clean, white paint and the floor carpeted a brilliant red.

"... this time?" a woman's voice shouted from somewhere up ahead. "I'm getting out of here!"

Another voice, a man, responded, "Where is Gohan? Has anyone seen or heard from Gohan?"

The power faltered again, and the lights flickered out. The machine didn't wind down this time, though, in fact if anything the vibrations grew stronger. People gasped in the distance as the floor shook so violently that I nearly stumbled. Metal squealed, followed by a series of booms, and through the window at the opposite end of the corridor I saw something break loose from the building face and fall.

The building's going to shake itself apart.

"Nix, is this it? Are they starting it?"

"No, these vibrations are abnormal," he said. "I believe the power fluctuations are weakening the machine's containment field."

"What happens if it fails?" Vamp asked.

"It could explode," he said. "Or, the gate could open out of control and begin to expand unexpectedly."

Something flickered through an open doorway to my right as emergency lights snapped on. More scaleflies stirred up when the light hit them, launching away to fill the air with buzzing and swarming black bodies. Metal groaned, followed by a low thump that made grit sift down from above.

"Come on," Vamp said. He pointed toward another set of double doors. "Through there."

I triggered the security scanner with Gohan's badge and we slipped through, closing the doors behind us. The large room on the other side was dark except for a single, buzzing light in one corner, and the glow from a bank of monitors on the opposite side. Structure-wise everything looked undamaged, but the tremors had knocked equipment down from a series of workstations and wall-mounted shelves. Computer stations lay on the tiled floor amid shards of broken plastic and glass. From the other side of the room, an electronic display cast a pulsing green glow.

"... breach in specimen containment units A through K," a voice said from outside the door as footsteps passed by.

"It doesn't matter. None of it will matter."

The voices, and the footsteps headed away; then I heard a heavy door bang. Footsteps echoed in a stairwell; then the door slammed behind them.

I crept into the room, trying not to crunch the broken plastic as I tiptoed through the mess and used one hand to wipe the soot away from the computer screen that displayed the green light.

"An A.I.," I said. I waved at the screen. "Hey, are you active?"

The screen flickered.

"Anyone home?"

The A.I.'s logo blinked on, skipping twice as a scalefly crawled across the screen.

"Rapture is ready for activation," the A.I. said. "All personnel should report to the lower floors and await reunification."

"How long?" I asked it. "What's happening out there?"

"A cascading failure of Hangfei's power grid appears to be imminent," it said. "In response to this, the foreign forces offshore have begun arming their missiles. In response to that, the haan defense shield has begun to power up as well."

"Holy shit," Vamp called from the other side of the room. I looked over and saw he'd wandered over to the bank of monitors.

"How was Gohan able to build this place?" I asked the A.I. "Who on the haan side helped him?"

"That information is unknown to me," it responded. "Please present your ID card."

I held up Gohan's card, and it scanned it.

"Guys!" Vamp called.

"My records show your ID has been used multiple times in disparate areas of the building," the A.I. said, a leery tone entering its synthesized voice.

"What?"

"Gohan is here," Nix said. "He has another badge and has used it to get access to the building."

"Please verbally give me your ID number," the A.I. said.

"Hang on." I crossed the room to join Vamp, while Alexei and Nix followed.

"What is it?" I asked, but then I saw the monitors, and I saw what.

They showed different areas of the building. On one of the screens, the camera looked down at a room lined with shelving and sitting in rows on the shelves were big glass specimen jars. Scaleflies crawled around on the inside of the glass of each one. On another screen, two people were pushing a floating platform along between them that had been heaped with big bundles. As they passed by the camera, I thought the bundles might be body bags.

"What the hell?" I muttered. Vamp tapped one of the other screens with his finger.

"Not that," he said. "This."

The monitor looked down into a room full of floor-to-ceiling tanks, rows and rows of them, all filled with fluid, with a mellow light shining down from the top. Floating in each one was a person, stripped naked with their toes a little bit off the ground. There were women, men, girls, boys, old and young.

Some of the tanks were empty except for a haze of bright red that had settled down near the bottom. Floating in one was the empty, wrinkled skin of a man that hung suspended like a deflated balloon. In front of one of the tanks that had been drained, a big plastic waste drum sat, full of clothing, and rubbery skin.

"It's them," I said, staring. "I saw them . . . haan constructs were getting rid of the clothing, down in the sewers under the tower."

"Are those . . . ?" Vamp asked.

"Haanyŏng," I said. "Gohan can see them. He's giving the infected safe haven here, to finish the transformation."

Qian might have been telling the truth, I thought. The haan might have been trying to undo, or at least control, what Sillith had done, while the whole time Gohan had been adding fuel to the fire. He could have been helping them, making sure their numbers grew, in an attempt to push us toward this point of no return. It could be true.

"Excuse me," the A.I. called, "but I'm afraid I have to inform you that if you don't recite your ID I will be forced to alert security."

"Sam, the coast is clear. We've got to get out of here," Vamp said.

"Yeah," I said. "Okay, let's—"

The words stuck in my throat as someone moved in front of one of the other monitors. "Sam, come on."

"Vamp . . ." I said, pointing. He looked, and I could tell right away he recognized her, too. Alexei did as well.

"Petra," he whispered, staring at the screen.

A little girl had stepped into the frame, carrying a pile of wet clothes that she dumped into the waste drum. When she turned and I got a good look at her face, I had no doubt. It was the little girl we'd found in the Pot months back when we'd been tracking down Dragan. He'd left Alexei with a friend, along with another girl he'd managed to free from Sillith's laboratory. A little blond girl . . .

"It's her," I said.

Back in the other room, the A.I.'s logo turned from green to red, and a klaxon sounded somewhere inside the building.

"Damn it." I waved for them to follow and made for the doors opposite those we'd entered. "Come on, we've got to move."

As soon as I stepped through, light stabbed my eyes and the vibrations grew strong enough to set my teeth on edge. For a moment, all I could do was stare.

The doors had opened into a huge, circular space that stretched up several floors before turning to a great dome. A machine filled most of the area, towering up to the peak of the dome and surrounded by shielded haan modules that connected to it via branching pipes and cables. The main tower ended two stories above us where a giant orb floated, its hexagonal plating throwing off reflected light like some kind of high-tech disco ball. Above the orb, a second spire floated. Several other, smaller orbs moved through the air at different intervals around the monstrosity, like tiny planets. Lenses of some kind stared back in toward the central sphere as they made their revolutions.

"Nix, can you tell what it is?" I asked, stepping closer. In front of the machine's base sat what looked like some kind of control console.

Nix stepped toward it, and I could sense his awe. Part of him, the part that consisted of shared memories from his fellow haan, recognized the machine.

He didn't need to tell me. I felt his recognition, his amazement, and his fear. Gohan had done it. He really had done it.

"My people would never allow a human control over such a device," Nix said, his eyes scanning the panel of contacts. "Only a haan can activate it."

"Gohan knows that," I said. "That's why he's creating this situation where—"

"I didn't create this situation," a voice said.

We turned to see Gohan Sòng himself standing just outside the doors. He stared at me, one eye wide, the other drooped as if half asleep.

Next to him stood a lithe haan female dressed only in a long, draping cloak. Her eyes glowed ember red, surrounded by blazing blue coronas.

"Ava?" I asked. She turned to me, and I felt her recognition.

"Hello, Sam."

"Ava, is it true?"

"I'm sorry," she said.

"Thank you for messaging me," Gohan said to Alexei. I turned and saw Alexei nod in his direction.

He'd contacted him. Alexei had contacted Gohan and let him know exactly where we were.

"No problem," Alexei said. Gohan turned his attention back to me.

"As I said, I didn't create this situation. You did."

"I—"

"In your desperate paranoia," he continued. "In your dreadful obsession to leave the haan exposed, to tear from them the one reliable piece of security they have left to them, you have spelled their doom."

"This isn't about the force field," I said. "It's about letting people see the truth."

"Even with the isolated blackouts, many have, by now," she said. "The city is beginning to panic, as we foresaw."

"Give them some time," I told her. "Have some faith."

"Faith?" Gohan spat. He looked amused. I ignored him, talking straight to Ava.

"Give us some credit, Ava. We can get through this thing."

"But the force field will drop," she replied. "And we will be exposed."

"Those yáng guǐzi barbarians waiting offshore are arming their nukes as we speak," Gohan said. "That force field is the only reason they haven't attacked, because they know it would be pointless. The moment they see their opportunity, they'll strike with everything they've got—"

"You don't know what they'll do!" I shouted. "They see what we can't, and they haven't come in yet! Nobody knows what they're thinking or what they'll do! We don't mean you any harm!"

"That would mean more without a gun in your hand," Gohan said.

I looked down at the pistol, having forgotten I even had it.

"Ava, I . . ."

"We will wait," Ava said. "But if we are exposed, and the foreigners attack, we may be left with no choice."

"Ava, you can't do this. . . . Gohan has been messing with your head. Look, look at the monitors, he's been letting Sillith's virus spread, he wants this to happen—"

"I know that, now."

"I did no such thing," Gohan said, raising his voice. Ava raised one delicate hand to silence him.

"The reality is," Ava said, and I felt a sort of empty sadness through the cluster, "that it doesn't matter. Whatever has brought us to this point, we are here, now."

"But he—"

"The Impact was a mistake," she said. "If it can be undone, if I could put right what went wrong, then perhaps it would be for the best."

"But what will happen to us?"

It wasn't until that moment that I noticed Alexei, who had been quiet up to that point, had begun to move away from us, and toward Gohan.

"If it is possible," she said, "if we could undo what we'd done, then our worlds would separate. We could each go back to the way things were."

"The way they were?" I asked. "Your planet is gone, and your accident collapsed our entire universe, there's nothing left for any of us to go back to!"

The sadness I felt from Ava ran deep with guilt, but I also felt her desperation.

"We are all too aware that your people don't want our solution," she said. "That, in order to preserve you in some form, we have to deceive you into it. Once you evolve, you will see the sense of it, but you are terrified to take that step, we know. I wonder if maybe it would be better to let you go."

"Ava, your people are the reason we're in this mess," I said. "You can't just wipe us out."

"I don't know if our people can coexist," she said. "Especially after what Sillith has done, I don't know if we will ever be able to coexist and my people have hung by a thread for so long. I am afraid of what our future holds."

"Have some faith," I told her, but even as I did I knew that what Gohan said might be true. It could be that the foreigners had stayed their hand so far only because they knew attacking with the force field still in place would hurt only the humans of Hangfei, and not the haan themselves. It could be that they, able to see the truth of what Hangfei had become, were so frightened by that prospect that they would try to destroy the haan, given the chance. Hadn't I known that all along?

"Faith," Ava said. "Do you still have faith in us?"

"Some of you, Ava, but you don't make it easy." Alexei had crossed the room by then, and stood halfway between us and Gohan. "Alexei, come away from him."

"Don't listen to her," Gohan said, holding out his hand. "Come here, Alexei."

"Alexei, come back here!" I snapped.

"Give me what I want, and you'll get what you want," Gohan said.

"And what is that, Gohan? Just what the hell is it that you want from me?"

"Tell me how the haan changed you," he said. "Tell me how you convinced them to bestow their blessing on you."

"What?"

"Please, I need to know," he said. "I need to. You don't understand. . . ."

Alexei had begun to walk faster, heading toward Gohan with a new determination, and I saw a flicker of confusion in Gohan's eyes at whatever he read on Alexei's face.

"Alexei!" I called.

He threw his gonzo robe off, and too late, I saw the remaining two explosive bricks strapped tightly around his scrawny waist. Gohan saw them, too, and the color drained from his face.

"Race traitor!" Alexei screamed, holding out a detonator in one small hand.

I stared, unable to process what I was seeing. I'd worried

he'd gone back to Dao-Ming's apartment to get them, but thought they were in his pack. I'd been wrong. Gohan put it together that he had not been using Alexei all this time, but that if anything, Alexei had been using him. Whatever he saw in the boy's eyes, it caused him to lose that detached calm of his.

"Alexei," he stammered, putting his hands up in front of him. "Calm down. Just . . . calm down for a moment and—"

"Those things killed my mother!" His voice cracked, and I saw tears had begun to stream down his face. "You let my people starve to feed them and they killed my mother! They took everything from us! Everything!"

His Mandarin had turned almost flawless. He'd thought about what he'd say if this moment ever came. He'd practiced it.

"Alexei!" I started toward him, when he spun around with one thumb on the detonator's trigger.

"Stay away!"

"Alexei, please," I said, stopping. I held out my hands to him. "Please don't do this."

"Sam, go away from here."

"No. Just . . . stop a minute, listen to me."

I stepped closer, the gun in my hand forgotten until Alexei waved his free hand at it.

"You gonna shoot me?"

"No," I said. I held up the pistol, aiming it away to try to calm him.

"Please, you can't . . ."

"Why not?" he asked. "Why shouldn't I?"

"I don't want you to."

His eyes welled with tears, but he didn't put down the detonator.

"Sam, go."

Alexei, I don't want you to go, please don't do this, please.

"Sam . . ."

Think of what this will do to Dragan, I tried. *He'll be devastated.*

"Go!"

"No," I said. *I won't leave you. I won't let you do this, Think about what you're doing. Think about me, and Dragan, and—*

How many of my people do you think Dragan has killed? he asked.

I saw then that whatever it was that had twisted inside of Alexei, it ran far deeper than I ever knew. He'd seemed like a normal kid, all things considered, but now I wondered if I even knew what normal was. While he'd gone to school, and talked about his day, watched cartoons, and even played and joked with me, something that had taken seed inside him had continued to grow without my ever seeing it. Real fear began to take hold as the realization set in that whatever was wrong with him had taken years to get him to this point, and I wouldn't undo it in a matter of minutes, or seconds.

"We die over there," Alexei said. "We die all the time, you know? I got no one left."

"You have me."

He shook his head, and one of the tears rolled down his cheek.

It's not enough.

"Please."

I don't want to be here. I have no one left at home, nothing left.

"This is your home."

He just shook his head and sighed, like a little old man. "I don't want to be here."

"Please," I tried again. It was all I could think to do, just plead. Tears ran freely down my cheeks, making my voice crack as I held my hands out to him, and took another step. "Please, I know Dao-Ming wanted you to—"

I wanted to, he said. *I need to do this.*

He turned back toward Gohan, and raised the detonator up over his head.

Vamp grabbed me from behind, trying to pull me away, to shield me maybe, but I wrestled free. Alexei held the detonator in one trembling hand, gathering the nerve to trigger it, and I knew that my time had run out.

I raised my pistol to Gohan's head, and pulled the trigger.

The sound of the gunshot startled Alexei, disorienting him as the bullet made a ragged hole in Gohan's cheek just under his lazy eye. An explosive spray of blood painted the wall behind him, and he stumbled back. His legs dropped out from under him, and he collapsed on the floor in a heap, a dark pool expanding around his head.

Alexei just stared, the detonator still in his hand. He looked like he didn't know what to do. He'd been ready to die, and now he didn't know what to do.

He moved his thumb back to the detonator, but before he could do anything else I rushed to him. I knelt, spinning him around, and hugged him to me. I squeezed, feeling the brick sandwiched between us, and buried my face against his neck.

"You have to let go," he said.

"No."

He put his arms around my neck, and I felt the detonator, still in his hand, against the back of my neck.

"Let go," he said.

"No."

I could hear Vamp calling to me, telling me to get away from Alexei, to leave him. I just held him, terrified. Terrified he'd trigger the detonator anyway, but equally terrified to let go. Over Alexei's shoulder I saw Ava, still standing there. She watched us, curious, and I felt a twinge through the cluster . . . I couldn't quite place what it meant. Sadness, maybe? Then the air warped around her, and she vanished with the explosive bang of air rushing in to fill empty space.

Alexei jumped at the sound, but a moment later I felt him sag, just a little, in my arms. I reached back behind my head. I put my hand around his, around the detonator, and when I took it gently from his hand, he let me.

Only then did I let him go. I rocked back on my heels, and he didn't resist as I removed the bomb harness from him. I opened my Escher tablet, and fed it through. The gate remote had been returned by either Dao-Ming or Shuang, and I took it, slipping it into my pocket. I closed the field and kissed Alexei on one cheek.

"It's okay," I told him. He looked down to Gohan's body, and I steered his gaze away. "It's okay. He's gone."

"He's gone," Alexei said.

"Yeah."

"You shot him."

I looked back at the body, and already Gohan's face had drained of color except for the bright red speckles where he'd landed. One eye stared down into the pool of blood that just seemed to keep getting bigger. I swallowed, and looked away.

"Come on," I told him. "Let's go find Dragan."

Chapter Twenty-Nine

"*. . . an attempt to destroy Rapture. Security teams report to the Rapture containment facility immediately. . . .*"

"Sam," Vamp said in my ear. "We have to go."

Alexei still looked a little shell-shocked, but when I took his hand and led him away, he followed.

"*I repeat: Gohan Sòng is presumed to have been injured or killed during an attempt . . .*"

"This place is being monitored," Nix said. "They're coming."

I stepped past Gohan's body, my legs weak and the room feeling like it had begun to spin around me. Some of the little planets revolving around the spire had begun to wobble. When I looked up at the towering machine, I saw that the ones near the peak had begun to move faster. The vibrations in the air had become more intense.

Groups of heavy footsteps echoed through the halls nearby, and I heard shouting as the guards began to close in. I let Nix lead me to the elevator, and I got in with them. When the doors closed, Vamp pushed the button for the ninetieth floor. As the car started up, and we began to pass the floors, I could hear shouting as news of what had happened spread.

Some were full of rage, some disbelief, while still others wailed in anguish. I rode the elevator, Alexei next to me, and tuned it all out until the car stopped and the doors opened.

The lobby led out onto a wide corridor where signs pointed to the aircar port. A big archway led into the terminal, where chairs and sofas had been arranged for people who were waiting to meet with arrivals. Most of the seats were unoccupied at the moment, but handfuls of men and women in white robes sat, some holding hands and some praying, with their eyes glued to the LCD screens. A Xinzhongzi security officer spoke, while displaying footage of the unconscious guard in the lobby as well as the moments leading up to the bombing, taken from cameras inside the room that housed Rapture.

"... if you see any of these people, stop them immediately and call security to ..."

My face appeared on the screen, then Vamp's, Alexei's, and finally Nix's. None of the people in the room even looked our way, though. They were too engrossed in the report to even notice as we headed straight toward the huge sliding glass doors at the terminal's far end.

The doors glided open, and a gust of wind blew over me as we stepped out onto the aircar port. Rows of matching, shiny white vehicles were parked there, stretching out toward the far edge, which accessed the skylanes. There, the port looked out into the open air above Hangfei, which sprawled into the distance. The civilian gonzos might not have been expecting us, but their security goons were. Several armed men in suits had taken up positions ahead, blocking any access to the skyway. The second they spotted us, they raised their weapons.

They never even tried to give a warning. Bullets thudded into the glass behind us as they began firing, and screams of surprise came from inside the terminal. One of the bullets grazed my cheek, tracing a hot line back toward my ear as I grabbed Alexei and pulled him down behind one of the vehicles with me. Vamp hit the deck right beside us as bullets thumped into the opposite side of the car, and the windows shattered, raining bits of safety glass down over us.

Nix took cover behind a truck in the row opposite us, his back to it as the hail of gunfire continued.

"We'll never make it," Vamp said. "We've got to turn back."

"We can't."

A bullet smashed into one of the vehicle's graviton emitters, knocking loose the fiberglass covering and sending it spinning across the concrete. I risked a peek around the back bumper and saw that the men had begun an advance toward us. I fired a couple of rounds blind to give them something to think about, but it didn't stop them. Two were moving to flank Nix's vehicle, two moved in the opposite direction to flank us, and the last two moved straight down in the middle to catch us once they flushed us out.

"The bomb," Vamp said. "Get it back out and tell them you'll set it off."

"I killed Gohan, Vamp. I don't think they'll care."

Dragan, I sent over the chat. *How much longer?*

We're beginning our approach, hang on.

"It's worth a shot!" Vamp said, as another volley of shooting started.

"Dragan's on his way," I yelled. "We just have to hold out a little while longer."

The sliding doors, now pocked with divots from the gunfire, slid open as three more men, all carrying guns, piled out. The one in the lead pointed toward us, and they all took aim.

Nix lunged toward them, and the air rippled in the space between. A ghost image of his hand flickered across the lot and I saw it clamp down on one of the men's arms almost twenty yards away. He screamed as it came apart at the elbow, the forearm and hand, which still held his pistol, flipping end over end before flopping down onto the ground.

The other two turned toward him as he stared at the stump in shock, but before either could react one of them jerked back off his feet and flew into the air.

He sailed backward over our heads, arms and legs peddling as he went over the lot's edge and into open air. His scream followed him down, fading as he dropped out of sight.

The last guy took aim and opened fired on Nix, who whipped his suit around like a cape to cover himself. Several slugs flattened against it and fell to the ground but some got through. Blood spattered against the pristine white of the vehicle behind him and he staggered back.

"Nix!" I called. I started to move toward him when Vamp grabbed my arm and stopped me. "Nix, run!"

Instead he leapt high into the air, arcing up over the rows of vehicles and then down onto the man by the stairwell. He crashed down on top of him, and the man crumpled. I saw his head hit the pavement, Nix's hand gripping his face as he forced it down. The man's skull splashed apart in an explosion of gristle, and Alexei screamed, cowering against me.

Several more shots struck Nix in the back as I turned away from the sight, bile rising in my throat. The other men had begun to close in.

"The terminal's clear," Vamp said, pulling me and Alexei along. "Come on, we need to take cover or we'll be dead before he ever gets here!"

Back behind the men, a vehicle peeled off from the sky-lane and accelerated toward the lot. As it did, blue and red lights began to flash from its underbelly and a siren whooped.

The remaining men turned and saw the approaching air-car. The two who'd been trying to flank Vamp and me ahead to the right both seemed to decide that if they were going to kill us, they'd better do it quick. They moved in to get a clear shot as we scrambled back to get around the other side of the car.

Before they could reach us, heavy gunfire filled the air from above as streams of shells began to fall, bouncing off the parked vehicles and pavement like hailstones. Several cars ahead of us were shredded, exploding in showers of metal and glass. The two men were thrown down out of sight in a cloud of red mist as the siren whooped three more times.

Blues and reds flashed off the pavement as the vehicle descended, then came down with a heavy thud. The doors sprang open and Dragan, along with two men I didn't recognize, jumped out with their guns ready.

"Drop it!" Dragan shouted at one of the two remaining pairs of men. When they didn't do what he said right away, he fired once and caught one of them right in the eye. His head pitched back and he fell onto the ground, dead. His partner dropped his gun and threw his hands up over his head.

The last two decided they'd done their duty and legged it back to the terminal entrance. Nobody tried to stop them as they ducked back through the doors.

"Sam," Dragan said, lowering his weapon. One of the other guys who'd come over with him went and zip tied the remaining goon's wrists behind his back.

I hugged him, my face in his chest, and Alexei ran over, too. Dragan scooped him up, holding him in one arm so that they were face-to-face.

Alexei said something in Pan-Slav, and Dragan just nodded.

"We'll worry about it later," he said. "I'm just glad you're okay. Okay?"

Alexei nodded, and Dragan turned to the rest of us.

"We have to go," he said. "Everyone, into the car, now!"

We piled into the transport, one officer staying up front with the pilot while the other two got in back with the rest of us. When the last officer got in, he slammed the door and called up front.

"Okay, let's go."

My stomach dropped as we leapt up off the tarmac, then spun around toward the skylane entry point. Through the window, I saw the rows of cars go whipping past as we picked up speed. Then the ground fell away and I stared a hundred stories down toward the streets of Xinzhongzi below. The tower began to fall away behind us, and as I turned back, I saw that the glass panels on its face had begun to shake.

"I'm getting some strange readings up here," the pilot said.

"What kind of readings?" Dragan asked.

"I don't know. Some kind of energy surge is messing with the nav systems. Hold on."

The tower's glass cracked, and I saw huge sheets of it break away, cracking apart as they began to fall down toward the streets.

"Rapture," I said. "The gate is opening."

I realized then that we weren't going to get a second chance. Whether the blackout happened or not, whether the foreigners attacked or not, the gate field would open and not even Ava could stop it any longer.

"Sam," Alexei said. "What's happening?"

Outside, the air around the tower began to ripple. A deep, electric crackle rose over the sound of the ship's engines, growing louder by the second.

I got out of my seat and moved toward the back window, scanning the skyline as though it may somehow offer up a solution. The bustle of Hangfei seemed as frantic as the thoughts sparking through my brain . . . flashing lights, streams of people, ground cars, and air traffic all flowing through a cityscape that sprawled as far as the eye could see in every direction. All those people, millions of people, unaware of what might be coming at any moment.

Will this be it? I thought, my heart hammering in my chest. *Will this be the last time I see Hangfei?*

I'd just wanted to hold the haan accountable. I'd just

wanted to show everyone the truth. In doing so, I'd played right into Gohan's hands and let him doom us all. The whole thing had been my idea. In mere minutes, or even seconds, I would be the woman who destroyed Hangfei, if not the world.

My eyes drifted over the city, toward the flats that led to the shore near Ocean Heights. I wanted to tell the pilot to fly away, to make a break for that blue horizon and the wall of foreign ships that waited there, but if a Second Impact really occurred, it wouldn't matter. It wouldn't matter where we went. The only safe place would be the tower itself, if even that.

I could think of only one thing left to do. I took the gate remote from my pocket, and dialed up the endpoint I'd placed in the sewers underneath Xinzhongzi. I aimed it at the deck of the transport, and opened a gate, small at first, just enough to see through. I eased it open a little wider, until a hole formed in the back of the vehicle, looking down toward the far-off ceiling of the power station on the other side. I saw cascades of flashing lights across banks of equipment, and monitors. I saw workstations, connected with miles of cable, and people. Men and women wearing white jackets, and hard hats. Before I could change my mind I retrieved the bomb, Alexei's bomb, from inside my Escher tablet.

A woman inside the substation noticed the gate, then. She started toward it to look through, and I threw the harness. I saw it go through, and then begin to fall back toward the gate as it adjusted to the gravity on the other side. The woman watched as two bricks of explosives jumped up from out of the floor in front of her, and her eyes went wide.

I closed the gate.

"Look out!" someone screamed.

Through the windshield, I saw a bright shell of light burst out from the Xinzhongzi tower, then stop, having encompassed the entire campus. A second shell expanded away from the first and as it bloomed, the buildings in its path flickered as if threatening to vanish. They phased out of existence, and for a brief moment, something else, a completely different landscape appeared in their place. Buildings, yes, but not of human construction. They were larger, and towered higher than anything we had ever conceived. I recognized them from the memories Sillith had shared with me just before her death. Not quite the same, but similar.

They're going to do it, I thought, staring. *They're really going to do it. . . .*

Time had run out. The expanding balloon of light had consumed all of Xinzhongzi, it looked like. The strange buildings solidified, becoming real, and I saw something begin to emerge from one of them. Something big, that wasn't like any haan I'd ever seen.

I put my thumb on the detonator, and squeezed.

The boom rose even above the racket outside, and through the side window, I saw what must have been the substation explode outward from one side. A ball of fire and smoke blasted through the roof of the structure, throwing up a huge plume of concrete, metal, and glass as the entire colony blacked out.

In the newfound darkness, an angry glow crackled from inside the cathedral tower. The light grew brighter until, shaken past its limits, the building began to collapse in on itself, crumbling down onto the campus around it as the twin bubbles of light winked out of existence. As they did, the haan oasis vanished. The colony phased back, but as it did, the buildings all went dark. The lights flickered out, and the buildings themselves grew black, and pitted as if decaying in front of me. Then, all at once, with a boom that shook the transport, the buildings were vaporized altogether.

Blocks and blocks of the colony exploded into rubble,

falling down into a growing black cloud that began to swirl like the storm at the Impact rim.

Was I too late? I wondered.

Before I could do more than wonder, the cloud rushed up and consumed us, raining ash over the transport and blotting out the light.

Chapter Thirty

In near darkness, something began to hum.

"Shen, get us out of this," Dragan called to the pilot.

"I'm trying, goddamn it."

The aircar engine sputtered, while outside the wind howled and what sounded like rain drummed against the hull.

"Sam?" Vamp said in a low voice. He groped and found my hand as Alexei shivered against me.

"I'm here."

"What happened?" one of Dragan's team asked. "What the hell just happened?" By the light of the dash I could make out the name patch on his shirt—Fong. The second man, Kao, shook his head as he stared out the window.

"I don't know," he said, sounding confused. "Somebody give me a status."

"The air filters are gummed up," a voice called back from the cabin. "The emitters are going into the red, and something fried the GPS."

"Can you tell where we are?" Dragan asked.

The pilot fiddled with the controls, frowning as the dash lights flickered.

"It's a mess out there," he muttered. "I can't see anything. If the nav logs are right, we should be a half kilometer inside the Xinzhongzi border, near the western gate."

"Can you keep us in the air?"

"Not for long. I'm taking a straight shot west, away from the tower."

"It's the Impact," Kao said under his breath. "It's the Impact all over again. . . ."

"Are we going to fall?" Alexei asked.

"We'll be okay," I told him.

Grit sprayed against the windshield, and I could see that in spite of him pulling up as hard as he could we weren't rising much. Not enough to get out of the dust storm.

"Can you find a landing spot?" Shen called.

"I can't see anything, I need to get us higher."

"Watch your altitude," Dragan snapped. "If the emitters fail we'll drop like a stone."

The pilot didn't listen, though. He kept taking us up as fast as he could manage until the smoke sifted away from the windshield, and for just a moment the headlights shined over the surface of the storm. Not long, but long enough.

The bright lights of Hangfei in the distance peeked through the swirling gray. At least part of the city still had power, and it wasn't that far. We could still escape.

An alarm sounded, and the dash lit up red. The vehicle bucked, then dropped back down into the cloud and lurched to a stop. A chemical smoke smell began to fill the cabin, as Dragan pushed Kang out of the way and shouted into the cockpit.

"The emitters are failing," he snapped. "Get us on the ground. Xinzhongzi has an airpad near the western gate, take us down there."

"I can't see—"

"Do your best; it's better than free fall!"

The pilot cursed under his breath but he started taking us down. The alarm continued to blare as the cabin grew warm; then the vehicle began to shudder. Through the windows, all I could see were the vehicle's own lights glowing feebly through the swirling smoke and ash.

Vamp crowded next to the window so that our cheeks were almost touching and I could see his reflection in it. I saw the dread in his eyes as his breath fogged the glass.

"Shit!" the pilot yelled from the cockpit.

"What's the matter?" I heard Li ask. "Can you get us down or not?"

"It's not that."

"Then what?"

"There's a problem with the navigation system. I'm at the airpad now—"

"Then take us down, what's the—"

"I can't, it's gone."

"What?"

"The airpad isn't there. Nothing is there."

The pilot was hunched over the controls, looking at the display while through the windshield I could make out an expanse of churning black and gray below us.

"What do you mean, it's not there?" Dragan called.

"The destination coordinates put us directly over it," the pilot said. "I'm telling you it's not there. We're going down, I'm looking for—"

The vehicle bucked again, and I felt it drop out from under us.

"Shit!"

"Can you make it to the wall?" Dragan yelled.

Through the window I saw the broken remains of smashed buildings jutting up out of the haze of black ash. Currents of gray smoke carrying black, burned flakes shrieked through the jagged edges of concrete, steel, and broken glass. What might have been the airpad had been reduced to an expanse of buckled and broken tarmac leading up to the squat remains of a terminal.

The scene through the windshield tilted to the left. A little at first, then everyone braced themselves as the angle turned steep.

"The left emitters are out," the pilot said.

"Kill the others, before we roll," Dragan said, squeezing between Vamp and me to approach the pilot.

"We'll go down."

"We're going down anyway, better on our belly than our back! Do it!"

Something under the deck sizzled, and sparks shot off in a trail behind us but the ship stopped tilting and the pilot managed to get it back under control. He evened it out, until the horizon formed a straight line again, but we were falling lower and lower toward the dust cloud below.

"This isn't good," the pilot muttered.

"Just keep us steady."

Ash and debris began to pepper the undercarriage as we sank, and I turned away from the cockpit, not wanting to watch.

"Brace for impact!" the pilot shouted.

We scrambled to the back and sat down as the ship fell. I planted both feet on the deck and pressed my back into the wall behind me. Dragan grabbed Alexei, and held him tight as the ship began to shake.

"Hold on!"

The hiss of ash against the hull turned louder the farther down we dropped, and underneath it all I heard machinery drum to life as the chemical smell filled the air again. The pilot was charging the remaining emitters for one last go.

The ship slowed, then stopped with a crash as the graviton spool blew its charge all at once. A loud bang sounded, followed by the squeal of metal as the housing, partially melted, gave way under the force. Part of the undercarriage tore free, and a fracture popped open across the deck in front of my feet. Black smoke began to billow into the cabin.

My stomach dropped as the vehicle lost the last of its power and fell to the ruined street below.

Chapter Thirty-One

The ship came down hard, sparks popping up through the crack in the deck as we skidded across a patch of warped pavement. The vehicle slowed, then hit something that jarred it to a stop. The back end came up off the ground like the whole thing might flip, then crashed back down.

A flashlight beam lit up the darkness, and I saw Dragan's face behind it. He swept it through the cab, checking on the rest of us.

"Cover your mouths!" he yelled over the sound of the storm. He moved to the back and pulled a metal crate out from under one of the rear seats, which he unlatched and pulled open. He took a gas mask from inside and fitted it over his face before tossing one to me. He put another on Alexei as I strapped it on, sealing the breather over my mouth and nose, then adjusting the goggles as Dragan distributed the rest to the others.

"Masks on, people!" he called. Li pulled his down over his face, then stood in the cockpit doorway, facing us. "Come on!"

"Where are we?" someone shouted, his voice muffled by the breather. "How far to the wall?"

"This makes no sense," the pilot said, staring at the console. "The facility is there, it's . . . there, right where it's supposed to be, but—"

"Get your mask on," Shen told him. "Now! We can worry about the rest once we get out of this shitstorm!"

I felt them through the surrogate cluster, just seconds before they came. Overlapping waves of pain, and hunger, and fear so intense that I stumbled, and fell to my knees.

"Sam, what's wrong?" Dragan asked, kneeling next to me.

"There are haan out there," I said.

"Haan?"

Haan, yes. A lot of them. I couldn't tell how many there were, but more than I could keep track of.

"Gohan had started to move them in . . . some of them are still alive, but . . ."

They weren't the haan I knew. How they'd survived what happened I had no idea, but they'd been so ravaged by it that their thoughts felt almost animalistic. They were in great pain, blind, and . . . hungry. Their hunger had turned so intense that it controlled them.

"Their bodies are attempting to regenerate," Nix said. "It is causing a massive calorie deficit. They need to eat or they will die, very soon. We are in very serious danger."

Something hit the side of the ship hard enough to move it. I felt it come up off the ground for a second and stumble as it slammed back down.

"What in the—"

The windshield shattered, thick shards of safety glass exploding into the cockpit on a wave of gray and black dust. Before it enveloped the pilot, I saw something lash through and hit him in the chest with a bone-rattling thud. The air in his lungs was forced out on a grunt of pain and I caught a glimpse of something, blood slick bone and guts, wrenched from out of his torso before the cloud flooded through to cover him.

Kao turned and raised his rifle, aiming into the cloud and firing as the struggle continued somewhere in the smoke. The copilot emerged from the smoke, his uniform spattered with blood as he pushed past Shen and into the cabin with us.

"What was that?" Vamp gasped. "What's happening?"

He looked around, rubbing his eyes as the lights flickered back on inside the cabin. They were dim, running on dying battery power, but better than nothing.

"Get the force field on," Dragan yelled through his mask speaker.

Shen headed toward the cockpit when something grabbed his leg and jerked it out from under him. He landed on his back with a crash; then something yanked him away, out into the smoke.

"Shit!"

My goggles were fogging over and even with the mask my nose and throat had begun to burn. Through the haze I saw Nix look around, assessing the situation. He took a step toward the copilot who pushed at the door to the cockpit, trying to close it when something slithered through the gap.

The black tentacle coiled around the copilot's arm from wrist to shoulder. He came up off his feet as it tried to pull him through, and he slammed face-first into the door. His weight forced it to slam shut on his own arm.

Before he could even scream, the arm came off with a series of meaty snaps. He stumbled back away from the door, the stump squirting blood. I turned away as he fell onto the deck, gasping and choking. Nix stepped over his body and slipped through the door, into the cloud of smoke that had filled the cockpit.

"Nix!" I called as he slammed the door behind him. "Nix!"

Dragan pushed past me and ran to the fallen man to try to staunch the bleeding, but he was too late. The pilot sagged, and then his legs, which had been shivering, stopped.

Something crashed on the other side of the cockpit door, and then I heard the low hum of a force field warming up. A second thud went through the floor, and I heard the rush of air begin over the moan of wind outside.

The vents. Nix is venting the cabin.

"What's going on out there?" I called back. "Can anyone see?"

Alexei tugged my shirt, and pointed as the rear door hinges of the transport groaned, and then snapped. The door tore loose, and then huffed away into the mist with one corner sending orange sparks across the pavement.

Dragan aimed his pistol toward the opening as a shape appeared from out of the smoke. A long tentacle came slithering through the open back of the vehicle and I could see more of them squirming in the fog somewhere behind it. It pawed at the floor and the walls, the tip moving purposefully like a sniffing nose as it passed between me and Vamp.

Dragan angled his weapon down at the part closest to him, when I grabbed the barrel. He stopped, looking up at me, and I shook my head.

It couldn't see us, at least not well. The haan knew we were inside, but not exactly where. Bullets weren't going to stop it, I thought. They'd only tell it right where Dragan stood. I waited, frozen, holding out my hands for him to stay still.

The tentacle squirmed across the floor like a huge band of living cable. The tip found the body on the floor, and coiled around one leg before snatching it out of the vehicle.

The cockpit door opened, and Nix stepped back through. The deck behind him was a mess of shattered glass, wet soot, and human remains but the empty windshield now shimmered with the faint blue of an active force field.

"The battery won't be able to power the field long," Nix said. "We need to get out of here and into shelter, now."

"The terminal," Dragan said. "It has to be close. They'll have shuttles in the lot. They might still work."

Something hit the side of the ship again. The floor lurched underneath us as we tilted up onto one side, then crashed back down again.

"Sam, Vamp," Dragan said. "Let's go, now!"

I stared into the cockpit. The battery was failing fast, but the console still glowed weakly, casting flickering shadows through the cabin. It was horrible. The pilot lay tipped over in his chair, his body slumped against the wall next to him. His eyes still stared in shock but his blood-spattered face was lifeless and pale. His shredded shirt had soaked through with blood and there was only a hollow pit where his chest had been. The copilot had fared even worse. His legs were still strapped in, but ended in nothing but ragged stumps. The rest of him had gone out the windshield. The walls and control deck of the ship still dripped, sloppy bits scattered across the dash.

Tentacles pressed against the force field, probing for any opening that might give access to the remains still inside.

"Sam, now!" Dragan shouted, his voice muffled through the mask.

He shook me, and I turned as Kao stepped out the back of the transport, sweeping an assault rifle back and forth as he went.

Dragan herded me and Alexei toward the storm, and we went. We ran from the ship, and out into the ruins.

I'd been to the Impact rim once before, and even though that time I'd landed in a special lot and gone straight into a base that had been set up there, I recognized it. Whatever the haan machine had done, the result was very similar to the original Impact. The wind howled through the ruins and the air was cold, despite the baking heat of Hangfei. In seconds, a fine gray powder covered my respirator's goggles. I wiped at them, trying to get oriented. Dragan had Alexei, and Vamp stood a few paces away. I couldn't see anyone else. We were near the middle of what was once a landing tarmac for aircars. The blacktop had warped, and been run through with fine cracks that left it in a slowly shifting mosaic. Up ahead I could make out the broken terminal, powder and smoke whistling between huge twisted girders and gaps in the brick and concrete. "I see the entrance!" Dragan shouted. "Follow me! Stay close!"

A low hiss filled my chest, and I turned around to see a shadow move down the tarmac, swirling the smoke in its wake. I saw the shape of a crumpled aircar move, and heard the heavy metallic scrape as its undercarriage was dragged across the broken pavement.

"This way!" Dragan called, pointing back toward the terminal. "Come on!"

Something struck Kao and he collapsed in a spray of blood. I heard two shots go off; then a leg rolled to a stop against a bent streetlight pole.

Dragan fired back behind us as Vamp and Nix both backed away from the shape, then began to run in the direction he'd pointed. I followed, all I could do to not lose sight of the dim terminal outline as I ran. As I panted behind the mask I saw the shattered entryway appear from out of the haze. I fumbled the gate remote from my pocket, ready to set an endpoint directly inside.

Then something grabbed my ankle and I pitched forward onto my palms, the remote tumbling away to be swallowed by the fog. The shape of the terminal and the glowing points of Nix's eyes fell away in front of me as the haan dragged me back across the broken pavement. I gagged as a mouthful of dust snuck under the mask's seal, and wiped furiously at the goggles as Dragan started shooting.

The haan constricted hard around my ankle until I thought my foot would snap clean off. It flipped me over and dragged me along on my butt as I reached for anything I could grab on to.

I pointed my pistol toward it and pulled the trigger, almost shooting my own foot off in the process as it sprayed a burst of rounds. Shells bounced off my respirator as bullets tracked across the thing's skin but it didn't slow it down at all.

The gun got hot in my hand, spraying bullets until it

clicked and the last shell flicked off into the gloom. The thing dragged me over a pothole and jarred me so hard the gun flipped out of my hand.

"Dragan!" I called.

A large shape emerged from the smoke as it reeled me in, and I saw a tangle of tar black strands, pocked with deep pores. Clusters of onyx marble eyes stared down at me as other arms grabbed me and lifted me off the ground.

An overwhelming sense of fear, not anger, filled my brain along with a desperate, crippling hunger. The haan didn't know where he was, that much I could sense. His blind panic threatened to send my own senses tipping over the edge as he pulled me in close, and I knew then that he intended to eat me.

Wriggling worms found me, squirming over my face, neck, and shoulders as the haan drew me in. I forced myself to focus, to focus all of my concentration on the mite cluster, and let some kind of message float through.

Don't . . .

The haan hesitated, but not for long before it began to squeeze. I felt the life being crushed out of me, and panic took over. I tried to scream but couldn't draw a breath. *We are like you,* I thought. *We think, and feel.*

At that last thought, the pressure building up around me stopped. I sensed hesitation through the cluster, and then loosening of pressure as the link grew stronger.

The surrogate cluster wasn't a direct form of communication, so I couldn't talk to the haan, but it acted as a sort of emotional conduit that had a language of its own. The haan on the other end remembered that language, that raw connection, from his time as a surrogate. In spite of the fear and hunger that he felt, I sensed him pull back from the brink. The bands around my chest let go, and I sucked in a breath as my feet touched down on the pavement again.

Something flashed past me on my left, and I felt the fab-

ric of Nix's suit slap against my shoulder. As the last strand
uncoiled from my arm, he scooped me up and whipped me
around.

Then Nix was running, moving as fast as an aircar until
the sound of gunfire rose up out of the racket, growing
louder as we rushed forward. Vamp had crouched on the
sidewalk, firing back down the street behind us. Ahead, I
saw the shadow of the terminal loom out of the smoke.

Nix skidded to a stop, throwing up clouds of dust, and let
me down next to Vamp.

"Go," he said, "Hurry."

Dragan fired off a few more rounds, keeping Alexei behind him as something big came rushing forward out of the
storm. It flashed along the broken street, and I caught a
glimpse of rows of haan arms scurrying it forward like the
legs of an insect. It reared up until it towered over us, and I
grabbed Dragan's arm, pulling him after me.

We ran for the terminal entrance. As we approached,
what looked like a guard station emerged out of the haze.
At the entrance, a strong gust of wind threatened to knock
me over, the cold biting into the exposed skin of my arms
and shoulders. I braced against it, skirting around the empty
hull of an aircar that lay on its back like a dead scalefly.
Then I raced through the open doorway on the other side.

It wasn't warm inside, but it felt a lot better being out of
the wind. I beat at my clothes, creating plumes of fine dust,
then bent over and shook out my hair.

Dragan moved his flashlight through the dark waiting
area, searching along the walls.

"There," he said. He shined the beam on a sign for the
shuttle lot, whose arrow pointed down a dark corridor.

Broken glass crunched from back behind us as something entered the terminal. Chairs toppled as something
heavy began to move in our direction.

"It's inside," I said. "Hurry."

Another sign guided us right at the corridor's end and

we followed it as more footsteps began to creep closer behind us. As we reached the top of a stairwell, it sounded like whatever had followed us was right on top of us.

"Where is the lot?" Nix asked.

"Should be just below us," Dragan said. He began to head down the stairs, into the darkness when Nix stopped, and stepped back into the corridor.

"Nix, what are you doing? Come on," Vamp urged.

Nix removed something from his jacket and pointed it at the floor. A white point of light appeared, and grew brighter until it cast frantic shadows down the hallway where dark shadows approached.

Dragan joined Nix, and aimed his gun down the corridor while the point of light expanded into a large hexagon that spanned the entire width of the hall.

"I don't have an endpoint in Hangfei," Nix said. "But this will take us to the lot below. Jump."

Eyes glinted in the gloom as the things crawled toward us, and I jumped into the portal.

After the moment of limbo, I fell through the air to land on a cold concrete floor. Vamp landed next to me, then Nix, then Dragan with Alexei. I looked up in time to see the gate closing, a cluster of black, marble eyes staring down through the shrinking hole until it vanished. Above us, something crashed.

"They will make their way down here soon enough," Nix said. "We must leave, now."

We ran through the underground lot, looking for a vehicle. A row of them had been parked at the far end, and having been shielded from the devastation above, they seemed to have fared pretty well.

"Here," Dragan said. He'd picked a heavy truck, a road vehicle, and used his security override to unlock the doors. We piled in, and he started the ignition as a jumble of footsteps began to echo from deeper inside the lot.

"There!" Alexei shouted, pointing out the back window.

"They're here, go!" I said.

Dragan slammed it into reverse and screeched out of the parking spot. The headlights flashed past something big as it headed toward us, and he slipped it back into drive.

"Hold on," he said, and stomped on the gas.

Chapter Thirty-Two

Something lashed against the rear of the truck and the vehicle bucked hard, jumping into the air as something stopped us. The rear bumper popped free, and I saw a black tentacle wrapped around it as we hit the ground with the tires still spinning. Rubber burned as the vehicle fishtailed, and then began to accelerate.

Dragan took us around the corner hard, brushing a row of parked cars and sending sparks flying as he picked up speed. The sounds behind us faded, until only the sound of the engine remained.

"We lost them," Vamp said, looking back through the rear window.

Dragan didn't slow down. He screeched around the next corner and headed up the ramp there. Ahead, I could see an empty guard station. A restraining bar jutted out from it, blocking the exit that looked out into a wall of raging gray smoke.

"Hang on," Dragan said.

He barreled straight into the rail, which broke loose and crashed onto the concrete in front of us. I felt it go under the tires, and then we launched out of the gate and back into the storm.

I reached over and brought up the GPS. The screen flickered, but it came on and it looked like it still worked. Sand showered the windshield like gray snow, and Dragan flipped on the wipers to keep it from accumulating too much. The headlights could make it only about a car's length, but I could make out a patch of street there. The broken line of the divider drifted between the beams.

"Try and turn left," I told him. "The western gate is left."

"How far?" he asked.

"Not far, if you—"

Dragan cut the wheel, causing the truck to lurch to the right as something big, a wrecked car I thought, huffed by. He found the road again and regained control, staring forward over the wheel with his knuckles white.

An intersection appeared out of the smoke and Dragan veered left, the broken pavement rumbling under the truck's big tires. Something glowed through the storm up ahead and I realized they were the lights of Hangfei, towering up over the security wall. As I watched, a portion of them flickered and went out.

"I can see the gate," Dragan said. The smoke seemed to be thinning. Ahead, an archway had appeared, spanned by a chain-link gate. On the other side, neon and electric light blazed.

The last of the cloud disappeared, and the uneven pavement turned smooth again as Dragan aimed for the gate, and picked up speed. In the distance, the city lights flickered.

"The power's going," Vamp shouted, pointing. "The failure's started."

A few blocks went dark as the truck's grille struck the gate and it crashed open.

Dragan stomped on the brake as people from the scattering protest appeared in the headlights in front of us. He leaned on the horn, revving the engine and then easing the heavy vehicle forward. The people scattered, some shouting and thumping on the side of the truck as he inched through the crowd. When he reached the end of the square he stopped at the side of the strip and killed the engine.

The doors popped open. As soon as they did I heard an

electric crackle rise up over the crowd noise. We all piled out, struggling to hold our ground as the mob surged past. People had come out of shops and clubs to try to see what was happening, spilling out onto the sidewalks and into the streets.

The crackle rose in pitch, and then ended in a single distant boom. The crowd turned their attention to the far end of the strip where street by street, the lights went out. The darkness came like a wave, extinguishing the lit office windows, neon signs, and streetlights. In seconds the darkness reached us, and as the last of the light faded with the winding down of machinery all that remained were the headlights of the vehicles on the street, and in the skylanes above us.

It kept the blackness from being complete, but being outside on the streets of Hangfei in such darkness stirred some primal fear inside of me. The people around us stared at it, transfixed, as drivers got out of their vehicles to see. Even Dragan stared, Alexei clinging to his side.

"Is this it?" I asked. "Did we do it?"

"We did it," Vamp said.

"The force field," someone nearby said, pointing.

I turned to follow the woman's finger and my eyes went wide. The haan force field, the glowing blue dome that had been part of the cityscape for my entire life, had gone. The top of the haan ship towered above the surrounding skyscrapers looking much darker and imposing without the veil of soft light.

"The force field is down," someone else said.

The air rippled around us, and the sudden dizziness that accompanied it made my stomach turn and my head ache. In the dim light, my surroundings began to change . . . colors became less saturated, and I felt disoriented as if blurry vision I'd lived with my whole life came into focus, and I had to struggle to compensate. Others around me experienced it too, I could tell.

"Sam . . ." Vamp said, and I could see that no matter how many times he'd told me he believed me, part of him hadn't been sure. Now that he realized it might be true, it scared him. I took his hand, lacing my fingers through his.

"Get ready."

The crowd gasped again as the sudden shriek of a jet grew to drown out everything else in seconds, and a dark shadow rocketed past above the dome. It zeroed in on the haan ship with a contrail stretching out behind it.

"They're attacking!" someone screamed. "The foreigners are attacking the ship!"

I stared, not sure what to do. There wasn't much I could do. An array of phones were held up over the heads of the crowd, all angled up toward the jet, trying to record it. Near the wall, I saw a robed gonzo, a young man, clasp his hands together and press his knuckles under his chin as he watched, terrified.

"Call someone!" a woman shouted, trying to be heard above the rising screams. "Call someone, they're attacking the—"

The crowd gasped again as a heavy boom shook the sidewalk, and a bright light flashed from somewhere up in the sky. A hole parted in the clouds, and through it, just for a second, I saw one of the distant, floating hexagonal plates that made up the defense shield. A huge beam of energy burst through the hole, wriggling like a live worm, then struck the jet.

I thought it would explode, but it didn't. Instead, it pulled up at the last second and debris flaked off the jet's undercarriage. The shockwave slammed into it, and sent it spinning out of control, back toward the square. Back toward us.

The crowd fell quiet, then began to shout and scream as the plane grew bigger and bigger in the sky above us. A piece flew off, and something came rocketing out. At first I thought it was a missile, but it wasn't—the pilot had ejected.

The plane, now a several-ton hunk of falling junk, broke in half and came screaming down toward the street.

Panic erupted, people scrambling to get inside as the shadow grew above us.

"Sam, Vamp, come on!" Dragan yelled, grabbing my arm. He pulled, trying to drag me away just as another light appeared in the sky, this time from the haan ship. The faint blue glow struck one half of the jet and a bubble of light formed around it. The second half, which had been whipping straight toward the square, stopped midspin, then halted. It had gotten so close, you could see the Western characters stenciled along the wing. Then it flipped back, end over end, and collided with the first half. The two hung there in the sky, and slowly crumpled together into a ball of metal.

The ball hovered, suspended in the field for a few more seconds, and then blasted away as if it had been shot from a cannon. It dwindled to a small dot in the blink of an eye, arcing out toward the ocean.

The flow of bodies slowed, stopping here and there as people realized what had happened. Fingers and phones pointed up toward the now clear sky where all that remained were clouds of black smoke, carried on the wind.

Then someone cheered. It set off a wave of cheering and fists pumped in the air around us, but when I looked at Vamp, he wasn't cheering. The guards weren't, either, along with some of the others. They looked concerned, and I understood why.

The implication that the foreigners might attack had been there for a long time, but now it had actually happened. Not a bombing carried out by one person or a few people, but an actual military strike. A foreign military jet had actually entered our airspace.

Looking around I could see a lot of people weren't sure what to make of it. The foreigners hadn't attacked us, directly. They hadn't gone after a military target or a feedlot.

They'd gone straight for the haan. The defense shield, built by the haan, had destroyed the jet. To most people's understanding, the haan had, for the first time in recorded history, just killed a human intentionally, or tried to.

"This is bad," I said, watching to spot where the jet had crumpled. The hole in the clouds had begun to slowly close in the current of the wind. I turned to Nix. "Nix, I—"

The air had already begun to ripple around him. As the air began to crackle, he gave me a quick nod.

"I have to go," he said. "Your truth will come soon. I hope it suits you."

He vanished. The air rushed in to fill the empty space with a loud clap, like thunder.

The air rippled again, more intensely, and again the wave of disorientation hit as the sounds of additional approaching jets began to grow. A series of booms echoed from offshore, followed by overlapping hisses.

"Let's get inside," Vamp said.

"No. I want to see."

Several bright points of light appeared in the sky, arcing up over the building tops. They were missiles, streaking toward the haan ship.

"Sam, Vamp's right. We should get off the street," Dragan said.

But before I could answer, a woman screamed.

At first I thought she had screamed because of the missiles, but she hadn't. When I located the source, I saw a middle-aged woman standing near the mouth of an alley. She clutched her face with her hands, eyes bugged out as she stared toward a big metal trash bin. Something stood next to it in the shadows, swarming with scaleflies. What looked like tar, or pitch, had been splattered over the bin's metal surface, leaving splotches on the ground and the brick wall behind it.

The woman sucked in a breath, and screamed again as the shape retreated into the darkness. I turned back to the street as more screams came. I didn't see any haan, they'd all been smart enough to make themselves scarce when they realized what had happened, but I could hear the sounds of alien voices, low, overlapping hisses with an undercurrent of insect clicking. They came from the haanyŏng.

I looked across the street and saw a young couple backing away from a dark shape. Unlike the haan I'd seen without the benefit of their disguise, it had a vaguely human outline but its torso was too long . . . its neck too thin and its head too large. It had tar black skin, and it walked toward them with an unnerving, shivering gait. Draped over what might have been its shoulders were the remains of a security uniform, as if it somehow had felt compelled to put it back on even after shedding its human skin.

The couple ran as others around the thing began to scream. The whole street began to scream, then the whole block. The sound grew until it sounded like all of Hangfei might be screaming. The haanyŏng turned to face the terrified people around it and something about its body language almost felt familiar. It seemed confused, and a moment later I did feel a pulse of shock, or confusion through the mite cluster. Rather than advance toward any of them, it did the opposite. It turned, and ran away.

. . . they often don't even realize the change has taken place. They sometimes cling to their old identities for weeks, even months, before they realize what they've become.

It doesn't know, I thought. The haanyŏng's imitation had become so complete, its disguise so convincing, that it still believed itself to be its host. It had fallen back on instinct, trying to calm the crowd like the security officer it had been, only to have them react as though they'd seen a monster.

"They're real," Vamp said, staring. "It's all real."

People ran, shoving their way down the sidewalk and across the street in panicked streams as more and more haanyŏng appeared, seeming as frightened as everyone else. Gunshots went off somewhere down the street, and I turned to see several human security officers firing at a dark shape on the sidewalk. Over the chaos, the sounds of the missiles began to lower in pitch as they plunged down toward their target.

I turned to Dragan.

"Dragan, we . . ."

A dark shape stood where Dragan had been only a moment ago. It stood, its too-big head angled down toward me as its long, limbs shivered. Black eyes, a cluster of them in the center of where a face should have been, seemed to focus on me, and I heard a low rumble of haan speech.

"No . . ."

Alexei still stood next to him, frozen in shock as he stared up at the creature that had suddenly appeared. My eyes moved to the tattered shirt still draped over the thing. It belonged to a security uniform, the crisp white stained black, and tears began to stream down my cheeks as I stared at the name patch still visible there.

SHAO

"No . . ."

Sam, wait.

The words appeared on the 3i chat. The message had come from Dragan.

He reached out to touch me and I recoiled, backing into Vamp who crossed one arm over my chest. He held out the other to stop the haanyŏng from coming any closer and right at that moment I felt a signal stream in through the surrogate cluster. I felt confusion, but also pain. The hurt, wounded feeling I picked up felt so honest and so real that my throat closed up, and fresh tears welled up in my eyes.

I'd lost him. At some point I'd lost him, and never known. The thing in front of me didn't even know.

How long? It was all I could think. How long had he been this way? Since the beginning? Since we rescued him from Shiliuyuán Station, or shortly after? Or had it happened more recently? How many afternoons had I spent with the haanyŏng? How many stories had we shared? Could Dragan truly have helped plan for this night, and never known what he'd become?

Sam, what's wrong?

The words appeared on the holodisplay between us, as the thing tried to approach again. Again I backed into Vamp, who took a step back himself. Again, I felt the hurt and the confusion.

Sam, it's me.

The missiles fell, while around us the city screamed as if it had just awoken into a collective nightmare. The truth of it threatened to send them over the edge, and me along with them. It wasn't just Dragan, they were everywhere. Some were being attacked by the crowd, and some were fleeing along with everyone else, but easily one in twenty of the people I saw weren't human ... on the sidewalks, under awnings, in vehicles. They were everywhere.

Everywhere.

The thing that had been Dragan took another step toward us and when I raised my own right hand out to stop it, I froze.

Everything ... the screaming, the sirens, the gunshots, the shrieks of the jets and missiles ... all of it faded as I stared down what seemed to be a long tunnel. My tears stopped as suddenly as if a switch had been thrown, and my legs turned weak. My mouth went dry, and I felt my lips part as my brain struggled, without success, to process what I saw. My left hand looked the same as it ever did, the same pale skin, the same tattoos, the same scars, but my right hand ...

My right hand had turned completely black, all the way to my elbow. The skin had turned rubbery, glistening as if wet. The nails had come off and the hand formed a gnarled claw, the tips vaguely pointed, with deep pores at irregular intervals over its surface. I stared in shock as a scalefly crawled out from a pore near the base of my palm, and flitted off above the panicked crowd.

I looked back at Vamp but he just stared at what used to be Dragan. I moved the hand down to my side so he wouldn't see, but I couldn't take my eyes from it.

In that instant, memories came rushing back, clicking into place as they came. Gohan had seen . . . it's why he took my hand, and kissed it in the aircar, then again, on the train. Qian had taken my hand as well, in the Gong district, and I'd seen a scalefly crawl from my hand to hers. At that moment, she'd become aware of my plan. The scalefly had shared my thoughts when it left my body, and entered hers. It's how they'd stayed one step ahead of me the whole time . . . I'd been telling them my secrets, broadcasting them, without even knowing.

I remembered the A.I. advertisers, pitching things like hand lotion, and scalefly repellent . . . they'd seen, matching on some pattern that told them the hand needed to be fixed.

"Tell me how the haan changed you . . . tell me how you convinced them to bestow their blessing on you. . . ."

My dreams of Nix, they weren't dreams. They were messages, information carried by scaleflies that I'd picked up through receptors I hadn't known I had. The dreams were my brain's attempt to interpret the packaged memories.

Fire bloomed in the air high above us as the defense shield sent out arcs of energy that licked across the falling missiles and caused them to explode. Most of them went up in flames but some continued to fall through the boiling smoke. Jets broke formation, some getting caught in the haan beams while others managed to escape.

All of it seemed to be happening far away. All I could see was my black right hand. Behind that stood the creature that had once been the only father I'd ever known. Behind that, far in the distance, loomed the mighty haan ship as thin white contrails crept ever closer.

Then, the angry orange light of the defense shield faded. Within seconds, the entire structure went dark, while at the same time the faint blue dome of light reappeared over the ship.

They're diverting the shield's power, I realized. *They know it can't stop all the missiles and they're using it as a power source to get the force field back up.*

The field that masked their real appearance stayed down, and the ship itself remained dark, but the glow of the force field grew brighter until the first missile struck. It exploded without penetrating, creating a cloud of black smoke and flame. Others fell into the expanding explosion and joined with it until a huge black spot bloomed across the shell of electric blue. Debris rained down the curvature of it, sending sparks spitting off into the night as the pieces struck and then bounced off.

In the time it took me to blink, my hand returned to normal. I still had it held down by my side like I wanted to hide it away somewhere, but once again it looked familiar, right down to the calluses and scars.

Dragan stood in front of me, his face a mask of concern ... worry for me. Around us, the city streets had returned to normal and people were beginning to stop running, to slow down and look around, confused as the world they'd always known returned just as suddenly as it had vanished.

"Sam," Dragan said. "Talk to me ... what happened? Are you okay?"

He reached for me, to hold me, or shake me ... anything that might snap me out of my shock, which he still didn't understand.

Before he could, I twisted out of Vamp's arms. I grabbed Alexei's hand and ran with him through the crowd into the darkness of Hangfei. I ran until I lost Dragan, until I lost Vamp, and until I lost even myself in the sea of confused and frightened masses, and a city gone mad.

Chapter Thirty-Three

I held the cigarillo in my right hand, between my index and middle finger, and closed my eyes.

"The universe you find your world in now is rejecting you. The decay will be slow, but certain. All life on this world that does not evolve will die. Stop fighting. Let us save you."

In my mind, I willed myself to move it, to move it away from me.

"... security deployed to the docks at Ocean Heights, where crates of rations that were provided to us by the haan have been dumped into the harbor by a group calling themselves the Hangfei Truth Initiative."

I opened my eyes and in the dim light I saw the smoldering ember of tobacco floating in the air between me and the TV. I could still feel it between my fingertips, but it hung there in the air in front of me. I pushed it out farther. I couldn't see them, but I imagined the fingers of my right hand extending, becoming long, thin tentacles coiled gently around the cigarillo's end.

I was getting pretty good at it.

I kept the volume low as I watched the news woman on the screen, not wanting to wake up Alexei. He'd been with me for the past two weeks. I wasn't about to let him go back to live with Dragan, and he wouldn't have gone even if I did no matter how much Dragan pushed for it. Since Dragan still didn't seem to know what had happened to him, he pushed a lot, but I got Alexei to tell him he wanted time to get to know me better. It seemed to work.

"... *streets of Hangfei will be off limits while the scalefly biocide is sprayed. For information about when your district will receive the application of biocide, go to* ..."

A window in the upper right corner of the screen showed more protest footage. The crowd had grown since the blackout, at least four times the size it had been and it had begun to spread into surrounding districts as well. The mob huddled together in unity, but also in fear. Their faces looked confused and angry as security kept them at bay but just barely. Already there had been more riots, more violence. I wondered if maybe Nix hadn't been right.

Sam, I'm here. Can you buzz me in?

The cigarillo snapped back into my hand. I closed Vamp's message, then switched off the TV and thumbed the button to let him in. I stood, and waited by the balcony door, looking through the glass to the outside. I kept the lights off, leaving the apartment to be lit through the windows by the city lights. It had been a week since the blackout, and I hadn't left my apartment once. Stacks of messages had piled up from just about everyone I knew, but I hadn't answered anyone until I finally called Vamp.

The official word regarding the blackout, and the events that followed, were all blamed on the foreigners. The governess held a series of press conferences where she explained that the foreign forces triggered the blackout through a cyberattack that caused a cascading failure of the power grid. She even went on to describe our attack in pretty good detail. The blackout was the first phase of a three-pronged assault ... the second was the deployment of an experimental psyops weapon developed by the Americans, which caused mass hallucinations and paranoia. While we'd been kept in a state of confusion, and unable to respond effectively, they'd launched their strike on the haan ship.

She'd been convincing, and a lot of people believed her, but not nearly enough. Too many people believed their own senses, too many to silence, and the mood of Hangfei had shifted.

I opened the balcony door and stepped out, listening to the distant roar of the protesters. Security aircars drifted past down below, much more than usual, and I could see the strobe of flashing blues between two buildings in the distance. Electronic billboards advertised vacation packages, which had suddenly become very popular. Travel ads, passport providers, and offers of transportation to the independent nation of Duongroi, which security would never allow anyone to reach. Already there had been hundreds of arrests as people tried to make contact with the foreigners.

All haan ads had been suspended. All haan colonies had been locked down, and there were no more haan out and about on the streets. LeiFang had even ordered the huge graviton lenses that were pointed at the haan ship powered up, even though she had no intention of ever using them.

When the knock came, I opened the door. Vamp stood outside, wearing black jeans and a T-shirt under a light suit jacket. He had a bottle of shine in one hand.

"Hey," I said. "Come on in."

He followed me in as I headed back to the living room.

"What happened to the locks?" he asked, nodding toward the front door.

"If they want to get in, the locks won't stop them."

I stopped in front of the sofa, and turned to face him. He looked around the dimly lit room.

"You want to turn on a light?" he asked.

"I like it like this, if that's okay."

"Sure."

I smoothed the lapels of his jacket, and then put my hands on his chest. He covered my hands with his, unaware that one of them was no longer the one I'd been born with.

"I've been worried about you," he said.

"I know. I'm sorry."

"It's okay, I'm just glad you're all right." We stood like that a while longer, and he added. "So . . . did you want to go out?"

"No."

"You want to order in or something? Dial up a movie?"

"Not really."

"You want to get drunk?"

I took the bottle of shine from him, and put it down on the coffee table.

"It's late," I told him. "I think I just want to go to bed."

He looked confused, and a little ticked off for a minute.

"Then why did you—"

I tiptoed up and kissed him on the mouth. Not a long kiss, but long enough. I broke it, resting back on my heels, and when I looked up at him, I saw he understood. When I turned, and walked to the bedroom, he followed.

We stripped down without saying anything, and then climbed into bed. I wondered if he'd just maul me right then and there, but he didn't. He just propped himself on one elbow, and looked down at me as I lay with my head on the pillow, looking up at him. He wasn't quite sure what to make of the whole thing, I think.

"Everything is different, now," I said. He stroked my hair, and I snuggled against him a little, despite the heat.

"Yeah," he said. "LeiFang is holding the American, the one who ejected from the jet, but people are pushing to hear what he knows. They're not satisfied with the usual bullshit, they want answers."

"I saw the riots on TV."

"Yeah, there are groups in pretty much every district now. Things are going to get ugly before long."

I sighed. "Maybe Nix was right."

"No," he said. "Since the blackout I've made some changes to eyebot's facial recognition software, so that if it can't identify a face it doesn't just mark it unknown. It flags anything that doesn't fit the human profile, and I've got everyone using it to look for anything strange and send a report back only to me. So far it's identified close to twelve percent of all recorded faces as haanyŏng."

I expected a wave of fear, or even panic, but it didn't come. I'd been expecting this. I think I expected it might have been even worse.

"That's in six months," I said.

"It will spread faster, the more there are," he said. "Even if the rate were steady, we could be looking at one in every four by year's end if the haan don't find a way to stop it."

"If the haan want to find a way to stop it."

"At least now we have a chance."

I settled back into the pillow.

"I thought for sure security would come for me," I said.

"Yun managed to implicate us, but that was it. When the dust settled there wasn't enough to prove anything, and Dragan pulled some strings. We should be in the clear."

As soon as he said Dragan's name, he winced a little. When the silence stretched out, he struggled to salvage the situation.

"Sam, I'm sorry about—"

"It's okay."

"It isn't, Sam."

I felt the pang in my chest, the familiar pang, but still no tears came. I hadn't cried since that night. I thought they would come sooner or later, but I still felt numb where Dragan was concerned. I didn't know how to feel about it, so I just didn't feel anything.

"He keeps calling me," I said.

"Me, too."

"He doesn't know. He still doesn't know what he is."

"He's worried about you."

"Is it weird that I feel bad for him?" I asked.

"It's a weird situation."

"I feel like I'm hurting his feelings."

"Maybe you are."

"But it's not Dragan. He's not even human."

"Nix has feelings."

There had been no word from Nix since the blackout, but every once in a while his 3i icon turned pink for just a second. He wanted me to know he was out there, and still alive. Maybe he'd gone into hiding, like me. Maybe he was just waiting for me to come out of hiding.

Vamp saw me getting upset, and changed the subject.

"You know, he's not the only one who's been worried about you," Vamp said.

"I know. How are the others?"

"Dao-Ming is having a rough time of it."

I tensed. Dao-Ming could rot in hell.

"How's Shuang?" I asked him.

"She'll be okay. She . . . decided to go back to Jangbong."

"And no one knows we were behind the blackout?"

"Just us."

"And Dragan," I said. Sooner or later, he would realize what had happened to him. When he did, what would he do with that information?

He nodded. "So what do you want to do? Do you want to leave?"

"Hangfei?"

"The country. Get out of their range of influence. I don't know. Defect to America or something."

"No."

"Are you scared?" he asked.

I shook my head. "No. Not anymore."

It surprised me to find that I meant what I'd said. My experiences in Shiliuyuán Station had left me frightened for months, and wound me so tight that I couldn't walk the streets of Hangfei without being almost paralyzed. I had begun to wonder if the fear would ever go away, and then, just like that, it had.

"After the blackout," I said. "After I ran, I came home. I locked myself in my room, in the dark, and sat in the corner. I stayed there all night, but when I woke up . . . I don't know. Something happened."

"Something?"

"I'm not scared anymore."

I put my arm around his neck, and pulled him close. I kissed him, running my fingers, my scaly, black fingers, through his hair, and it felt like it always did. With my left hand I took his, and held his palm against my breast. When we broke the kiss, I could feel the tension coming off of him.

"Sam, I . . ."

"It's okay," I told him. "I want to."

"Are you sure?"

"I'm sure. I want this. I want you."

He kissed me, soft at first, then harder until the dam broke and the bed became a sweaty tangle. I felt his rough face on my neck, and at my ear, and when he touched me I felt myself begin to lose control. For all his pent-up energy, he took his time, and I let him, until he tipped me over the edge and I forgot, finally, about anything else.

Maybe, when we got around to sharing the uglier parts of our lives, the parts we still kept secret even from each other, maybe then he would decide he couldn't be with me. Maybe after losing Dragan I'd lose Vamp, too. Maybe, though, he would accept me as I was, like he always had before.

Maybe he would accept, too, that I had changed even since the blackout. That I had decided the blackout would be only the beginning and that the haan would, if not pay, then answer for Dragan, and everything else. We might have been spared from Gohan's Impact, but the haan's plans for us, their original plans for us, were still in full effect. We were going to have to try to stop them.

When that happened, things would get worse. They would get far, far worse.

I clutched Vamp's back, and pulled him close.

But not tonight.

About the Author

James K. Decker was born in New Hampshire in 1970, and has lived in the New England area since that time. He developed a love of reading and writing early on, participating in young author competitions as early as grade school, but the later discovery of works by Frank Herbert and Isaac Asimov turned that love to an obsession.

He wrote continuously through high school, college, and beyond, eventually breaking into the field under the name James Knapp, with the publication of the Revivors trilogy (*State of Decay*, *The Silent Army*, and *Element Zero*). *State of Decay* was a Philip K. Dick award nominee, and won the 2010 Compton Crook Award. He has since written *Ember*, *The Burn Zone*, and *Fallout* under the name James K. Decker.

He now lives in Massachusetts with his wife, Kim.